ALSO BY C. C. BENISON

Twelve Drummers Drumming

Eleven
Pipers Piping

Eleven Pipers Piping

A FATHER CHRISTMAS MYSTERY

C. C. Benison

DELACORTE PRESS  NEW YORK

Published in the United States by Delacorte Press, an imprint of The Random House Publishing Group, a division of Random House, Inc., New York.

DELACORTE PRESS is a registered trademark of Random House, Inc., and the colophon is a trademark of Random House, Inc.

Library of Congress Cataloging-in-Publication Data

Benison, C. C.
Eleven pipers piping: a mystery/C. C. Benison
p.   cm.
ISBN 978-0-385-34446-3
eBook ISBN 978-0-440-33984-7
1. Vicars, Parochial—Fiction.   2. Devon (England)—Fiction.   I. Title.
PR9199.3.B37783E44 2012
813'.54—dc23   2011042715

Printed in the United States of America on acid-free paper

www.bantamdell.com

246897531

First Edition

Book design by Karin Batten

For Marjorie Poor, constant reader

Cast of Characters

Inhabitants of Thornford Regis

The Reverend Tom Christmas	Vicar of the parish
Miranda Christmas	His daughter
Bob Cogger	Retired farm labourer
Florence Daintrey	Retired civil servant
Venice Daintrey	Her sister-in-law
Liam Drewe	Owner of the Waterside Café and Bistro
Mitsuko Drewe	His wife, an artist
Briony Hart	Shop assistant
Victor Kaif	Homeopath
Molly Kaif	His wife
Becca Kaif	Their daughter
Caroline Moir	Owner of Thorn Court Country Hotel
Will Moir	Her husband
Adam Moir	Their son
Ariel Moir	Their daughter

Penella Neels	Co-owner of Thorn Barton farm
Colm Parry	Organist and choirmaster at St. Nicholas Church
Celia Holmes-Parry	His wife, a psychotherapist
Declan Parry	Their son
Roger Pattimore	Owner of Pattimore's, the village shop
Enid Pattimore	His mother
Fred Pike	Village handyman and church sexton
Joyce Pike	His wife
Charlie Pike	Their son
Madrun Prowse	Vicarage housekeeper
Jago Prowse	Her brother, owner of Thorn Cross Garage
Tamara and Kerra	His daughters
Karla Skynner	Postmistress and newsagent
Tiffany Snape	Her assistant
Eric Swan	Licensee of the Church House Inn
Belinda Swan	His wife
Daniel, Lucy, Emily, and Jack	Their children
Mark Tucker	Accountant
Violet Tucker	His wife
Ruby Tucker	Their daughter

Visitors to Thornford Regis

The Reverend Hugh Beeson   Vicar of St. Barnabas,
Noze Lydiard

Colin Blessing   Detective Sergeant, Totnes
CID

Derek Bliss   Detective Inspector,
Totnes CID

John Copeland   Gamekeeper and shoot
manager at Noze Lydiard Estate

Judith Ingley   Retired nurse

Nick Stanhope   Home security company
owner

Màiri White   Police Community
Support Officer

Eleven
Pipers Piping

The Vicarage

Thornford Regis TC9 6QX

10 JANUARY

Dear Mum,

I hope you're prepared for snow! I switched on the radio once the
Teasmade had done its job this morning and the Met was issu-
ing a severe weather warning for the entire country. We are to
be ~~inindat inud~~ inundated! And we WILL be by the time this letter reaches you, so I hope you and Aunt Gwen are all right in
Cornwall. You must have Aunt Gwen phone me if you think
there's anything I can do at this end, though last time we had an
enorm~~us~~ous dump of snow in the West Country the phones went
down. And the electricity went off too. It really was quite a to
do, wasn't it! I know lots of folk have no weather memories, can't
remember what year had what conditions. In fact, Old Bob
asked me while I was getting a loaf at Pattimore's the other day,
when was the Great Storm of 93? It was in 1993, Bob, I said,
not batting an eye. (I do think he's not very well.) But that was
a great wind storm. Both you and I remember the last great

snow *storm, don't we? Maureen did pick her moments. No one could drive out of the village. No ambulance could get in. Dr. Philpot had got himself stuck in Torquay. And it was Christmas Eve day. I can still see the spot on Mr. James-Douglas's dining room rug where Maureen's water broke. Well, not "see" it as such. Of course it cleaned up easily. Poor Mr. J-D, I think at first he was more worried about the state of his Tabriz rug than the state of Maureen. And he did go out and shop for that enormu~ ~ous canopy bed soon after Maureen gave birth to Tamara on his old one. (What a trial it was getting that bed into the vicarage!) Anyway, you and I did splendid work as midwives, didn't we? Even Dr. ~~Fuss~~Philpot couldn't find a reason to caution us later. And now your granddaughter is at university at Exeter. Time has flown, hasn't it? It was so lovely seeing her at Christmas with all of us in Cornwall. She's coming down to perform in Totnes with her old group Shanks Pony tonight, but I can't go, as Mr. Christmas has the Burns Supper at the hotel and Miranda is having her first sleepover in the vicarage with some of her friends. I'm not sure Mr. C is looking forward to the haggis. I once fed him my very good braised lambs' kidneys with onions. He ate most of it, but I could sense organ meats weren't his cup of tea. I think Miranda fed most of hers to Bumble! I was not pleased! Anyway, I think Mr. C will be surprised at the B. Supper, but I shan't tell him what the surprise is and spoil it. Molly Kaif is cooking the Supper, by the way. I don't think she's the best caterer hereabouts, but it's good that she's coming out of her shell, poor woman, though it's a bit odd she's chosen to do so at the Moirs'. Well, Mum, I must get on with the day. I'm doing a special meal for the girls this evening and I've been asked to contribute something to the B. Supper, so there's that to cook too, and Mr. C has a wedding in Pennycross this afternoon, which will keep him busy. Mum, I just glanced at the window and even though it's so dark this early in the morning, I could see a snow-*

flake fall on the glass. I expect it's starting. Oh dear, I wonder what the next days will bring? Last time, with all the snow, it felt like the whole village was ~~maruned~~ marooned. We coped wonderfully, though, didn't we? Still, I wouldn't wish for the sort of drama we had last time. A cosy fire and the sudoku machine Mr. C bought me for Christmas will suit me until it all blows over. Cats are well and still sulking over the dog, though Bumble does try to make friends. Love to Aunt Gwen. Glorious day! We hope!

Much love,
Madrun

P.S. I'm still investigating the Yorkshire problem! I'll let you know when it's solved.

CHAPTER ONE

"Did they not feed you after the wedding, Mr. Christmas?"

"I dropped into the reception for only a minute," Tom replied, conscious of the passing figure of his housekeeper, as he continued his contemplation of the bounty in the vicarage refrigerator. "I didn't have a chance for a bite."

He barely knew the young couple he had married that afternoon—Todd and Gemma—other than to have a brief preparatory discussion with them the month before. He had never seen them in church, nor had he seen their families or friends, and didn't expect to see them again, unless the couple wished their baby baptised—which mightn't be far off, given that the bride, wearing a meringue with a train half a mile long, had fairly waddled up the aisle at St. Paul's, the second of the two churches in his charge. Her plump face, when she'd pushed back her embroidered veil, had looked much like a blazing beetroot, he recalled, staring at a jar of the pickled variety inside the door of the fridge. Sweat had sparkled in tiny beads along her exposed hairline—this despite the glacial damp of the nave in January—which some might have construed as the effect of energy expended getting up the aisle, but which Tom interpreted as a dew born of anticipation and triumph.

The groom, however, had been a figure of bemusement, his face a kind of Belisha beacon, one moment as blanched as that leftover rice pudding in its puddle of cream on the second shelf, the next as pink as the Virginia ham one shelf below. Tom shouldn't have fancied their chances at marital success—they were much too young; he was a farm labourer and she was a health-care aide of some sort and they were living with his parents—but for some reason he did, and could only chalk it up to a decade's experience splicing couples of varied sorts. He imagined them receiving their sixtieth-anniversary card from the Queen (or the King, as would most probably be then) where other couples, more advantaged, would fall by the wayside. "When betrothal is brief, the marriage lasts long," he recalled his father-in-law saying, quoting some bit of Jewish wisdom when he was trying to reconcile himself to his daughter's elopement. How wrong he had been, at least in Tom and Lisbeth's case.

"The reception was at The Pig's Barrel," Tom told his house-keeper.

"A January wedding and a pub reception. Sounds a hurried affair."

"A little, perhaps," Tom responded noncommittally. He rarely went to wedding receptions anyway, unless he knew the family well. Receptions could murder the best part of a Saturday afternoon, and it wasn't as though he didn't have anything else to do—polish his sermon, for instance. He'd dropped in at Todd and Gemma's only because he'd seen the very attractive village bobby, Màiri White, pass through the The Barrel's doors when he went for his car after the ceremony and couldn't resist the allure of a chance encounter. But, alas, when he arrived, Màiri was ensconced, back to him, at a table full of—damn!—*men*. Anyway, snow, ominously forecast to bung up northwestern Europe for the weekend and more, was beginning to fall in earnest and so getting home to Thornford seemed more imperative than being stood like a lemon at The Pig's Barrel.

He looked past the edge of the refrigerator door, wondering if Madrun was about to launch into a mini inquisition over the newlyweds. Customarily, she would have ushered them into the vicarage study when they came for their marriage interview, but the wedding had come together all in a rush during busy Christmas week, which Madrun had spent with her aging mother in Cornwall, thus depriving her of an opportunity to inspect and pass verdict on events at home.

But Madrun's back was to him. He could see one hand resting against one cheek as she contemplated the array of cookery books marshalled behind the glass of a ceiling-high barrister's bookcase. He guessed her preoccupation lay not with the hapless couple. The Sunday before, after her return from Cornwall to Thornford Regis early in the New Year, she had cooked a joint, accompanied with roast potatoes and parsnips, green beans with caramelised shallots, and, of course, Yorkshire pudding. Tom and Miranda had been in the sitting room with their guests, Will and Caroline Moir, their daughter, Ariel, their son, Adam, and his girlfriend, Tamara, when their conversation had been riven by a piercing cry—such as he had never heard before—from the kitchen. Heart racing, expecting to find Madrun horribly burned or cut, Tom dashed into the kitchen, the others at his heels. Instead, they found her, oven-gloved, staring aghast into a steaming dish, the door of the Aga behind her a yawning maw. Nestled inside the dish's black and aged sides was a vast and even expanse of tawny gold—quite lovely to look at and smelling heavenly. Despite his still-coursing adrenaline, he had felt his stomach growl.

And then Miranda, on tiptoe, glanced into the pan and declared: "Oh, it's a dropdead!"

A kind of moan slipped from Madrun's throat as she turned and placed the hot dish onto a trivet on her worktable, next to the roasted beef and several bowls of thawing berries, which a little later spilled around a heavenly pavlova.

"But I'm sure it will *taste* wonderfully," Caroline had interjected quickly, and the others had murmured concurrence. *Dropdead* was his daughter Miranda's coinage for a Yorkshire pudding that failed to rise. Her mother's often hadn't. Lisbeth had been a blasé sort of cook whose Sunday lunches were sometimes a fiesta of Waitrose ready meals. When Lisbeth died, their French au pair, Ghislaine, tried her hand at English fare but could never quite get the knack of certain dishes, Yorkshire pud among them. Tom, who had never made one in his life, couldn't understand how a simple concoction of eggs, milk, and flour could be so temperamental and cause so much distress. There had been much crestfallenness back in Bristol when the Yorkshire, pulled from the oven, looked more like Norfolk-in-a-pan than Staffordshire-in-a-pan—flat rather than hilly. Lisbeth would feign indifference, but Ghislaine wept at her first failure. But then they were all in shock in the wake of Lisbeth's sudden, violent death.

Madrun's, on the other hand, were always a tremendous success—puffy and light, glorious umber hillocks set against deep golden valleys, a sponge to sop the rich brown gravy she would produce from the organic beef acquired from the farm shop at Thorn Barton. But not last Sunday. The pud simply looked . . . sad. After her initial distress, she had pulled herself together and brought forth an otherwise fine Sunday lunch in the dining room, although she remained subdued throughout. Since then, she'd had Fred Pike, the village handyman, in to look at the Aga, which Fred had pronounced fit as feathers on a duck, scrutinised the sell-by dates of the flour and milk, and had a barney with Roger Pattimore down at Pattimore's, the village shop, over the freshness of his eggs. She had adjured Tom to check on his computer to see if there were any chat rooms or forums devoted to Yorkshire pudding—the word *failures* didn't pass

Madrun's lips; *mysteries* was substituted—and there were a few, not unpredictably, in the Internet age, but he had white-lied and said there weren't because—and this he didn't say out loud—for heaven's sake, it was *too* silly. All this bother for a simple—and not wholly necessary—side dish.

"You heat fat in the pan first, don't you?" Tom had asked a couple of days later when he found Madrun lifting her glasses from the chain around her neck with one hand and pulling the very pan to her face with the other for close examination. "Then why don't you do a pudding now and experiment with some vegetable oil? That's a sort of fat, isn't it?"

"Really, Mr. Christmas," Madrun had snapped, her tone indicating the suggestion *infra dig*. "It must be *beef* fat." And then her eyes shot open behind the lenses and a flash of enlightenment lit up her features. "I shall have to have a strong word with the girls at the farm shop."

Tom later learned from one of his parishioners that there had been some unpleasantness up at Thorn Barton when Madrun arrived at the shop to question the aging of their beef, or lack of aging, or some such thing. Sainsbury's had made a larger-than-usual food delivery to the vicarage on Thursday, so Tom suspected Madrun and the women at the farm shop were keeping a bit of space between them for the time being.

"Sometimes, Mrs. Prowse, things happen for no reason," Tom said finally, trying to keep exasperation from his voice.

Madrun flicked him a disapproving glance, as if he were being theologically unsound, and said, "It's an omen. I feel it in my bones."

Tom, who at the time was struggling to put the lead on Bumble preparatory to a walk up Knighton Lane, had bit his tongue and said nothing, because, of course, there was nothing to say: He was disinclined towards omens, particularly if they came in the form of collapsed savoury puddings.

Now his housekeeper had pushed back one of the glass doors of the bookcase and pulled out a cookery tome. Opening the book to the index at the back, she studied him a moment over the rims of her spectacles. "You'll let all the cold out, if you keep the refrigerator door open like that."

"Yes, sorry."

"You may be pleasantly surprised this evening, you know, Mr. Christmas."

Tom made a demurring noise as he closed the door. "Perhaps if I lined my stomach with a glass of milk."

"Mr. James-Douglas used to love the Burns Supper."

"I expect from his name he had a bit of Scots in him."

"You don't have to be Scottish to enjoy the Burns Supper."

Oh, don't you? Tom thought. It might help. He didn't know who his natural parents were. He didn't *feel* somehow they could have been Scottish, if one were permitted to feel such things. He himself felt thoroughly English, and if he were about to give allegiance to another people, it would be the French or the Italians, who had wonderful food, not the Scots, who could only have been led by a ghastly climate and impoverished soil to think a celebratory dinner should consist of offal and oatmeal stuffed into a sheep's stomach then boiled, turnips—his least favourite vegetable—boiled, and potatoes— yes, boiled. Without reopening the refrigerator door, he could see in his mind's eye the ham, the leftover cheese-and-onion pie, the last of the turkey orzo soup Kate had made after Christmas—any of which would make a fine Saturday-evening meal.

"He was hardly fit for the pulpit the next morning," Madrun continued almost fondly, licking her thumb and turning a page.

Giles James-Douglas, who preceded Tom, but for one, as incumbent, had been vicar in the village for over twenty-five years before his death. A lifelong bachelor of considerable private means and epicurean tastes, he installed Madrun as his housekeeper when she was a young woman, turned her into a superb cook, and left both the large late-Georgian vicarage—which he bought outright from the

Church—and its housekeeper to his successors. Tom, therefore, had more or less *inherited* Madrun Prowse, who, though a spinster, retained the honorific *Mrs.* He was grateful for the help, being a busy priest and a widowed father, but there were moments when she did get on his wick a bit, especially when the matchless Mr. James-Douglas slipped into the conversation. He felt, to keep up, he should get as much malt whisky as he could down his neck Saturday then spend Sunday morning conducting services at two churches with a throbbing headache and a dry mouth, and trying not to gag over the Communion wine. He didn't fancy it. In fact, he didn't fancy attending the Burns Supper at all, but he was chaplain to a regional pipe band and Roger Pattimore, the pipe sergeant, expected him to come and deliver the Selkirk Grace. It was churlish to say no. Having been in Thornford less than a year and still finding his way in the parish, Tom didn't want to offend for small reasons. What he wasn't keen on was the food—the tatties and the neeps (potatoes and turnips, so called) and that acme of culinary horrors, the haggis. When he had been a curate in Kennington, he'd had an old parishioner who told him that in Botswana, where he held some rank in the colonial administration, they had used haggises (or was it *haggi*?) to poison hyenas.

Really, Tom thought, he should have gone to that pub reception, after all, and at least had a couple of greasy pasties. With such bricks in his stomach he might have an excuse to only nibble at the forthcoming supper.

He glanced at a couple of trays on the counter and wondered what was under the linen cloths covering them. He was about to step over and lift one when, unexpectedly, tantalizingly, the aroma of roasting meat tickled his nostrils. He began to wonder if hunger was driving him to fantasy. His glance moved to the oven.

"Am I smelling beef? Are you back up on that horse, Mrs. Prowse?"

Madrun glanced up from the cookery book. "I don't know what you mean."

"I thought perhaps you might be cooking a roast with a view to making a Yorkshire pudding."

"Well, it's true I'm cooking beef, but it's beef Wellington . . . of a kind."

"Beef Wellington!" Tom gave a passing thought to his food budget. "You're serving the children beef Wellington?"

"It's . . . an adaptation of beef Wellington." Madrun frowned at something in her book. "Minced beef, which I shaped into a ball and roasted earlier. Now it's cooking enclosed in chopped mushrooms and puff pastry."

"It's *en croûte*, Daddy," a voice behind him said.

Miranda had pushed open the kitchen door, followed by the vicarage cats, Powell and Gloria, who began a lewd and mewling pace in front of the Aga.

"Yes, *oncrew*," Madrun murmured. "That's the word."

"We're having our own Burns Supper," Miranda said brightly, moving to the counter to examine the contents of various bowls.

"I shaped the mince to look like a haggis," Madrun explained.

Tom frowned at his daughter. "I'm surprised that you and Ariel and . . . who else is coming to your sleepover?"

"Emily and Becca."

" . . . had the faintest interest in Robbie Burns."

"Oh, we don't. Or at least *they* don't," Miranda added obliquely.

"Then . . . ?"

"It's because of Zak Burns." Miranda shook her head so her pigtails slapped against her cheeks.

Tom turned to Madrun helplessly.

"I believe he was the last winner on *X Factor*." Madrun raised a censorious eyebrow.

"It's because of Emily." Miranda shrugged. "She thinks he's . . ."

Oh, blast, Tom thought: *The word to follow is probably* cute, hot, *or* cool. He sighed inwardly. There was something awfully cunning about Emily Swan. Perhaps having two older brothers and an older sister, and living over a pub, made her more worldly wise than the other two girls joining Miranda at the vicarage for her first sleepover: With a brother nearly a dozen years older moved away from home, Ariel Moir lived the life of an only child, like Miranda, while Becca Kaif had lost her only brother to suicide, in August—a terrible tragedy for the village, and it had—cruelly—made Becca into an only child, too.

" . . . nice," Miranda said at last. "Emily thinks he's nice."

Nice seemed a good noncommittal word to latch on to, and Tom did. He couldn't help not wanting Miranda to leave the sweet, dreamlike realm of early childhood, to be swallowed up in schoolgirl pop-star crushes, with bedroom walls covered in posters of boys with peculiar haircuts and ludicrous trousers, though, come to think of it, his bedroom, when he had been ten years old, had been covered with posters of *men* with peculiar haircuts and ludicrous trousers. But all of them were magicians and magic had been his passion in those days. It had led to a career in magic—for a time—so at least his bedroom walls had not proved a waste of space, so to speak. He glanced at Miranda's furrowed little brow and wondered what was passing through her furrowed little grey matter.

"And do you think this Zak Burns is nice?" Tom asked.

"Oh . . . he's okay, I suppose."

He watched her reach into a bowl by the sink, pull out a finger of raw potato, and bite into its end.

"Are you making chips?" he asked Madrun, trying to keep yearning from his voice. A plate of hot chips slathered in salt and malt vinegar would go down a treat at this very moment.

"Yes, chips for tatties," she muttered over her cookery book; then she looked up. "You really can't expect little girls to want boiled potatoes, can you, Mr. Christmas."

How gratifying to be schooled about children's tastes when he had spent not a little time easing Madrun into the notion that Miranda's—nor his—tastes did not run to Gordon Ramsay on a daily basis.

"So, I suppose you could say your Burns Supper is a kind of posh burgers and chips."

Madrun looked up again. "Well, if you must."

"Then may I stay? Please."

Miranda giggled. "Emily says, 'No boys allowed.'"

Except, presumably, for the spectre of young Mr. Burns, crowned with fifteen minutes of fame, Tom grumped. "Then what are you doing for neeps?"

"I've made fruit crumble for pudding," Madrun answered. "Bramleys, Bosc pears, wortleberries, blackberries, yewberries, tayberries, strawberries—I've had quite the run this week on the frozen berries I picked and put down in the fall—"

"Clever Mrs. P. They'll never detect turnip in that." Tom was full of admiration.

Madrun looked enormously pleased, if enormous pleasure could be counted in a slight upturning of the lips. "Mind you don't say anything." She shook a warning finger at Miranda.

"I won't." Miranda paused, then raised her own finger to her lips. "Well, I won't until *after*."

"After will do. I suppose it's one way to have children eat their vegetables." She addressed Tom.

But Tom's attention had been drawn to Miranda, who had skipped to the kitchen door and was looking through the glass into the garden. "*Papa! Regarde la neige! N'est-elle pas merveilleuse?*" she said, falling into French, as she often did when she was excited. In the darkness of early evening in January, the farthest end of the sloping garden, where trees screened the millpond in summer, seemed a void, soft and black, but where light spilled from the vicarage windows, demarcating the base of the old pear tree and two wicker chairs, all blazed white, diamond bright.

"Yes, it is marvellous, isn't it," he responded, joining Miranda to witness the thin veil of snow shimmering in the air. He put his hands on Miranda's shoulders and felt the straps of her dungarees. He could sense her anticipation: This would be her first full experience of snow, though in the garden outside it was neither particularly deep (patches of stiff grass were visible) nor terribly crisp (wet, more like) nor very even (the terrace had less than the lawn). But it might be before long, if the weather folk read the signs and portents correctly. Shifting weather partly informed his unwillingness to tarry at the wedding reception at Pennycross. Temperatures had dropped through the afternoon; patchy ice had formed in the lanes between Pennycross and Thornford, and the landscape glimpsed between the hedgerows was bleached and undifferentiated in the watery winter light. Perhaps the snow wasn't so marvellous, after all. Perhaps Madrun had been right: A fallen Yorkshire doth herald tempests drear. Or suchlike.

His stomach growled in response to the thought of food.

"Lions and tigers, Daddy," said Miranda whose ears brushed his shirt below his chest.

"You could hear that?"

"I could hear it over here, Mr. Christmas. You could have a biscuit, I suppose . . ." Madrun began, making Tom feel not unlike Bumble, soon to be rewarded for being a good doggy.

He turned. Madrun was studying her watch.

". . . or perhaps not. Best not to spoil your supper. Aren't you expected soon?"

Tom glanced at his own watch. "Oh, yes, I suppose." Then he glanced again, longingly, at the fridge—a huge double-door chrome American model, surely the largest fridge in the village outside the commercial ones at the Church House Inn, the Waterside Café, and the Thorn Court Country Hotel. "But isn't there much standing about first, drinking whisky and the like?"

"I wouldn't know. I've never been to a Burns Supper."

Startled, Tom was about to ask how she knew, more than he, what he was to expect from such an event, but Miranda interjected, "Are they no-girls-allowed?"

"They are," Madrun replied stoutly.

"That's not fair," Miranda said.

"But yours is no-boys-allowed," Tom protested.

"Really, Daddy!"

"Really, Mr. Christmas!"

Faced with remonstration to what he thought was reasoned observation, Tom backed down, supposing, in a split second of reflection, that most of human history was no-girls-allowed. Even Jesus, whom he thought a rather forward-thinking chap, hadn't put a woman among His disciples. He was a bit snippy with His mother, too.

"Never mind. There's Bumble off his head." The sound of a frenzied Jack Russell barking could be heard on the other side of the kitchen door. Powell and Gloria stiffened into parodies of alert felines. "Someone must be coming to the front door. Race you!" he called to Miranda.

And yet somehow Miranda made it to the front door first and pushed it open. Ariel Moir and Becca Kaif seemed to pitch in on a gust of wind as Bumble darted between them and dashed into the front garden.

"Bumble! Get in here!" Tom shouted over their heads.

But the dog, now a scurrying, grey shadow against the black stone of the wall dividing the vicarage grounds from Church Walk, had turned dervish in the novel ground cover. Tom could dimly make out four wiry legs wriggling in the air as Bumble churned his back in the snow and made happy growling noises.

"Bumble!"

"Yes, Bumble, there's a good dog," called another voice, feminine but authoritative, clear and ringing, and Tom's attention turned to a shadow moving up the path, various soft shapes hanging from each hand. Caroline Moir emerged into the halo of the light over the porch, her cap of fine, fair hair blazing almost as white as snow itself. In the same light, her pale heart-shaped face and large, luminous blue eyes lent her a tentative, fragile air, but Tom had been deceived before by this tender vision. In his first week in Thornford, on an exploratory evening walk towards one of the green lanes that radiated from the village into the countryside, he had witnessed Caroline tear after—then tear into, politely but very firmly—a young man whose bullmastiff had fouled the road and who had paid no heed to the bright red dog-waste bin, not five feet away, which the parish council provided. She had not seen Tom pass during the encounter, and he was glad, for she had been introduced to him earlier as a member of St. Nicholas's choir, and he simply couldn't remember her name—a hazard of early days in a new parish. The man with the mastiff had glimpsed him, however, and though they occasionally crossed the same path, the man always turned his head away, as if tugged by some string of embarrassed memory. Bumble, too, seemed to know the effect of her voice, for he flipped right-side up at her command, darted over, and leapt up to imprint her camel coat with his damp paws.

"Stop it, Bumble—inside!" Tom commanded, and this time the dog obeyed him, inserting himself between the girls who were taking off their jackets.

"Oooh, he's all wet!" one of them shrieked.

"These are Ariel's," Caroline said, handing him a purple backpack and a rolled sleeping bag. "And these are Becca's." She handed him a second set, this one pink, then brushed some snow from her hair. "Are you sure you're ready for this, Tom?"

"I'm afraid it's Mrs. Prowse who will bear most of the burden of the sleepover." Tom dropped the girls' gear on the deacon's bench. "I'm going to the Burns Supper at your hotel."

"Of course. What was I thinking?"

"Would you care to come in for something warm?"

"I can't. I mustn't linger. I think I'm parked illegally in someone's spot."

"Oh, you drove the girls here." The hotel wasn't far up the road.

"I'm going into Totnes to join Adam and Tamara for supper. Tamara and her group are performing at the Civic Hall. Although if this snow keeps falling I may have a sleepover of my own, in town." Caroline cast him a faltering smile. "Anyway, it might be best to leave you males to your own devices. Burns Suppers have a certain reputation."

"Perhaps," Tom responded lightheartedly, tugging at his dog collar, "their chaplain will be a restraining presence."

A look of half-startled wariness seemed to cross Caroline's face. She stared at Tom a moment, as if entertaining some private care. "Oh, I should doubt it," she responded at last, forcing an awkward laugh.

"Caroline," Tom began, puzzled by her response, "are you feeling all right?"

"I'm fine." She paused. "I'm . . . perhaps a little concerned about making my way to town. It was quite slippy coming round the lane a moment ago and I wonder how the roads will be out of the village. I don't think I've seen so much snow outside of a ski holiday the family took in Switzerland before Ariel was born."

Responding to the sound of her name, Ariel said, "Mummy, have you got my camera?"

"Oh, yes, dear, it's right here." Caroline reached into her coat pocket. "Now, you remember what we talked about."

"Yes, Mummy," Ariel said with a sigh.

"And mind," Caroline continued, bending down, drawing her daughter into her arms, and lowering her voice, "how you behave towards Becca."

"Yes, Mummy." Ariel sighed again, enduring her mother's hug.

Caroline held on to her daughter for a moment longer than the wriggling girl seemed to wish, then released her. "There. Now be good." She rose and addressed Becca. "The pair of you. I'll be having Mrs. Prowse give me a full report."

She gave a tentative smile as the girls, divested of their outerwear, raced down the hall towards the sitting room.

"And speaking of Mrs. Prowse, any more fallout from the great Yorkshire debacle?"

"Oh, it's a puzzle being pondered at some length."

Caroline's smile managed to widen. "I see. Anyway, I shall leave you to it. Best of luck."

St. Nicholas's bells rang the quarter hour as she turned back down the path, reminding Tom that six thirty was the appointed time for the Burns Supper to begin. Holding Bumble by his collar, he regarded the departing figure with disquiet. Through the demands of managing a hotel, Caroline carved out the time to lend her rich, slightly breathy alto to the church choir, faithful to the Thursday-evening practices and Sunday-morning services, where her white robe and silvery-blond hair lent her an almost ethereal air. But lately she'd had episodes of missing both, excusing her absences lamely, uncharacteristically—usually some consequence of short staffing. She and Will had closed their hotel after Christmas for renovations to take advantage of the low season, and this had given Tom the opportunity to have them for a meal, in part a belated thanks to Will for organizing Race for the Roof, the half-marathon fund-raiser for the church in the autumn. But that afternoon—unexpectedly, for he had found them simpatico on other occasions, imagining that Lisbeth, if she had been alive, would have taken to the accomplished and astute Caroline—conversation had not flowed with particular ease. He had a sense of another conversation, private and passionate, adjourned, to be resumed after tendering good-byes at the vicarage door. At the table, Caroline had seemed to watch Will like a sparrow hawk.

"Come on," he muttered to Bumble, closing the door, "we need to get you dry." He lifted the seat of the deacon's bench, pulled out an old bath towel, and began rubbing down the dog's rough coat. Looking up, he noted Madrun coming down the hall from the kitchen bearing a tray with four fluted glasses containing what looked like champagne.

"Surely, Mrs. Prowse, that isn't—"

"Heavens, Mr. Christmas! Of course it isn't."

He followed Bumble into the sitting room, where the three girls—minus the never-on-time Emily Swan—were gathered around the games table, which held two silver trays laden with Lilliputian versions of provender—tiny sausages, mini savoury muffins, chicken goujons, grissini, baby quiches. He was about to reach for one of the pizza fingers when he heard someone—Madrun—say "tut" followed by "those are for the *girls*, Mr. Christmas."

Becca and Ariel regarded him warily over their flutes of ginger ale, as children might when confronted by a transgressing adult, particularly if that adult was a priest.

He had an idea. He gently brushed his hand by Miranda's head, then exclaimed, "Look what I found! Miranda's got ten pence behind her ear."

"Oh, Daddy," Miranda groaned, as he showed the coin to the others.

Ariel and Becca's expressions brightened with curiosity as Tom made quick movements with his hands.

"Oh, look, the coin's disappeared. I wonder where it went? Perhaps Ariel has it behind her ear. Good heavens, yes! Only Ariel has *fifty* pee behind her ear."

Ariel shrieked as Tom once again demonstrated the coin, then, with more brisk handwork, caused it to disappear. When he pulled a two-pound coin from behind Becca's ear, both girls chorused, "How did you *do* that?"

"It's magic."

"It isn't," Miranda said firmly.

"It's a magic trick, then. Shall I teach it to you?"

"Don't you have another engagement?" Madrun regarded him over the top of her glasses.

Tom sighed ostentatiously and moved with theatrical reluctance across the rug, as he might have done upon the stage. "Yes, I suppose I do. Well, girls, enjoy your fine supper. Mrs. Prowse has outdone herself, as usual. I pray I shall enjoy the humble meal that awaits me at the hotel."

He turned into the hall and quickly crammed three pizza fingers into his mouth. Heaven! His heart and mind may have obeyed St. Paul's counsel to put away childish things when he gave up his career in magic for the priesthood, but for his stomach there were moments of apostasy.

CHAPTER TWO

❉

"No, Bumble, you can't come." Tom edged out the door of the vicarage so the dog wouldn't escape. But he had barely slopped four steps into the damp snow when he heard the door open and Bumble's victorious bark.

"Mr. Christmas, you forgot this."

Madrun was pitched forward under the lamplight, restraining the dog with one hand and holding forth a box suspended from a loop of string.

"What is it?"

"The sweet. You're to take it with you."

"Oh, lovely! All is not lost, then." Tom took the box, a light cardboard affair, such as one might get in a baker's shop, and tucked it under his arm.

"Someone might think you . . . Scotophobic, Mr. Christmas."

"No one loves a bit of Dundee cake more than I, Mrs. Prowse," Tom responded to the closing door. He refrained from informing her that *scotophobic* referred more properly to fear of darkness, cases of which seemed to be rare in Thornford—a good thing, as street lighting was entirely absent and likely to remain so, especially with the Thornford Regis branch of the Campaign to Protect Rural England so vociferous on the subject of light pollution.

"And Mr. Christmas . . ."

The door opened again. Madrun leaned out.

" . . . you have red sauce on your upper lip."

The door closed.

Rumbled, Tom thought, reaching for the offending stain with his tongue. *Blessed is the man that endureth temptation,* wrote James. *Not me, miserable pizza pirate that I am.*

He looked up through the scrim of dancing snowflakes towards the night sky, its curtain of low-hanging clouds silvered by the floodlights illuminating the blunt Norman tower of St. Nicholas's. He glanced at it fondly as he switched on his torch and turned the beam of light down the path towards Church Walk. In the short time he had been in Thornford, he had grown to love the little village church with its freshly lime-washed walls, its crooked aisle, its delicately carved reredos with the signs of the Four Evangelists, its wineglass pulpit, and its Victorian stained glass, and almost thought of it as his own property, a covetousness that he was reminded to banish in prayer. The Church House Inn, which hugged the corner of Church Walk and Poynton Shute, shone as a beacon, too, its leaded windows glowing gold and its perimeters delineated by Christmas lights, which Eric Swan, the landlord, had yet to take down. But beyond, as he crossed Poynton Shute, the village lay in velvety blackness, punctuated only by tiny bright squares here and there jumping with television.

At the corner, stopping to dig snow from the inside of his shoes and regretting that he hadn't worn his wellies instead, Tom noted a distant silhouette, limned in a torch's beam, moving down Poynton Shute, the gait—lumbering, rolling—recognisable. Roger Pattimore was rotund and pink-faced and projected an air of amiable distraction. In his kilt, resting below an unzipped Barbour too small for his girth, he looked like a hairless Clarissa Dickson Wright. In one hand he held a large black case containing, Tom presumed, a bagpipe; in the other, almost lost in the meatiness of his palm, was a mobile phone.

" . . . then I expect we won't see you for another fortnight," he overheard Roger say into the device.

Roger followed this with a grunting noise; he was close enough now for Tom to see him roll his eyes.

"Yes . . . well, cheerio, then," Roger signed off, sounding less than cheerful. He snapped the mobile shut. "Bless! That's *three* cancellations I've had!"

"Some don't want to chance the weather."

Roger shone his torch over the snow accumulating by the stone walls. "Doesn't seem too awful, does it?"

"Reports beg to differ."

"I haven't been paying attention. I've been so busy and Mother has got one of her migraines what with the barometer falling. Fortunately, Tiffany Snape's come off her shift at the post office. She's minding the shop for the next few hours."

"Ah," Tom said, hoping the response was sufficiently sympathetic. Enid Pattimore practised hypochondria the way Steven Gerrard practised football—with finesse. Most villagers thought her simply possessed by morbid thoughts of her own health, and, after several pastoral visits, Tom was inclined to agree, though he wasn't sure: Enid did have, besides migraines, the most remarkable nosebleeds, even if the timing of the red tide seemed curiously opportune. Method or madness, however, the effect was the same—to keep her only child, a six-foot-two, seventeen-stone, late-fiftysomething man on a short leash. "Is there anyone to look in on her?"

"Karla said she would pop up. Poor Mother," Roger added—ambiguously, Tom thought. Worry over his mother? Or worry over being visited by Karla Skynner, churchwarden, postmistress, and unrepentant bossyboots?

"What's that in your hand?" Roger flashed his torch against the box in Tom's hand as they turned to trudge through the snow on Pennycross Road.

"A sweet of some nature." Tom bent into the wind and wrapped the collar of his coat tighter. "Mrs. Prowse's contribution."

"Oh? I thought we were having . . . well, anyway, perhaps your Madrun's making amends for that bollocking she gave me the other day. Those eggs were fresh. And so was the milk!"

"Pride cometh before a fallen Yorkshire. I'm sure she'll recover her sensibilities before long."

Roger made a dismissive noise. "Is your lip bleeding?" He had turned his torch on Tom's face.

"Oh, is that still there?" Tom blinked into the blaze of light and rubbed around his mouth with his free hand. "I had a bit of pizza before I left."

"That's cheating."

"Well . . ."

"You might be surprised, you know." Roger squinted against the falling snowflakes.

"Mrs. Prowse said 'pleasantly' surprised."

"I'm not sure I can supply 'pleasantly.'"

"Oh?"

"I don't mean the food. I mean the atmosphere, sorry to say."

"I thought a Burns Supper was an experience not to be forgotten."

"I wouldn't go that far, Tom, though we've had some great fun over the years. Bless, it's one of the few times of the year I seem to get out of an evening. But . . . oh . . . I don't know." Roger trailed off, flaring the darkened windows of the Tidy Dolly Internet Tea Room with an absent flick of his torch. "I suppose Poppy is still on holiday in America."

"Until the end of the month, apparently."

Late middle-aged and fussy Poppy Cozens had owned the tearoom for decades, but when she installed the Internet she transformed her life, meeting an agreeable Californian on an online dating service.

"Perhaps it's time to call it a day."

"Really?" Tom was surprised. "I thought Poppy did rather well with her tearoom—all those coach tours coming in and so on. And if you don't have a computer, it's the only place in the village to—"

"No, no. I meant us—well, not you—us, the band. Although Poppy is actually selling the Tidy Dolly. I heard the other day—"

"The Thistle But Mostly Rose South Devon Pipe Band?" Tom cut him off. "You're an institution!"

"So were Lyons Corner Houses and look what became of them."

"Can't be that bad. Whatever's the problem?"

Roger seemed to ponder the question as they continued through the snow. "Will, in part, I think. And I'm sorry to say it. When he joined five years ago, when he and Caroline came to Thornford and bought the hotel, he seemed to inject a new energy into the band, especially when he became pipe major. Well, you know—he's Australian and a cricketer and all that, energetic, very positive, sort of a large personality, you understand. He sometimes seems too . . . large for the village. But lately—"

The muffled tinkling of "Ode to Joy" rose above their footfalls. Roger tucked his torch in his armpit and reached into his coat pocket. "Bless, another one, I expect." In the blue light cast by the mobile's screen, Tom could see Roger's face crease with disappointment. "It's a text. Look."

Tom squinted at the tiny lettering and read, CYN SAYS 2 MUCH SNO SO U CANT GO SORRY DAVE.

"Well, give him a point for rhyming," he said, handing the phone back to Roger.

"He lives at Upper Coombe Farm. It's all of three miles away!"

Roger slipped the phone into his pocket and sighed. "I'm not surprised. His wife hates the pipes. In better weather, we sometimes practise in Dave's four-acre field and have a barbecue afterwards. Cyn straps one of those music player whatsits—"

"iPod?"

"—to her arm and wears an enormous pair of earphones."

"Not to everyone's taste, I suppose."

"I don't know how that can be. When I hear the triumphant skirl, my heart simply rises in my chest. There's no sound as splendid as the pipes in massed formation. When we played the marine festival at Weymouth—"

"You're not Scots, though."

"Must one be? Bless, there's pipe bands the world over. I read in *Pipe and Drum Monthly* of a band of some Indians or other in the Amazon who play the bagpipes and they've never stepped out of the jungle or the rain forest or whatever it is."

"And all kitted out, too? Kilt? Sporran?"

"I'm not sure of that bit. I can't recall a photograph with the article."

"Wool would be awfully scratchy in that heat."

"Kilts can be surprisingly cool. I can almost see the attraction of skirts to women. The ventilation, you know."

Tom glanced to his right to see Tilly Springett's plump face framed in a bright mullion of her sitting room window. Her home—April Cottage—sat at an angle to the road and afforded her long views over the low wall of her garden, in summer a sea of blue delphiniums, towards the cottages and Purton Farm, the community field, opposite. Her eyes were raised heavenwards, pondering the snowfall, Tom guessed, and he lifted a hand to wave in greeting before remembering that he and Roger were but imperceptible shadows trailing cones of torchlight.

"Tilly's husband was a band member, wasn't he?"

"A stalwart," Roger responded. "Until a stroke took him and he couldn't move one side of his body, poor fellow. He was the one who got me started on the pipes. Bless, that's years ago now."

"It always strikes me as an odd instrument to want to learn, unless you're part of a regiment or such," Tom mused. "You wouldn't take a bagpipe to play at a party."

"Gracie Fields took a harp to a party."

"But nobody asked her to play, if you recall the song."

Roger grunted. "At least a third of our little lot—the younger men at any rate—was drawn to the bagpipes because of *Star Trek*. Apparently in one of the films someone plays 'Amazing Grace' on the pipes at the funeral of one of the characters—the one with the pointed ears. Can't think of his name."

"Spock."

"That's right. That's what inspired Victor, although he's one of the few with any Scots in him. Bless, but you wouldn't think it to look at him. His mother was Scottish. Or perhaps his gran. I can't recall. He must be Asian on his father's side. Hence the last name, Kaif."

"Is Victor the only thistle, then?"

"You might count Will, though he was an adopted child. But his adoptive mother was of Scottish descent, I believe, so I guess we could count that. Moir is Will's mother's name, by the way. Did you know?"

"No."

"Apparently his adoptive father did a bunk shortly after the adoption. Bless! Can you imagine? Then she emigrated to Australia, fresh start likely, who could blame her?"

"Not me," said Tom, who disliked tittletattle. "So you *are* mostly rose."

"Mostly, yes. With a smidge of lotus."

"Then Victor will be at the Supper, will he?"

"Oh, I think so. After all, Molly—oops, I don't want to spoil the surprise, the *pleasant* surprise, that is."

Tom raised an enquiring eyebrow, but realised it would be invisible in the dark. "Well," he said, uncertain what Roger meant, "perhaps Victor's attending tonight means fences have been mended as much as they can be."

"Bless, I hope so. We missed Victor at band practice through much of autumn, but you can hardly blame him for not coming."

"I think the sun rather went out of the sky for Victor and Molly the day Harry died."

Tom could hear Roger sigh deeply. "Poor lad. So tragic. I don't know why he would have signed up for cricket in the first place. Hardly seemed the type."

"To please his father, perhaps. Or try to be like the other boys. But that isn't why—"

"I wonder if Will hadn't laced into him so that day . . . ," Roger interrupted, on his own train of thought, then left the rest unsaid.

"I think all of us must stop wondering that, Roger. I know one thing followed swiftly on the other, but . . . "

Tom, too, left the rest unsaid. At a Friday-evening practice in late August, Will Moir, who coached the Under-15s, one of the youth teams at the Thornford Regis Cricket Club, had flared with rage at Harrison Kaif in language unbecoming an adult charged with children's welfare. For one reason or another none of the other fathers was present to restrain him, but one of the boys captured part of the rant on his mobile and posted it to YouTube under the title "Coach Goes Mental." Five days later, after the boy was last seen Saturday afternoon in Totnes, and a frantic search mounted, fourteen-year-old Harry Kaif's body was found floating in the River Dart at Baltic Wharf. No note had been left anywhere. Some folk had conjoined the two events, but Tom knew that self-inflicted death invariably came at the end of a long period of suffering. He knew, too, but could say to no one, that Will had seen him privately as his priest and had agonised over his outburst and possible hand in young Harry's death.

"Anyway," Roger said, "Will and Victor seemed to have patched it up. They each brought their daughters to the Christmas pageant, remember? They seemed to have a civilised conversation."

"Yes . . . I presume." As chaplain of the pipe band, Tom had, at Will's request, arranged a pastoral meeting with the two men. They had joined together in Tom's study on a rainy Saturday afternoon in late October, Molly having made it plain she wouldn't let Will cross the threshold of her home and Will feeling too much the supplicant to ask Victor to cross his. Will had been ashen-faced, abject in contrition; Victor had responded with an almost impassive civility. A chat, a prayer, a handshake, and it was done and dusted. Tom was certain forgiveness had been sincerely sought, but uncertain it had been genuinely granted.

Will had departed the vicarage first. Victor had lingered a time, the stoical mask slipping around the edges as he touched on life at the home front: Molly lashing out at Harry's school for its ill vigilance against bullying, at various children for various cruelties, and at him, mostly him, Victor, for pushing their son into sport when it held only terrors for him and pulling away from the boy's genuine passions. All of which he denied to Tom with rising indignation and sprinkled asides about Molly's coddling her elder child and not the younger. Tom interjected with an earnest offer, rebuffed in the days after Harry's death, to pay a pastoral visit on Molly, or meet with both of them, or do anything he could really, to help deliver them from this hell. But Victor drew in his shoulders and shook his head. No point, he said with ill grace as he tugged on his jacket and turned to leave. Tom watched him make his long-legged stride down the path to the gate to Poynton Shute, worried. If Molly and Victor didn't soon join together to address their problems, assuage their grief—and forgive each other their trespasses—walls would rise around their hearts and shut out love. He knew this. He had once gathered a few foundation stones himself in his own marriage.

"A penny for 'em, Vicar."

"Oh, it's nothing. I was just . . . ruminating."

Tom glanced to the left, towards the village hall, the windows of which were black and lifeless. "Looks like film night's cancelled," he remarked as Roger's mobile tinkled out "Ode to Joy" once more. *Singin' in the Rain* had been scheduled for seven thirty. As Burns himself attested, the best-laid schemes gang aft agley, though fickle weather may not have been uppermost in the great poet's mind. If the Burns Supper had been scheduled at the Thorn Court Hotel for January 25, Burns's actual birthday, then Roger's mobile might be less harrying. But as Will had explained to him, many of the Thistle But Mostly Rose hired themselves out to entertain at other Burns Suppers nearer the date, obliging the band to schedule its own celebratory meal well before or after.

"Another cancellation?"

"No, that was Mother, wondering if I'd arrived safely. Apparently they interrupted some programme she was watching with a weather bulletin."

Tom could see a frown forming on Roger's face, illuminated by a pale light over the sign that announced their destination. Pennycross Road curved to the right forty feet or so beyond Tilly's cottage and then ascended sharply around a high stone wall that defined the western boundary of Thorn Court Country Hotel's expansive grounds. Cut into the wall at the base of the small hill that the hotel crowned was a gate of filigreed wrought iron adorned with the letter *S*.

"It can't be good if they're interrupting TV."

"The snow's heavy." Tom pocketed his torch and pushed at the gate. "Goodness, perhaps this gate's iced up somehow. Here . . . " He handed the box of pastries to Roger, dug his shoulder into the curlicued metal, and heaved. With a reluctant shriek along its hinge, the gate budged a few inches, creating a nascent fan shape in the fallen snow.

"Bless!" Roger remarked. "Perhaps we should go round to the upper entrance."

"Wait! I'll get it."

Tom pushed harder against the resistant metal, finally gaining sufficient room to slip through. "There!" he said with some satisfaction, turning to Roger, who was calculating his belly width against the gap's.

"Tom, I think I'll have to get in the other way."

"Oh, don't. I'm sure we can get this bloody thing to move. Caroline drove the girls down to the vicarage earlier and said it was quite slippery. She likely meant the stretch up the hill."

As if to confirm this, at that very moment the sweeping oval headlights of car flared against the wall opposite, followed by a black bullet shape that careened around the corner and roared towards the heart of the village.

"Bless!" Roger gasped, backing against the wall.

"He might have taken out the side of the village hall at that speed! How irresponsible! Did you see who it was?"

"Too dark, I'm afraid. A sports model of some nature, I think."

"Well, you're not going up that hill. Here . . . " Tom grasped two of the gate's bars and immediately regretted not wearing gloves. The cold metal seared his skin. " . . . now that I'm on this side I can pull. If you put your things down, you can push."

But before Roger could divest himself of his burdens, the gate gave way with a sickening snap and Tom found himself tossed onto a low box hedge.

"Tom! Are you all right?"

"I'm fine," Tom croaked. "Just a little wind knocked out of me. Give me a minute."

The denuded branches stabbed at his backside and thighs while his head brushed against a mound of wet snow on the other side of the hedge. He was afforded, however, a view of the starless heavens through mediations of falling flakes.

"Good thing I'm not wearing a kilt," he remarked between breaths, feeling pinpricks of snow tickle his skin. "Otherwise—"

Roger interrupted him with a noisy sigh. "Bless, Vicar, I hope you're not going to do what's-up-your-kilt jokes this evening. We've heard them all."

"Sorry."

"May I give you a hand?"

"Another minute."

"You remind me a bit of the time Will fell over Mrs. Dimbleby's hedge."

"When was this?"

"In the autumn. At the Race for the Roof. I was minding the water station halfway and held out a paper cup to him as he was going by and somehow he lost his footing when he was reaching for it and fell over the hedge. He was quite shirty about it, blamed me."

"I thought Will looked put out at the finish line. I think he came in fourth."

Tom allowed his body to slide off the hedge, a task made easier by the slippery surface along his waxed jacket. He landed in a heap in what in better weather would be a bed of roses, but was now a quilt of snow.

"Still," he continued, scrambling up and brushing damp clumps from his sleeves, "Will raised a very good sum for the church roof repairs. The Race for the Roof was a splendid idea and he was willing to organise the entire event, as you know."

"Perhaps that's why . . ."

"Perhaps that's why what?"

"Why Will has become so snappish of late. He takes too much on. He manages this hotel with Caroline." Roger pointed up the steep path through the marshalling of cypress trees towards Thorn Court, as sinister as a sorcerer's castle behind the veil of snow but for the redeeming glow from the ground-floor windows. "He rehearses twice a month with us pipers. He plays cricket *and* coaches the Under-fifteens—well, used to coach. He's a member of the amateur dramatic society and been in all the plays, except the last one."

"Why not?"

"Oh, Harry's death, I think. Didn't want to be too much in the public eye, though he was marvellous the year before in *Abigail's Party* as the henpecked husband." Roger handed Tom the box of pastries. "And Will sits on the parish council, though . . . I expect there's a bit of self-interest there."

"Why do you say that?"

"Will is anti."

"Vivisectionist?"

"No, development."

"Of course, yes, I did know that."

Indeed, at lunch on Sunday, Will had been agitated about Moorgate Properties, developers based in Newton Abbot, making discreet enquiries into available parcels adjacent to Thornford on which to build new homes—forty or fifty of them, all with white masonry and slate roofs, all identical, all as sore on the eyes—Will declared in his Australian twang—as a rank of sheep pens. Thornford's frail network of narrow lanes would be flooded with more cars, a hazard to children and horse-riders, and a swath of fields designated an Area of Outstanding Natural Beauty would be spoiled. Will didn't say, but seemed to suggest, that such a development threatened to devalue the village as a holiday destination, no hotelier's wish, and his every gesture and twitch seemed intended to solicit Tom's agreement.

Tom, however, thought the fence a fine place to perch that afternoon. Yes, despoiling the English countryside was an idea with little merit; he could understand that—he loved his walks in the countryside with Bumble. But, he said, rising to open the wine, mightn't there be an argument for new housing? He meant, of course, affordable housing, of which there was little in the village. Marg Farrant, one of the steadfast and true of the Flower Guild, had remarked to him only the other day how desperately her daughter and her husband wanted to live in Thornford to be near her, but found themselves priced out of the market. From the corner of his eye, as he poured the wine, he had seen Will rapping his knuckles in random jumps along the edge of the dining table until Caroline's slim hand slipped across and squeezed her husband's larger, sinewy one, not wholly successfully, into submission. Tom barely had time to register surprise at Will's agitation—and acknowledge his own yearning for such a tender wifely touch—because it was that moment in which Madrun sounded her grief over the Yorkshire pudding. Afterwards, the subject was forgotten. Will was, if anything, subdued through the meal. They talked about the weather, a political scandal that was the lead story in *The Sunday Times,* the vagaries of fund-raising for a country church, and the controversy over national curriculum tests—tacitly avoiding parish council news, food failures, and cricket.

"What are your views?" Tom asked Roger as they stepped up the sloping path. By their feet, solar garden lights, tiny perfect circles illuminating the unblemished snow, guided the way through the darkness towards the hotel's front door.

"Of a new housing development? Bless, I don't know. I must say I could use the trade. It's all very well everyone wanting me to be open at seven in the morning if they run out of milk, or open at eight at night if they've run out of fags, but then they go off and do their main shopping at Totnes or Paignton."

"Well, here we are." Tom heard Roger grunt when they had reached the hotel's forecourt. Here the snow, glimmering in the soft golden glow of the coach lamps on either side of the entrance, was blemished by a splodge of footprints. Narrow trails of tyre tracks disappeared into the darkness. "Good, we're not the first." Roger shone his torch down the forecourt towards the old stable block, converted to a hotel garage. "Not many cars, though," he observed.

"I expect the weather is slowing people down." Tom glanced up through the tumbling flakes of snow to Thorn Court's belvedere tower, his attention caught by the upper window's sudden illumination. "I wonder who's gone up there at this time of the evening?"

Roger followed his glance. "Whatever *would* one do with it, I wonder?"

"With what?"

"The tower. Oh, sorry, Tom. I was reflecting on a conversation I overheard in the shop before Christmas. Two men were discussing this property, Thorn Court . . . for development." He turned his beam onto the garden they'd passed through moments earlier, now a hummocky white blanket spreading down to Pennycross Road below. "Bless, you could put ten cottages here, I expect. More."

"Oh," Tom exclaimed, startled by the idea of the hotel's grounds, ravishing in the spring and summer with vivid tangles of flowers, vanishing into slate and mortar. "Do you know who the two were?"

"I've not seen them before. Moorgate Properties types, I shouldn't wonder. Funny what you hear standing in a shop all day. People think you're invisible. Anyway, they were saying the hotel could be converted into flats, then speculated about what to do with the tower."

"But wasn't Thorn Court designed by some notable nineteenth-century architect?"

"I think so."

"It must be at least Grade II listed. They'd have to leave the tower, but more to the point," Tom continued, "Caroline and Will can't possibly be thinking of selling. He spoke so strongly against development last Sunday lunch, and, of course, they're going to all the expense of renovating and upgrading."

"Bless! Caroline would never sell. Except for the period between her father selling it and her buying it back, her family has held this property for nearly two hundred years. I'm not sure there's anything she loves more."

CHAPTER THREE

om, I don't believe you've met my brother-in-law, Nick Stanhope." Will motioned to his right. "Caroline's brother," he added
unnecessarily.

"Half brother." Nick shifted his whisky glass to his left hand,
took Tom's in his right, and shot him a taunting smile. His grip was
firm, crushing, as if testing Tom's mettle while his eyes, blue, bright,
and sharp, held Tom in an ironic thrall. Tom glanced from them to
Will's, which were similarly blue, but clouded, opaque, as if he had
something else on his mind. Only a slight twitch of Will's eyebrows,
so light and blond as to be almost invisible, suggested irritation with
Nick's gratuitous explanation.

"We share a father. Or shared, rather. But sod that." Nick took a
draining gulp from his glass. "More to the point, Vicar, are you ready
for a night of debauchery?"

"I think Tom has an early call in the morning," Will interjected
in a weary tone.

"Old Giles used to crawl up the pulpit Sunday morning after, I hear."

"Nick is building a home security business—a point of conversational interest," Will added, frowning as his brother-in-law shook his empty glass in his face. "And Tom, of course, is the incumbent at St. Nicholas's. The Reverend Tom Christmas."

"Father Christmas? Oy, where's my prezzie, Father Christmas? I asked for a shiny new shotgun and never got it."

"Nick, shut it."

"Just bring the bottle over, Will. There's a good lad," Nick called as the kilted figure departed towards a sideboard, then muttered darkly, "misery guts." The hard grin snapped back. "You'll want topping up, too, Father Christmas."

"I wouldn't want to slur the Selkirk Grace," Tom demurred. So this, he thought with a spurt of envy, was Nick Stanhope, paired for a spell—said wagging tongues—with Màiri White, the village bobby (more properly known as the Police Community Support Officer) who materialized in the village at intervals on her electric bicycle, a caution to those contemplating anti-social behaviour but a temptation to Tom contemplating the privations of his widowhood. He felt an unaccountable skip in his veins if, say, he glimpsed her outside Pattimore's shop holding one of her informal "surgeries" about village issues. There would go his silly bloody feet, carrying him witlessly down Poynton Shute when his appointment was in the other direction, past PCSO White, all for the chance to exchange a smile and a greeting and have a glimpse of her open, attractive face under her regulation bowler hat. Giddy teenagers had more poise.

He thought he sensed a reciprocal heed on her part—her smile seemed awfully warm—but he felt constrained, even after ten months in Thornford, to make some sort of overture. In part, he wasn't sure he was ready to let his heart be vulnerable a second time, expose it to a chance of breaking. Before he had been called to priesthood, before he met Lisbeth, his heart had been a buoyant sort of thing, quick to bounce back from failed affairs. But his love for Lisbeth had been swift, sudden, surprising, and all-consuming, and it had been his shield through the years against cassock-chasers, more even than the clerical collar banding his neck. His fingers strayed to its surface, starched and ironed at Madrun's hand. He was a man in holy orders and yet, without a wife, he was a man lingering, uncertain, on the shores of some sea of romance. Others might set sail in pursuit of love untroubled; few were as formally constrained as he.

"Ever get hot under the collar?" Nick smirked, gesturing towards Tom's neck, splashing a drop of whisky on his Prince Charlie jacket.

"Only when I bathe," Tom responded dryly, having entertained the hackneyed question more than once. What, he was beginning to wonder, had Màiri found so winning about Nick Stanhope? "That must be an ancestor of yours." Tom gestured towards a large, gilt-framed oil portrait over the mantelpiece of a solidly prosperous Victorian gentleman in a frock coat and high collar nudging long side-whiskers. Shared with Nick was the generously curved mouth with its hint of petulance and the short fringe of jet-black hair, glossy as an animal's, combed forwards to cover the incipient widow's peak. Shared, too, was the faintly bumptious gaze.

Nick turned to look. "I haven't a clue."

"It's your . . . " Will had reappeared with a crystal decanter and was holding it over Nick's glass. "Great-great-grandfather Josiah Stanhope. The son of the man who had Thorn Court built. It was painted by William Gush."

"Worth anything?"

"It doesn't matter what it's worth, Nick. We're not selling it."

"Oh, for Christ's sake, have a drink, Will."

"And it's firmly affixed to the wall, too, so don't get any—"

"What do you take me for?" Nick said through his teeth. His neck bulged over his black bow tie. "Let me remind you again, brother-in-law, that you owe me—"

"Gentlemen," Tom interrupted in a low voice. "Perhaps another time . . . ?"

Will turned to him, his mouth a grim line. "I'm sorry, Tom."

"If you think you've landed in the middle of a family row, Vicar, you have." Nick trained his laser eyes on him.

"Nick, for God's sake!"

"Caro and Will forget that I didn't grow up here in this sodding pile so why would I be sentimentally attached to it? Great-Great-Grandfather Josiah can go fuck himself. There, I've said my piece, and I'm not saying any more on the subject tonight." Nick snatched the decanter from Will's hands, splashing scotch on the Axminster. "Give me that. You don't seem to be drinking anyway." He pasted back on his hail-fellow-well-met grin. "We're going to enjoy ourselves this evening, Vicar, depend on it. Now, let's see who else needs a drink."

Tom flicked a glance at Will. His face, under the shock of straw-coloured hair, bore the marks of strain: pallid skin stretched tightly over the strong sharp bones, smudging in the hollow of the eyes.

"I'm sorry, Tom," Will said again.

"Is there anything I can do?" Tom responded reflexively.

Will shook his head and smiled wanly. "Happy families, eh?"

Tom returned a sympathetic smile. "All alike, according to Tolstoy." Then, before he could think, the rest of the quotation slipped from his lips: *"Every unhappy family is unhappy in its own way."*

The skin below Will's right eye twitched suddenly. "Yes, I . . . I think he's probably right." He turned to look over the room. Tom followed his gaze. When Thorn Court was the private residence of the Stanhopes, he thought this might well have been the drawing room. The proportions were agreeable—the space was neither grand

nor boxy—and the predominant colour was equally agreeable—
a gentle sage-green wash over the walls, setting off the gold and dark
red chintz of the upholstery. With the sconces turned low, the drap-
eries closed, and the fire blazing, the room seemed to pulse and
glow, like a cocoon lit from within.

Will turned back to Tom. "Caroline and I foolishly involved
Nick financially in the business when we purchased Thorn Court.
He was content to let us run things when he was in the army, but
since he was . . . discharged two years ago . . . anyway, he's not happy
about us renovating."

"I must say, Will, in this light the room looks very handsome."

"Good, though I can't really tell. It all looks more or less brown
to me. Thank God for Caroline's good taste." To Tom's puzzled
frown, he added, "I'm colour-blind, didn't you know?"

"Sorry, I did. Cricket ball to the head was the culprit, wasn't it?"
His eyes, roaming helplessly over Will's head looking for a dent,
landed on his broken nose.

"It was to the back of the head," Will explained. "I've been hit
more than once. Anyway, we had the reception rooms redone five
years ago, when we took over. They're fine. No, it's the bedrooms
and bathrooms upstairs that need upgrading. Some of the plumbing
is from the early sixties, when Caroline's grandfather had the house
converted to a hotel."

"Enterprising of him."

"It was. I have to admire the old bugger. Most characters like old
Arthur Stanhope—"

"Caroline's grandfather?"

Will nodded. "—were driven to paralysis by the new tax regime
after the war. Running a hotel's expensive and complex, though, but
Caroline loves it. It's like she was born to it."

"I thought she was, in a way."

"True." Will permitted a short laugh. "She spent the first ten
years of her life here, and it always remained a kind of . . ."

"Eden?"

"When we were in Australia and Adam was very small, she would describe it to him as though it—and Thornford—were something out of some old children's story. *Swallows and Amazons*. Enid Blyton. Anyway—"

Will's attention was caught by the sight of two bluff men entering the room, rubbing their hands from cold, brushings of snow falling from their outerwear.

"Gentlemen," he called, moving to greet them, "there's a coat tree in the lobby."

The two were unknown to Tom, but he wasn't surprised. Having lived less than a year in Thornford, he still found many villagers were unfamiliar to him. At times, he rather wished that folk would wear those little sticky HELLO, MY NAME IS ____ badges for a season, so he could get caught up. Several of the other band members, all of them clad in Devon tartan green kilts and black Prince Charlie jackets, he did know. He had talked briefly with two of them—Jago Prowse, Madrun's younger brother and owner of Thorn Cross Garage, and Mark Tucker, his new treasurer on the parochial church council. Victor Kaif he could see slouching by the brass guard at the fireplace, the light from the crackling fire bronzing his attenuated, tawny features. His glass held no translucent liquid. Orange juice, Tom suspected, and wondered if Victor, being a homeopath, took no alcohol. He was in conversation with a man whose back was to Tom, but he recognised in the broad shoulders and the black hair shot with grey the figure of John Copeland, sidesman at St. Nicholas's, a man like himself both an adopted child and a widower. Well, he thought, at least one member of the Thistle But Mostly Rose besides Nick had braved the weather. John was gamekeeper and shoot manager at the Noze Lydiard Estate, ten miles north of Thornford.

His hand hovered over an oatcake with smoked salmon and what tasted, from the previous two he'd eaten, like crème fraîche.

Would it be piggy to have yet another one? he wondered, mindful of the dreaded meal to come. Roger joined him at that moment, frowning at his watch and then glancing at the carriage clock over the mantel.

"Tut," he said, lifting an appetizer from the platter. "You'll spoil your supper."

"And what would you be doing?" Tom watched him pop the entire morsel into his mouth.

"This is my first one! I've been seeing everything's all right in the kitchen."

"I believe your sporran is ringing."

"Bless!" Roger fumbled with the leather pouch at his crotch and pulled out his mobile. "Olly!" he shouted heartily, then frowned. "Well," he sighed, snapping the phone shut, "that's the last one reporting in. How disappointing. We don't have the numbers we should, and we have so much food."

"How many, then?"

"Let's see. We have no drummers. We have"—he glanced around the room and counted on his fingers—"eleven pipers. And we have you. That makes twelve."

"That's all right, then. Thirteen at a dinner is said to be bad luck."

"Perhaps we should seat you in the middle, like the Last Supper."

"If you're thinking of da Vinci's picture, then we'd all be sitting on one side, which might be a bit odd."

"Bless, it'll be more like the Mad Hatter's tea party, with all of us crowded at one end. Perhaps I should suggest to Will that Kerra remove a number of the place settings."

"Or, when we want a clean plate, we could all simply shift down one."

"If you recall the story, Tom, only the first person had the advantage of a clean plate. Everyone else was lumbered with someone else's dirty one."

"You're quite right." He wasn't sure if it was hunger or the whisky or the effect of the whisky on an empty stomach that had enjoyed little more than a finger of pizza in the last several hours, but he was starting to feel a bit giddy. "When does the show begin?"

This time Roger looked from the clock, the big hand of which nudged seven thirty, to his watch.

"Shortly," he said. "I'll just have a word with Will."

"Some hae meat and canna eat," Tom recited. *"And some wad eat that want it."* He had practised his accent for the Selkirk Grace with Màiri, who happened to be a Scot. They had met by chance in the snaking returns queue at M&S in Torquay the day after Boxing Day, he returning a shirt a size too embarrassingly tight, which his mothers had bought him for Christmas (Madrun's cuisine was ruining his boyish waistline, which retreated spinewards the moment he espied Màiri), she returning an electric underblanket (she already had one). They had whiled the time rolling *r*'s and adding epenthetic vowels until Tom impetuously suggested a coffee afterwards at the shop's café and Màiri declined, as she had a briefing with her sergeant. He should have known. She was wearing her uniform.

"But we hae meat and we can eat," he continued, banishing Màiri from his mind, larding the line with an enthusiasm he didn't feel for the haggis to come.

"Sae let the Lord be thankit."

A murmur of amens arose from around the table. If reciting four lines was singing for your supper, Tom decided, sitting back down in his chair, then he might take more bookings.

"Very good, Vicar," said a voice to his left, as the rumble of male voices in Thorn Court's private dining room rose in scattered conversation.

Tom was distracted momentarily by the sight of Kerra Prowse, smartly dressed in a black skirt and blouse, appearing from the door leading from the kitchen, and walking past the unpeopled end of the table where place settings for those absent had been removed. Under her upraised palm was a very large, laden tray. *Real food at last!* he thought, taking a deep breath, seeking some satisfying aroma in the atmosphere. And oddly, the aroma *was* satisfying, quite satisfying. He thought he caught a whiff of . . . but, no, it couldn't be, he reconsidered, as Kerra removed a plated soup bowl from her tray and placed it in front of him.

"Thank you," he said belatedly.

"You're welcome, Mr. Christmas," Kerra responded crisply, slipping a steaming bowl in front of John.

"I intended that for you," Tom murmured to John, as Kerra passed on to Will, seated at the head of the table. "Hmm," he added, inhaling the heady aroma, grateful for its unchallenging familiarity, "chicken soup."

"Cock-a-leekie."

"Of course." He picked up his soupspoon and poked it into the broth, pausing over the garnish, which appeared to be a crosshatch of glistening black leather.

"Prunes," John said, either reading his mind or noting his hesitation.

"Ah. I'd been told to expect a surprise. I doubt this is it, though." Tom avoided the garnish and lifted a spoon of the broth. "I didn't realize until we had the Moirs at ours for lunch Sunday last," he said in a low voice, seeking a conversational gambit, as John, he had discovered at PCC meetings and at church services, was a man of few words, "that Will's son worked with you at Noze." He flicked a glance at Will, concerned lest his host think he was talking out of turn. But Will was looking away, engaged with Roger, who sat to his left.

"Adam's been with me for a while now. He's a good lad."

"Just he and you?"

"That's it. These days, you don't need the full-time staff to manage a small shooting estate like Noze. On shoot days, we hire locals for beaters and pickers-up and such."

"Quite the operation."

"Nothing like when I was young. My father was gamekeeper at an estate up north, much bigger than Noze. There were seven men on staff." He turned to look at Tom. "Why do you ask?"

"About Adam?" Tom lifted his spoon. "At lunch, he told us about a professional forager, so called, Fergus somebody, camping out on your land—"

"Not my land. Earl of Duffield's."

"—harvesting dandelion leaves and chickweed and berries and the like—some of it for sale in town at the Tuesday market. Something about you nearly shooting him?"

Tom smiled, but John looked offended. "I thought he was a poacher—"

"And he turned out to be a fervid vegetarian, his jacket stuffed with purslane or something."

"I didn't 'nearly shoot him.'" John flashed a dark glance in Will's direction as he bent towards his soup. "I don't know how that got about. But he was trespassing, so I escorted him off the estate. In my dad's day, you could still crack a few heads, but the law's different now." The last words were tinged with bitterness.

"A friend of Adam's, it turns out, this Fergus."

"Took courses in gamekeeping with Adam in Hampshire, but some anti turned his head."

That prefix again, Tom thought, lifting his spoon. Anti-development? -vivisectionist? -war? "You mean, not keen on shooting?" he asked.

"An anti-blood-sports townie bitch, is what I mean."

"Ah, *cherchez la femme*," he responded, startled by John's uncharacteristic eruption of feeling.

John bent towards his soup and nodded. "Jago's daughter holds the same views," he said in a low voice.

"Kerra?"

"No, the older one. Tamara. She's up at Exeter these days, at university."

"Yes, I know. She came to lunch with Adam. They seem to be paired."

"Which is why Adam said nothing to me about this Fergus character trespassing. Tamara has her hooks well in."

Laughter rose in Tom's throat. Tamara struck him as eminently sensible, Adam as rather gawky. Love-and-marriage, horse-and-carriage, a cosy-cottage-just-for-two seemed an unlikely outcome. They were both so young.

"Are you suggesting Tamara is out to convert Adam to all things green and environmental?"

"Not if I can help it."

"Be patient."

"I've learned to wait." John leaned away as Kerra came up behind to retrieve their soup bowls. Tom glanced at his profile and thought his words oddly freighted. There was a certain gravitas to John Copeland; his seriousness helped lend Sunday-morning services at St. Nicholas's an added dignity. He suspected John still carried the burden of at least one private sorrow: His wife had died more than a decade before; they'd had no children. He had not remarried. Perhaps he was reluctant to commit himself, or, Tom thought worriedly, watching Kerra round the table and pick up Roger's and Nick's bowls, perhaps John had worn a rut down life's pathway and become set in his ways.

A high-pitched shriek snapped him out of his reverie. He glanced through the candle flame to see Kerra jerk her body, her laden tray tipping dangerously towards the unfamiliar man seated to Nick's left. The shadowy light captured the smirk on Nick's face;

little imagination was needed for anyone on Tom's side of the table to suss what had passed. Seated on Nick's right, however, Jago merely raised a startled glance.

"Kerra?" he said.

"It's nothing, Dad." Kerra's free hand straightened her skirt.

"Nick!" Will barked. "We're having none of that here."

"It's just a bit of fun." Nick cast his brother-in-law a look of cold disdain.

Understanding flickered across Jago's face. "You keep your bloody hands off my daughter." He elbowed Nick's shoulder.

"Dad, it's all right!" Kerra was insistent.

"Sorry," Nick muttered, his sour expression giving lie to his words. Then he shot out of his seat. "I'm going for a pee," he announced, petulant as a child.

"Nick, for heaven's sake, we're about to have the haggis. And that's the *servery* door . . . oh, never mind."

"Make sure that's all you do out there!" Jago shouted after him as Nick pushed through one of the two doors on the far wall. He folded his arms over his chest and glowered.

"I apologise for my brother-in-law's behaviour." Will's cheek twitched below his left eye.

Jago shrugged. Roger, to his right, shifted his bulk. "Vic?" he prompted. "You might—"

But Victor Kaif was already rising to leave. Tom watched him pass through the second door into the connecting hall, an awkward silence descending in his wake. Tom glanced at the other pipers down the table, men he didn't know, roast-beef faces above black bow ties red with discomfiture or drink. Many, as if orchestrated, reached for whisky glasses all at once; others found a point of interest in their silverware or the arrangement of thistles and heather in a crystal bowl in the centre of the table.

And then, suddenly, everyone broke into conversation, as if kindled by the tension in the room. Mark Tucker, who was sitting to his right, said in Tom's ear: "Did you know the ancient Romans had a kind of haggis?"

"I was rather hoping it was confined to a single ethno-cultural group." Tom glanced at Mark, who seemed to be fiddling with something along the side of his leg.

"Your first?"

Tom nodded. "You?"

"Third. I've been with the Thistle But Mostly Rose for four years, but Ruby was born at the New Year two years ago, so . . ." He trailed off. "Anyway, I was going to say that there's a story that Marcus Aurelius poisoned his co-emperor, Lucius somebody or other—can't remember the chap's name—by using a knife smeared with poison on one side. You see, he gave old Lucius the half touched by the poisoned side of the blade. Clever, yes? Well, wicked, of course, but quite clever. I think I could use that."

"Should you, though? The consequences might not be wholly agreeable."

"No, I meant in some writing."

Tom regarded his seatmate. Mark was almost ridiculously fair-skinned, round-jawed, and cherubically curly on top. With his black horn-rims, he looked every inch a young accountant, which he was. He had accepted an appointment the previous year as the new treasurer on the parochial church council and Tom was enormously pleased with his proficiency at accounting and his ability to explain some of its more abstruse aspects without making everyone else in the group cross-eyed with boredom. It was as though Mark were born to accountancy. Both his father and his uncle were accountants, and he worked for them at Tucker, Tucker & Tucker in Totnes. Tom suspected he had been a sweet, agreeable little boy who had never questioned following in his father's footsteps, until recently. He was reminded that Violet Tucker, Mark's wife, and a young member of the Flower Guild, had broadly hinted that she wished he might sit down and have a bit of a man-to-man with Mark, who was having his midlife crisis well in advance of his peers. Mark, it seemed, was thinking of throwing accountancy over to—and here Violet rolled her eyes in despair—write. And not simply novels, but "bestsellers." Possibly including poisoned knives.

"You're not by any chance reciting the address to the haggis, are you?" he asked Mark.

"How did you guess?"

"Well, for one thing, you just pulled that knife out of your sock."

"Ah, my *sgian dubh*."

"And your anecdote about Marcus Aurelius suggests research."

Mark lifted the black-handled knife, the tip of which looked worryingly sharp. "Yes, I was rooting around. I wanted to make sure I *plunge* the knife in just so." He made a stabbing motion with the instrument. "There was some jolly useful stuff on YouTube."

"I thought the master of ceremonies made the address."

"Yes, well . . . " Mark hesitated. "Will called earlier in the week and asked if I wouldn't mind. And of course I didn't. I've been practising for days. You did well with yours."

"Mine was only four lines."

Mark patted his chest. "No danger. I've written it out, just in case. I've always fancied a bit of acting, but putting bits of Gaelic to memory is a task."

"I wonder why . . . ," Tom began, then stopped himself. The change of personnel was none of his business.

"Because . . . " Mark seemed to intuit the question, then hesitated, adding in a low voice, "He said he simply didn't feel up to it."

They both stole a glance across the gleaming linen at Will. The low light cast unforgiving shadows on his lean features, accentuating the heavy lines on his brow and the bracketed flesh around his lips, downturned now as if he had descended into some private rumination. His lids then sank slowly over his eyes, not, Tom thought, in fatigue, but more in prayer attitude. But when a weary sigh followed, and Will's body slumped a little in his chair, Tom felt an odd flicker of alarm. Indefatigability was Will's usual mien. But then, Tom reflected, Will had seemed preoccupied much of the evening, as he had been at lunch the previous Sunday. He was about to turn back to Mark and lob a question about his adventures in writing when Will's eyes shot open. He stared at them.

"What?" he said.

Mark replied. "I was just telling Tom that I would be addressing the haggis."

"Instead of you," Tom added.

Will cracked a small smile and scratched his nose where a vicious bouncer from a fast bowler had broken it during a cricket match when he was younger. "I thought I wouldn't make you Poms suffer Scottish with an Aussie accent. Pretty awful. And shouldn't you be out there, Mark? You're part of the procession. Fill your glasses everyone," he added in a raised voice.

"Oops!"

Mark scrambled out of his seat and out the door to the corridor. Shortly after, an unearthly wheezing noise intruded. From behind him, Tom sensed the French doors to the main dining room opening; in front of him the candles flickered, teased by the onrush of new air. The noise expired, mercifully, but then a rude wail burst forth, so loud and uncannily thrilling that Tom jolted against the back of his chair, nearly tipping it. Everyone at table rose at that moment, Tom following, and began clapping in rhythm. The wail formed into a recognisable tune, and then, there was Victor Kaif, his cheeks puffed before a reed, his expression concentrated, his arms cradling what looked like a black velvet pig jabbed with sticks, rounding the table followed by, of all people, his wife, Molly, in cook's whites, holding a silver platter high over her head. Tom hadn't seen husband and wife in the same room together for months. Mark trailed behind. They rounded the table twice—Tom prayed the archangel Michael would manifest with earplugs—then Molly set the dainty dish before Mark's seat. The haggis, unadorned as it was by any sissy garnish, resembled nothing so much as a pale, perspiring football, insufficient to feed twelve men. Tom's stomach lurched.

Molly stepped back into one corner, while Victor stood sentinel in another. Nick returned through the servery door with a mumbled "sorry" and resumed his place. Everyone sat, and Mark, with great solemnity, began,

> *Fair fa' your honest, sonsie face,*
> *Great chieftain o' the puddin-race!*

After which, as the second verse piled on the first, Tom's mind went a bit walkabout. Perhaps one needed a Berlitz course in Scots dialect to appreciate the finer aspects of Robert Burns's verse, though Mark, he noted, was performing the wild-eyed Scot with admirable aplomb.

> *His knife see rustic Labour dight,*

Mark continued, picking up the dirk, which flashed gorgeously in the candlelight. His voice rose to a fierce grunt on the words,

> *An' cut you up wi' ready sleight,*

and he plunged the blade through the bladder's taut skin, sending a plume of steam into the air, followed by another smart cut, St. Andrew's cross fashion.

> *Trenching your gushing entrails bright,*
> *Like ony ditch;*
> *And then, O what a glorious sight,*
> *Warm-reekin', rich!*

Reekin', yes. Tom suppressed a gag, his salivary glands uninspired by the—several descriptors suggested themselves: *reek, stench, stink*—that the dish emitted. He didn't think he was a fussy eater, but there was something awful about offal.

> *Ye pow'rs, wha mak mankind your care,*
> *And dish them out their bill o' fare,*
> *Auld Scotland wants nae skinking ware,*
> *That jaups in luggies;*
> *But if ye wish her gratfu' prayer . . .*

Mark paused dramatically. Tom hastened to pick up his whisky glass, as the others were doing.

> *Gie her a haggis!*

he concluded with a shout of bravado.

> *Gie her a haggis!*

the company roared in response.

"Fuck!" A furious Aussie quack rose above their dying words, as the bright ping of shattering glass pierced the air. *"Jesus!"*

CHAPTER FOUR

✦

*I*t's only a bloody glass, Will," Nick boomed. "Get another one. We can't sit with our arms in the air all night. Sod it, I'm having mine anyway."

Nick tilted his head and took an inch of the amber liquid in one gulp. Everyone else hesitated while Will bent and tucked his arm under the table, producing the ruined glassware, a jagged half-moon piece vanished from the rim as if bitten off by some animal.

"That's all right, Molly." Will took the large piece she had retrieved near her feet and dropped it into the crystal shell. "The Hoover can get the bits in the morning."

As Molly exited the room, Will rose awkwardly and turned to the sideboard, the containers on which twinkled and gleamed.

"C'mon, mate!" Nick began a slurred chorus to the tune of "O Come All Ye Faithful." "Why are we waiting? Why are we . . . Will, there's whisky right here on the bloody table."

"There's Oban here, Nick."

"Then what's this swill we're drinking? Here I thought you were serving the best whisky first. It's like that wedding in the Bible, eh, Vicar?"

"At Cana," Tom responded. Will's arms were raised like black wings as he poured scotch from bottle to fresh glass. "The custom was to serve the best wine first, but after they'd nearly run out and Jesus changed water into wine, the steward complimented the bridegroom on saving the best for last."

"He turned the water into scotch." Nick mangled the Johnny Cash song.

"Nick," John growled, setting his glass down, "have some bloody respect."

"The first miracle, yes?" Mark twiddled his *sgian dubh*.

"There are no miracles." Will turned back to them, gripping the crystal tumbler close to his chest, his expression overtaken by some emotion Tom couldn't identify. A drop of scotch snaked down the side and dripped onto his jacket. "None." Will raised his glass, which blazed like a bowl of fire in the candlelight. *"Gie her a haggis!"*

"Gie her a haggis!" they roared—again—in kind. As whisky slipped down a dozen throats, Kerra reappeared through the servery door, this time with a platter groaning with plates.

When she set his before him, Tom couldn't help but stare. In the enormity of the white china sea sat three tiny balls, one brown, one creamy white, one yellowy white, daintily crowned with a sprig of green, possibly coriander, and artfully bordered by two puddles, one chocolate-coloured, one golden. Nonplussed, he glanced around the table at the others jawing their way through this mingy bit of nosh. *Is this it? Can this be supper?*

Jesus wept.

Eschewing the two whitish balls, which could only be the tatties and neeps, he braved the brown ball, forking half of it into his mouth, while holding his breath against the unfamiliar aroma. Mealy, he thought. Dry. Not quite so nasty as he'd imagined, though.

The oats and onion helped, though the chopped liver gave the concoction an unpleasant mouth-feel. He reached for his whisky for a cleansing dram, then pushed the remainder of the haggis ball through the chocolate puddle, which he hoped was gravy. It was, and he was grateful. The potato ball and turnip ball he polished off in short order. The other puddle helped. An orange-honey reduction, it quite nicely disguised the bitterness of the neeps.

"Would you care for more?" Mark asked, gesturing towards the plattered haggis, from which curls of steam still rose.

"Oh, no, I've eaten heartily," Tom lied preposterously. The whisky really was getting to him. He glanced at Mark's plate. "You've hardly eaten any!"

"I love potatoes, but the rest . . . " He grimaced.

Tom looked around the table. Hardly anyone had finished his haggis ball.

"The haggis is just for show," Mark confided. "Pretty horrible stuff. Nobody really likes it."

Tom's heart sank and stomach protested. Surely pudding would be glorious, and ample.

"I'll have more," Will said above the rumble of other voices.

"Except for Will," Mark added. "Will always has more haggis. He—"

"Trying to prove something," Nick interrupted, reaching for the platter and pushing it down a path past the candelabra, whisky decanters, and Roger's plate towards his brother-in-law.

Will ignored the jibe and silently thrust his spoon into the innards of the haggis, scooping a sizable portion onto his plate. He ate with concentration.

"I forgot something." John rose, dropped his napkin by his plate, and sidled behind the other diners to the corridor exit. At the same time, Kerra popped through the servery door and began removing the plates. John returned after a few moments and resumed his seat, wearing, Tom noted, a preoccupied frown.

"Problem?"

"Oh!" John started, rubbing at something in his left hand. "No . . . nothing. I . . . took a quick look outside. I think we're in for it. I've never seen snow like this. Monday's shoot will be cancelled for certain. It may be a task getting back to Noze tonight."

"It looks like it might have been a task getting *into* Thornford." Tom cast his eyes around the table. "I don't know those gentlemen well"—he nodded towards those farther along the table—"but I think other than Nick you're the only one here who doesn't live right in the village."

John followed his glance. "If Nick drinks much more, he won't be able to drive anywhere. My Land Rover's fit for most weather, but I'm not sure about this. It was getting icy when I came down a few hours ago and now the snow's getting deep." He opened his hand and removed what appeared to be a pink tablet. "Antacid," he muttered, popping it into his mouth and chasing it with sip of whisky.

"I sympathise. Haggis is rather—"

"It's not because of the haggis, Tom."

"Oh, I'm sorry." He knew some people suffered terribly from acid stomach. But John shot him a smile that seemed to invite enquiry.

"What?" he said, but before John could reply, the door from the servery opened yet again, and this time both Kerra and Molly Kaif stepped forth with trays of steaming china. Some wisp of aroma reached Tom's nose. His heart soared. Yes! That whiff he had caught earlier! He hadn't been wrong. Faces on the other side of the table beamed in the buttery light as heaped plates were placed before them. When Molly placed Nick's before him, he shouted,

Gie her a curry!

A roar of approval followed, fit to bring down the ceiling. Tom smiled upon the fare as he watched Kerra set Will's plate down, then

John's, then his own. Glory be! Curry! And it looked beyond splendid. Perfumy basmati rice and what looked like chicken jalfrezi swimming in red and green peppers. A creamy golden lamb korma. Dal with tomato and courgette, sprinkled with fresh-chopped coriander. This is what he had been missing. One of the middling deficits of village life was not being able to pop out for a curry takeaway. He lifted his fork and tried the dollop of tamarind chutney on the plate's edge. Piquant. It was bliss.

Roger caught his eye and said across the table, "Surprised?"

"I am! And happily. Do you always have curry for your Burns Suppers?"

"It varies. But with the supper being here in Thornford this year and with the hotel staff being on . . . hiatus, right, Will? And, bless, with Molly being a dab hand with garam masala . . ."

Tom leaned over his plate to look down the table. "Cheers, Victor. This is brilliant. You're a lucky man."

But Victor returned only a doleful glance. Tom realised his indiscretion in an instant and felt a fool. Of course Victor mightn't account himself a lucky man these days, not in the aftermath of his son's death, not with a marriage strained and foundering.

By the end of the main course, having drunk much water along with the whisky to cool his tongue, Tom felt the need to—as his proper grannie in Sevenoaks would say—"spend a penny." Crossing the lobby on the way to the men's, he detected a shadow moving along the floor of the reception room, which was now dimly lit, the fire burning low. He peered in to investigate. What he saw was the back of a plump female figure in a pink ski jacket and black trousers, a bob of silvery hair brushing the exposed collar of a roll-neck jumper as her head tilted up towards the portrait of Josiah Stanhope.

"Hello," he called.

"Oh, hello." The woman turned, a slight jerk to her movements indicating that he had startled her from some reverie. The first thing Tom noticed were her cheeks, plump as red apples. She looked as grandmotherly as a figure on a biscuit tin, but for the girlish set of her hair, parted to one side and pinned back with a pink butterfly hair slide, and the brassiness of her lipstick, almost as red as her cheeks. As he stepped towards her, he was further shaken from his grandmotherly imaginings. Behind her gold-rimmed spectacles he could see the sharp shrewd eyes.

"You're not the manager, surely."

Tom fingered his clerical collar, the object of her scrutiny. "No, I'm not." He hesitated. "Are you wanting to stay at the hotel?"

"Well . . . yes." Her puzzled frown told Tom she thought he was dim. "If it's not a bother."

"I think the hotel's—"

"I did ring the little bell on the desk out in the lobby some time ago, but there was no response. I expect no one could hear it over the noise."

"There's a private function tonight. A Burns Supper, as it happens."

"Really? For the staff?"

"Er, no . . . perhaps I should fetch the owner. He's hosting the supper. If you'll have a seat, Mrs. . . . . Miss . . . ?"

"Ingley. Judith Ingley. Mrs."

"I'm Tom Christmas. I have to make a slight detour, Mrs. Ingley, then I'll get Mr. Moir directly."

"Moir? Then there are no Stanhopes?"

"Will Moir is married to a Stanhope, so, yes there are Stanhopes . . . You know the family, then?"

"A little." Judith Ingley's smile was indecipherable.

A few minutes later, Tom returned to the reception room with Will, who said: "I'm very sorry, Mrs. Ingley, the hotel is closed for renovations."

"Oh, dear . . ."

"We haven't been taking any reservations for the New Year. I hope someone on staff didn't make a booking by mistake."

"No, I . . . really, I drove down on a sort of whim. I didn't think at this time of year . . ."

"Where did you come from?" Tom asked.

"From Stafford. I didn't imagine the weather would turn so."

"That's a fair distance in these conditions." Tom glanced at Will, wondering if he might make some accommodation at Thorn Court for the traveller. But Will's attention seemed directed inwards. His large, bony hand pressed into the chintz fabric on the armchair set before the dying fire, as if he were making an effort to keep himself upright. Judith, too, was studying him.

"Are you well, Mr. Moir?" She reached down for the handle of a bulging handbag.

"I think maybe the curry hasn't agreed with me." Will placed his hand against his stomach.

"Discomfort or pain?"

"A little discomfort. It's nothing."

"Upper abdomen?" she persisted, opening the clasp of her bag. "Are you feeling any pain or discomfort in your chest, perhaps? I trained as a nurse," she added with a look that brooked no argument.

"You do look a bit peaky, Will," Tom added.

"Really, it's nothing," Will said, asperity rising in his voice. "All it is, is . . . wind."

Judith peered at him coolly. "Well, if you say so." She snapped the clasp shut. "Now, I wonder if there's a bed-and-breakfast . . . ?"

The few there were in the village—Weir House, the Moon and Stars, and Red Cottage—paraded across Tom's mind, but he knew that in this, the lowest weeks of the low season, their owners had not unwisely flown off to the Caribbean or Florida or the Algarve for a bit of sun. Once upon a time the Church House Inn had a carriage trade, but Emily Swan had three siblings, a mother, and a father who was the inn's landlord. There were no rooms at that inn.

"You mightn't get any joy." He shot Will another prompting glance.

But Will was merely prompted to embellish the current condition of Thorn Court: "Much of the furniture has been moved to storage and the heat is off in the bedrooms, so you see . . . "

Judith's shoulders sagged. "Well . . . " Her voice trailed off as she cast her eyes around the warm, comfortable room.

"I have an idea," Tom found himself saying. "I know we've barely been introduced, but you would be welcome to come and stay at the vicarage, if you like. We have extra bedrooms, and there's only my daughter and I . . . and the housekeeper."

Saying that, a panicked thought crossed his mind: How would Mrs. Prowse take to an unexpected guest? Were the extra beds made up? Would she have wanted to run a duster over the place? Or put in fresh flowers? God knew, there was enough food in that monstrous refrigerator to feed another mouth.

"I was a stranger and you took me in." She beamed at him.

Tom smiled back. "Then, in keeping with Matthew, have you eaten?"

"I had a little something at Newton Abbot."

"We're about to have pudding, aren't we?" He glanced at Will for agreement and decided to ignore the faint irritation ghosting his features. "Would you care to join us?"

"Are you sure?"

"If you don't mind being the only woman present as a guest."

"Oh!" Judith tilted her head in a way that was almost coquettish. "I shouldn't want to put you out of your fun. My husband once belonged to the Stafford Rotary and often attended such dinners."

"Your husband isn't with you on this adventure?" Tom asked as they passed into the brightness of the lobby. Judith removed her coat and added it, a burst of pink, to the crowded tree of green Barbours.

"I'm afraid my husband passed away, in November."

"I'm very sorry."

"May I join you in a few moments? If you'll tell me . . . "

"The ladies' is just there." Will gestured down the hall to the right of the desk.

"And we're off to the left," Tom added. "First door. Just follow the voices. I hope I haven't been presumptuous," he murmured to Will when she'd passed from earshot.

"No, it's . . . fine." But Tom could hear the lie in the hesitation. "Anyway, thanks for taking her in. Staying here wouldn't be . . . " He seemed to grope for the word. " . . . wise."

"Bless," said Roger, grinning at Tom after Judith had been introduced to the assembled. "I do believe, Mrs. Ingley, that you're the thirteenth at table."

"Oh, am I? Oh." Judith's expression turned to one of faint discomfit, though her appearance had undergone a recent refurbishment, the lipstick newly bright, the silver hair freshly combed. "Then I mustn't be the first to rise. It's bad luck to be the first when there's thirteen, isn't that right? Where shall I sit?"

"We've had a place set here." Roger pointed to the end of the table next to Will. "We wouldn't want you to have to suffer the company of the rabble down that end."

Laughter followed Judith to her seat. "I'm sure I've suffered worse. This looks lovely," she added, settling into the chair pulled out for her, indicating the tall fluted crystal glass with contents layered white, red, and gold, set on a crested china plate arranged with a plump berry pastry. "And you had an extra. What luck!"

"Bless, it's not luck, Mrs. Ingley," Roger said. "We have cranachan for twenty-two, but the snow put a stop to half the band.

Which reminds me—Lads!" He raised his voice. "There's seconds of this, if anyone wants."

"You've got more pluck than some of our lot," John said to her.

"I think it was more fright that kept me going." Judith plucked a raspberry from the top of the cream-and-oatmeal concoction. "When I left Newton Abbot, the snow had become quite startling. I simply clung to the steering wheel for dear life and didn't stop the car until I saw the Thorn Court sign. I passed quite a few drivers who had skidded off the road."

"Did you manage to find anywhere to park?" John asked.

"Oh, yes." She gestured with her spoon as she surveyed his face. "In the converted stables."

"Then you've stayed at Thorn Court before?" Will asked.

"I grew up in Thornford."

"Bless, did you now?" Roger rested his spoon on his plate. "But Ingley is your married name . . . "

"I'm Judith Frost that was."

"Oh."

Roger's slightly surprised tone made Tom glance up. Both Roger's and Jago's heads tilted as if they were searching for some memory.

"I'm older than you both." She laughed lightly. "You wouldn't remember me. And I left to take up training for nursing at St. James's Infirmary in Leeds when I was eighteen—many years ago—and I've never been back. Until now."

"Mmm, these are splendid," Roger interrupted, biting into the tartlet. The berries left a red stain on his lips. "These must be the baking Madrun sent along with you, Tom. You're not eating yours, Will."

"You have no family in the area?" Will's fingers hesitated over the pastry.

"I was an only child. Both my parents died when I was young."

"Bless! Not at the same time, I hope."

"No, not at the same time." Judith turned to Will. "You're Australian, of course. Yes, the accent did give you away. How did you come to own a hotel deep in Devon?"

"I married into it." Will contemplated the tartlet. "My wife's father and grandfather had this place," he added, taking a large bite. "This is very good. Are there nuts in these?"

"Your wife is . . . ?"

"Caroline. Stanhope before she married me."

"Oh, then she must be Arthur Stanhope's . . . granddaughter. He was one of the bigger landowners in the village, wasn't he?" She frowned in thought. "Then your wife's father has to be Clive Stanhope. Where has—"

"He snuffed it." Nick interjected loudly, pouring himself another whisky. "About five years ago, six."

Tom studied Judith as she jerked her head in the speaker's direction. She looked startled, yes—at Nick's crudity—but he was intrigued to see another, cooler, emotion—a scrutinising intelligence—glittering behind her lenses.

"He was my father, too," Nick added.

"Oh, I see. I'm sorry. So many names when I was introduced. I guess I didn't catch yours."

"Different mothers, though," Nick muttered thickly. "Excuse my fingers." He leaned past Roger and handed his tartlet to Will. Flakes scattered to the tablecloth. "You eat this, Will. I'm bloody stuffed."

"I expect you knew Clive Stanhope," Tom said to Judith. Will was frowning at Nick's offering. He looked to the tartlet on his own plate and wondered if he had a cranny left for anything more.

"Everyone knew everyone then," Judith replied. "But—"

Will pushed his chair back, stopping her. He rose unsteadily and gripped the edge of the table. The flickering candlelight cast his features into sharp relief and shadow. "Gentlemen . . ." His voice slurred. " . . . lady . . ." He nodded to Judith. "I think a short break is in order here before we get on to tonight's entertainments. I think you all know what you probably need to do, so," he continued over the laughter, "shall we reconvene in about fifteen minutes?"

Will popped the tartlet into his mouth. Tom popped his into his. He had done what needed to be done a little earlier.

"Have you been in Thornford long?"

Tom let the front window drapery fall back into place. He had pulled the heavy fabric aside to look at the deepening cradle of snow visible in the porch light and worried if, in the morning, his route to the second church in his benefice, St. Paul's, in Pennycross St. Paul, a little over two miles north of Thornford, would be cut off. In fair weather, the drive took about seven minutes. But what about foul? He could walk, he supposed. That would take about forty-five minutes. But how long would the journey be in deep snow?

"Less than a year." He turned to Judith. "I was in Bristol for several years before that."

"And how are you finding it?"

"Quite different and oddly very much the same. A rural parish has its peculiar challenges, and yet the problems of people are usually a slightly different edition of a universal fact—suffering of some nature."

"All the world in a snow globe, I would say on an evening like this." Judith lifted the curtain herself and peered out. "You're quite sure you don't mind having me to stay?"

"Not at all. The vicarage was built for a nineteenth-century priest with a wife, six children, and scattering of servants."

"Do you mean the vicarage is still the Georgian pile between the churchyard and the Old Orchard? I thought the Church was dedicated to selling off such properties."

"It is. But the arrangement here is unusual. A previous incumbent—Giles James-Douglas—did you know him—?"

Judith shook her head. "I have been gone a long time."

"—had considerable private resources, so he bought the property and returned it to the Church in his will as a gift of sorts with sufficient moneys for its upkeep and so forth. Our housekeeper has a flat on the top floor and Miranda—that's my daughter—and I have the run of the other two."

"I hope you don't think me over-inquisitive, but is there no Mrs. Christmas? That *is* a wedding band, is it not?"

Tom glanced at the circlet of gold on his ring finger. "Technically, there never was a Mrs. Christmas. My wife was a pediatrician and kept her maiden name, Rose. But in any case, there is no Mrs. Christmas. Lisbeth died two years ago."

"Oh! I'm so sorry."

Tom smiled tightly. He could feel the force of a lively curiosity: The wives of men not yet forty, the mothers of young children, do not die in any way that is not tragic. And yet he was loath to offer details freely. Lisbeth had lost her life to a stranger, some madman—yet to be run to ground—who stabbed her beating heart with a knife as she passed through the south porch of St. Dunstan's, his church in Bristol. That dreary autumn afternoon, she had borne a gift, a doll, that was to be Miranda's birthday present, better concealed from their precocious daughter's eyes in the church office than in a cupboard at home. The horrible concatenation of events haunted him still, troubled his sleep and pierced his waking hours. Anytime he relived the details for strangers, he felt as though he were somehow reburying them. And, of course, he often found the pity unbearable.

"You must have loved her very, very much," Judith continued. "The ring has remained."

"I've never taken it off."

Judith studied her own rings, heavy old gold, one set with small diamonds. "I doubt I shall ever remove mine. At my age I don't expect to marry again." She looked up at him and cocked her head.

"But you're a young man . . . " She didn't need to say more. The implication was clear: *You could marry again.*

"Odd," he said. "You're the first person to remark on this. At least in my hearing."

"I don't mean to offend."

"Don't apologize. I have wondered from time to time what I should do with it . . . the ring. I expect in some way, I'm not really quite ready . . . " *To let go, to move on,* he thought, which removing the ring would imply. "I wonder for instance what my daughter will think . . . "

"You do have your own life."

"Yes . . . yes, of course."

"Don't mind me. I'm being intrusive." Judith laughed lightly. "You have other family, I'm sure."

"Yes, at Gravesend. Shall we?" He gestured in the vicinity of the private dining room. "They were all down at Christmas," he continued, hoping to abandon the topic of rings. "My wife's parents live in London and dote on their granddaughter. And then there's my wife's sister—she used to live here in the village, but she moved to Exeter in the summer, which is a shame, but, still, she's near enough. So on the whole, I'm not . . . ill commoded when it comes to rellies.

"And you?" he added conversationally. "Do you have children?"

"I have a son," she answered as they passed into the dining room where Kerra was finishing setting out the coffee service.

"And where does he live?"

"My son? Oh! In Shanghai."

"So far away. That's a pity. What does he do?"

"Oh, what do they call it? IT?"

"Ah, computers."

"I'm afraid he's not able to come home very often." Judith resumed her seat.

Tom glanced around the table as the other guests returned to the room, now chilled slightly in the absence of human bodies and the weak flame in the fireplace. Nick trailed after the others—a little drunkenly, Tom thought—and threw a couple of slender logs onto the glowing embers, which received them with a sudden crackle and flare.

"I've never been to a Burns Supper before," Judith remarked, watching Roger pour coffee into her cup from a silver pot. "What happens now?"

"The toast to the immortal memory, for one," John explained.

"Which is John's task," Roger said.

"Toasting the immortal memory of Robbie Burns, I presume." Judith lifted the creamer.

"Yes, and then there's a toast to the lassies. To Molly, who cooked our fine meal, and to Kerra, who served it. And bless, to you, too, now. That's my job."

"How kind. But I've done nothing but intrude."

"We must toast Her Majesty first," Mark interjected, reaching for the whisky decanter. "I'd better top up."

"That's Will's job, as host," John explained, glancing at the empty chair to his left. "Where is Will, by the way?"

"Will!" Nick roared.

Jago jerked his body away as if hit. "Christ! Would you *stop* it!"

"Get your Aussie arse back here!" Nick continued, oblivious, grinning at his own wit.

"There's a lady in the room, you idiot," Jago snapped.

"Sorry." Nick appeared uncontrite.

Conversation faded around the table as guests poured themselves coffee or whisky and reached for cheese and biscuits, which had been left on the table. Soon an expectant silence fell, broken only by the hiss and crackle of the burning logs and the gentle ping of china cups nestling on china saucers. After a few moments, Tom was certain he could hear a faint humming of "O Come All Ye Faithful." Soon it grew louder. Then, like a dam bursting, several at the table, led by Nick, began again to chorus loudly, "why are we waiting, we could be fornica—"

"Is Will in the kitchen with you and Molly?" Jago interrupted loudly, leaning around Nick to address Kerra, who had arrived with a fresh pot of coffee.

"Not now, Dad. He came in for a minute after you broke before coffee, but otherwise . . . "

"Odd," Roger remarked. "Perhaps he's in the hotel office. Could you look in, Kerra?"

But she was back in a minute with no joy.

"Odder still." Roger's hands travelled under the table into his sporran, then reappeared with his mobile. "Bless if Mother hasn't called four times." He frowned at the screen, then listened to the messages. "Weather reports. Heavens! They might even close the airports if this keeps up. Anyway . . . " He punched in a number and waited. "Can anyone hear a phone ringing in the hotel?"

Everyone strained to listen. "We're a bit insulated back here, Roger," someone remarked.

"Yes," Judith added. "None of you could hear the front desk bell when I rang it."

"Gone to message," Roger said after a moment, closing his phone. A thoughtful look settled over his fleshy features.

"Will probably switched his mobile off, if he's even carrying it." John reached for the cream.

"He's probably bladdered, is what he is," Nick sneered. "Fell over something. He's been doing a bit of that lately anyway."

"I don't think he's had any more to drink than most of us—excepting you," Jago snapped.

"Perhaps he's gone next door," John suggested. The Moirs lived in the Annex, the gatehouse of Thorn Court when it was a private residence, converted and enlarged. Though semidetached, it had a separate entrance, accessible only from the outside. "Shall I go and look?"

But he, too, was gone only a moment. "I looked out the door." He brushed wet flakes from his black jacket. "But there's been much snow in the last hour and there are no new footprints. He has to be in the hotel somewhere."

Tom glanced around the table and sensed in that instant that everyone shared the same premonition, that something was terribly wrong. He could see it in the drawn brows and arrested movements. Even Nick, whom he expected to be loudly dismissive, had fallen to silence. Tom's eyes fell on Judith's. A certain intelligence passed between them.

"I think," he said, pushing his chair back with more force than he intended, "we'd best go and look for him."

CHAPTER FIVE

It's really the only place left." Tom's eyes travelled the narrow, carpeted staircase, which disappeared into darkness above.

"Bless, why would he go up there?" Roger voiced the question on all their minds.

Three—Mark, Roger, and Tom—had delegated themselves to find Will. Tom had invited a fourth—Judith—reasoning, but not worrying the others at the table, that her medical skills might prove useful. Nick tried to bully his way into joining them—he produced the master key to the rooms from the hotel office—but his bellicose shouting of Will's name finally drove amiable Roger to steer him back to the private dining room.

Many of the bedrooms and suites on the first floor needed no keys, as there were no guests. Bed frames, wardrobes, chairs spilled awkwardly into the hallway, a concession to renovations, presumably, for the rooms Tom entered—and he entered with trepidation, switching on the light with foreboding—all were empty but for an amorphous shape or two covered in tarpaulin, a ladder, or a nest of tools. Workmen had not penetrated the smaller chambers on the second floor—once upon a time servants' quarters, now single rooms with single beds—but many of the doors were unlocked, too, suggesting that renovation was nigh. Dark turned to light with the flick of a switch, but no cry of discovered horror came from any lips.

And now the three men were gathered on the landing of the hotel's central staircase, attenuated in its rise to the belvedere tower above.

"Will?" Roger leaned against the wall and twisted his head upwards. His call held hope more than expectation. "Olly olly oxen free!" He turned back to them, his features falling. "I thought perhaps . . ."

He met silence. Will wasn't the type for this sort of game, Tom thought. If hide-and-seek were the evening's entertainment, he would have organised it properly.

"What *is* up there?" he asked. "I've never been past the ground floor."

"Nor I," said Mark.

"Never," Roger added. "Odd, given how long I've lived in Thornford."

"I have." Judith's voice came from above their heads. "A long time ago."

They turned to see her standing at the top of the staircase, bathed now in a soft light that poured along the walls. She had been in the tower room and had needed no key. Tom studied her face, but her expression telegraphed nothing. He had heard no yelp or muffled cry from above as they had searched the second floor; neither had Judith dashed down the steps calling for them to come quickly. Each little indicator in its way filled Tom with a new hope. It was absurd to be worried, he told himself.

"Is Will up there?" Mark asked the question on all their minds.

Judith descended a few steps and rested her hand on the banister.

"I'm so very sorry," she replied, "but it's the worst you might imagine."

Tom felt his feet as weights as he climbed the stairs behind Judith, his heart contracting with pity, his mind flown to Caroline, somewhere in Totnes, or perhaps gone to Noze, where her son, Adam, lived, and to Ariel innocently tucked up in her sleeping bag before the fire in the vicarage sitting room with his daughter and the other girls, all three Moirs unaware of this shattering change about to overtake their lives. When he entered the chamber, he felt the chill immediately. The windows on each of the four sides were opened to the night. They framed the ceaselessly falling snow, drawing in the icy air. His eyes were first taken by the unconventional seating, a chocolate-brown banquette around three of the sides, peppered with bright pillows and blankets, punctuated at each corner with a floor-to-ceiling mahogany bookcase untidily crammed with books of all heights and thicknesses. He envisioned for a moment the pleasure of retreating here on a rainy afternoon, letting his eyes run from the page of some beloved text to a contemplative view of the garden below or over the roofs of the farther cottages towards south Devon's soft hills. But then he willed his eyes to travel towards the very human shape lying in shadow under the south window, and felt pity anew.

"Lord have mercy," he intoned, looking down on the recumbent figure of Will, first at his kilt tidily pleated around his legs, his Charlie jacket buttoned and smoothed, his hands with their elongated fingers resting neatly across his chest, like the figure of a knight on a tomb. Tom let his eyes close before permitting himself a look at Will's face, and he must have wavered in his stance for suddenly he felt something warm press firmly against his stomach. Startled, he opened his eyes and realised it was the palm of Judith's hand; he should have felt at least disconcerted, but instead he felt strangely restored.

"I don't know why it works, but it does," Judith told him, withdrawing her hand. "Better?"

"Yes, thanks."

"It's the shock, you see."

Tom now looked upon Will's face. The overhead light in the tower room was perfunctory and unflattering; it was a room for daylight hours, but tiny halogen reading lamps had been integrated into the décor, and it was one of these that sharpened the skeletal scaffolding of Will's cheeks and the pale plain of his forehead where the mop of silver-white hair had fallen back. "Thou most worthy Judge eternal," he murmured, the familiar words of the petition swiftly on his lips, "suffer us not, at our last hour, for any pains of death, to fall from thee." But he thought he saw in the set of facial muscles that very thing—the vestige of some pain of death, some final suffering—and he felt a rush of sorrow.

"There was some . . . strain in his face," Judith said. "But the muscles have begun to relax. I arranged the body—"

"You did?"

"Force of habit, I'm afraid."

"I see." Tom imagined few in expectation of death arranged themselves so tidily, though he was surprised at the capabilities of this small and elderly woman.

"It's the training," she explained, as if reading his mind. "When you work as a nurse . . . "

"Did he suffer much, do you think?"

Judith was clinical. "There would have been some suffering, yes. I found him curled in something more of a fetal position."

"But Will was so fit. In his late forties, but still . . . He was an athlete. A cricketer, a runner. How could this happen?"

"I'm afraid these things can happen to those who appear to be the healthiest of people, Vicar. You're too young to remember the

American James Fixx, who started this running lark in the seventies. He died one day out on his daily run. He wasn't very old."

"Heart attack?"

Judith didn't respond. She silently studied the body.

"You saw signs earlier in Will," Tom pressed. "We both did, really. This is so awful. We should have done something then."

"I'm not sure there's much we could have done in the circumstances. Is there a doctor living in the village?"

"I'm afraid not."

"And look at that snow." She gestured out the window. "I don't think any ambulance could get through. Not tonight. And I'm sure they'll be taken up with all kinds of accidents and other emergencies in these strange conditions."

"But there must have been something—"

"Oxygen, if the hotel has any. Had him chew aspirin. If it were a heart attack."

"You don't think it was?"

"I'm a nurse, Vicar, but not a doctor."

Tom looked again at Will's body with grief. "Why did he come all the way up here?"

"Perhaps this room held some memory for him." Judith cast him a faltering smile, then added quickly: "Or perhaps . . . well, some creatures seek privacy when they sense they're going to die, don't they?"

"Perhaps," Tom responded reluctantly, though if he had such a foreboding in his middle years, he wondered if he wouldn't fight death with all the power at his command. Will had been so vital; it seemed so odd for him to retreat in death.

"I think I should like to offer a prayer," he said. "Will you join me?"

"Of course."

Tom sensed all eyes upon him as he and Judith stepped into the reception room. Conversation ebbed at the same moment, swallowed up into a ghastly calm with a muted sobbing the only interruption. In the far corner of the room, next to the window, Jago was consoling his daughter, whose pretty young face was puckered with misery. Tom felt almost grateful for Kerra's reaction, so ingenuous, so apposite, so fundamentally female. Judith had reacted to the death of a stranger as a professional caregiver might; Molly was absent, perhaps in the kitchen. But the men wore their stoic masks, scarlet with drink and heat and tight collars, rigid with suppressed feeling. Only their eyes hinted of troubled depths—shock and grief in most, as was natural, but disconcertingly, in a few, less expected sentiments: Victor, reinstalled by the fireplace, flicked him a glance fraught with anxiety, then turned to jab the dying embers with a poker. John seemed to look through him, as though working out some puzzle in his head. Nick had splayed himself across one of the couches and peered at Tom through half-closed lids, like a lizard sunning on a wall, his expression a disturbing amalgam of indifference and contempt, though possibly—Tom reached for a charitable thought—the man was anaesthetised by drink.

"It was his heart?" John spoke first. His tone made it plain that Roger and Mark had carried Judith's conjecture downstairs with them when they relayed the terrible news.

"It would seem so." Tom looked to Judith for confirmation.

"At the end, in any case." Her mouth fell into a grim line.

"I don't understand."

"I can only reiterate," she responded to Tom, "that I'm not a doctor, so I mustn't make pronouncements. Now," she continued briskly, addressing Roger, who was clutching his mobile, "have you tried to get help?"

"Bless, but there is none, I'm afraid. I phoned triple nine and described what has happened, but the man in dispatch said their resources are pressed to the limit what with all this snow. Some ambulances have even got stuck. This is awful, but they suggested we leave . . . Will where he is until they can get someone here."

"Christ," a snickering voice said from the couch, "he'll stink up the place worse than in life."

"Mr. Stanhope," Judith snapped before anyone could protest. "I have no brief for corporal punishment, but I think the sharp crack of a whip against the backside would do you a world of good."

"Dead kinky."

"Shut it, Nick!" Jago hugged Kerra to his chest.

Judith moved on: "Where is Mrs. Moir? She'll need to be told."

"Nick tried phoning Caroline just before you got back downstairs," Roger replied. "It went to message."

"I hope you were judicious with your message, Mr. Stanhope," Judith said.

"*I* left the message." John regarded Nick with something akin to disgust, handing him back his mobile. "I asked Caroline to call me as soon as she got the message."

"Caroline is in town," Tom explained to Judith. "At a performance at the Civic Hall, but surely it's over by now. Perhaps she went to Noze with Adam and Tamara. It's closer than Thornford."

"We've tried to reach them, too, after we tried Caroline," John said with a nod towards Jago, "but the phone service went off suddenly. The snow may be buggering the mobile towers in the area."

"Landlines?" Tom asked.

"Gone to message."

"Bless, but this is sad," Roger remarked, his face sagging.

"I'll go get her." Nick struggled up from the soft couch.

"Who?" Tom had a hideous vision of Nick barging into the vicarage to fetch young Ariel.

"Caro."

"You bloody will not!" John glared. "You're not fit to drive anywhere."

"And if an ambulance can't get in, how do you think you'll get out?" Mark interjected.

Nick fell back into the cushions and regarded them sourly.

"I find the idea of Will being in the tower alone unbearable," Tom said. "I'm prepared to sit vigil."

"Bless, Tom, you have two services in the morning," Roger responded gently. "And what about Ariel? Shouldn't Caroline be the one to tell her?"

"Of course. If I'm not home, they'll wonder."

"I can stop here for the night," John offered. "Then, if Caroline phones—"

Nick interrupted. "You are not stopping here for the night—"

"—then I can run up to Totnes or Noze in the morning when at least it's light out and bring her home."

"You are not stopping here for the night," Nick repeated heatedly. "This is my property. Caroline is my family. If Caro phones I can sort it out. And *I* can run up to town or wherever."

"And what are you driving, Nick?"

"The MG."

"Not your van?"

"Sorry," he slurred, "yes, I'm driving the van."

John regarded him coldly. "Well, good luck to you in any case."

"Gentlemen," Roger interposed. "I have a suggestion. We've had a tragic end to this evening. I wonder . . ." He faltered. " . . . I wonder if we might play something, as we had intended to do. But in Will's memory."

Tom pushed the door open against the accumulating snow and stepped onto the hotel's forecourt. He welcomed a rush of cold air against his cheeks, so sweet and clean that he couldn't help but lift his face into the night and draw a great purifying gulp deep into his lungs. It was an instinctive animal act, but he felt faintly faithless, as if he were signaling his relief at being liberated from the bright, heated claustrophobia of the hotel and the last terrible hour. Outside, in the hush, the evening felt as holy, good, and peaceful as a prayer, the village below slumbering in vaults of snow, oblivious to the sad news to come. He paused for another faithless moment to savour the cool, then quickly switched on his torch. Judith had preceded him and was pushing purposefully through the drifts towards the garage, disappearing past the glow of the hotel windows into darkness.

"Wait! We'll help you with your bags," he called after her, turning to John, who had followed him out the door. They were the last to leave, but for Roger and a couple of the other men who had kindly volunteered to help Molly and Kerra restore order to the dining room and kitchen.

"Are you sure you don't mind my kipping at the vicarage, too?" John switched on his torch and together they traced Judith's footprints in the snow, the beams of lights crisscrossing.

"I don't think it's worth you getting stuck trying to get to Noze in the dark. Besides, it would be good to have you in church tomorrow as usual. You might as well leave your vehicle here."

"I'll have to wear the kilt in church."

"I could lend you some trousers."

"Tom, I've got ten years and at least a stone and a half on you."

"Well, some detractors say a cassock looks like a party frock, so you won't be the only one in a skirt. Here, let me," he said to Judith, reaching into the open boot of her car and gripping a valise.

"Thank you. I'll take the other."

"I can take it," John said.

"You've got your bagpipe case."

"I have two hands."

"You do all insist on chivalry." Judith handed over the case. "Give me your torch, then. I should have thought to bring one. I forgot how dark it gets in some villages. And if there's a moon, it's not visible."

They all looked at the starless black sky emptying its burden. The falling snow seemed unceasing.

"I didn't expect 'Waltzing Matilda' to be quite so . . . moving on bagpipe," Judith continued after some moments passed. They had reached the gate at the bottom of the garden, still open and now firmly rooted in a drift of snow. "It was the *lento*, I expect."

"We can pull together when we need to." John grunted, sidling through the opening with the luggage.

"One person told me I would be pleasantly surprised by the Burns Supper," Tom added. "And another said I would be simply surprised. I didn't expect to be so shaken. I can't think what this will do to Caroline . . ."

"Is Mrs. Moir a blonde?" Judith interjected.

"Yes," Tom replied, startled. "Why would you ask that?"

"Oh . . . I knew her father when I was young. He was very blond, although I suppose for a man I should say 'fair-haired.' "

"A not unusual hair colouring in these isles," Tom pointed out.

"No, I suppose it isn't."

"And with Will being blond . . . fair-haired, too, they're . . . they were a very striking couple."

"Odd, whenever I imagine Australians, I always think of them as blond. My good friend Phyllis, in Melbourne—I was at school with her at Leeds—she married an Australian and, of course, he's blond. Or was, rather." Judith flashed the torch down Pennycross Road. "Look, the Tidy Dolly! And the Church House Inn! How everything looks unchanged! It's like a dream."

The pub windows' golden glow beckoned in the darkness. Beyond, at the end of Church Walk, past the lych-gate, the tower of St. Nicholas's rose above the tangle of the ancient yew, burnished by a floodlight timed to shut itself off by eleven. Tom realised he had paid little heed to the hour, but it couldn't yet be eleven if the pub was still open. How unimaginably long the evening felt, now that he was just about on the doorstep of his home.

"I hope Nick doesn't take a notion to run up to town or to Noze," Tom said, his mind shifting again to Caroline. That she couldn't be reached by telephone, that she didn't know her husband had died, seemed horrible and deeply unfair, but Nick as herald seemed insult to injury.

"No danger there, Tom." John gripped Judith's case under his arm, reached into his pocket, and pulled out a set of keys, which Tom illuminated with his torch. "I took these from Nick's jacket when I went for my mobile. That young idiot's not going anywhere tonight."

"Wise man."

"Is Nick's mother living?" Judith asked as abruptly as she had earlier.

"She predeceased his father," John replied. "I think. Do you know, Tom?"

"I know very little about Nick Stanhope. Other," he added grimly, "than what I've learned tonight."

The illumination from the pub window traced the stone wall separating Church Walk from the vicarage garden. "If the girls aren't asleep, and—" Tom glanced at the flicker of light against the sitting room window drapes. "—and they may well not be, then we must be very careful what we say and how we behave, for Ariel's sake."

"Poor poor child," Judith murmured. "Do you have children, Mr. Copeland?"

"No, I don't."

The wooden gate moaned when they pushed it open, eerily amplified in the night landscape. Tom swore he had oiled the hinges before Christmas; he swore, too, it had made no sound when he'd passed through earlier in the evening. Did alien snow and cold have the power to alter such things, he wondered as maddened, muffled barking in the recesses of the vicarage reached his ears.

Bumble had heard the squeaking gate.

And Madrun heard Bumble. Tom had barely touched the handle on the front door when the porch light flashed on and there she was, standing before him, gripping a tea towel. It took just one look into her spectacled eyes for him to know that the village drums had already been beating.

The Vicarage

Thornford Regis TC9 6QX

Dear Mum,

I've never written a letter by candlelight before, which I'm doing right now, but then I can't remember the last time the electricity went out. I was going to try and make my way down to the kitchen in the dark to the fuse box, but I think the whole village is gone out. Usually, if I look out my windows winter mornings, I can see a light from one or other of the cottages up Poynton Shute towards Thorn Hill, but the village is as black as Tobey's ~~arse~~ bottom, as Dad used to say. My faithful Teasmade didn't wake me, but of course with no electricity it couldn't very well, could it? so I am a bit behind getting ready for my day. Short note then, Mum, sorry. Though I wonder if any letters will get through if the rest of the country has as much snow as we do? Shame I don't have a battery radio up here. I'm without news of any sort. I am glad, though, that I haven't gone and got a com-

puter as Mr. Christmas has suggested. You don't need electricity to run my faithful old Olivetti! Though you do need ribbons, which I'm almost out of. You'll have to pardon typing mistakes. Candles aren't the best light and I don't want to spill wax on the typing paper. Or set it afire! Anyway, it looks like ~~its~~ it's going to be a very different sort of Sunday here in the village. The worst news is that we've had an unexpected death. Will Moir died of a heart attack last night. It's such a shock when someone dies well before his time, and Will was very fit-looking, not someone you'd think would die in his forties. It happened at the Burns Supper he and the Thistle But Mostly Rose were having at the hotel. Mr. Christmas is their chaplain. What is very sad is that little Ariel is with us here at the vicarage and doesn't know what's happened and we must be SO careful how we behave. I'd only got off the phone last evening with Enid who had called Roger at Thorn Court earlier and learned the dreadful news when Mr. Christmas came through the door—with two unexpected guests. John Copeland was one, and you know about him! The other was introduced as Judith Ingley. What a good thing I always keep the extra bedrooms at the ready! Knowing what had happened, I took Mr. Copeland and Mrs. Ingley into the kitchen for a nice cup of tea, while Mr. Christmas stayed in the sitting room with the girls, who were having that sleepover I mentioned in yesterday's letter. It hadn't gone 11 and they were still up watching a DVD and I thought I would just let them go on until they dropped while I played ~~sadukoo~~ sudoku in the kitchen when Mr. Christmas returned. He helped them roast marshmallows in the fireplace and managed to get them settled into their sleeping bags. I wonder if you remember Judith Ingley as she was Judith Frost before she married? Her father's family worked for the Stanhopes at Thorn Court, but he died young and there are no Frosts in the village now. Judith left the village when I'd barely started primary, so I have no recollection of her. There's a story

there, I'm sure, but I didn't like to ask as we were much taken up
with what had happened to Will. Perhaps Karla knows. Or
Venice or Florence Daintrey might, but then they're always
rather short with me, so there's no point asking. I thought to look
through Dad's history of the village—which I'm nowhere near
finished typing out of course—but by the time I got our guests
settled into their rooms I was too tired. And, of course, now
there's no light and no time. Good thing we have the old
wood-burning Aga or it would be a cold breakfast for everyone
on a cold day and no Sunday lunch! I'm doing French toast for
the girls, which I can stretch out for the extra guests and for Mr.
Christmas who usually only has a bite of toast before rushing out
of here for 8:15 Communion at Pennycross, which surely will be
cancelled. But what will happen to the refrigerator with no electricity? I hope this is only temporary. At least we have lots of
food in stock as who knows how long folk will be staying? We
must keep Ariel with us until either her mother or her brother
can fetch her. Poor child, losing a parent at such an age, and we
don't dare tell her ourselves. It wouldn't be right. I can tell,
though, that Miranda thinks something is wrong. She gave Mr.
Christmas a sort of "look" when he returned last night. She is
such a clever girl and she and Mr. Christmas seem to be able to
read each other's moods. Anyway, the sun won't be up for another
hour so I must see what we have in the way of candles. And I
wonder if we'll have enough hot water? I hope you don't have as
much snow as we seem to have! The cats aren't at all fussy about
going out of doors. They've never seen snow before! I don't think
Bumble has, either, but he loves it. He tries to get out and roll in
it any chance he gets. Love to Aunt Gwen. Hope you have a glorious day in beautiful Cornwall!

Much love,
Madrun

P.S. I don't usually cook roast beef two Sundays in a row, but Mr. C says I should get back up on that horse as regards my Yorkshire, so fingers crossed, Mum!

P.P.S. I just had a terrible thought! What if this weather means Karla and I can't get to Tenerife this year? We're to leave in 10 days.

P.P.P.S. Have you thought any more about getting one of those mobility scooters? Mum, I really think they might be the thing as long as you mind how you go on the hills!

CHAPTER SIX

S orry to be so early, I'm missing my Becca," Molly said in a rush when Tom opened the door to her, her anxious eyes lightening at the sight of him.

"Come in," he responded unnecessarily as she slipped into the vestibule, a whisper of the cold clinging to her jacket trailing into the small space as she passed. Tom glanced into the front garden at the pure sweep of white, broken only by the hieroglyphic of Molly's footsteps from gate to stoop.

"The sight of all this snow is . . . stunning, isn't it?" He closed the door and waited as Molly unzipped her jacket. "Everyone's in the kitchen. Have you eaten? Mrs. Prowse has plenty."

"I had a little something earlier, thanks."

"Your cooker is working, then?"

"Yes."

"So is ours." Tom received the coat from her—noting how thin she was out of her cook's uniform of the previous evening—and placed it on a crowded hook over the deacon's bench. "Come through to the kitchen. It's warmest there."

"Perhaps I best wait here." Molly pulled off a black crocheted cap and shook her head to release an abundance of carefully crimped spiralling hair, which fell down the back of the olive-coloured cashmere sweater she was wearing over rust jeans.

Tom wondered if he should take her choice of apparel as a hopeful sign of better mental health. Molly's pedigree was pure Anglo-Celt, expressed in her fair skin, fox-red hair, and dusting of freckles across her nose, but she had long been gossiped about in the village for wearing dresses over trousers in the Indian style, for the multiplicity of gold bracelets along her arm, the embellishment of a sari on festive occasions, and even, sometimes, a caste mark on her forehead, which she really had no business wearing. She reminded Tom when he first arrived in Thornford of a religious convert who took on the trappings of new faith with zeal, though she came to St. Nicholas's intermittently, placed Becca in Sunday school, and made no practice of alternative faith. He suspected the thoroughly assimilated Victor tolerated this sort of show in his wife, and wondered what his views were on the new Molly who had emerged recently from her fabulist chrysalis as a garden-variety village mum in jeans and jacket—though the gear looked, to Tom's undiscerning eye, to be the *best* sort of jeans and jacket.

"I'm sorry to be early to pick her up, but I wanted to know she was all right."

"Becca's fine, Molly," Tom said gently, leading her into the sitting room, where he had earlier lit a fire against the chill. Sleeping bags, articles of clothing, DVD cases, and detritus of some board game were scattered over the rug. He glanced at the open door to the hall and lowered his voice. "The girls don't know what's happened. We haven't said anything."

"Oh, I am relieved. I thought about coming for Becca last night."

"I'm very glad you didn't," Tom replied evenly. He was startled that Molly would have considered intruding upon the girls' party, and imagined the effect. What worse signal could there have been that something had gone disastrously wrong?

He regarded her with pity. She had suffered the most appalling loss a parent could suffer. Briefly, after the shock of her son's death, she seemed to come to grips with her loss, resuming some of the rhythms of her old life, managing the Totnes branch of GoodGreens, one of a chain of health-food shops in the West Country owned by her parents, and event catering, which allowed her to parade her culinary talents.

But soon, it was as if the full realisation of what she had suffered had reached out and pulled her into a grey mist. He had heard from Madrun that she abrogated her few duties to GoodGreens and turned down catering contracts. Victor would bring Becca to Sunday school; Molly retreated to Damara Cottage, her and Victor's home on Orchard Hill, doing Tom knew not what, spurning all help. He recognised the signs of sorrowful depression; he had seen it in not a few parishioners during his pastoral work, dealing with the aftereffects of loss; he had experienced its relentless grip himself in the bitter days after Lisbeth's murder. The wonder—and perhaps another hopeful sign—was that Molly had roused herself to cater a large meal at Thorn Court.

"We'll keep Ariel here until we can somehow get Caroline back from town," Tom continued. "Or Adam, at the very least."

"There's Nick."

"I'm not sure Caroline would want her brother to be the one to tell Ariel."

"She'll wonder why she can't go back on her own, you know. The hotel's only up the road." Molly perched on the edge of a wing chair by the fire, tugged Becca's sleeping bag towards her, and began rolling it, squeezing the air from the down as she went along. "Or why her father can't come and fetch her."

"Thankfully, all the girls are very excited about the snow, so I think we can keep them preoccupied for a while. There's talk of building a snowman this morning. But I don't know what we'll do if Caroline is stuck in town. John Copeland is going to try and get her in his Land Rover. He thinks he might be able to get through.

"It's all quite awful, isn't it?" he added, watching her long, slim fingers bind the straps on the bag. When she didn't respond, he asked, "Would you like a cup of something—tea?"

"Do you have anything herbal?"

"Mrs. Prowse seems to stock everything known to man . . . or woman. Anything in particular?"

"Genmaicha?"

"Well," said Tom, who had never heard of it, "I'll see what Mrs. P has on offer. Are you sure you wouldn't care to join us?" Her face, as she surveyed the room in search of more of Becca's things, betrayed in a flicker an emotion he didn't expect to see—excitement? pleasure? he couldn't quite pin it down—which vanished the instant she realised she was being observed.

"No, Tom. Really, I'm fine here on my own."

He returned a few moments later with a tray Madrun had laid out. She had indeed had Genmaicha, amazing woman, and had thoughtfully added several of her homemade walnut biscuits. She had nearly sailed out the kitchen with it, too, but Tom felt a need for a private conversation with Molly, not least because Becca had groaned at hearing of her mother's presence and hinted that Tom should intercede to let her stay with her friends and build a snowman in the vicarage garden.

"I should say—because there really was no good moment last night—that the curry was brilliant." Tom placed the tray on a low table next to Molly's chair and caught a whiff of the tea, which smelled like hot, soggy cereal. "A wonderful substitution. Was it your idea?"

"Oh . . . Victor's, I think. Or was it mine? I really can't remember." She frowned and sipped her tea. "I think Will was a bit stuck for someone to cater the Burns Supper when he and Caroline decided to close Thorn Court for renovations, and it being too late for the Thistle But Mostly Rose to book somewhere else."

"Well, it was as good as anything I've ever had in a restaurant." Tom bent to add a log to the flames. "And you made the haggis and the rest, too?"

"No, the haggis was Roger's contribution. He always does two, Victor tells me. One's for the what-do-you-call it—the address. The other's for the chef to plate in the kitchen. All I had to do was boil them. The potatoes and the turnips were simple to do and so was the cranachan. Hardly an episode of *Top Chef*."

"Well, anyway, Molly, it was very good to see you, you know, out and about. How are you feeling? If there's anything I can do . . . "

"I've been seeing Celia, actually." Molly tugged at an invisible thread on her sleeve.

"Oh? I didn't know."

"She's really very good."

"I'm sure she is," Tom responded evenly, sensing he was being baited. Celia Holmes-Parry, wife of St. Nicholas's music director, Colm Parry, had trained as a psychotherapist though she took on few patients now, preferring country pursuits, horses chief among them. "The clouds are lifting a little, then?"

"Perhaps. A little." Molly looked up and favoured him with what looked like the shadow of a brave smile.

"Excellent. I hope last evening's events didn't distress you too much." Tom shook his head, still confounded at the tragedy. "It really was a terrible shock."

Molly regarded him with a new, alert expression. "It's karma, isn't it."

"I'm sorry, what did you say?"

"Karma."

He'd heard her the first time—she voiced it as a statement, not as a question—and he couldn't suppress his irritation. Mind troubled by misgivings over Will, stomach made queasy by excess food and drink, he had not slept well.

"Karma? You can't possibly mean you think Will was punished with untimely death for some deed in some supposed past life."

"No, in this life."

Tom was aghast. "That's very harsh, Molly, don't you think? Will's outburst towards Harry was a single episode—terrible, true, but deeply, deeply regretted. And anyway," he continued, watching her face stiffen, "Christians believe in grace, not karma."

He was immediately sorry for rebuking her. The apology was on his lips when he heard heavy footfalls in the hall. John poked his head into the sitting room.

"Tom," he began, "I'm going to—"

But he stopped himself as Ariel slipped around him and headed for the games table.

"—go. On that errand we talked about. With luck, I should be back in time for the service. Hello, Molly," he added, taking a step into the room. "That was a fine meal you provided last night. And Ariel . . ."

Tom watched this normally taciturn man struggle for a cheery salutation.

" . . . I've had an idea. Perhaps walnuts would do for the snow-man's eyes. I saw some in a bowl in the kitchen. What do you think? You could paint them black first."

Ariel, in her small and female way as ruddy-cheeked and sturdy as John, seemed to mimic his movement, tugging at the floral coat of her pajama set. "But Frosty's were made out of coal." She frowned up at him as she squeezed a small purple plastic camera into the coat's front pocket. "Mrs. Kaif"—she turned to Molly—"would it be okay if Becca stayed with us to help make the snowman?"

Molly flicked Tom a reproachful glance, then granted Ariel a tight smile. "No. I'm sorry. Becca needs to come with me. I don't want her—"

"Ariel," Tom interrupted, fearing Molly would be indiscreet, purposefully or not, "three's just the right number to build the very best snowman. Becca can come around later, perhaps, and view your work, yes?" He looked to Molly for agreement, but silently, with short, sharp movements, she plucked up Becca's things and began to thrust them into her backpack.

CHAPTER SEVEN

*I*n the end, John's expectation that he could drive to town and
return to Thornford in time to take up his sidesman duties at St.
Nicholas's was misplaced. Tom wasn't surprised. The sunless world
he stepped into when he left the vicarage that morning was even
more choked with snow than he had imagined it might be when he
woke and stumbled to his bedroom window, stupidly expecting to
assess road conditions in the pitch black of a January morning. The
stone walls bordering the vicarage garden were buried up to their
haunches, and when he tramped through the drifts into Church
Walk, the first things to greet his eyes were two great anonymous
white humps, which he presumed concealed two parked cars. Past
the lych-gate, in the churchyard, only the tops of the more ostenta-
tious markers showed, like black buoys in a still, white sea, and even
they wore crowns of snow.

It was as they were saying the Creed together that he noted John
Copeland take his customary pew near the back by the baptismal

font. His return was well timed. Earlier, Tom had wondered if he should include the Moirs in the Prayers of Intercession, to follow shortly upon the Creed. It was clear from the murmured conversations, when people began to trickle in, stamping snow from their footwear and rubbing ungloved hands for heat, that news of Will's death had reached some in the village, though not all. Before the service began, as congregants received their copies of *Common Praise* and the order of service and moved to their favoured places, it was a secondary topic of neighbourly exchange. But it quickly surpassed the first—the remarkable weather—as shock and dismay travelled from pew to pew. Should he, though, acknowledge the community's painful loss before God, when Caroline herself remained oblivious of her widowhood? Strangely, it felt like a breach of etiquette.

John answered his question. Tom searched out the man's grave eyes as he intoned the final words of the Creed and received a deep nod, which he took as confirmation that Caroline had been found, and had been told. With a heavy heart he said, when the moment came:

Comfort and heal all those who suffer in body, mind, or spirit, especially Caroline Moir and her children, Adam and Ariel, who yesterday lost husband and father; give them courage and hope in their troubles; and bring them the joy of your salvation.

Somewhere near the south window, someone released a short, sharp cry of pain.

"Thank you for taking on that task," Tom said to John, at last able to have a private conversation. After the Dismissal, a few were always wont to linger and chat, none more so than on such a day of peculiar weather and sad news, even though St. Nicholas's, like the rest of the village still without electricity, was drained of welcome heat. "It can't have been easy telling Caroline."

"No," John replied without elaboration, methodically fitting copies of *Common Praise* back into the low shelf along the transept aisle.

"Where did she get to in the end? Noze?"

John nodded, nothing more. Tom could understand the man's preoccupation. There was nothing more cheerless than the task of relaying news of the death of a loved one.

"I expect the roads were poor."

"You might imagine."

"I hope they've been able to get at least a mortuary van in."

"Yes, finally one arrived."

"Good. It's been troubling thinking of Will's body simply lying there, in wait."

"Caroline is taking a little time to compose herself, then she'll come and fetch Ariel." John bent to rehang a hassock. "She asked me to tell you that."

"How is she?"

"As you might imagine."

Tom sighed. He turned in the direction of the vestry to remove his vestments, then turned back. "What of Nick Stanhope, by the way?"

"Sleeping it off somewhere, is my guess. We saw hide nor hair, not even when the mortuary people arrived. And . . ." A shadow crossed John's broad features. "I've still got his car keys. I must get them back to him."

"If you like, I could give them to Caroline."

"It's fine, Tom. I'll drop them off at Thorn Court on my way back to Noze. But . . . " He bent for another hassock. "I think I'll stop at the pub for a bit."

"Good idea," Tom responded sympathetically. "I'd join you, but I should wait for Caroline at the vicarage."

As it happened, as they stepped along the path beaten through the snow on Church Walk, they glimpsed through the scrim of gently falling flakes, the figure of Caroline, in yesterday's camel coat, making her way cautiously down Pennycross Road, avoiding the centre, where it was iciest, instead trudging through the drifts accumulated by the high stone walls at the side. Her movements, the high steps and the uncertain grasping of sprigs poking through the stone, made her appear delicate and vulnerable, like a deer in disaster. John, who was slightly in the lead of Tom, quickened his pace, as if moving to reach her and guide her, but by the steps of the Church House Inn he abruptly stopped.

"Perhaps you best go," he called back to Tom. He raised his hand towards Caroline, in a kind of tentative wave of acknowledgement, and heaved his body up the steps and through the door. Mildly startled at the man's behaviour, Tom moved across Poynton Shute and met Caroline across from the Tidy Dolly.

"Thank you," she said breathlessly, taking his proffered arm. "It's quite treacherous, isn't it?"

"Caroline, I'm so sorry." As he glanced at her, she raised her face to his. She was snow-pale, her eyes puffy and red-rimmed, her expression grave.

"I've tried so not to cry, for Ariel," she said, touching the skin below her eyes with a gloved hand. "I mustn't let on, until I can get her safely home."

An older couple, unknown to Tom, crossed Poynton Shute in front of them, heads bent into the cold.

"Oh, Mrs. Moir, we're very sorry for your loss." The woman turned a sympathetic expression to them.

"You're very kind, thank you."

"If we can help in any way, please let us know." The man added a solicitous smile. "Vicar." He nodded acknowledgement, glancing at Tom's exposed collar. They passed on, crossing the street towards the pub.

"Francis and Beth Hamilin," Caroline told Tom. "They supply honey to us. I guess the whole village knows. However shall I get Ariel through this?"

"Children are surprisingly resilient." Tom reflected on Miranda's response to her mother's death, more than two years ago.

"I meant, how will I get Ariel back to Thorn Court through a gauntlet of well-intentioned people. I have a feeling that with the electricity down, many will be headed out for a pub lunch or some warmth."

"Oh, I see. Well, I'll be very happy to accompany you and Ariel back. I can fend folk off with a fierce look or a growl or something."

Caroline made a feeble laugh. "Would you? That would be a great help. How . . . " She stopped herself, as if needing a moment to stanch fresh tears. "How did you tell Miranda?"

"Well." Tom sighed deeply at the memory. They had reached the vicarage's front gate. "I don't think I had a plan. It's not something you ever expect to have to do, is it? So you can't really have anything rehearsed. And even if you did expect something like . . . well, this, I'm sure anything you might plan to say would fall by the wayside anyway, if that makes sense. I'm sorry, I'm not being at all helpful."

"No, that's all right. Of course, Miranda was about—what?—seven?"

"Almost. Her seventh birthday was a few days hence. Lisbeth, you see, had brought her birthday present to the church I was serving in at the time to hide it there. She was then to pick up Miranda after school, but when she never arrived, Miranda . . . " He hesitated. The memory still felt raw. "Miranda took herself off to the library, took out a book, went home, and made herself a sandwich.

She was in front of the TV watching some kids' show when I arrived. She was so resourceful. I was so proud. And then—"

His eyes teared unexpectedly. Caroline sensed his distress and moved her arm around his back.

"I think I'm supposed to be comforting you," he said, his voice thick.

"Never mind. Have a moment, then tell me."

They stopped at the vicarage gate. "Well, I told her that something had happened, that her mother had died. She really didn't understand, I don't think. Not at seven. For days afterwards, she would ask when her mummy was coming home. Of course, Lisbeth's death was . . . unusual, and eventually that had to be explained, too."

Caroline, silent, looked past Tom down Poynton Shute towards the entranceway to the Old Orchard, which abutted the vicarage property to the east. She seemed lost in thought.

"Please tell me if I'm being intrusive, Caroline, but . . . was Will having heart problems?"

Her eyes turned to meet his. "Not that I know of."

"Or was there heart disease in his family? Again, stop me, if I'm being rude."

"That's all right, Tom." She shook her head. "I couldn't say. Will was adopted. Did you know?"

"Roger mentioned it to me yesterday."

"Will's adoptive father wasn't even around long enough to give Will his name."

"And Will's mother? Did she know anything of his natural parents' health?"

Caroline turned her attention to her shoes, which she shook to remove snow. "She'd died before I met Will. If she knew anything, I don't think she told Will. I . . . I can't say I even know what took her, really. Or I can't remember, not that it matters."

Tom frowned as he pushed through the squeaky gate then

ducked to avoid a tumble of new snow from the arch. It wasn't that he thought it odd not to know the circumstances of one's mother-in-law's death—it was possible, if you had never met the woman, and you might forget after twenty-odd years of marriage—it was that he heard the lie in Caroline's voice.

"I hope the girls behaved themselves," she said as they reached the vicarage door.

"I've had no reports of problems," Tom replied, pushing through the door into the vestibule. He stamped the snow off his shoes, aware of the absence of a now familiar sound, that of Bumble skittering down the hall and scrabbling into the door that opened onto the central hall.

"Hello!" he called, opening the door. "Anyone home?"

"What a gorgeous smell of beef." Caroline came up behind him. "Every Sunday?"

"No, not usually. But you were witness to the Yorkshire debacle last week. Mrs. Prowse has been worrying the problem all week. I thought it best she try again, soon, and for some reason she won't make Yorkshire unless there's a roasting beef. You know," he added, noting the absence of footwear in the vestibule, "I expect they're all in the back garden. Snowman-making was the order of the day." He looked at his damp shoes and Caroline's wellies. "Perhaps we should go round the house, rather than through it."

Bumble greeted Tom and Caroline first, racing towards them with his usual desperate energy, kicking up the snow, yelping with every bound and whirl.

"Bumble!" Tom commanded the dog to silence, but he paid little attention. Clearly, Tom thought, not for the first time, Bumble's previous owner, the late Phillip Northmore, had exercised an authority over the animal that he, Tom, didn't seem to possess.

But Bumble acted as early warning, so when Tom and Caroline rounded the corner of the vicarage, they came upon three figures under the old pear tree's snow-smothered winter branches who were turned towards them in expectation—four figures, if one counted the deathly white, strangely rounded, inanimate form in the middle.

"Mummy," Ariel called excitedly, "come and see our snowman!"

"It's brilliant, darling," Caroline responded. The forced enthusiasm in her voice was detectable. Tom could see Judith Ingley studying her with some intensity and then remembered his manners and introduced·them.

"Judith grew up in Thornford," he added.

"But left many years ago," the older woman explained. "Before you were born. My maiden name was Frost."

"Oh?" Caroline's brow crinkled, as if she were winkling out some memory. "Well"—she cast Judith a wan edition of a hotelier's smile—"I do hope you enjoy your stay."

"Where's Emily?" Tom asked Miranda, suddenly conscious of a missing child.

"She went home." Miranda looked at Ariel and they exchanged wicked grins.

"Has something happened?"

Miranda wiped her wet mitten across her nose. "Emily thought we should make a snow princess."

"Ah," said Tom, halfway to understanding. The princess force was still strong with young Emily Swan, who had been lobbying for months to be crowned queen at next Saturday's Wassail in the Old Orchard.

"We did try, Daddy," Miranda continued, "we really did . . ."

"We really did," Ariel echoed.

" . . . but . . ."

And they both burst into giggles.

"But . . . ?" Tom prompted.

"They couldn't—" Judith began.

"We couldn't," Miranda interrupted with another sudden frown, "stop the . . ." She looked down the front of her jacket. " . . . *chests* from falling off." The frown quickly shot back to a shining grin.

Tom grinned back. It was too silly.

"Did Emily go off in a huff?" Caroline asked.

Judith nodded.

"Oh, well." Tom glanced at Bumble finding olfactory treasure at the snowman's base. "Never mind. She'll get over it soon enough. Besides, yours is properly . . . traditional. As it should be."

They all turned to the masterwork, three not-entirely-spherical spheres, piled one atop the other. It was more head, thorax, and abdomen than any humanoid assemblage, poor legless thing. A line of black buttons, likely plucked from Madrun's sewing basket, bisected the thorax to suggest a jacket; a bright red knitted scarf of ludicrous length (possibly one of Giles James-Douglas's from the box under the stairs) swaddled the neckless neck and draped over the tree-branch arms, which ended in gardening gloves. An exceptionally broad-brimmed straw hat, likely another of Giles's leavings, crowned its head. Madrun must have raided the larder to give the face expression: A couple of Cox's Pippins denoted eyes with staring calyx-pupils; the traditional carrot, this one straight as a file, served as the nose; a banana formed the mouth, which curved upwards into a lopsided grin. The effect was of a dapper, portly gent, going nowhere and nowhere to go—not unlike a cleric or two he'd known in his time.

"Well done, you," Tom enthused. "I can see you've gone to a lot of work. However did you lift those great balls of snow?"

"Mrs. Ingley helped," Ariel piped up.

"I may pay for it tomorrow." Judith clutched the small of her back.

Tom looked down the garden, at the strips of exposed grass poking through the white covering here and there where the girls had rolled their balls, then up through swirling flakes at the denuded trees weighted with accumulated snow. Above that was leaden sky, punctuated by a flock of rooks spiralling and climbing, finally vanishing, leaving only the promise of yet more snow. Nature seemed shrouded in a single tonality, its riotous summer palette shrunken to grey and white and brown, and it made the world feel claustrophobic, hushed as a tomb. Small sounds—the squish of nylon rubbing nylon of the girls' anoraks, Bumble's doggy yap—were curiously amplified, which may be why he started a little at Ariel's querulous question:

"Mummy, have you been crying?"

"Oh, dear, no. I just . . . didn't sleep well, that's all." Caroline flicked a finger along her eyes. "Come, we need to pack up your things and leave Mr. Christmas and Miranda and . . . Mrs. Ingley to their lunch. Goodness"—she reached for her daughter's mittened hand—"your things are wet, aren't they? I don't want you catching cold."

"I'm sure Mrs. Prowse has some extra mittens or gloves," Tom responded, glancing at Miranda, who was wearing the same sceptical expression she had worn the night before, when he arrived with John and Judith. *My child can read atmospheres too well,* he thought, as he wondered aloud where Mrs. Prowse was.

"She went in just as you were coming round the back," Judith replied.

But Madrun had seen them and come to the door, wringing her hands on a tea towel. At her feet, Powell and Gloria sniffed the air and backed away in disgust at their new, changed world. "Shall I lay more places, Mr. Christmas?" she called.

"No, thank you, Mrs. Prowse," Caroline answered in his stead. "Ariel and I must be leaving. And thank you for everything you've done . . . for Ariel, for the girls."

"Mrs. Prowse," Tom added, "I'm accompanying Caroline and Ariel back to Thorn Court, so—"

"That's fine, Mr. Christmas." Madrun was pushing the cats away with her feet preparatory to closing the door. "I won't put the York-shire in until you've returned."

"I hope all goes well," Caroline murmured.

Tom smiled wanly and replied, "There are worse tragedies than a fallen pudding."

Tom's heart sank when Madrun offered Caroline one of her casse-roles, frozen in preparation for her absence, but proffered in condo-lence, without, of course, phrasing words of condolence, Ariel being within earshot. Caroline meekly accepted it, but Tom ended up car-rying the heavy, bright orange, two-handled dish up Pennycross Road, Caroline being lumbered with Ariel's sleeping bag and Ariel with her backpack. Miranda had viewed the passing of the casserole at the vicarage with even more visible suspicion, peering at the let-tering on the lid—it was part of Madrun's very good Le Creuset set—and then peering at Tom. He knew that she was remembering when her mother had died, when a swarm of well-meaning parish-ioners had descended upon their home bearing Pyrex. Robbed of hunger, he could barely tolerate the rich aromas of their contents. *What became of all those casseroles?* he wondered as he stepped care-fully on the road's icy surface. Someone—Ghislaine?—must have consigned their contents to the bin, then returned the dishes to their owners. He felt a flicker of guilt for the wasted food and the scorned cooks, and wondered what would happen to this casserole, though he was sure, given the chef, that its contents were superb. It was Madrun's best *boeuf bourguignon,* after all.

"Taking your lunch for walkies?" one wag remarked in passing.

Tom was sensing that the freakish weather and the assault on the mod cons was, perversely, beginning to cast a spell over the village. He noted as he passed the gate to old Mr. Sainton-Clark's cottage that Mr. Snell from next door was shovelling the snow from his front walk. The two, he was told, hadn't spoken in ten years, having battled bitterly over intrusive tree roots. Mrs. Ewens, who was normally reserved, greeted them effusively as she cleared the pavement in front of her cottage, clearly unaware of what had befallen Caroline and Ariel, and just as happily looking forward to the worst old man winter had to offer—all very spirit-of-Dunkirk and such. They were hailed more than once along the way, with the expectation of cheery conversation, but Tom, feeling Caroline's growing anxiety, cut each visit short. Mercifully, only Tilly Springett, sweeping the walk of April Cottage, the last one before Thorn Court, was aware of the tragedy, having heard the news in church. She glanced at Ariel, then, reading the anxiety in Caroline's eyes, murmured "good day" before turning back to her solemn task.

Against the low grey sky of midday, Thorn Court appeared as a colourless silhouette, its hip roof and the witch's caps over the bow windows snow-burdened, its Elizabethan garden a zoo of hilly white shapes, broken only by a tall cypress. Fresh footsteps—John's and Caroline's earlier traversings, presumably—cut a narrow path through the snowy walk up to the hotel forecourt. Tom gave a passing thought to Nick, who might have taken the trouble to clear the snow, but when they stepped onto the forecourt, as if thinking made it so, there Nick was, still in his kilt, his shirt crumpled and half open, and his hair plastered awkwardly to one side of his head. A blanket was draped over his shoulders.

"I saw you coming up the path," he said, then yawned extravagantly and scratched his head. "Christ, it's colder than a witch's tit. Look at all this sodding snow! Can you credit it?" He regarded them peevishly. "What? What's the matter? You look like—" Then a certain alertness crept over his dulled expression. "Oh . . ."

"Don't say another word, Nick." Caroline spoke with a kind of suppressed fury, shepherding her daughter. "Not a word. I have something I want to talk about with Ariel."

"Where's Daddy?" The child's tone was sulky, suspicious.

"Not a word, Nick," Caroline repeated, turning towards the Annex. "Come along, Ariel. Let's get you warm and dry. Tom"—she glanced back at him over her shoulder—"thank you very much for your help."

"Please let me know if there's anything else I can do," Tom responded.

"I will. Come around tomorrow morning, if you can."

"What's that you've got, Father Christmas, sir?"

Tom followed Nick's gaze to his own gloved hands, then looked hurriedly at the retreating figures of mother and daughter. He was loath to disturb them. "Here, you take this, Nick. It's something of Mrs. Prowse's."

"Tarts?"

"Beef bourguignon, I think."

Nick burped, then pulled the blanket around his shoulders. "No thanks, mate. Don't think I could manage that sort of grub, the state I'm in."

"It's not meant for you *specifically*." Tom shoved the dish at him. "Or *now*," he added, annoyed. "Have you only just got up?" He studied Nick's face. He had his answer. The man's skin was sallow, his lips dry and cracked. The evidence of sleep crusted the corners of his eyes.

"Yeah, Christ, that was some night, wasn't it?"

"Then you slept through the mortuary van arriving and people going up the tower to fetch Will's body?"

"Yeah, must have."

"Will you please take this?" Tom pushed the casserole dish against Nick's shirt.

"Will's dead."

Tom glanced again at Nick's face, alerted by the tone of his voice, which was—shockingly—wondering, almost pleased. He sensed a mind rising out of somnambulance and calculating some marvellous

effects of changed circumstances in the House of Stanhope. Then,
as quickly, he appeared to snap out of it.

"Coming in for a drink?"

"Good God, no," Tom responded brusquely, taken aback, then
realised how ungracious his words sounded. "Sorry. I'm wanted back
at the vicarage for lunch."

"Suit yourself." Nick, his hands full, shouldered the door closed.
The rich clunk of wood on wood resounded through the muffled
landscape.

Tom took a purifying breath and turned to retreat down the
path, but the view from Thorn Court's rise arrested his step. *See,
amid the winter's snow, born for us on earth below*—the lines of the
Christmas hymn slipped unbidden into his head. The village amid
the winter's snow appeared transformed, the sharp edges of its cottages and boundary walls softened into curves. It was as though
someone had poured castor sugar over the village and let it settle
into satiny valleys and peaks. How unblemished and pure it all
looked—at least from a distance.

And then he glanced down at his feet, and noted how that im-
placable purity could be so quickly blemished. There were his own
footprints up the central path, combined with Caroline's and Ariel's,
and presumably John's and Caroline's made earlier, creating a hard,
crude trail down to Pennycross Road. And there, to his right, was
another crude path, a diagonal extension of the central one, veer-
ing to the Moirs' residence. It crossed through a couple of sets of
deep, parallel ruts, evidence of recent vehicular traffic. To his left,
however, the snow was still blissfully untrammeled, beautiful in its
simplicity, a blanket stretching to a series of pristine, snowy mounds
that could only be smothered cars.

It was only some time later that he realised how peculiar that
was.

CHAPTER EIGHT

No throaty outburst from the kitchen accompanied this Sunday's lunch. As usual, Madrun backed into the dining room with her trusty serving cart, its top tier crowned with the joint resting on a platter and accompanying sauce boat, the second tier with an assortment of covered serving dishes, which contained the roast potatoes, vegetables, and anything she considered complementary to the main affair. All seemed bright and beautiful, and smelling heavenly, until she turned to them, her long, straight face stamped with disappointment.

"Oh, Mrs. Prowse, not again!" Tom was standing, holding the carving knife, preparatory to doing his masculine duty, but let it drop to its silver rest.

"I simply can't understand how this could happen twice, and in a row! I've done everything the way I've done it for years . . . forever!"

"Pauvre Madame Prowse." Miranda regarded her dolefully, her elbows improperly on the table propping up her head.

"Whatever is the matter?" Judith looked wildly about the room.

"A dropdead," Miranda said.

"A what?"

"Mrs. Prowse has been having a spot of bother lately with her Yorkshire pudding." Tom lifted the knife.

"Hardly a spot, Mr. Christmas! The pudding hasn't risen, not a titch." She addressed Judith. "Today, nor last Sunday."

"Oh, is that all," their guest remarked, glancing into her lap and adjusting her napkin. "I thought somebody had died." She looked up sharply, instantly conscious of the effect of her casual remark in light of events of the last twenty-four hours. "Sorry!"

Miranda shot her a puzzled frown.

Madrun remained oblivious to the nuance. "Quite all right." She lifted the meat platter, then paused in reflection. "Perhaps I should have Fred look at the Aga again."

"And yet the roast appears to be done to perfection." Tom rather wished Madrun wouldn't hover about holding the thing. Hangover worn away, he was surprisingly hungry.

"Do you make your batter earlier and refrigerate it?" Judith asked.

"Always. The night before."

"There's your answer, then." Judith reached for her water glass. "With the electricity off, the fridge and its contents have been getting warmer."

Enlightenment flashed in Madrun's eyes. "Yes . . ."

"Mrs. Prowse—"

"Perhaps that *is* the reason."

"Mrs. Prowse," Tom began again. "The roast might find a place here, in front of me."

"But the electricity worked last Sunday," Miranda pointed out.

One of Madrun's eyebrows rose. "That's true."

"I'm sure it tastes like manna, even if regrettably horizontal." Tom moved to take the meat platter from his housekeeper's hands.

"I'll carve and you go fetch it, Mrs. Prowse. Wouldn't we all like some anyway?"

"*Oui, s'il vous plaît,*" said Miranda.

Judith nodded, remarking when Madrun had left the room, "I confess I've used a packet Yorkshire mix for years. It seemed to work well enough, though perhaps the result was a trifle dry."

"I think Mrs. Prowse regards any food in a packet with the gravest scepticism," Tom said, lifting the carving knife once again. "At any rate," he continued, anxious to leave the agony of the Yorkshire behind, "I'm not sure you said what brought you back to Thornford after all these years."

"Oh, didn't I? Sorry, it was Madrun I must have told, while I was peeling potatoes. Anyway, what brought me was a bit of a whim, really. As I told you last night, my husband died last autumn. I've decided I'll retire this spring, and I'm going to sell the care home Trevor and I owned. Expecting I might be at loose ends, I'd been looking for a little business to run—in the West Country, I thought, as I was from here. I was looking through some estate agents' sites on the Internet and saw that the Tidy Dolly Tea Room in Thornford Regis was for sale. Or the Tidy Dolly *Internet* Tea Room, as it's now called."

"Everything's up to date in Thornford Regis," Tom intoned, helplessly riffing on *Oklahoma!*, the musical his mother Kate was particularly fond of. "They've gone about as far as they can go. I mean to say"—he cleared his throat—"the Tidy Dolly's entered the twenty-first century."

"I hope not too much. The estate agent's site said all chattels included in the sale, and not much looked changed in the pictures posted."

"I can assure you it's little changed." Tom sliced into the beef, which curled tenderly onto the plate. In fact, he found the atmosphere of the Tidy Dolly almost shudderingly mimpsy-pimpsy: the tiny tables, the lace tablecloths, the flower-pattern china, and, of course, the dolls, everywhere, large and small, blond and brunette, white and white-ish, staring at you with emotionless eyes while you sipped tea or ate a light lunch. He'd tried to steer his Wednesday Holy Communion service flock to the Waterside Café down at the millpond for their coffee morning. The food was inventive and excellent and the décor plain and pleasant, even if the proprietor, Liam Drewe, was irascible. But he couldn't be seen to favour one village institution over another and since almost all of Wednesday morning's flock were women and thought the Tidy Dolly delightful, he found himself on too regular a basis passing through its etched-glass doors and noshing on fairy cakes with coffee in translucent cups and saucers, often as not the only male in the place and feeling faintly gargantuan.

"The girls like it, I think." Tom glanced at Miranda, who responded by scrunching up her face. She had dragged him through the doors early on their arrival in Thornford and had seemed delighted then, but children's tastes change.

"I wonder what the Tidy Dolly would be like with only candles for light?" Miranda responded, staring into the lit tapers on the table. With electric light absent and daylight feeble, the dining room glowed golden with candlelight and flames from the fire built to defend against the vicarage's growing chill.

With different company, Tom mused, this could be the setting for a romantic meal, then immediately expelled the poignant thought to respond to Miranda: "A little disturbing, I expect."

"*Macabre.*" Miranda let the sound roll over her tongue in her excellent French.

"New word, darling?"

"*Je l'ai lu dans le nouveau* Alice Roy—Alice et la poupée chinoise."

"*En anglais,* Miranda. Alice Roy is a kind of French Nancy

Drew." Tom addressed Judith as he passed her the meat platter. "If you're familiar with the American books about the teenage detective."

"Not really." Judith's response was clipped. "Anyway, as I was saying, I loved the Tidy Dolly when I was a girl and thought it might be just the ticket."

"To what?" Miranda asked.

Judith looked up from the platter. "Well . . ." She cast Miranda an exasperated frown. " . . . to new life, I suppose."

"Poppy Cozens, who owns the Tidy Dolly, is holidaying in California, I'm told." Tom reached for the sauce boat and passed it to Judith. "She has a friend there."

"Well, my notion had been to take a quick look, then treat myself to a night or two at the Seven Stars in Totnes and contact the estate agent if I think the Tidy Dolly worthwhile. At worst, this would have been a pleasant little getaway."

"And then came the snow." Tom watched Madrun reenter bearing the lacklustre Yorkshire.

"Yes, then came the snow."

Tom found Miranda among the drifts deep in the back garden, standing with utter stillness in front of the snow-laden woodpile. Her stance, her head bent almost as if in reverent prayer, her dark hair fallen forward, seemed to demand caution, and so, when he stepped up to join her, he whispered, "What is it?"

"Regarde, Papa."

Tom looked. At first, against the dun and tawny colour of the aged logs he didn't see the shape of the tiny bird. And then he did: It was one of the brave wrens that made the woodpile their home, despite the patrolling vicarage cats. Its eyes, two perfect black beads, stared unseeingly; its feet, two tiny pale brown twigs, poked into the air in a way both tender and comic.

"Poor thing." He put an arm over Miranda's shoulder and drew her to him, feeling her warm cheek against his.

"*Est–il parce qu'il fait si froid?*"

"The cold? I expect so." Or old age, he thought. Or possibly both. This tiny casualty of bitter weather reminded Tom that the village might experience other casualties if the electricity didn't return soon and snow didn't cease floating down from the heavens. Who had heat and who didn't? Who was able to make a hot meal and who wasn't? Who needed to get out of the village, to Totnes or Torquay, to a medical appointment? He expected some of the answers—and an action plan—would be found at the pub. But first there was something to tell Miranda.

"Shall we give him a decent burial?" he asked. "Probably best. Powell or Gloria won't be respectful, should they ever manage to brave the weather."

They found a spot near the bottom of the garden, where Madrun cultivated white roses, now thorny clots of denuded branches swallowed in snow. Tom made a clearing with the garden spade, then pierced the ground, overturning clots of rich red soil until he had created a hole sufficiently deep. Miranda fashioned a bier of a loose piece of bark and solemnly scooped the tiny corpse, a mere handful of feathers, into its arc. *She is not squeamish,* Tom observed, watching his daughter carry the small frame down the garden path; a legacy, perhaps, of her mother, who'd been unfazed, as a doctor must be, by the squish and squash of corporeal existence. Miranda bent onto her haunches, gently let drop the wren into its modest grave, then rose and reached for Tom's hand. Together they passed a moment's silent reflection to the tiny lifeless creature, then Tom asked, "Shall I say a prayer?"

"May I, Daddy?"

Pleased and delighted, Tom replied, "Of course you may."

"Amen," he echoed her when she had finished her simple invocation. He took up the spade and returned the soil to its place. Miranda made a rough circle of stems and leaves around the edge of the tiny mound.

"Come, let's sit on the swing a minute. I have something I want to talk to you about."

"I think I know," Miranda said when they had brushed the snow from the old oak seat and squeezed in side by side.

The roped swing, which Tom suspected his predecessor Giles James-Douglas had installed for his own pleasure, and not—because of its seat length—for any child's, groaned under their combined weight. He glanced up at the brawny branch askance and asked worriedly, "Do you?"

"Last night you looked like you did after Mummy died."

"Oh." Downcast, Tom pushed off and they began to swing gently. "I'm sorry, darling. We couldn't say anything in front of Ariel. We had to find Mrs. Moir first. It's something she must say to her daughter, as I once said to you. Do you see?"

Miranda was silent a moment, then asked, "Will they move away?"

"The Moirs?" Tom said, startled by the question. "I don't—" And then he did understand. Displacement had followed upon Lisbeth's death; it must seem an inevitable consequence. "Do you miss Bristol?"

"I miss Mummy."

"Oh, my darling girl, so do I." He watched the trail his longer legs were carving through the snow and held Miranda closer. "So do I."

A formidable wall of anoraks, waxed jackets, and damp tweed met Tom's eyes as he stepped into the Church House Inn and stamped the snow off his shoes. The pub was as packed as a rush-hour railway carriage.

"Usual?" Eric Swan, the licensee, shouted into his ear when Tom had squeezed through the last knot of folk and collapsed against the bar. Without waiting for a reply, Eric pulled a pint of Vicar's Ruin and slid it across the bar's damp surface.

"I would describe you as wreathed in smiles." Tom lifted the glass.

"The muscles in my cheeks feel tighter than my wife's brassiere." Eric stretched both arms expansively to enfold the universe into his bosom. "This boozer hasn't had a day like this since . . . since . . ." His arms fell and the good cheer vanished from his expression. "Well, never mind."

Tom grimaced. A curious murder in Thornford the spring before had attracted undesirable numbers of day-trippers with nothing better to do than dabble in crime tourism. Of course, after filling their metaphorical boots gawping at this or that site, they all ended up at the pub. This had a beneficial effect on revenues that, by ancient custom, were shared with St. Nicholas's, but it was an unintended consequence of evil that filled Tom with despair.

"At least it's only a natural disaster this time that's bringing the punters in. That's a good thing. Here, have a sausage roll."

"Unless this is a consequence of global climate change, which means we humans are to blame—a bad thing." Tom bit into the flaky crust.

"The trouble with you, Vicar, is you think too much."

"Being the moral conscience of the village is my trade."

"It's a tough job, but someone's got to do it."

"These aren't half bad, you know. Have you got Belinda up to her elbows in pastry in the kitchen?"

"No. Roger sent them over. Seems things in the shop's freezer are starting to thaw. This keeps up and I can serve everything else he's got."

"Your cooker works, then. Are you not having too many problems? It's decently warm in here." Tom turned to look into the lounge bar at the glowing logs on the hearth heating the space between kippered ceiling and stone floor.

It felt like a cosy cave with a primordial fire. Some faces, red with drink and heat and exertion, flickered in shadows cast by the flames from the fireplace; others were anchored in the cool light filtered through the window mullions.

"I really came in to see what might be being done for those who haven't got any heat or can't make a hot meal," Tom said.

"If they've no heat or meat, they're probably here, and what with the hotel closed there's no place—other than the Waterside." Eric swiped a damp rag across the bar. "I was very sorry to hear about Will Moir, by the way. John Copeland was in earlier and told me. You were there at the dinner, too."

Tom nodded.

"Hardly credit it, can you? I should be the one popping my clogs before I'm fifty." Eric grasped his considerable belly with his meaty hands and gave it a jiggle. "Didn't see Will in here much—he's got a boozer of his own—but he always looked fit as a fiddle to me. Just goes to show, I suppose. This is going to be hard on Caroline."

"Well, the death of a spouse . . . "

"That, yes, of course. But I was thinking about Thorn Court. I couldn't manage this place without my wife. The hotel's an even bigger operation."

"There's Nick Stanhope."

"Don't make me laugh, Vicar. I don't know how he'll get that home security business of his up and running without cocking it up. Besides." Eric leaned so close to Tom, the latter could pick out the red hairs in his nose. "Half the village knows Thorn Court's been struggling lately. Meanwhile, they're doing all these renos, which must be costing a bob."

"Spend money to make money?" Tom suggested.

Eric shrugged. "It's getting the money in the first place that's the trick. Banks aren't giving it away these days. Look"—he moved to serve another customer—"if you're wanting to see what's being done for folk in this storm, you might check that lot out over there. Thornford Winter Emergency Response Party, they're calling themselves. What's it called when you take the first letters of each word and—"

"Acronym?"

"Right. That'll give you a clue." He pointed to several people grouped nearest the fireplace. "There's talk of making the rounds to see who's short of rations or warmth or the like, but they look fairly tucked in. Funny, if Will were alive, he'd be in the thick of organizing something, wouldn't he?"

After another protracted cha-cha through the madding throng, Tom managed to squeeze into a seat in the inglenook next to Old Bob, as much a fixture of the Church House Inn as the three-hundred-year-old mummified cat in a glass box on its wall. Old Bob undoubtedly had a last name, but probably only the postman and the parish clerk worried about knowing it. He was short, thickset, his nut-brown face a deep crisscross of lines that spoke of a life spent out of doors—fishing, in the days when commercial fishing was viable along the river, farm labouring, in season, and whatever else he could turn a hand to in between. Most arresting, however, was his eyewear: It wasn't simply that the thick lenses magnified his irises—a cloudy blue—to an alarming degree, it was that the frames were indecently large, as rectangular as a department store window, and pink. If you thought he'd snatched up his wife's spectacles from her night table, you'd be wrong: He had no wife, nor ever had.

"Father, hear tell Judith Frost be bidin' wi' you," he said without preliminaries.

"Yes, she arrived out of the storm last night." Tom took a swallow of ale and glanced over towards the TWERP members on the other side of the fireplace, which had been his intended destination. "Word does get about. She's Judith Ingley now."

"Remember years back when she were a girl. Worked with Bill, 'er dad, sometimes. Up't Thorn Court."

"Before it was a hotel?"

"Aye, and after. She were a bright one, always busy. She lost 'er mam, you see, when she were born. I remember . . . "

Tom was only half listening. He was counting the number of empty beer glasses on the TWERPs' trestle tables, four of which had been pulled together. *If we're going to engage in good works,* he thought, *we'd best do it in daylight.* It was already past three and the sun would vanish from the sky by four fifteen. But somehow, and with a modicum of guilt, he felt resistant to the notion of getting off his backside. The ale was mellowing. Sweetly scented logs from an old apple tree crackled in the fireplace, throwing up little showers of sparks now and then, which danced before his mesmerised eyes. He felt well sunk into his cushioned seat, warm and dry and soft and safe, and realised the TWERPs were sinking into the same torpor.

" . . . but I 'spect she's tol' you all this," Old Bob was saying.

"No, I haven't had time to really get to know Mrs. Ingley," Tom responded. He shifted slightly and glanced at the text woven into the wool of Old Bob's bobble hat, which he knew covered a knobby head bearing a few tufts of hair. "Do you follow North American ice hockey?"

"No." Bob patted his cap. "What do it say?"

"DETROIT RED WINGS."

"Oh, it were one of Ned's. Got it at the jumble after 'e died."

"If it weren't for Ned, I mightn't be here," Tom reflected.

"I remember. You took th' funeral. I were there."

"So you were."

Almost two years earlier, five months after the death of his wife,

Tom, who along with Miranda had been visiting his wife's sister in Thornford Regis, had through force of circumstance taken the funeral at St. Nicholas's of one Ned Skynner, a former Conservative parish clerk who had come out in a Marxist rash after a stroke. It had been the strange and sweet peace of the moment in the pulpit, looking out over the nave, radiant with shifting streams of light through stained glass, that had decided him for a rural parish, which, by another force of circumstance, turned out to be Thornford.

"Odd," Tom added, "I didn't know Ned, but I wouldn't have thought him keen on professional ice hockey."

" 'E weren't. 'E reckoned t'were some sort o' commie outfit like."

"Ah, *red* wings. I see. Probably a fledgling group, taking flight or something."

"Whatever they say about Ned, he were always 'opeful—'specially after the stroke. Zat right 'ere most nights." Bob pointed at the seat they were occupying. "We knocked about as lads, me and Bill," he continued, "though Bill were a bit older."

"Oh, yes?"

"He married a lass up Tiverton way, lovely girl. She could 'ave 'ad any lad, but . . . "

Old Bob trailed off. Tom saw a flicker of some ancient regret in the magnified eyes.

"But she died fairly young, I think you were saying earlier," he prompted.

"Aye. Giving birth. Weren't twenty-two, don't think. Terrible, it were."

Tom felt a pang of regret for Bill Frost. Like himself, he would have been a young widower with a young daughter to raise on his own.

"I'm not entirely clear what it is Bill Frost did."

"He were all round—handyman, driver, gardener, the like for old man Stanhope. He lived over t' stables . . . well, garage."

"That explains Judith's familiarity with the hotel." Tom quaffed his ale. "Did he remarry? I seem to recall Judith saying she left Thornford when she was about eighteen."

"Aye, after 'er dad died."

"Good Lord, then he must have died young as well."

"Aye. Very young."

"What happened?"

"He were up th' tower at Thorn Court, fixin' th' weathercock, same one tha's still there. It had got broke in a storm, see. I remember this—it were round time of tha' zex scandal in London, that Profumo who left Parliament for lyin'. Aye, that were before you was born."

"I did read about it later, in—"

But a peculiar noise, a combination of hissing and pinging, diverted his attention, as it did everyone else's. Conversation trailed off as everyone looked about the room, seeking the source of fresh disaster. Then, abruptly, the wall sconces and the lamps back of the bar switched on, casting a new shine to the fire glow on the moulded beams and horsebrasses. A great hurrah erupted.

"Three cheers for the Western Power Distributors!" shouted one voice above all.

"I wouldn't go that far, mate!" another voice responded to a tide of laughter. Everyone shifted in his seat to study the view outside to see if windows glowed from the cottages up Thorn Hill. They did. The atmosphere inside the pub soon grew heavy with a sense of renewed obligation to old responsibilities; at the same time, everyone seemed loath to move from the pub's warm womb, Tom included.

He turned back to Old Bob. "I pray you're not going to tell me Bill fell from the tower to his death."

Old Bob wiped his mouth along the sleeve of his shirt. "No, Father, I wouldn't tell you tha', because it weren't true."

"There's a mercy."

"Bill didn't fall, Father. 'E were pushed."

The Vicarage

Thornford Regis TC9 6QX

Dear Mum,

I know you'll be as ~~agast agahs~~ shocked as I am over this, but my Yorkshire pudding came out of the Aga yesterday as flat as a flounder. I was VERY crushed. It's the second Sunday in a row for this to happen, and the second in front of ~~guests~~ a guest—this one being Judith Ingley who thought the batter might have got bruised in the fridge as we had no electricity for most of Sunday, but I'm not convinced. I thought the weather might have something to do with it, as this is the stormiest January we've had since I can remember, but then last Sunday's Yorkshire went all flat and the day was perfectly normal for the time of year. Mr. Christmas says I must remember the Battle of Britain and keep my chin up and if I walk through a storm I must hold my head up high and not be afraid of the dark or words to that effect and of course he's right and so I shall, though I'm not sure if I really want to cook a joint next Sunday as beef three weeks in a row *may get a bit wearying and I have a recipe for lamb that I plucked out of Woman's Own that I've been wanting to try. Anyway, we shall see. The electricity came back not long before teatime yesterday, which was a great relief as I was growing concerned about all the fruit and veg I had put down in the chest freezer from last year's harvest. How are you, Mum? I switched on the radio once the power was back and no reports of yours being out. I'll give Aunt Gwen a phone call later today to see you're all right, though I'm sure this letter won't get to you for days. I expect there'll be no post today and there won't be any school either, which would have thrilled me to bits when I was Miranda's age, but she was downcast when the announcement came over the radio yesterday. She likes school most times, bless her, but I think she was particularly looking forward because her whole class was to begin making lanterns for next Saturday's Wassail. I said we might make a start at home but now I'm not sure we have anything to make a lantern of. I shall have to look in the cupboard under the stairs. Thank goodness it's stopped snowing. It's black as pitch out this minute, as it's only after six o'clock, but no flakes are landing on my window ledge. I wonder if we shall have the Wassail if this snow doesn't melt? Did I tell you that Tamara is coming down to entertain with Shanks Pony at the Wassail? It will be lovely to see her again so soon. Jago says to tell you that she just received her results and did well in her autumn term. If Tamara is here I expect we'll see Adam Moir again, too, as we did at lunch last Sunday. As you know he's smitten with your granddaughter, although of course now I think on it he will come in from Noze to support his mother now his father's gone, poor lad. Adam's quite different, really, than his father. Not a chip off, I wouldn't say. He more favours Caroline in looks—shorter, though fair-haired like both parents, and he's not at all the outgoing sort like Will, or like Will was until the last while, but I've told you before about his being a bit moody.*

Actually, Mum, I think Adam's a bit gormless. I'm not sure what Tamara sees in him, but it's none of my business, is it. Ariel will more likely favour her mother too, at least in figure, although you can never be sure at that age. She has such thick, dark hair, almost black, quite a contrast to the other 3 Moirs. Oh, Mum, yesterday's breakfast was hard to get through! All we adults knew what was to befall poor little Ariel, but we had to keep cheerful because it was her mother's place to tell her, not us. Ariel was sitting beside John Copeland and he was very good with her. He never seems the type to know what to say to a child, but he rather came out of his shell on this occasion. And then Judith Ingley, our guest who I told you about in yesterday's letter, asked Becca Kaif if she had any brothers or sisters, which is the sort of thing you might ask a little girl you didn't know, but Becca burst into tears and it was all a bit awkward and then Molly Kaif came far too early to fetch Becca and so that the cat was set among the pigeons in a way—that is, I could see Miranda thinking something was not right. Anyway, the girls were very excited by the snow, so we bundled them up, Judith and I, and had them making a snowman in the back garden. Judith showed them what to do. They must get more snow in Staffordshire than we ever do! Anyway, I could see Miranda had got her back up a bit. I think she thinks she could figure out how to make a snowman on her own, without being told by someone! Judith does have her views, but she seems nice enough. She's had her trials since leaving Thornford R all those years ago. She and her husband owned a residential care home in Stafford for many years, but then her husband got ~~Parkingto~~ Parkinson's disease, when he was only in his 50s, and ended up in care in their very own care home! At least they were together to the end, Judith said. She didn't have to PUT *her husband into care. He died in autumn. She has a son named Tony who lives in China and doesn't sound very helpful, and no grandchildren. She doesn't seem to have maintained any connections with Thornford, either, but then she was an only child and so was her father, though I might look in Dad's history to see if there's any mention of Frosts past. Who knows? There might be second cousins or third cousins about somewhere. And I realise I've forgotten to ask about her mother's people! Anyway, she was very interested in the Moirs and the Stanhopes, and asked all sorts, but that's understandable, I suppose, as she once lived over the Thorn Court's garage. She was surprised family still owned the hotel, though of course there was that gap after Caroline's father sold it and took them all off to Australia. Anyway, must go and start the day, though it won't be a normal one. Mr. C has his Monday off, but there's deanery synod this evening, though I expect that's cancelled now. I was going to nip into Torquay for a bit of clothes shopping, but I think we're all marooned in the village for the ~~foreseeable~~ next few days. Cats are well, though I had to push them through the catflap yesterday so they would go out and do their business. I'm not having a litter box in my kitchen! Bumble loves the snow and has been trailing nothing but wet through the vicarage. He can be a very messy dog! Love to Aunt Gwen. Have a wonderful day!*

Much love,
Madrun

P.S. Yesterday, after lunch, Mr. Christmas had a talk with Miranda about Will Moir's death, which must have been a hard thing to do, poor man, even if it isn't the first time he's had to do that awful task. I could tell from the way they were sitting on the swing in the back garden that's what they were talking about. And afterwards, after Mr. Christmas went off to the pub, I watched Miranda take the banana off the snowman. I had

given it to her for its mouth and it made the snowman look very
jolly, even though it had gone black from the cold. But Miranda
chipped away at the snowman's head for a bit then and replaced
the banana. Only upside down! Which made the snowman's
mouth turn down and look very very downcast, which was sad.
Worse, Mitsuko Drewe came around a little later, as she's taking
photographs for one of her "art projects" of all the snowmen in the
village. I said to her, if only you'd come an hour ago! But she
thought it was the most interesting one she'd seen all day!

CHAPTER NINE

Tom pretended an interest in *Country Life*. He flipped past the estate agents' adverts for million-pound homes and fine art galleries' adverts for exquisite *objets* to fill said homes, and noted that Miss Isabella Pimlott, nineteen, pashmina-wrapped and flawless-skinned, was reading history of art at St. Catherine's College, Oxford—but little else registered. He slowed his page-flipping a bit, though, when he came upon a feature story on Thornridge House, a Nash-designed jewel on fifty acres outside the village overlooking the river, owned by Colm Parry, a flash in the pop-star firmament of another era. He did let his eyes fall here and there upon its contents, speculating that Colm's ambitious wife, Celia, was the likely force behind this peacock display of acquisition. Yes, there was a picture of the façade and another of one of the reception rooms, and the dining room, and another of the gun room, which Tom had never visited, and there were two of the magnificent gardens that were

Colm's real passion. And there was Colm, who was music director and organist for St. Nicholas's Church in Thornford Regis. It said so, right on page forty-two. The issue was two years old, and so it had been printed in a happier time for Colm, before the death of his daughter, last spring. This bitter January day in England, Colm, Celia, and their son were sunning themselves in Barbados, while Tom was ensconced in the lobby of Thorn Court Country Hotel, trying not to let his attention be drawn by the raised voices on the other side of the wall, in the hotel's office.

He had rung, once, but, like Judith Ingley on Saturday night, he had not been heard. He earlier tried the Annex; the front door was left open to the chilly air, as if someone had departed in a hurry, and when he called, a small figure, Ariel, emerged from the hall's shadows, her eyes brightening for the time it took a candle flame to flare, then die. In his battered Barbour, his back to the blaze of snow-white light, he realised that in silhouette he might be any male, her father returned perhaps, and his heart went out to her. He quickly learned—without asking—that Mummy had gone next door, and before he could offer any words of kindness, Ariel had vanished back into the hall's gloom. Tom gently closed the door and slogged through old footprints to the hotel entrance, noting that among the cars parked outside the old stable block only one—Judith's, he presumed—remained an inert mound of snow.

That Caroline had most likely been summoned by her brother was evident in the first clear words to reach his ears. The tone was agonised but laced with fury: "I must get back to Ariel! There's no need to talk about this now!"

Nick's response was lost in a baritone rumble.

Then Caroline again: "You are *not* a partner in this enterprise. You loaned Will and me money—and we're grateful *and* we'll pay you back—but the decisions are *ours. Mine!* You've no business snooping into our accounts!"

"Look, Caro . . ." Nick's voice, now audible, rose menacingly. "I need some bloody money and I need it soon, do you understand? It's a matter of life and death!"

"Don't be so melodramatic! How could it be?"

Again, Nick's voice was lost.

Caroline's fell, too, until Tom heard her snap: "Well, I believe, Nick, that where there's a will, there's a way."

"And now you have no Will."

"Of course I have a will. We both have wills."

"I meant your husband—Will—is gone."

Tom could hear the sneer in Nick's voice, and felt his own temper rise in the beat before Caroline cried, "Stop it, Nick! Where did you learn to be so absolutely heartless?"

"I'm merely pointing out the truth, aren't I? How do you think you're going to run this bloody money-pit of a hotel on your own? Without Will's drive? Sell the bloody thing! Moorgate Properties is prepared to make you an offer."

"And how do you know that?"

"I *know*, that's all."

"They'd never get planning permission."

"Oh, wouldn't they? I can think of one anti no longer on the parish council: your husband!"

"Nick, I'm not selling to anyone. This is my *home!*"

"Then I know of some private investors."

"Would they be the same toads who have invested in your company, Nick? I know exactly their game. You won't have yours for long if you deal with the likes of them."

"Look, Caro, you're going to have to do something! There's the insurance money, yes? We both know Will's worth more dead than—"

"How dare you! Are you suggesting—?"

"Wait a minute, I'm getting a call."

Sound from the office fell to a muttering. Tom closed the magazine with a thought to slipping out of the hotel, then reentering, as if his witness to this cringe-making conversation could be rubbed from his mind. But then the door opened abruptly. Nick was visible, half turned, sliding one arm into a businesslike black Burberry.

"I can't think you'll get wherever you're going in all this snow."

"I'm not going far. Besides, I have a decent motor—not like *yours*." Nick turned and called over his shoulder, "We'll continue this conversation later."

"No, we will not."

Nick's eyes fell on Tom. "Ah, Vicar." He leaned back in to the office. "Vicar's here, Caro. Put the kettle on, why don't you.

"Get an earful?" he snarled, moving quickly past Tom, not waiting for a reply. Tom noted the flash of disdain in his eyes and felt vaguely assaulted. He dropped the *Country Life* onto the seat beside him and rose to his feet as Caroline stepped from the office. She gave him a tentative smile.

"Tom," she murmured. "Perhaps we should move to the Annex."

Caroline was wearing black jeans, wellies, and what looked like a pajama top. Her hair, usually an immaculate cap, was pulled back into an unkempt chignon. When she approached, he could see the skin puffed around her eyes and a dullness along the sclera, the effect, perhaps, of a sleeping pill. She folded her arm into his and leaned into his shoulder, as if she needed his physical as well as his moral support.

"I'm so glad you've come. I'm afraid my brother isn't really someone capable of offering much sympathy. He rather takes after our father in that way. Or did the army knock it out of him? I'm not sure I know."

"How are you?"

"Oh, numb, I think."

"Don't you have a coat?"

"I'll be fine."

They stepped out the door into the cold air as Nick's van, HOME-

CASTLE SECURITY emblazoned on the side, zipped past them, sending a spray of wet snow landing at their feet.

"And how is Ariel?" Tom asked, frowning after the retreating car.

"Oh! Isn't that Miranda?"

Tom glanced past Caroline to see his daughter, in her scarlet quilted jacket, trudging up the path from the road. He had left the vicarage with her earlier, but she'd parted company with him to fetch Emily Swan and go to Fishers Hill—which, it was rumoured, had been turned by the ice and snow into a glorious slide. Madrun had disassembled a cardboard box to act as toboggan.

"This is very thoughtful," Caroline murmured.

"Would Ariel want a visitor?"

"I don't know. I really don't. When I told her yesterday that . . . well, what had happened, she asked if she could go back out and play. I was so surprised, I said of course, but in any event she chose to stay in. We ended up watching *The Lion King,* her favourite film. She ended up comforting *me.* I'm afraid Mufasa's death scene set me off terribly." Her mouth sagged. "How odd, how unreal this all is. I can't take it in that my husband is gone. And this snow on top of it—it's all part of some horrible ghastly unnatural—"

"You're shivering, Caroline. We need to get you inside."

"I thought Ariel might like to come and slide on the hill." Miranda regarded them both solemnly, her cheeks red with exertion and cold. Silver puffs of air emitted from her mouth as she spoke; then her lips curved into an impulsive smile. "It's really fun! I thought—" She seemed to catch herself, as if sensing the remark lacked sensitivity. The smile fell.

"Let's ask her, shall we?" Caroline led the way to the Annex, calling out to Ariel when she pushed open the door, but Ariel was in the shadow of the hall, waiting, her brother, Adam, barely visible behind her, his hands resting on her slender shoulders. Caroline caught her breath. "Oh, sweetheart! You startled me. Miranda wants to know if you would like to go out and play."

The two girls regarded each other shyly.

"Should I?" Ariel asked her mother, her dark eyes telegraphing a tumult of emotion.

"Yes, of course. But only if you really want to. Your brother and Mr. Christmas will keep me company. You mustn't worry."

"How about this," Tom offered. "You and Miranda go out for an hour or so—there's a wonderful icy slide on Fishers Hill that Miranda will tell you about—and then we'll come and fetch you both."

"Or I could go with them," Adam suggested, though his tone held little enthusiasm.

"Adam, darling, why don't you take yourself off to the pub." Caroline switched on an overhead light and reached for Ariel's jacket. "You can drop the girls off first, if you like. I expect there's lots of adult supervision on the hill."

"Are you sure?" Adam's mouth twitched, then fell back to form a thin, unhappy slit.

Tom studied him as Caroline fussed with her daughter. He was fair-haired like his father, and resembled him, too, in build—tall and lean, rawboned. Yet somehow he seemed a less vital edition of his sire, his face thinner, more attenuated than Will's, his hair, though clipped ruthlessly short, unable to disguise a hairline in early retreat. Dull despair, marker of misery, flecked his watery grey eyes. It was that, more than the presence of a child who didn't need reminding, that quashed the words of condolence forming on Tom's lips. Instead he said: "You managed to get through all right, I see."

"Yes," Caroline answered for her son, "Adam drove in earlier this morning. It's so good to have him here."

"How are the roads?" Tom asked.

"The A435 is passable, Bursdon Road less so." Adam shoved his stockinged feet into a pair of wellies and reached past his mother's head for a waxed jacket.

"I think you and John are the only people I know who've breached the parapets of snow . . . other than the—" Tom remembered the mortuary van and bit his tongue.

Adam cast him a troubled frown as he fumbled with his zipper, flicked an undecipherable glance at his mother, and stepped around the girls. He turned at the door, his narrow frame traced by the light, and said, "Perhaps a walk would be better."

"Yes, a walk." Caroline handed Ariel a pair of mittens. "The pub probably isn't a good idea."

"Hard to be around people being jolly in a pub," Tom remarked, glimpsing the three moving down the path before Caroline closed the door. "How is Adam?"

"Oh, you know, bottling it up." Caroline turned and smiled weakly. "As you might expect. I'm not sure I can . . . reach him. He's not a little boy anymore. I'm more worried about Ariel, how this will affect her. She's being very . . . watchful. She wanted desperately to come to the office with me earlier, but with Nick being . . . " She left the rest unsaid.

"Miranda became watchful for a time, too," Tom told her. "My diary seemed to absorb her. She was concerned I be home by certain times, which is hard to do when you're a priest with evening meetings and such. Fortunately, she has three doting grandmothers, and Ghislaine, our au pair at the time, was wonderful."

"You were lucky to have her. I'm hoping I can get my mother to stay here for a good while. Come through, Tom," Caroline said, gesturing down the Annex's central hall towards the kitchen. "Will you have coffee or tea?"

"Either will do," he replied, following her. Coffee in the morning was preferred, but more important was the comfort the ritual provided the bereaved. "Your mother lives in Australia, does she not?"

"Yes," she replied, lifting the kettle. "She very much took to Australia. More so than my father, who was the one who took us off there in the first place." She paused over the taps. "I telephoned her last night. So awkward, the time difference between England and

Australia. Anyway, I suggested she wait a bit before booking a flight. Has Heathrow reopened? I'm not sure. Are the trains running? What about the roads?" She placed the kettle on the hob with a metallic scrape.

"I can't imagine this snow lasting long." Tom studied her face, creased with anxiety. "It doesn't usually. Not in this part of the country."

"And what does all this mean for the funeral?"

"The weather?"

"Yes, I . . . why? Is there something else?"

Some look of doubt must have registered in his expression, for he saw consternation in her eyes. "Well," he began gently, "Will was still a young man, really. I expect there'll be a . . . "

"Postmortem? That's all right, you can say it, Tom. I'm not squeamish. And why don't you sit? We might stay here. It's cosier, I think."

"Sorry." Tom took a Windsor chair next to an old oak refectory table that was the centrepiece of the room. "For some people, the notion of a postmortem comes as a shock. I suppose it did for me, in a way."

"Because of your wife."

"Yes." How Lisbeth had died had seemed obvious, hardly in need of examination. He had come across her supine, life's blood drained from her, with a knife, a crude shiv of razor and duct tape, clearly visible, penetrating the flesh that he had adored with all his being. That her body had been thus desecrated had been unbearable at the time. It was hardly less so now. "There could be an inquest, too, Caroline."

"Inquest?" He noted her body stiffen.

"I'm sure it would only be a formality, but it may mean a delay."

Her back was to him. He watched one hand reach for a glass canister and remove its top. Then she reached up into an overhead cupboard, where she took a cafetière from a jumble of mugs and cups. Silently, she spooned coffee into the beaker. Her head was bent, exposing the vulnerability of her neck, with its wisps of untidy blond hairs.

"How . . . ," she began after a moment, her voice tentative. "How did Will . . . die?"

Tom let a moment pass. "I'm not sure we properly know."

"No, I mean, what happened at the supper?"

"Did John say nothing when he fetched you at Noze?"

"When he . . . ? Oh! No. Well, I think you know what a man of few words John is. And Nick couldn't tell me much. I gather he was very drunk."

"I'm afraid we'd all had too much—even your priest, who had promised to set a good example. We were fortunate Judith Ingley arrived when she did. She sort of took charge and I think most of us were grateful." He gnawed at his lip and gave a passing thought to the Last Supper and those obtuse disciples who didn't seem to notice that anything was wrong; surely a woman among the Twelve would have been sensitive to Jesus's mood. "Caroline," he said, "I feel very much that we could have done something for Will."

"What do you mean?" She placed two mugs on the counter and turned to him again.

Tom ran his fingers along the polished edge of the table. "He wasn't himself, really, much of the evening." Although, saying it, he could well describe Will as not really being himself the last several months. "He seemed preoccupied, but later he looked—well, I said peaky, but Judith, when she met him in the lobby for the first time, seemed to immediately think something wasn't right, and said so. She'd trained as a nurse, you see. But Will was adamant that nothing was wrong. 'Wind,' he told us. We should have insisted on fetching a doctor or calling an ambulance right then and there. It might have made all the difference." He found himself wringing his hands. "Caroline, I'm so sorry."

Caroline seemed to look through him as she held his gaze. "I don't think there was anything you could have done," she responded finally. Her tone gave no clue to her feelings.

"I wish I could be sure."

"The weather, Tom. It's not likely anyone could have reached Thornford in time. And with no doctor in the village . . . "

"Possibly. But you don't know, do you, until you try."

"Where there's a will, there's a way," Caroline murmured.

"What?"

"Oh, nothing. Just a little joke between Will and me. It was a play on his name, of course. As long as he was around, there was a way." Tears spurted from the corners of her eyes. "I'm sorry," she said, her voice thick.

At that moment the kettle's hiss became a scream, filling the kitchen with its insistence.

"Sit," Tom commanded, rising. "I can make the coffee."

Caroline did as bidden, while Tom poured the hot water into the cafetière and placed it on the table.

"I should say," he said after a moment as he waited for the grounds to settle and for Caroline to compose herself, "because Nick may well tell you in any case, that I happened to overhear a little of your conversation earlier, in the hotel. You said, 'Where there's a will,' et cetera, to Nick. I do apologise."

"Oh." Caroline, wiping at her eyes, gave him a wary glance. "Well, I expect it's nothing that isn't being gossiped about in the village anyway."

"As I said, I heard very little. It's none of my business, and it will go no farther."

"You really are a bit of a townie, aren't you?"

Tom laughed, glad to see her smile for the first time. "Yes, I suppose. I do have trouble with the tittletattle that seems endemic to village life."

"As opposed to the tittletattle that seems endemic to Church life?"

"You may have a point there." Tom pressed the plunger into the blackening liquid. "But really, Caroline, will you be able to manage?"

"I don't know . . . No, that's not true: I do know. I will manage, and I'll manage just fine. It's what Will would expect of me, yes? Now," she added with a new resolution in her voice, "do you take coffee black or white?"

"Black."

"I'll have cream. No, I'll get it," she said, rising and moving to the fridge.

Tom brought the mugs to the table and sat down.

"And the tower." Caroline placed a matching milk jug on the table. "You found Will in Thorn Court's tower."

"I'm sorry. You didn't know?"

"No, I was told, and went up before the mortuary van arrived yesterday."

"Oh, Caroline—"

"I just . . ." She shrugged and sat down.

Tom understood the strange hunger for details. He had felt it, too, in the wake of Lisbeth's death.

"It was Judith who found him, really," he explained. "She insisted on going up first. To spare us, perhaps, she being a nurse, but, really, there was nothing to spare us from. Will looked simply as if he were resting. Caroline, are you sure you want to hear this?"

"Yes." She poured coffee into Tom's mug. "I do."

"I suppose," Tom continued, watching the liquid swirl against the side of the china, "I wondered why he went up the tower, but I can only think now he knew something was fatally wrong, knew we were trapped in snow, and didn't want to cause concern. It's remarkable, really."

"Men." Caroline's tone conveyed a world of meaning: the fear of losing face, the felt need to hide pain or suffering.

"It's the training, I expect. I mean the process of making soft boys into hard men, but I suppose it's more acute when you're an athlete as Will was."

"Yes." Caroline poured coffee into her own mug. "I witnessed the pickup match where the cricket ball hit broke his nose. I'd have been shrieking in pain, but not a peep from Will. And of course, it's not simply physical. I'm told he never complained about the blow fate dealt him when injuries ended his professional career so early, though that was before my time."

Tom knew the story. Stress fractures in his lower back had sidelined Will; when he completed a long rehabilitation process, he opted to coach the game rather than play it professionally, first in Australia, then in England.

"I adored the tower as a child." Caroline stared off into the middle distance. "It was my *Secret Garden*—you know the book? Like Archibald Craven, my grandfather had had it closed, sealed off. I was never sure why. Anyway, when I was about eight or nine, I happened to find the key in the back of an old desk in the living room here in the Annex. There's a modern one now, but then it was a Yale style—ancient—and somehow, with some childish intuition, I knew exactly which lock it fit. I remember it was summer holiday, August, actually a rainy day, which may be why I was poking about indoors, and I remember me waiting for my grandfather to take his nap, which he did religiously in the afternoons when the hotel was at its least busy. After my parents married, he moved out of the Annex and into rooms in the hotel proper—near the stairwell to the tower—so I had to be careful."

She paused to pour cream into her coffee. "Oh, Tom, it was magical, slipping in the key, opening the door, then going up and being bathed in this glowing light. The clouds had lifted and the rain had stopped by this time and I could look down over the village towards the South Downs and the patchwork fields. I felt like the queen of the castle. I remember I even considered growing my hair so I could be Rapunzel."

"I sense an instance of all good things coming to an end," Tom remarked, noticing her expression falter.

"Yes and no. Of course, as you might expect, I couldn't resist inviting a friend or two up. Soon enough word got back to my grandfather, and he was quite adamant I never go up there again, but after some considerable fuss on my part—really, I think I was quite awful about it—he relented and let me play in the tower whenever I wished, as long as I played alone." She sighed. "Unfortunately, he died not long after—when I was ten—and my father almost immediately sold Thorn Court and moved us to Australia.

"My grandfather was a wonderful man—at least he was to me. He made my childhood here an idyll. I never knew it as a private residence, as he had—only as a hotel, but I loved it so—all the guests and the activity, eating in the dining room with all the formality, the wonderful gardens, the swimming pool, the elegant wedding parties, the ladies' lunches, tours to Dartmoor and the coast—all the sorts of things Will and I were trying to restore." She took a sip of coffee. "I suppose all the activity around the hotel and my grandfather's skilful intervention were what kept me from the truth: In Australia, with just the three of us, I realised how unsuccessful my parents' marriage really was. Of course, it didn't last long after that. My father had a notion of investing in a shooting estate in western Victoria—you can see how Adam might come by his interests—but he really didn't have the patience—or the interest, really—in the work and so he returned to England after the divorce. My mother, as I said, found Australia very much to her liking, liberating, I suppose—she had been a vicar's daughter—I must have told you this—and her home life, as she tells it, was repressive. Naturally, in those days, one stayed with one's mother."

"You'd rather have been with your father?"

"Oh, no, my mother was the much better parent. I love her dearly, though she's a bit flighty. I'd rather have been in England, though. I could never quite get used to Australia. Perhaps if we had moved when I was four or five, but at ten . . . Australia seemed so alien, like another planet—all the plants and animals are so unlike anything here, the heat can be absolutely scorching, and of course in school, you're teased unmercifully for being a Pom. Once we moved to Melbourne after the divorce it was better, but my first years were spent in a little village called Edenhope, where we were very much the outsiders.

"However"—she regarded him slyly—"the boys were very attractive. Not quite so . . . tentative as here."

Tom smiled. "I recall you saying that at the marriage preparation course in autumn."

With the Reverend Barbara Boswell, vicar of All Saints in nearby Hamlyn Ferrers, he had invited engaged couples in the area to a Saturday gathering, in the Old School Room, to help them build the foundations of a lasting marriage. Caroline had gamely volunteered herself and Will to join them and be the "old marrieds" and offer the wisdom of their experience. The icebreaker had been for each couple to tell the story of how they met. Tom, though without his better half, volunteered his: A hopeless non-swimmer, he'd been pitched off the punt he'd been guiding down the River Cam by some clever dick grabbing the top of his pole as he passed under Clare College Bridge; an awfully attractive young medical student, possessing a very good senior swimming certificate, reading by the bordering lawn responded to his helpless flopping about and saved him from drowning in the water's green gloom.

Somewhat less farcical was the meeting of Caroline Stanhope and Will Moir: Will had returned to Australia from England one blazing December to be in a friend's wedding party. To the wedding rehearsal dinner, he wore shorts and a polo shirt, a coordinated ensemble of brown and maroon he had bought in the hotel men's store. At the door of the restaurant an attractive woman shot him an amused glance and said, "Are you dressed for supper or are you dressed for Christmas?" To those untroubled by colour-blindness, such as the attractive woman named Caroline, he was wearing bright red shorts and an electric green shirt. And so it began. Within six months they were married.

As Will had related the story in his twangy accent, Tom had been struck forcefully by a wellspring of tenderness flowing between them. He thought Will possessed by wonder and a kind of irrational pride at having captured the heart of a woman of Caroline's poise. At the start that morning, he had been fidgety, restless, as if he didn't really wish to submit to this kind of public inspection, dragged to this event by his wife, but Will had relaxed as Caroline, seated beside him on one of the Old School Room's dilapidated couches, placed her hand over his and seemed to press it into the chink between cushions with a kind of restrained passion. The set of her features, next to Will's, was perhaps less decipherable—pleasure and embarrassment at the tribute being paid, yes, but something, too, of regret, a tenderness of pity in her lowered eyes. Perhaps other memories had penetrated her thoughts then, for as the morning progressed, in an exercise on forgiveness that placed the men on the opposite side of the room from the women, Caroline revealed that beds of roses do contain thorns: She and Will had parted company for a time in their marriage, though the details, at least within Tom's earshot, were not forthcoming.

Now, as they sipped their coffee in silence, Tom wondered what had pushed them apart and what had returned them each to the other. *Married lives are communities in miniature,* the Queen Mother had once said, an observation he had woven into a sermon. Her Majesty hadn't elaborated, but she had provided him the seed. Marriages had private and public identities, and like communities were marked by constant renegotiation and recommitment.

"I haven't offered you a biscuit," Caroline said, breaking into his reverie.

"I shouldn't." Tom shifted in his chair. "I'm sure I gained half a stone over Christmas."

"Are you sure? I have some pastry here, which I think your housekeeper must have made—it certainly looks to have Madrun's touch. Nick brought it over yesterday—he's been staying in the hotel—along with some leftover curry, although how he could think either Ariel or I would have an appetite for something like that . . . and something associated with that terrible dinner, I really don't know. He is remarkably obtuse," she added with a flash of anger. "Anyway, I binned it all. I did keep these tartlets, though. Were they part of the meal?"

"They accompanied the cranachan."

"Oh."

"You might bin them, too."

"I think I will. Sorry, I know what fine work Madrun does, but . . . oh, and there's the casserole she very kindly gave me yesterday. What—?"

"I handed it to Nick. You needn't feel obligated, Caroline. I know at times like this simple foods are best."

"Well, it will be eaten in time. She's such an awfully good cook." She sighed. "Will and I had been planning to hire a new chef, you know. This break for renovations was giving us a chance to make some personnel changes. But now . . . " Her hand fluttered in a vague manner. "I've just remembered something: The belvedere tower was the first place in the hotel I took Will when we came to view it. I sort of raced him up the stairs. The estate agent was rather startled. I think it was the view that brought Will around."

"You mean, Will wasn't keen on the purchase?"

"Well, he needed a little persuading. He had a good job with Sport England, but we were living in Toot Hinton, near Oxford, where I managed one of the Van Haute hotels, and it was a long, wearying journey in and out of London each day. Ariel was about to turn five, so it seemed like a good time to settle into a new place with a good school. And of course, we had some money after Father died. Still, Thornford had none of the associations for him that it had for me, but he gave in to my enthusiasm and grew, I think, to love this village as much as I. Perhaps that's why . . . "

She trailed off, but her implication was clear: Perhaps that's why Will had sought the comfort of the tower. It held for him, too, a cherished memory. But what would he have seen on a January night? Tom wondered. Pitch black broken only by twinkles of light from this window or that. A snow-burdened sky devoid of moon or stars. He hewed to his initial notion: that Will must have sensed he was dying, realised the impossibility of getting help, and like a canny animal, sought solitude for his final moments. Thorn Court's tower was a place of convenience, as Gethsemane, despite its later cultural accretions, had been a place of convenience for Jesus, a place to be alone with His fears and His prayers. He glanced at Caroline. Her expression was forlorn. He said nothing. Those who grieve need comfort.

CHAPTER TEN

*I*t's Nanette of the North!"

"Isn't it Nanook of the North?" Màiri White gasped between gulps of air. Her breath hung in the chilled air like little silver clouds.

"Probably," Tom agreed, regarding the village bobby's footwear with considerable interest. "Where on earth did you get those?"

"From my neighbour. From my neighbour's wife, I should say. When Griff finds these gone, he won't be pleased. But Roz—his wife—has finally got her wish to rid their cottage of these things." Màiri's feet were encased in a pair of wellies, which in turn were lashed by what appeared to be loops of leather to two large, curved wooden frames strung with crisscrossing grids of rawhide strips, all of which was clotted with fresh, wet snow. "They take a bit of getting used to."

Tom imagined snowshoes did. He had managed to distract himself from the travails of the weekend watching Miranda and half the other children in the village sliding, slithering, glissading, toppling, and pranging into one another on sledges improvised from cardboard and plastic on the *piste* that was now Fishers Hill. The frosty air was pricked with shrieks and laughter, underscored by the wail of some smaller child crushed in the melee, and the insistent yelps of delighted dogs. Adults, mostly mothers, gathered in conversational knots, sipping takeaway coffee from the Waterside Café and Bistro, occasionally sending forth an emissary to arbitrate some dispute or other among the children. (Many of the fathers, Tom suspected, had drifted towards the pub.) As Fishers Hill was the only route to the quay and the Waterside, Tom, too, found his bottom planted on what looked like someone's draining board and careening down the icy road, narrowly avoiding the smaller, lighter hominoids in his path, feeling vaguely foolish but helplessly happy. It had crossed his mind to suggest Caroline join him on this downhill adventure, but he could tell from her strained expression that she was anxious to avoid awkward exchanges with other villagers, who would, of course, cast opprobrium on a new widow's carefree behaviour. She'd parted from him at the top of the hill when she had gathered Ariel.

When he reached the bottom of the hill he had noticed in the middle distance along the snowy path by the millpond a figure vaguely familiar by shape and haircut, but quite unfamiliar in her gait, which was more of an unhurried but comic bowlegged hobble. It was only as she drew near that he realised with a fizz of happiness that made him smile that it was Màiri White slogging along in a pair of snowshoes.

"Why would this Griff own footwear like this?"

"They lived in Canada—in Quebec—for many years. Griff loved it. He was an engineer. Roz hated it, and couldn't wait to get back to England. Do you not know them?"

Tom shook his head. "They don't come to St. Paul's," he said, referring to his second church, in Pennycross St. Paul.

"Griff brought back a wee crate of souvenirs of their time in the colonies to decorate their home," Màiri continued, removing her woollen Nepal hat and giving her abundant hair a shake, "all of which Roz is burning in her back garden."

"Would I be correct in thinking Griff is not home?"

"Trapped in London. Not many trains running to the West Country." Màiri's lips curved into a smile. "He's a bit of a bully, Griff. According to Roz, he told her Devon would need to freeze over before he'd let her take down any of his precious mementos. Well, Devon's frozen over"—she gestured towards the millpond and its surface of thin ice like a grey skin—"and she's taken him at his word. I helped her heave the moose's head that used to be over the fireplace in the sitting room onto the flames."

"Burning fur?" Tom grimaced. "Must give off a pong."

"There's only me to smell it. I rent the little stone cottage attached to the farmhouse Griff and Roz had converted. You've never been, have you? Well, you must one day." She gave him another fetching smile. "Anyway, Roz came round to warn me what she was planning to do, and that's when I saw these great buggers and thought they'd be just the thing."

"For what?"

"Getting about on, of course. Although I think my ankles will be playing up before long."

"Come and have a coffee at the Waterside," Tom suggested. "You'll want to take those off first, of course. Can I help?" he added, as Màiri crouched to untie the leather bindings, which appeared damp and unyielding. He looked down on the top of her head, at her chestnut hair, which was becomingly tossed.

"Och, these are tight."

Tom stuffed his gloves in his pocket and bent to work on the bindings of her left snowshoe. With half an eye on her nimble fingers working the right, he said, "Saw you at The Pig's Barrel on Saturday."

"Oh? You should have come over and said hello."

"You looked engaged."

"Workmates, that's all. What were you—?"

"Wedding. The snow made me think better of lingering at the reception." Tom struggled with a knot. "What's brought you down from Pennycross?"

"You," she grunted.

"Really?" Tom couldn't keep the delight from his voice.

She flicked him a glance he couldn't interpret. Their faces were so close he could smell the lovely scent of citrus coming from her. "It's business. Of a sort."

Business? he thought, disappointed. *Of a sort?* "Sounds a bit dire."

"There! Got yours?"

"Yes," Tom replied, giving the leather strand a final loosening tug. He rose in tandem with Màiri, who stepped out of the snowshoes. "How did you find me here?"

"Caroline Moir. I was about to turn into the gate at the vicarage when I spotted her and Ariel coming up Poynton Shute. I went over to give her my condolences, and she said you were here."

"So you know . . . "

"I didn't hear it from the bush telegraph, if that's what you're thinking, Tom." She picked up the snowshoes and clacked them together. Snow tumbled out in little balls. "It's something else."

"From dire to ominous."

"I'll tell you when we get inside. You've a very unhappy snowman, by the way. I snowshoed through your garden to the millpond path."

"That's Miranda's doing. She feels badly for Ariel. I'll just pop over and let her know where I'll be."

"You're getting to be Thornford's favourite server." Tom smiled up at Kerra Prowse, trying for light effect. Madrun's niece, dressed in jeans and a black polo neck, looked faintly harried, pushing a loose strand of hair behind one ear with her pencil. Most late weekday mornings in January, the Waterside would be blessed with little more than a few pensioners eager for distraction, but this late week-day morning, all the tables but one farthest from the cash register, which he and Màiri had nabbed, were filled with cherry-cheeked folk, jackets and coats opened against the warmth of the room, all chattering away.

"Liam called and asked if I would do a shift," Kerra said, flipping to a new page in her pad. "With school closed, I had hoped to do nothing at all, but . . . " She shrugged, her pencil poised.

"And how are you getting on with His Nibs?" Màiri asked. "You've lasted longer than most."

Kerra glanced down the room at Liam Drewe. The Waterside's owner was rubbing his shaved bullet head and frowning fiercely at something in his hands, while an elderly couple leaned away, as if expecting a gale force of displeasure.

"Looks like someone's dared question the bill," Tom remarked before Kerra could reply.

"Stuff him," Kerra snapped, then amended her remark: "Liam, I mean. I got an A-star in my GCSE maths. I can sort it out."

"Then we'll try to be quick," Tom continued. "Two coffees and . . . oh, let's see . . . " His thumb absently pushed his wedding band around his finger. "I don't know what I want."

Màiri glanced at his hand and shot him a teasing smile. Throat-ily, she said, "Don't you?"

Tom blinked, amused by the subtext. "I suppose I do know what I would *like*. The question is whether I should indulge myself."

"Might you be on a sort of diet?"

"Let's say I am obliged to live by certain rules."

Màiri's eyes twinkled. Her smile widened. "Och, you know what they say about rules."

"Aye, lassie," he mimicked her accent, "but there are conse-quences to breaking them."

Màiri threw her head back and laughed. Brow furrowed, Kerra tapped her pencil along her pad.

"Sorry, Kerra, the vicar is dithering. Very vicarish of him. Just bring us something nice. Off you go, now. Poor lass," she remarked as Kerra edged between the crowded tables towards the front counter. They watched her shoulder her way past Liam, snatch the check from his fingers with a withering glare, and smilingly address the customers.

"I take that back," Màiri observed. "Looks like she's tamed the beast."

"She served at the Burns Supper at Thorn Court. She was very good, quite capable. Her father's one of the Thistle But Mostly Rose—Jago Prowse, you must know him—and she very ably got him to *not* thump Ni—one of the other men who pinched her bottom. I'm not really a ditherer, you know," he rushed on, not wanting to bring Nick Stanhope to the altar of conversation.

"You dithered just then."

"Last thing I want is to be a dithering priest. Two cats, a bicycle, and a housekeeper is caricature enough."

"You do have Bumble."

"Saved by a dog."

Màiri smiled. "So Nick was misbehaving at the Burns Supper." She removed a paper napkin from a holder on the table.

"I—"

"I know he's a member of the pipe band, Tom. I don't know if you know this, but I did see him for a wee while—"

"Er—"

"Not long, mind you. I soon realised he wasn't boyfriend material." She began to fold the napkin. "I also realised any connection with him wasn't going to do my career any good."

"Really?"

"I'm thinking of taking the training to become a police officer.

Being associated with Nick wouldn't exactly burnish my résumé. They check."

"But he's ex-army. He's started a home security business."

"I've already said too much."

Tom regarded her solemnly, deliberating whether to ask her the question that had troubled him at the Burns Supper as Nick grew increasingly obnoxious: What on earth had been her attraction to him? He glanced around at the other tables, noting that not a few Waterside patrons were casting eyes his way with what could only be described as avid curiosity. Marg Farrant acknowledged his glance with a teasing wave, while Anne Willett's eyebrows perched above her glasses in a censorious arch. He felt rather on display.

He sighed, returned his eyes to Màiri, who continued making elaborate folds in the napkin, and asked the Nick question, prefacing it with a "I hope you don't think this intrusive, but . . . "

"But?" Màiri looked up and smiled. "I know what you're going to ask. Well, I could say Nick was a great laugh and could tell a good joke—and all of that isn't untrue, particularly if he hadn't had a skinful. But"—the smile broadened, crinkling her eyes—"I would have to say this: Nick Stanhope is a very fit lad—aye, a *verra* fit lad, and a girl"—she rolled her *r*'s extravagantly—"has needs."

Tom sensed the blood pulsing up his neck, which seemed to bulge dangerously against his constraining clerical collar. He was struck by a riotous vision of Màiri naked, and then himself pantless, and then . . . At the same moment, he felt, on the cusp of his forties, suddenly, horribly, devastatingly middle-aged, and unprepared for this sort of flirtation—if flirtation it was and not simply reportage—and where it might lead. He must have looked like a beetroot with tumid eyes, for Màiri's head fell back; laughter came in silvery ripples, fading only when Kerra—bless her!—interrupted with a tray bearing two cups of steaming coffee and a plate with two pear-and-chocolate croissants.

"Mr. Christmas." She set a cup before him. "Are you feeling okay?"

"Fine," Tom croaked. "I'm fine."

"That's exactly what Mr. Moir said to me Saturday night and look what happened."

Màiri's laughter ceased abruptly. "When?" Tom asked, startled.

"After the pudding, when everyone left the dining room for a break. He passed through the kitchen."

"Kerra," Tom said gently, "you're not to feel badly. A few of us thought he didn't look well, but he seemed determined to ignore our concern."

Kerra received this in silence as she set a coffee cup in front of Màiri. "Adam thinks someone could have done something."

"You've talked to Adam?"

"No, to Tamara. She says that's what Adam thinks."

"Oh." Tom grimaced as Kerra twisted her body towards a woman importuning her at the neighbouring table.

"Of course, he would share his feelings with his girlfriend," he said to Màiri. "I saw him earlier this morning at the hotel and he didn't have much to say. Stoical, his mother indicated. But I expect he's angry as well as grieved. Odd," he murmured, a thought suddenly coming to him, "that John didn't drive Adam back from Noze when he went to get Caroline yesterday."

"Sorry about that." Kerra turned back to them. "Anyway, these are fresh this morning. I hope you like them."

"They look brilliant," Màiri responded, taking a croissant and biting into it as Kerra moved away. "Now, where were we?"

"I think," Tom said, reluctant to return to their previous topic, "you said you came down to Thornford on some business."

Màiri, taking another bite, didn't reply immediately. "Tell me about the Burns Supper," she said finally, licking at a dab of chocolate that had fallen on her finger.

Tom stared helplessly at her lovely tongue.

"Tom?"

"Sorry?"

"The Burns Supper?"

"Oh, yes, quite. Well, you know the tragic part already."

"Indulge me with the rest."

"All right," he began, mildly challenged, his mind roving over the course of the evening, uncertain upon which detail to alight, "let's see. There was the haggis—"

"A haggis at a Burns Supper? Fancy that."

"Well, it was a novel experience for me."

"And . . . ?"

"It was . . . interesting."

"Tom, that's the sort of word the Queen uses when something bores her cross-eyed."

"Then put it this way." Tom pulled his croissant in two, better to get at the rich filling. "It wasn't as bloody awful as I expected, but I still wouldn't feed it to swine."

"I wouldn't touch it with a caber, either. Haggis is the reason I turned vegetarian."

"But you're—"

"Doesn't mean I have to eat it! I remember my parents plunking haggis in front of me when I was eight. The reek! I refused. That's when I announced for vegetarianism. Lips that touch the flesh of poor wee lambs shall never touch mine. But enough of the bloody haggis. What else happened at your doomed Burns Supper?"

"It didn't seem doomed at the time. Not really. Although there were undercurrents." Between sips of coffee and bites of pastry, Tom went on to describe the evening.

"Interesting," Màiri murmured when he had finished.

"Is that a royal 'interesting'? Or a genuine 'interesting'?"

"Genuine."

"I hadn't been to a Burns Supper before, but except for the dramatic and very cheerless ending, I'm not sure it was much different than any other Burns Supper in the realm."

Màiri ran her fingers along the rim of her coffee cup. Tom stared at them, at their pink tips and pearly manicure, as he waited for her to respond. Faintly mesmerised, he wondered what it would be like if those very fingers travelled along his . . . well, really, any part of his anatomy would do.

"I was having a chat on the phone with my sergeant at Totnes station," Màiri began after a moment, "sorting out what presence we could possibly have in this weather—which isn't much—when he happened to say that the postmortem results were in on Will Moir."

"Mmm . . . ?" Tom was only half attentive.

"Will had a heart attack, all right. However . . . "

Tom refocused on her face. He saw the muscles settled into sombre lines and felt the first bloom of unease.

"I don't have the precise details, but . . . " She glanced at the other tables and dropped her voice. "Something was found in his system."

"Something . . . ?" He leaned nearer to hear her better.

"Taxine."

The word resonated from hospital visits or, possibly, conversations with his late wife. "Isn't it a cancer drug or the like? Or is it Taxol? Don't tell me Will had cancer and didn't tell anyone?"

"No evidence of that in the PM. Tom, I'm telling you this on the quiet because you may be personally affected by the consequences. Or your household may be."

"Now you have me frightened."

"Do you remember our first real conversation, last spring, at the village hall, at the opening of the art exhibition?"

"Yes."

"Your housekeeper had prepared some pastries for the event and was helping Kerra serve them. Do you remember what they were?"

Tom frowned, worried. "Yes . . . "

"And did you not have the same thing for afters at the Burns Supper, with the cranachan?"

"Well, yes . . . I mentioned them a moment ago when I described our meal."

"Tom, taxine is a poison. It's made from the leaves, bark, seeds, roots—in fact, any part but the berries—of the yew tree."

"Oh, God!"

CHAPTER ELEVEN

It wasn't a conversation Tom anticipated with unalloyed pleasure. After lunch, after a perfect winter meal of Tuscan bean soup, crusty bread, and Devon Blue cheese, after Miranda drifted away to her room to read her latest Alice Roy and Judith retreated to hers for a postprandial nap, Tom found himself trailing about the kitchen, clearing plates and running a cloth over the cooker, tasks that wouldn't normally preoccupy him, given the press of church work on any given day—even on a Monday, his usual day of rest.

But this wasn't a usual Monday. The entire village, indeed the entire island, was bogged off from its usual patterns of production and consumption and driving around like mad, and though endless paperwork awaited him in his study, Tom felt he could rightly break from his patterns as well. When he asked Madrun if he might lend a hand by loading the dishwasher, she regarded him askance.

"No, Mr. Christmas, I think it best if you didn't."

"Oh."

"You're not very good at it, you see."

"I'm not?"

"No, you're not. I've observed you. You need to be more . . . punctilious. You should always load from the back, thus, with the larger plates first." She demonstrated. "And then you should nest the cutlery—see, the spoons in this part of the basket and the knives in this. And then . . ."

"I *am* schooled," he said humbly when she had finished.

"We had the dishwasher installed in Mr. James-Douglas's day. For a time he would put in a single cup and saucer and then start it running. I had to put a stop to that, of course!"

"Yes, I agree, a terrible waste."

Madrun made a dismissive noise and peered at him. "Would you like me to make you a fresh cup of tea to take away with you?"

"Tea would be very nice."

"Then I shall bring it along to you in your study." She bustled, reaching for the kettle.

"Actually, Mrs. Prowse, I wondered if you might join me in a cup?"

"Oh?" She was arrested plugging the instrument into the socket and frowning at the clock. "It's only gone two."

"Yes, I know it's not your teatime, but if you would indulge me." He took a deep breath. "There's something very important I'd like to discuss with you."

Madrun's eyebrows slipped up her forehead. "Your study, then, in ten minutes, Mr. Christmas?"

"Unless there's somewhere else you'd care to talk?" His study—the thought occurred to him—had a sort of intimidating formality, yet the other rooms in the vicarage seemed suddenly too public, easily breached by daughter or guest. He was anxious this conversation be confidential and nonaccusatory.

Madrun seemed to read his mind. Her features betrayed a flash of concern. She said sceptically, "Mr. James-Douglas sometimes joined me in my rooms when he had something important to discuss."

"If you'd like ..." Tom responded, a little startled. Thornford Regis's vicarage had been his home for less than a year, yet he had never been in Madrun's suite of rooms on the top floor, which seemed somehow inviolate.

"Take the back stairs, Mr. Christmas. I shall be up in nine minutes."

Tom's searching eyes couldn't help going first, upon entering Madrun's aerie, to the mahogany desk and round-back chair by one of the dormer windows where, he was sure, lay the instrument that visited his every daily awakening. Yes, there it was. Red, surprisingly, as red as a pillar box, a colour he didn't associate with typewriters. And the design was modern, in a mid-twentieth-century way. He had somehow expected an Edwardian contraption with tiny round keys that required a thorough bashing; it was the only way he could account for the *clacketty-clack* that carried down to his bedroom. He peered closer. OLIVETTI said the raised letters at the back, and above the keytop VALENTINE—the model presumably. This likely accounted for the colour, but had it, too, been a gift with some sentiment attached? This wasn't the hour for wondering such things. Inserted in the carriage, peeking above the paper guide, was a piece of stationery with THE VICARAGE clearly visible at the top, tomorrow's letter to old Mrs. Prowse in Cornwall at the ready. Tom grimaced at what it might contain.

The rest of the desk was a paean to tidiness, like the rest of the vicarage (expect for his own office), with its aligned stack of stationery to one side, pens and pencils gathered in a neat spiral in a Royal Wedding 1981 souvenir beaker, and a set of bronze lion-head bookends squeezing together precisely ranked copies of the *Oxford English Dictionary, Roget's Thesaurus,* Bartlett's *Familiar Quotations,* and, curiously, *Black's Medical Dictionary.* There was an ivory box with envelopes, an array of photographs in silver frames, while farther along, on a large blotter, was a pile of spiral notebooks, the cover of the top one grubby with what looked like oil stains. He peered at the crabbed handwriting on the front and thought he could discern THORNFORD REGIS, A PARISH HISTORY, VOLUME VII. This had to be Madrun's father's fabled local history, which he'd scribbled between oil changes and brake repairs at Thorn Cross Garage before he died, and which Madrun was dutifully transcribing to type.

An unenviable task, Tom thought, turning and absorbing an aspect of the room he hadn't quite noted when he'd crossed it. It was very red, boldly so. The sitting room walls were covered in an unpatterned red silk wallpaper, the chairs in a red fabric. Pillows were red, curtains were red, the highly patterned Turkish rugs and chintz sofa were predominantly red, woven through with a British racing green, the accent colour for the room, most apparent along the wainscoting, mouldings, window sashes, and chimneypiece. He looked back at the Valentine-model Olivetti. The room's appointments struck a note of professional attention—the handiwork of one of Giles James-Douglas's many nephews, perhaps?—and he didn't wonder that the catalyst to artistry wasn't the shiny red typewriter.

Tom was still standing by the desk, noting the winter pansies in a goldfish bowl on the window ledge, when Madrun arrived with a tray of tea things, which she set down on a low table between the couch and two Queen Anne chairs opposite.

"Is everything well with Miranda?" she asked.

"Yes, I think so." Tom's response was automatic. "Why?" he asked anxiously. "Have I missed something?"

"I watched her make the snowman's smile into a frown."

"Yes, well, she feels badly for Ariel. I expect it's just her way of . . ." Tom trailed off. "Actually, Mrs. Prowse, it's Will Moir's . . . circumstances I wanted to discuss with you."

Madrun gestured towards a chair opposite and sat on the couch, gathering the folds of her skirt under her.

"I don't quite know how to begin," he said, pausing to watch Madrun's expert hand move to the milk jug and begin to pour milk into two teacups. She looked up at him enquiringly.

"It seems Will Moir's death isn't quite as . . . straightforward as it might appear."

"He was very young, wasn't he." Madrun lifted the knitted cosy off the teapot. "Is there heart disease in his family? Or was he an adopted child. I can't—"

"It's none of that, Mrs. Prowse," Tom cut in. "It's this: Some poison was detected in Will's system. There's been a postmortem."

"*Poison?*" Madrun looked at him sharply. The spout of the teapot veered from the cup, sending golden, steaming liquid splashing onto the tray. "Oh, dear heavens, Mr. James-Douglas's best rosewood! But how could there be poison? Food poisoning? Something he ate?"

It was the very question.

"Yes, Mrs. Prowse, it was something he ate—something it *appears* he ate . . . or ingested in some fashion," he quickly amended.

"The curry? Was it very spicy?"

"No, Mrs. Prowse, not the curry. Or at least most *likely* not the curry," he amended again. Certainties beyond that of taxine poisoning as cause of death were pretty much absent.

"Perhaps the poor man took some medicine incorrectly." Madrun resumed pouring the tea.

Tom waited until she had handed him his cup and saucer. "No, not medicine. Well, at least it's highly doubtful." He took a polite sip, then replaced the cup. He cleared his throat and said the awful words.

"It appears, Mrs. Prowse, that Will died from a poisonous substance that is found in most parts of the yew."

Madrun was on the point of reaching for her tea, but her arm stopped midair, as if suddenly clamped by invisible jaws. Her eyes shot to his.

"Mr. Christmas! It's impossible!" Her features, for a flying moment stamped with incredulity, swiftly hardened to stern stubbornness. She sat up, rigid as a statue. "You've seen what I do!"

"I know, Mrs. Prowse," he responded gently. He had described Madrun's method with yewberries to Màiri earlier at the Waterside, how she harvested the red fruit from the lower branches of the ancient tree in the churchyard in the late summer, how she meticulously tweezered out the poisonous stone from each berry, how, as an added precaution, she made an inventory of the stones against the berries, then flushed them. She would let no one help her in this task, refusing even Miranda's enthusiastic offer, barring Bumble and cats, and turning the kitchen almost into a white-coated laboratory. As he'd said to Màiri, he thought it was mad to expend so much time and energy on something so calorically insignificant. He had even hinted as much to her, but Madrun Prowse, a force unto herself, eschewed cost–benefit analysis in her food preparation. Madrun fancied a forage now and again. She foraged for blackberries, wortleberries, bilberries, tayberries, tummelberries, cherry plums, elderflowers, wild mushrooms, wild garlic, and a number of other goodies from the fields, woods, and hedgerows around the village and up on Dartmoor.

"I'm only telling you this," Tom continued, "because as soon as the roads are passable there'll be an inquest—and most likely some awkward questions."

"But I've been making sweet things with yewberries for years and years." Madrun's tea sat untouched, its thin vapours drifting into the air. "It's impossible," she said again, "simply impossible! It *must* be something else. How do you know this, Mr. Christmas?"

"Well—"

"PCSO White! I saw her coming through the garden this morning down to the millpond wearing those . . . tennis rackets."

"Snowshoes," Tom amended. "Màiri has impeccable sources for her information, as you might imagine, Mrs. Prowse." As Madrun opened her mouth to protest, he added, "Her concern was that you be prepared."

"For what?"

For the worst, he wanted to say—*helping the police with their enquiries, becoming a person of interest,* and other such sugarcoatings. "For questions," he said instead. "For people's reactions. It will become publicly known."

If he had expected Madrun to collapse in grief and fear and tears, he was relieved she evinced nothing more than compressed lips and a red splotch on each cheek. In his ministry, he seldom found people's reaction to shocking news to be utterly predictable. Brutish men wept like children at the loss of a pet; sympathetic women turned stony at the loss of a parent. "At least he didn't take anyone with him," one woman had remarked to him matter-of-factly after her son had turned a shotgun on himself.

"Mr. Christmas, this can't be true. I'm much, *much* too careful for this to happen."

"Mrs. Prowse, I want you to know that I believe you are. I know from sharing this house with you that you're meticulous in every way." He stopped himself before he got to the damning coordinating conjunction *but—but* accidents happen. Life can change in an instant. Horrible, terrible things can befall you and send your life hurtling down some unforeseen path.

He had a thought. "Do you always make a contribution of your baking to the Burns Supper?"

"What?" Madrun frowned.

Tom repeated the question.

"No." She shook her head vaguely. "This was the first time."

"Oh? Well, it was kind of you to do so, a nice addition to the traditional offerings, except for . . . "

"I was asked to supply some berry tartlets. I don't think I would have thought to offer them myself. Mr. James-Douglas always said he got so full at the main course, he could barely tuck into pudding, so—"

"You mean someone *asked* you to supply the pastries?"

Madrun nodded.

"Who asked you?"

"I don't know, really. I thought it was Roger."

Tom frowned, confused. "I always think the way Roger speaks rather distinctive."

"No, Mr. Christmas. The request came in the form of a note, not over the telephone."

"You mean, in the post?"

"Not as such. But it was among the letters in the first post, in an envelope pushed through the letter box . . . last Tuesday, I think it was."

"And you weren't sure whether Roger had written it?"

"It wasn't signed."

Tom caught his breath. Unbidden came a sharp memory of standing at his cluttered desk at St. Dunstan's one spring afternoon in the year that Lisbeth died, telephone jammed between ear and shoulder (he had been talking to the archdeacon), absently opening the post he'd retrieved moments earlier from the church office in-box. Among the letters and flyers, too, had been an envelope, unsealed, unaddressed, unremarkable, really, until he fished out the note within, unfolded it against his thigh, and casually scanned the first sentence, disbelieving scanned it again, his eyes racing over words that followed, the phone receiver, his interlocutor forgotten, slipping from his shoulder and crashing to the desk, along with a fluttering of another paper tucked into the note's fold. His stomach clutched with disgust at the invective, the blast of pure extruded hate, the assault on Lisbeth as a woman, as a Jew, as his wife—and its implications. Half blindly, oblivious to his name barked anxiously through the phone receiver, he sank against a rank of filing cabinets, hand groping—with dread—for the other thing, the thing that fluttered, the thing—a photograph—that would, for a time, shatter his faith in their marriage.

"Mr. Christmas?" Madrun regarded him curiously.

"Sorry, I . . . " Tom pushed the awful memory away. "I was going to say, how odd this is. Did you think it odd at the time?"

"I did think it a bit previous, Mr. Christmas." Madrun took a more confident sip of tea. "But as the request was for the Burns Supper and as Roger is pipe sergeant of the Thistle But Mostly Rose and an old friend, I assumed he was busy in the shop and dashed off the note and had it delivered . . . and forgot to sign it."

"The telephone would have been quicker."

"There were three twenty-pound notes in the envelope—perhaps that's why. I put the money in the offertory box in the church."

"That's very generous, Mrs. Prowse, thank you." Tom thought a minute, glancing absently at a cabinet against the wall between the two windows filled with china figures. "But it couldn't have been a note from Roger. He was curious about the box you gave me to take up to Thorn Court on Saturday."

A silence descended on the room, broken only by the sound—muffled by snow and the vicarage's stone walls—of St. Nicholas's chimes sounding the time, two thirty. Faced towards the south windows, Tom glimpsed through net curtains the pale midwinter light already waning as the sun edged towards the folds of the hills, his mind niggled by this queer departure from the Burns Supper customs, the curry notwithstanding. Who among the Thistle But Mostly Rose so adored Madrun's pastry he had to have it at the meal, an addition to the traditional cranachan? He glanced at Madrun, whose fingers were worrying the hem of her jumper, her face now as stubbornly inexpressive as an Easter Island statue.

"Was the note handwritten, Mrs. Prowse?"

She blinked. "It was typewritten."

"Really?" Tom had a notion that typewriters had all kinds of minor idiosyncrasies that could be spotted—cockeyed *e*'s or smudgy *n*'s or wonky *t*'s.

"Not like my Olivetti, mind. More like a page in a book."

"A computer printer, then," Tom groaned. The note he'd received that day at St. Dunstan's had been similarly devised. "The printing's usually very tidy—although I suppose there are experts who do forensic identifications. Oh, well, perhaps the writer of the note will come forwards at the inquest, though I shouldn't wonder that he keeps mum."

"I'm not sure that will help me, Mr. Christmas."

"No, I suppose not." Tom bit along his lip. "You didn't happen to keep the note, did you?"

Not keeping his had been a mistake. Rage had triumphed over shock then. Foolishly—for he could have provided some scrap, some lead, to police after Lisbeth was murdered—he had torn the evil thing to shreds and flushed them down the loo, watching to ensure every bit was consigned to oblivion. But the damning photograph—a drab image on copy paper, surely captured by a mobile phone lens, of Lisbeth in the passionate embrace of another man outside a restaurant on Bristol's harbourside—he had slipped into his pocket.

"I'm not sure." Madrun's brow furrowed. "I remember folding it into the pocket of my apron. No. I did take it out again, and used the back of the paper to make a grocery list."

"Was there letterhead? Distinctive paper?"

She shook her head impatiently. "Mr. Christmas, what I don't understand is why Mr. Moir wouldn't have *noticed* seeds in one my berry tartlets. Yew seeds would be hard on the teeth, I'm certain, and—I gather, I've never had one—really quite bitter. And"—she warmed to her argument—"you would need many seeds, many—a tablespoon at least, I should think—for it to be—"

She stopped herself; the word *fatal* hung in the air between them. But Madrun's contention had been Tom's, too. How much taxine *did* it take to fell a man the size of Will Moir, surely weighing more than thirteen stone? Màiri didn't know. The finer details of the postmortem remained undisclosed. But Tom recalled a story from his childhood in which a neighbour girl had ingested some yewberries, seeds and all, and had been rushed to hospital to have her stomach pumped. This prompted a warning from his mother about the dangers of noshing on the alluring red berries that formed on the yew in September. "Not even one!" she had warned, though it had taken more than one to make the girl ill.

"Well, Mrs. Prowse, let us hold on to that thought. If it takes that many seeds, there must be some sort of mistake."

What he didn't report to Madrun was the remark Will made at table when he bit into one of her tartlets: *"Are there nuts in these?"*

It was the plural that was troubling.

The Vicarage

Thornford Regis TC9 6QX

13 JANUARY

Dear Mum,

Something dreadful has happened—much, MUCH worse than my troubles with the Yorkshire pudding. Mr. Christmas told me yesterday that Will Moir ~~died~~ may have died of the sort of poison produced by parts of the yew. Remember last week I told you I had got a note asking if I would send some of my berry tartlets up to Thorn Court to the Burns Supper? Well ~~everyone thinks~~ ~~some folk think Mr Christmas thinks~~ it's thought that perhaps I didn't tweezer out all the seeds from the berries and that Mr. Moir swallowed some of them. I can't believe this could be true. Mum, I can't believe that EVEN ONE slipped my notice! I went over and over in my mind how one could have slipped through my counting system. And even if one or two slipped through, which can't have happened, I can't believe there would be such a horrible ~~a~~effect. The only creature I can remember being affected by yew was one of the heifers at Thorn Barton who ate a Christ-

mas wreath some fool had tossed onto the property. There's to be an inquest, Mr. C says, and all this will come out and people will think my tartlets were to blame and how will I be able to look Mrs. Moir in the face? Or Ariel? I can't bear the idea of the child blaming me for losing her father. Or Adam. I can't think how I shall hold up my head in the village after this. If it's true, which I can't believe it is. It can't be, so you mustn't worry, Mum. I'm sure it will be all right in the end and Mr. Moir will be shown to have died of something else entirely. But perhaps this morning I ought to rid the freezer of the remaining yewberries. I don't think I shall have the heart to bake with them again, and also who will want to eat them now? Anyway, I mustn't dwell on this. I talked to Aunt Gwen on the phone last night, as you probably know, and decided not to mention it. She says you are both well and untroubled by all the snow, which is a great relief. It's good to know you have such good neighbours. I'm glad you didn't have to go out in it. I know Florence Daintrey sprained her ankle on some ice on the path outside their cottage. No school again today. The snow stopped early yesterday and some of the roads are beginning to be cleared, and for many of the village children, like Miranda, the walk to school isn't far. But perhaps the teachers want a day off more than anyone, even if they only just got back from their Christmas holidays. I know Miranda is anxious to get back, especially so she can make her lantern for the Wassail. I did look in Karla's shop yesterday morning when I posted your letter to see if she had any lantern-worthy ~~miterial~~ things, but no. I am feeling more optimistic that the Wassail will go on as planned on Saturday. The radio last night said mild air is on its way from the Azores, which promises to make short order of all this snow. Soon it will be like a dream, I suppose. Judith Ingley is still our guest at the vicarage while she's waiting for someone from the estate agents to get to Thornford and she's been making herself useful. She likes

*a good natter the way Mr. James-Douglas did when he was
alive, which is such a pleasure as Mr. Christmas does tend to
frown on what he calls "tittletattle." I've been filling her in on
various village doings and such, though much has changed in the
years she's been away—at least as far as people go. The buildings
are much the same! She's been curious mostly about those she met
at the Burns Supper, so I told her about Mark and Violet's lovely
baby and Roger's ~~marterdom~~ martyrdom to his mother, and how
the poor Kaifs lost their son last autumn, and why John Copeland comes to St. Nicholas's rather than to the perfectly good
church at Noze, and why Nick Stanhope's stint in the army got
short shrift. She was curious about Clive Stanhope, but as it's
thirty years or more since any one of us last saw him, I couldn't
say, other than how he died, ~~poor silly~~ poor man. I'm not sure I
told you this as it only came on my "radar" recently, but apparently about five or six years ago he was at his second wife's funeral tea at a country hotel somewhere in Cumbria where he had
landed up after coming back from Australia when he took it
upon himself to drive himself home and ploughed straight into a
tractor as he was tearing through the hedgerows. I expect he was
very drunk. This meant Caroline was planning a second funeral
within days of the first, though of course it wasn't her mother
who had died the few days before, but then I expect Nick is fairly
useless at such things—or perhaps he was in the army then. I'm
not sure. Now that's made me think that Caroline must plan a
funeral for a loved one and perhaps I am the cause, though I
simply know I cannot be. I did tell Judith last night after teatime what Mr. Christmas told me, as she must have seen I was
not my usual self, though I did try to hide my upset at least for
Miranda's sake. She told me she thought Mr. Moir looked a bit
off BEFORE they sat down to pudding and Judith trained as a
nurse so I'm taking heart from this though I think Mr. Moir has
been "off" in a way for some months. When he was at lunch*

Sunday before last he wasn't terribly cheerful, the way he used to be. Anyway, I must buck up and get on with things, breakfast to start with. It will be nice when there's light in the morning. January is always a bit of horror isn't it, Mum. So dark! We are all well otherwise here. Even Powell and Gloria are bearing the snow a little. I hope you have a very good day. Love to Aunt Gwen.

Much love,
Madrun

P.S. Mr. Christmas has a little bee in his bonnet about Old Bob's spectacles. Do you remember them? Large, with pink frames, very the thing twenty years ago. I'd forgotten they were originally yours, Old Bob's been wearing them so long. I expect he found them at a jumble sale. I think when Mr. Christmas takes him for his next medical appointment, he's going to see if he can get him fitted with some new frames, something better suited a man, I suppose. I can't think Mr. Christmas will have much luck. Old Bob is awfully attached to those things for some reason.

CHAPTER TWELVE

Madrun had suggested he roll socks *over* his wellies to give him some traction if he were going to attempt walking over black ice, which was indeed his intent. But the notion of strolling through the village to the Daintrey cottage thus shod struck Tom as haberdashery beneath the dignity of the priesthood—an invitation to ridicule. Still, he understood Madrun's wisdom now, as he began to climb Thorn Hill. The road was covered here and there between the snowdrifts with the most remarkable sheet of ice, almost invisible, as if the macadamised surface had been given little more than a light polish. Adding to the delicacy of his task was the object he was toting with him—hot soup in a large plastic container itself inside a Morrisons carrier bag, which, should he take a tumble, would most likely burst its lid and cover the ice with steaming stock and vegetables.

"You look like you're in trouble, Father," remarked a cheerful male voice behind him.

"Yes, I suppose I am." Tom released a sort of embarrassed chuckle and stopped, resting his free hand on one of the crooked stones in the wall lining the road. It was Rorie, the postman, whose bright red cagoule proclaimed him and whose last name eluded Tom. He was usually to be seen dashing through the village, so much like a cartoon blur that Tom had little firm idea of the man's physical appearance. Now he did. Rorie was short and stocky with a fringe of dark hair over a large, ruddy face split by a huge grin.

"The entire country's virtually shut down." Tom eyed the large red bag slung over the man's left shoulder.

"Neither snow nor rain nor heat nor . . . something, something . . ."

"Isn't that an American saying?"

"Yes, but a good one. As it happens, the road to the village has been cleared, some trains are getting through from London, and there's mail!"

But Tom was more interested in Rorie's footwear, Doc Martens embossed with ROYAL MAIL on the heelcap, but wrapped in a crisscrossing of steel chains.

"I used to work in North Yorkshire," Rorie explained, following Tom's eyes. "Terrible black ice we would get. These work a treat. You know, Father, if you put socks over your—"

"Yes, I've heard that," Tom interrupted with rising impatience.

"Here," Rorie continued, shifting his bag so it hung down his back. "Let me help you. Take that carrier bag in your other hand. There, that's the way." He took Tom's hand in his own beefy one and led him up the slope, half pulling him, encouraging his progress with lively invocations. The question was whether it was sillier to wear socks over your boots or hold hands with your postman. Tom wondered if he would be rewarded with a sweetie for being a good boy when they reached the Daintreys' gate. He wasn't. He was rewarded with a sheaf of letters.

"Here. Give these to the girls, would you, Father?"

The girls? "One moment, Rorie." Tom steadied himself on the gatepost. "If someone gave you an unstamped envelope and asked you to take it to someone down the road or across the village on your rounds, would you do it?"

"Well, we're not supposed to. We're not carrier pigeons, Father. But if someone asked and it was on my way, I might. Why? Is there something . . . ?"

"No. I was just wondering . . . You haven't delivered something under those circumstances in the last week, have you, by any chance?"

"Can't say I have." The postman paused. "No, I tell a lie. Mr. Sainton-Clark asked me to pass a note to Mr. Snell next door. You know they refuse to speak to each other? There was some urgent need of communication. Still, that was about four months ago. Shall I leave you here? Will you be all right?"

"Yes, thank you for your help. Will we see you in church?"

"You saw me Christmas Eve."

"So I did," Tom white-lied.

"Our Theo was one of the shepherds at the Crib Service."

"Of course, yes." Tom poked through the deck and picked out the right card: Young Theo had used his crook to hit one of the other shepherds; unholy screeching ensued. "I hope you'll come again."

"Easter, I should think, Father."

Of course. More C & E than C *of* E.

"Hello?" Tom poked his head through Uphill Cottage's door into a small square hall with a small round table with a small parched poinsettia dead centre, on which he placed the Daintreys' post. "Hel*lo*?"

A muffled response came from behind the closed door to the left. Tom stepped out of his boots and padded across the hall in his

Barbour. A blast of warmth rushed along his face when he opened the door. Not only must the central heating be cranked up, but a fire in the grate was blazing at good mid-tempo. One hand went automatically to his zipper.

"Oh, hello, Vicar!" Florence Daintrey boomed from one of the two identical couches perpendicular to the fireplace. She was lying flat, her greying head to the fire, swathed in a patchwork quilt. She placed the book she had been reading onto her stomach. "How kind of you to visit."

"I heard you were under the weather." Florence's foot, which was partly exposed from the quilt, was dressed in a makeshift splint and an argyle sock, resting on a nest of pillows.

"Bloody council can't be bothered to salt the road, can it? Take off your jacket, Tom. You'll probably find it warm in here."

"I have a bad code," Venice Daintrey announced thickly. She was huddled under a quilt of her own on the couch opposite. Her eyes blinked at him rheumily.

"You have a bad cold, Ven. Co*ld.* Say it!"

"Code."

"And it's not that bad."

Tom interposed. "Mrs. Prowse sent me over with her very good homemade soup to buck you up." He held up the carrier bag with a gesture of triumph.

The two women traded sharp glances.

"Oh," Venice wheezed.

"What?" Tom said, suddenly conscious of an atmosphere.

"I'm sure it's lovely," Venice said in a hoarse voice.

"As long as it isn't yew noodle!" Florence cackled.

"Florence!" her sister-in-law managed to croak, then sneezed loudly.

Tom caught a breath. "How could you possibly . . . ?"

"Know? Really, Tom! How long have you lived in Thornford?

Anyway I know you don't approve of tale-bearing, so I shan't disclose my source."

From the corner of his eye, Tom noted Venice's mouth moving with exaggerated effect. He deciphered a name.

"Judith Ingley," he intoned.

"No one can accuse you of being thick, Vicar."

"But how—"

"Judith telephoned this morning. I think she's looking to connect with people she once knew in Thornford, and happened to let the news slip. I knew her a little when I was young. Or knew *of* her, rather. I'm somewhat older than she is, and I can't say our families travelled in the same social circles."

Venice rolled her eyes at Tom, then sniffed loudly. Florence turned her head and cast her sister-in-law a suspicious glance.

"For heaven's sake, Vicar," Florence continued, "you're stood there like a lemon. Take a pew."

"I'll make some tea." Venice wrestled with her quilt. A chubby pink foot appeared briefly from beneath a fold.

"Why don't you rest?" Tom suggested, pushing out of his coat. "I'll make it."

"But you won't know where things are."

"He may be a man, Ven, but he's not a complete boob. He can boil a kettle!"

"Nevertheless, I'll make it. The vicar is our guest." Venice's feet found the carpet and slipped into a pair of pink, rabbit-ear slippers. She pulled back the blanket to reveal a pair of loose pink trousers and a matching sweatshirt. "Goodness," she added, patting her permed snowy hair, "I must look a sight."

"Truer words, Ven!" Florence cackled again.

Venice gave Tom a look of long suffering as she took his jacket. "You might try to have more sympathy," she called over her shoulder to her sister-in-law. "I sympathise with your ankle."

"You're not *that* bad off, Ven. It's a simple cold."

"I have no appetite. It might be flu."

"You should cancel that appointment."

"No!"

Venice shut the door behind her with audible force.

"And losing a stone wouldn't go amiss," Florence remarked airily. "As you seem to refuse to sit down, Tom, would you mind throwing another stick on the fire? Venice doesn't have flu, you know," she added, as Tom pulled a beech log from a basket by the fireplace and felt the blaze of the flames against his bedewing forehead. "It's her way of saying she won't be touching Madrun's soup. Nor will I, come to that."

"But Mrs. Prowse is a superb cook."

"I know . . . or, rather, I've heard."

"You can't tell me you really do think poison has found its way into her soup."

There was a beat of silence. Tom looked at her sharply as he sat down on a wing chair placed near the end of the couch. "Florence?"

"Of course not. I was simply testing you, Vicar. I really have trouble imagining Will Moir dying from a misplaced yew seed or two. If that's what it was. I know a *little* of poisons, having worked for a time for the ministry." She paused, running her fingers absently over the spine of her book. Protuberant veins, like purple twine, ran over the back of her hand. Florence had mentioned working for the ministry more than once in his presence. Which ministry remained the mystery, but it seemed to trump anything in an exchange of views.

"You mean, you don't know?" she enquired.

"Don't know what?"

"Exactly. This is my point: This is what happens when you disassociate yourself from intelligence-gathering."

"You mean gossip."

"I mean what I said, Vicar. If you mean to tend your flock diligently, then it's best you know all you can about them, don't you think?"

"Well . . . " Tom shifted in his seat, which was lumpy and unforgiving.

"Anyway, before Venice returns, as she doesn't care to be reminded of this episode . . . You of course know that Madrun's mother is deaf."

"Yes. Something to do with being struck by lightning, wasn't it? At the May Fayre, thirty years ago or so."

"And did you know that my brother Walter—Venice's husband—was killed by lightning?"

"I had heard." From whom? he wondered. In his first weeks at Thornford, he had been bombarded with details about the village's *dramatis personae*. Seems lightning had an unusual affection for Thornfordites.

"Well, as it happens, the same bolt out of the blue—or out of the grey, as it happened—that turned Edith Prowse deaf also felled Walter. My idiot brother was having an affair with her."

"Oh."

"Oh, indeed. Some fools in the village thought it was divine punishment. Not me of course. Too medieval. Still, you can see why Madrun's gift is unwelcome."

"I don't see, really. Madrun is innocent of any trespass."

"Memories run deep in Thornford, Vicar. We don't forget."

"You might forgive. As Jesus said, *If you forgive sins of any, they are forgiven.*"

"Well, He would say that, wouldn't He. He didn't live in a village."

"He did too live in a village. Nazareth was a village."

"It wasn't an *English* village, was it?"

Tom opened his mouth to remonstrate, but the protest of an

unoiled door hinge and the discreet rattle of china announced Venice's return. Tom rose and offered to carry the laden tray, but Venice seemed wont to prove her strength despite a dangerous waver in her step, though she did sink back onto the couch with a sigh after placing the tray on the table.

"What were you talking about?" she asked, frowning at the tea things.

"You! Ha!" Florence smirked.

"I was remarking to Florence how I thought for the longest time that you two were sisters." Tom decided he could afford the cost of a white lie.

"Oh, our names." Venice sniffled. "Tom, would you be mother? I'm hoping not to spread any more germs."

"And I said I was named after one of Father's aunts who was probably named after Miss Nightingale." Tom caught Florence's knowing glance as he poured the milk into the cups. She seemed to be enjoying this small deception. "But Venice's parents named her after the city."

"My parents were dedicated Italophiles, despite Mussolini and the coming war," Venice explained, pointing Tom to the tea strainer. "My poor older brother was lumbered with Arno, after the river, of course—did Flo tell you?—but as a boy he insisted on being called Arnold."

"Imagine if you had married Venice's brother?" Tom addressed Florence as he aimed the teapot spout over a cup.

"Too silly, Vicar. Besides, chance there would have been none."

"My brother died in the Korean conflict, you see." Venice took a proffered cup from Tom and passed it over to her sister-in-law, who looked unwilling, or unable, to shift herself. "Battle of the Imjin River. He was with the Gloucestershire Regiment. His picture's on that shelf, if you'd care to look."

Passing another cup to Venice, Tom dutifully rose and examined the sepia-toned photograph, set in a nest of other family pictures, of a very fresh-faced young man, khaki shirt opened at the collar, posed jauntily, hands on hips, pipe in mouth.

"His loss must have been very painful for your parents, and for you, of course," he said.

"Nick Stanhope was in the same regiment," Florence remarked.

"Not at all, Flo. Nick was with the Royal Green Jackets when it merged with other units and became . . . The Rifles, I think they're called."

"Yes, I know, Ven. But the Glorious Glosters were part of the merge, so—"

"I'm not going to argue with you about anything as Byzantine as the army." Venice blew on her tea, then coughed. Her face reddened.

"He was discharged, wasn't he? And not with honour, I believe. Told an officer he would shoot him if he put him on guard duty again, can you believe it!" Florence scowled at her sister-in-law. "He's something, that one. Like his father."

"You knew Clive Stanhope?" Tom returned to his seat.

"Well, yes. He was younger than I so I can't say I paid him too much mind. But Clive did have a reputation for cutting a swath through the local girls, for one thing. Anyway, I was gone and living in London by the time he finally settled down with one of them, a vicar's daughter—Dorothy somebody—from somewhere near here, I believe."

"Caroline and Nick are really quite different from each other," Venice snuffled. "Not that I can say I really *know* Nick Stanhope. Have a biscuit, Vicar."

"Different mothers," Tom remarked, reaching for the plate.

"Same father, though," Florence murmured throatily.

"Whatever do you mean by that?" Ven glanced over her teacup.

"Caroline may seem like an angel, but . . . "

"Really, Flo! The woman has just lost her husband! I lost my husband when I was in my forties, too. I feel for Caroline terribly. I wish there was something I could do."

"You might take her a casserole," Florence said dryly. "When you're up to it."

"I think not."

"My question is," Florence continued, oblivious, "who benefits?"

"What? Do you mean money? Florence, really! This is all because you're reading that nasty mystery novel."

"It's not nasty. It's very good, and it makes the mind ponder, you know. Who benefits? Wives do, for one—when their husbands die."

Tom felt a drop in temperature instantly. This he did know, as indeed did most of the village: In best male primogeniture fashion, Walter Daintrey had inherited very nice Uphill Cottage in Thornford and a few other properties that were part of his and Florence's parents' estate when they died, with the time-honoured expectation of continuing the male line. Reproductive challenges (apparently) and a bolt of lightning put paid to that notion, marking the end of the Daintrey line, but left Venice the beneficiary of Walter's estate, cottage and all. Florence had inherited a sum of money from her parents, but, on the eve of her retirement from her mysterious government ministry, she found most of it vanished in the Lloyd's debacle. Her sister-in-law very kindly, and perhaps unwisely, invited her to share what had been her family home in Devon, and the two had lived in uneasy companionship ever since, each regarding the other, Tom suspected, as interloper.

"Money is no balm when a loved one dies," he swiftly interjected, perhaps more vehemently than he intended.

Venice wheezily released a held breath and set her teeth to the rim of the cup, as if willing herself off a coughing jag or attempting to keep her temper. Florence, however, was either oblivious of the effect she had caused or studiously pretending she wasn't.

"Perhaps Will Moir was *deliberately* poisoned," she announced.

"For the money? Really, Florence, you are the limit." Venice tugged a tissue from the sleeve of her sweatshirt and dabbed at her nose. "The Moirs are . . . *were* a very loving couple. Wouldn't you say, Tom?"

"Yes, I would, actually. I know they've had their ups and downs like all married couples, but—"

"Marriages are much like icebergs," Florence interrupted. "Ninety percent is below the water."

"And you would know this, would you? You being a spinster of this parish."

Florence, looking mildly miffed, said, "I wasn't necessarily suggesting Caroline would—"

"I'm not sure there's a lot of money to go around," Tom interjected cautiously, recalling his earlier conversations with Caroline. "And anyway," he added, though he wasn't quite sure he believed this: "How could it be anything more than a terrible accident? It was only chance that Will ate the offending tart."

"Was it?" Florence shot back.

"Flo." Venice put down her teacup. "Don't be silly. Why would anyone *want* to poison Will Moir?"

"Well, there's the rub." Florence motioned towards the biscuit plate imperiously.

"Perhaps we should talk about something else," Tom said with a sigh, leaning over and passing the plate.

"Quiet! I'm thinking." Florence snatched a biscuit. "Who was at the supper?" she said at last.

"Flo," Venice wheezed, "it was the Thistle But Mostly Rose, which you know perfectly well."

"Yes, I do know that! But who? *Who* specifically?"

"At least half the band had to cancel," Tom said after listing the guests. "Because of the weather. Almost everyone was from the village or within short distance. The only guests from farther afield were Nick, who has a flat in Torquay, and John Copeland who, of course, lives at Noze Lydiard."

"Well, no love lost between Nick and Will." Florence popped the remainder of the biscuit into her mouth and chewed thoughtfully. "John Copeland, though . . ."

"Florence . . . ," Venice murmured warningly.

"John's been making sheep's eyes at Caroline for years. Haven't you noticed?"

"No, I haven't," Venice snapped.

"Ven, you have too noticed. We've discussed this. There's a perfectly fine little church at Noze that John could be attending, and they would be happy to have him, but instead he comes here every Sunday."

"Because of the quality of worship at St. Nicholas's."

"Oh, Ven, really! Giles James-Douglas was practically gaga the last few years before he died, and the only folk who found that smarmy Peter Kinsey compelling were women too young to know better."

"Tom's doing a splendid job."

"Mmm," Florence murmured, as if doubting it. "But he's had the living for less than a year. John's been coming to St. Nicholas's for five and he started coming when the Moirs took over Thorn Court. And . . ." She quelled her sister-in-law with a lifted eyebrow. "And! John's wife died some years before that. He's been a widower for a very long time—with no new woman in the picture—"

"There's that Helen whatsername—from Noze."

Florence waved a dismissive hand. "Oh, she just lays on the lunches for the shooting parties for him."

"I'm not sure—"

"—and you know what men are like." Florence aimed the question squarely at Tom.

"No," he said, startled, "what are men like?"

"Not without a woman for long!"

"Florence!" Her sister-in-law's warning tone was amplified. A new redness crept up her neck. "Don't you dare . . ."

"You have been observed, you know, Tom," Florence barrelled on.

"Oh, I can't bear this." Venice dropped her teacup, scuttled back under the quilt, and flung the top over her face.

"With PCSO White. At the Waterside."

"Yes," Tom responded slowly, uncertain whether to be irritated or amused.

"She's not suitable, you know."

"Florence," came the muffled voice, "would you kindly stop it."

"Not suitable for what?" Tom asked.

"Florence." Venice flipped the quilt back from her pink baby-doll face. "You're being abominably rude to the vicar. And you're embarrassing me."

"I'm being perfectly forthright with the vicar. A priest is a public person, a community leader, a—"

"Màiri White came to see me yesterday on a private matter." Tom decided to affect amusement, though he didn't feel it. "People often seek counsel from a priest. Even in restaurants."

"There, Flo, you've had your answer."

"I'm merely concerned that proprieties continue to be observed." Florence sniffed.

"Chance would be a fine thing," Venice muttered.

"What?"

"I was agreeing with you, Flo. Proprieties ought to be observed. In *all* quarters, at *all* times," she added between clenched teeth.

Florence eyed her sister-in-law doubtfully, then twisted her mouth. "When is that quack to arrive?"

"Dr. Kaif is *not* a quack."

"Well, he's *not* a doctor."

"Is this the appointment that was alluded to earlier?" Tom interjected, bewildered.

Venice nodded, then addressed her sister-in-law: "The Queen uses a homeopath, and you can't say she isn't a sensible woman. Dr. Kaif said he would come later this morning."

"Now, there's someone with a knowledge of poisons," Florence boomed.

"Florence, you know perfectly well that homeopathic remedies contain only the teensiest, tiniest bit of . . . "

"Poison."

"I don't accept the word."

"Well, Ven, it's poison when it's a large quantity and Victor, I daresay, has large quantities of all the poisons he puts into his whatever-you-call-them."

"Tinctures. And are you suggesting, Florence Daintrey, that Dr. Kaif poisoned Will?"

"No, I wasn't suggesting that at all. I'm simply assuming that Victor knows a great deal about poisons—"

"Medicines."

"—and that we can pump him for information when he's here." A sharp, alert look entered Florence's eyes. "Although . . . !"

"Florence, these speculations are making me weary, and they're most unkind. I don't think it would be at all fair to ask Dr. Kaif about what quantities of . . . *whatever!* it could take for someone to die."

"I'm afraid I have to agree with your sister-in-law," Tom said to Florence. "Perhaps we should talk of other things." He clicked his fingers. "I'm reminded to give you a copy of the parish magazine."

Florence handed her empty teacup absently to Venice, who received it meekly and enquired if she wanted more. But Florence didn't respond. Instead she addressed Tom. "But he was at your Burns Supper—Victor, I mean."

"So was Molly, come to that," Tom responded with some exasperation, then immediately regretted the imprudence of saying so.

Florence cast him a probing glance. "Really? As a what? Did she dance a Highland fling?"

"No, she cooked the meal."

"Where's Thorn Court's chef then?"

"On hiatus, along with the rest of staff during the renovations."
Tom set the copy of *Thornford Regis News* next to the tea tray.

"Of course, I forgot. But Molly? I thought she had finished with
that catering lark of hers. She was only ever showing off!"

"Molly did a splendid job. We had wonderful curries—"

"Ha! I'm not completely surprised. I think she must have gone
native when she married Victor Kaif."

"Really, Florence." Venice cast a worried eye at Tom. "You're not
fit for human company."

"But she is the most peculiar creature, Ven, gadding about in
those pajamas or whatever they are and wearing saris to the May
Fayre and such. You must agree. Molly's as English as God!"

"Perhaps her husband likes her in those clothes. Besides, I think
it's a refreshing change from the usual cardies and anoraks. Well, it
was. She seems to be dressing more conventionally these days."

Florence shifted her leg and winced. "Victor only married her
because her parents own those GoodGreens shops. Probably gets a
discount."

"Flo, that's outrageous. You know no more about the Kaifs' relationship than you do the Moirs'."

"Hmm, curry, you say." Florence ignored her sister-in-law.
"What an odd choice for a Burns Supper."

"No one cared much for haggis, although we did have a taste of
it," Tom said.

"Can't say I blame you." Florence wrinkled her nose. "You could
doctor up curry quite nicely, couldn't you, if you had a mind to. It
being so hot and spicy, you'd never know there was something
tucked inside. I expect taxine tastes rather unpleasant. What do you
think, Vicar?"

Tom felt a respite from thinking might be in order. In Florence
Daintrey's presence, he felt a little like a battlement under bombard-
ment.

"I don't know what to think, really," he responded, placing his empty teacup on the tray. He added a note of caution: "Probably best not to speculate too much about all this in public. And now I really must leave you two. Thank you for the tea and—"

"There'll be an inquest, of course," Florence interrupted.

"Yes."

"Perhaps I'll attend."

"I shouldn't think you're going anywhere in your condition." Venice looked mildly horrified. "Tom, I'll see you out."

"No need."

"Nevertheless." Venice struggled from out of her blanket as Tom retrieved his coat, his backside relieved to be out of the very lumpy chair.

"Lovely to see you, Vicar. Call again," Florence called after them as Venice closed the door to the sitting room. Tom welcomed the relative coolness of the air in—and the unclaustrophobic atmosphere of—the hallway.

"I do apologise for Florence," Venice told him in a low voice. "She's always been . . . outspoken, but she seems to be getting worse."

"I expect being confined is getting on her nerves. She is all right?"

"It's only a mild sprain. I took a St. John's course years ago and I was able to fix her up. We'll have the doctor in when the roads are cleared."

"Rorie the postman says we're not so cut off now. Roads are ploughed. Look, there's post." He pointed to the hall table.

"Oh . . ."

"Is there something else?"

Venice appeared to be in the throes of a decision. "I do wonder at times," she said, "if Florence has had, oh, perhaps the tiniest stroke or something. As I say, she's always been outspoken, but she seems to be becoming less restrained, and I can't account for it, really."

"I am sorry. Perhaps the doctor . . . ?"

"Well, I don't think it's come to that. I mustn't worry you, Tom. And perhaps you're right. It's just her being confined. She likes to be active, so when she can't be, bees start buzzing in her bonnet. She's been reading that novel all morning and become fixated on the sadness at Thorn Court."

"I'm sure it's on villagers' minds in one way or another," Tom responded, reaching for the door handle.

"I can only imagine what Flo might have said to you. It's she who's so taken against the Prowses. She won't even let Jago service her car. She and Walter were twins, you see, and so I think she's always taken his loss harder than I." She shook her head. "It's all so long ago now anyway. But you know the past—it seems to do nothing but intrude on the present, doesn't it?"

CHAPTER THIRTEEN

*T*om stood outside Uphill Cottage's gate, looking unseeingly down the road he had climbed with Rorie the postman's help little more than an hour before, his thoughts stirred by Florence's provocations. He found himself unaccountably resistant to the notion of Will's death being anything other than a deeply regrettable misadventure. Even at the Waterside the day before, when Màiri White had given him the unhappy news, conversation had not strayed into other, darker realms of speculation—though now he wasn't sure why, unless Màiri was sparing him pain, and he, for his part, preferred the safe harbour of denial. But surely his reaction then, and now, was natural and customary; to think otherwise was to entertain the appalling notion that the village sheltered a scheming intelligence, prompted to homicide by mischief or malice.

But a notion acknowledged cannot be unacknowledged.

There was but a single boon, he decided as his mind refocused on the practical task of getting down icy Thorn Hill: Madrun would surely be absolved from any culpability. She couldn't possibly hold malice towards Will Moir or any of the men at the Burns Supper, unless some buried secret will out (*but surely not!*) and she was certainly incapable of mischief, even of the most trivial sort. He couldn't imagine her even as a child shorting a bed or making a prank phone call.

He studied the road, a narrow shute bordered by stone walls, wishing he had the piece of cardboard he had used yesterday at Fishers Hill with Miranda. Hugging the walls, stepping carefully, and gripping gateposts along the way looked the best means of descent without suffering Florence's fate, until he considered that the rubbery bottom of his boots, useless for going up anything slippery, might be just the thing for going down. Certain he was unobserved, he crouched slightly, so that his weight settled along his thighs, then led off, letting the ice whisk him down the road. It worked! It was a merry experiment in locomotion, unhappy thoughts of loss and grief seeming to peel away as his new smiling face sliced through the breeze. If he kept his balance and manoeuvred with some grace, he could spin around the point where Thorn Hill met Pennycross Road, then continue his descent into the village, like a skier at Klosters, though Pennycross, on second thought, was decently salted and would force a stop.

A stop, however, was forced sooner. A figure in a sombre overcoat and bowler hat stepped from the shadow of the stone stairs that offered pedestrians a shortcut from one ascending road to the next, his head bent to the breeze. Tom shouted, but it was too late. Like a car meeting a light-dazed deer, Tom careened into the man, sending him sprawling face-forward into a snowbank by the tiny wedge-shaped memorial garden, and sending the black case he had been holding soaring into the air. Tom, landing on his back, watched the case crash onto the garden's low stone wall and burst open at the latch, flinging some of its contents onto the snow and ice, and some onto stone with the unpleasant tinkle of shattering glass.

Oh, bugger, was Tom's first unhappy thought. His victim was no mystery. Only Victor Kaif wore a bowler hat, and he wore it when he was on the job, either in Totnes, where he shared a clinic with another homeopath, a naturopath, and an iridologist, or when making house calls in the village, which of course he was doing—the road from his bungalow in Orchard Hill to the Daintrey cottage ascended the very set of roads Tom was descending. Why Victor favoured a bowler hat—headgear few had worn, even in the City, for generations—remained a mystery to Tom (he didn't like to ask), though established Thornfordites were long past noticing or caring. Duelling eccentricities, he postulated: Molly appropriated bits of Indian dress, her part-Indian husband appropriated English dress. Whatever the reason, the fact was—as Victor probably knew—he looked uncommonly handsome in the hat, which matched his jet-black hair and set off his sharply cut features, his fine straight eyebrows, and his dark, bluish brown eyes. Though not without suggesting a certain rakishness, his attire projected self-possession and respectability—perhaps, Tom mused, a deliberate counterbalance to homeopathy's dubious reputation. Anyone else wearing a bowler in a village in the twenty-first century would be branded a nutter, but Victor somehow carried it off—with aplomb.

"I'm very sorry, Victor," Tom said, pulling himself up and brushing snow off his battered wax jacket. He plucked the bowler hat from its landing place by the forsythia that dominated the tiny garden. "Victor?"

Tom experienced a moment's panic as he bent to attend to the fallen figure, but Victor chose that moment to roll over.

"Hardly 'bump.'" The homeopath shielded his eyes, though the noon sun was a pale disk in a pale sky.

"'Hit,' then."

"'Collide,' I would say. 'Crash into.'"

"Victor, it wasn't my mission this morning to knock you over in the road. Are you all right? Nothing broken? You really should get up. The snow is rather wet, and it won't do that coat of yours any good."

"I think I'll just lie here awhile."

Tom stood over Victor with his bowler in hand, feeling very much like a gentleman's gentleman. "It might have been a car coming down the hill, you know. You weren't exactly looking when you stepped off the stairs."

"I was somewhat preoccupied, if you must know." Victor jack-knifed his body upwards like a spring, then rose with elegance to his feet—which, Tom noted with wonder, were shod in polished black wing tips with no evidence of traction-making aids.

"I was preoccupied, too, actually. Sorry, I was sort of blaming the victim, wasn't I?"

Victor silently took the hat from Tom and settled it on his head, angling it ever so slightly. He flicked Tom a worried glance. "What's preoccupying you, then?"

"At the moment? Will Moir."

Victor looked away, at his bag, which lay at an ungainly angle in the snow, and at the scattered glass vials. "What about Will? Tom, look at what you've done."

"His . . . stoicism." Tom wondered if word of the taxine poisoning had reached the man's ears. "I am sorry about this, Vic. Here, let me help you." He bent to pluck a glass vial from a patch of snow.

"Bloody hell, some have broken!"

"Sorry." Tom apologised again. "Really."

"Never mind!" Victor retrieved his case and took the vial from Tom's hand. With his foot, he pushed the glass shards against the base of the garden's stone wall. "What do you mean, his stoicism?"

"Will must have known he wasn't well, but he didn't ask for any help."

"A heart attack can come on suddenly."

"Then why did he go up the tower?"

"Perhaps he wanted a lie-down. Makes sense, if he wasn't feeling well."

"There are couches in the reception rooms, bedrooms on the first floor."

"I'm sure I don't know," Victor said with evident pique, stooping to collect scattered vials. "There's not always an accounting for other people's behaviour, is there?"

"No, I suppose not." Tom plucked another vial from the road. The label read AGARICUS, which sent his mind like a rocket to tedious hours in fifth form under Mr. McKechnie's tutelage declining Latin nouns. *Agaricus, agarici, agarici, agaricarum* reverberated through his brainbox. It was probably the wrong declension. "What's this for?"

"Disorders of the nervous system." Victor snatched the vial from Tom's hand and gave it a quick study before shoving it back into his case.

"Ah," Tom responded noncommittally, picking up another vial, this one labelled ANTIMONIUM TARTARICUM. He had no argument with homeopathy, though the notion that patients could be healed through the administration of the substances that caused their symptoms, diluted to the point where the remedies contained barely a molecule of the original product, seemed, on the surface, a damp squib.

"I expect Will wasn't one of your patients, was he?" he asked Victor.

"No, he wasn't. Although you phrase it oddly." Victor frowned. "Is there a reason why he wouldn't have been?"

"Sorry, I didn't mean to suggest he wouldn't see a homeopath. Will wasn't that old, so I can't help wondering about the state of his health."

"Difficult to know. As I say, he wasn't my patient."

"Lisbeth—my late wife, whom I've probably mentioned—used

to say that she envied homeopaths and naturopaths and the like because they seemed able to take so much time with their patients, talk to them, and really get to know them, whereas the NHS always seemed to pressure her to get through as many patients as she could in a day."

"But if you're asking me if I had some understanding of Will's underlying health, I can't say that I did."

"But you observe, surely. You and my wife, for instance, because of your training, can read things in faces or mannerisms or speech. I'm told optometrists can read your health in the backs of your eyes."

Victor moved impatiently onto the garden's flagstones and set his kit down on the top of a bench that offered sitters a view down Pennycross Road's descent into the village. Fastening the latch, he said, "I think there was something not quite right about Will."

"Saturday evening? I thought he looked a bit peaky much earlier in the evening."

"I didn't pay much attention to him Saturday." He looked away. "No, I mean longer than that. His temperament was changed—as you know." Victor's lips formed a grim line.

Tom did know. Though he had decided not to watch the "Coach Goes Mental" YouTube video, the anonymous posting of which he thought intrusive and cruel, the episode at the cricket pitch had been well described to him by several parishioners who had watched it.

"He and Caroline have some challenges in their business, as you know," he said. "The economy is pressurising people for one thing. Money woes often put a strain on a marriage."

"That might be it."

"But you're not sure."

Victor shrugged. "I'm sorry, Tom. I do have worries of my own."

"Yes, of course, I don't mean to be a bother. Might I ask you in turn what's preoccupying you?"

Victor cast him a penetrating glance, then looked away. "Oh, it's nothing, really."

"Well, if you ever think I can be of any help," Tom responded. "That must be yours, too," he added, noting a burst of colour against the grey stone and white snow. It was a bound sheaf of paper that must have flown over the wall and landed in the garden. "It's got a bit damp, I'm afraid," he continued, retrieving it, shaking a clump of clinging wet snow from its surface. He was about to hand it off to Victor, but then snatched it back. Something about it caught his attention, its colour and texture strangely evocative. He frowned over it, staring, and then he remembered and felt a momentary chill that owed nothing to the winter air.

"Are you going to give me that?" Victor said to him impatiently.

"Sorry. I was . . . admiring it," he lied lamely, passing it to Victor. "A prescription pad, of a sort?"

"Of a sort." Victor's deep-set, dark eyes regarded him. "It's multipurpose. I'll write a scrip on it, for instance, for a patient to take to GoodGreens or Boots to get it filled."

"It's certainly distinctive," Tom added.

It was. Lisbeth's prescription pads had a number of clever security features—VOID would appear if anyone tried to photocopy a prescription, for instance—but superficially the paper looked unremarkable: plain and white, the lettering sans serif, brisk and businesslike. Victor's, he noted, was more like the letterhead he used at the vicarage, with address at the top in a pleasing script and no other markings. Victor's, however, was not a discreet white or pale blue. It was a delicate shade of lavender.

"Certainly not my choice." Victor shoved the pad into a pocket lining in his case. "We moved the Totnes clinic to new premises on Castle Street in November, so new cards and stationery and scrip pads were in order. One of my colleagues chose this. Only a woman would pick such a bloody *ridiculous* colour. Hardly dignifies the profession, does it? Bloody women," he muttered.

Tom felt a smile tug at the corners of his mouth, pushing out thoughts of the pretty paper.

"What's so amusing?"

"You, Victor. You've had a row this morning with your wife, yes?"

"Is it that obvious?"

"You show not untypical signs—misdirected anger, laddish misogyny—"

"Then *you* try living with Molly!" Victor's voice and the case's clasps snapped simultaneously. "I'm not sure how much longer I can."

"I'm sorry to hear this, Victor. I was praying that with time—"

Victor grunted.

"—and Molly's getting some counselling from Celia Parry, which seems a good thing."

"She told you that, did she?"

"Have you thought of—"

"No!" Victor's eyes flashed. "I have my own way of coping with these things, and that includes my working and getting on with my life and not . . . not hanging about the house, talking and crying and arguing all the *bloody* time."

Tom bit his lip. The expectation, he thought, is that the loss of a child naturally binds a man and wife together in grief. But the dismal reality, as his pastoral work had taught him, was too often the opposite: Grief tore people apart with all the heedless abandon of a tempest. He recalled vividly—because it came only a fortnight after Lisbeth's death—a funeral he had taken at St. Dunstan's for a three-month-old boy. So devastated were the young parents, whom he had wedded not thirteen months before, by the cot death of their newborn (their first real encounter with profound loss), their marriage cracked like a dry branch. Derrick and Zoë had made the traditional vow at the altar—*Till death us do part*—but the words resonated in his heart in a new way when he learned of their separation.

And now he wondered, glancing at Victor's choleric expression with dismay, if a death would part Victor and Molly. He wanted to say that even the most loving couple may each pull away from the other in time of grief, but with mutual forbearance and understanding, they could restore the intimacy and kindness of an earlier time in the marriage. But it sounded a bit of a bromide in his head, and as Victor didn't appear awfully receptive, Tom reached for something more concrete: "Molly ventured out to cater a big supper for more than twenty men. That seems a good sign." He added a hopeful smile.

The blaze vanished from Victor's eyes. Hopeless frown met hopeful smile. He tugged at his case and turned to go. "I wish," he said to Tom over his shoulder, "I thought that were true."

CHAPTER FOURTEEN

Are you suggesting that *we* jump?"

"I'm simply saying that I thought it might be a good thing if we—I mean those of us on the PCC—took a leadership role. But of course you're not expected to jump, and you needn't jump, if you don't wish to. I recognise it is a rather daunting prospect."

"Mr. Chairman." Karla Skynner cast Tom a withering glance from across the table. "I can't think of any circumstance in which I would be persuaded to fling myself out of an airplane. *None.*"

"You'll be wearing a parachute," Fred Pike, the assistant verger, piped up. He was studying a raisin biscuit he'd taken from a platter Madrun had sent over with Tom to the parochial church council meeting in the Old School Room. Tom wished people would *stop* examining food that came from the vicarage kitchen.

Karla shot Fred a look that would have scorched the fur off a small rodent, then turned back to Tom. "You, of course, will be jumping."

"Of course," Tom replied, drawing from some well the sort of feigned enthusiasm he'd mustered in his days as The Great Krimboni when confronted with a surly audience indifferent to his feats of magic. "I think it will be great fun."

"Absolutely!" Mark Tucker chimed in.

"I'm sure Colm will join in."

"He's not here to say, is he, Mr. Chairman?" Karla snapped.

"Well, no. But I think Colm's sort of the type."

"The type for what?"

" . . . adventure?"

"And John, too," Mark added, then frowned. "Well, perhaps. I'm not sure about the others not in attendance this evening."

"I can't think why John couldn't be here tonight." Karla reached for a biscuit and did not examine it. "I hear he was the only one able to drive out of the village on Sunday, and now that the lanes are cleared of snow, there's no excuse."

Tom looked around the table. "I'm certainly not pressuring any of you to take part in the jump. I'm sure it will be challenging to both body and spirit, and many of you may feel you're not . . . up to it."

"I'm not dead yet, Vicar," Jeanne Neels, the matriarch of Thorn Barton, the former manor farm, declared. She was a woman in her late sixties and lean, with masses of greying hair tied in a loose bun. "And I've got one good hand to pull the rip cord." She held up one hand, her right—she had been born without her left—and pushed at a few strands of hair that had worked loose to dangle across her face.

"I'm not dead yet, either," added Russ Oxley, a semi-retired archaeologist who had moved to Thornford two years before. His face, covered in a hundred minuscule wrinkles, bore what looked like a permanent mahogany tan visible from the top of his open-necked shirt to a line three-quarters of the way up his forehead.

"And of course you know I did my National Service in the Parachute Regiment." Michael Woolnough, MBE, puffed out his chest. "Saw action in Cyprus in '56."

Tom didn't know, but considered Michael the least likely on the council to participate, given his age, closing in on eighty. Though he seemed in excellent health, except for incipient deafness.

"Bless, I feel faint simply thinking about it. You're hurtling through the sky at some ghastly speed, aren't you? What if your parachute doesn't open?" portly Roger Pattimore asked.

"I've been assured," replied Tom, "that your odds are much greater being struck by lightning."

"That doesn't assure me in the least." Karla removed her glasses and began polishing them against her sleeve. "Lightning has had quite a deleterious effect on some people I can think of in this village."

"I'm willing," said a squeaky voice on Tom's left. "I'll get everyone at GoodGreens to sponsor me."

"Lovely, Briony, thank you." Tom glanced down at her nimble fingers dancing over the keys of her little notebook computer. The last PCC secretary took notes in a shorthand of his own devising and presented minutes at subsequent meetings that shot fairly wide of the mark for accuracy. Briony's were letter-perfect and swiftly approved at the next meeting, saving the council half an hour's worth of amendment aggro. So good to have some folk on the council *not* old enough to vividly remember when President Kennedy was shot or when England last won the FA cup. Briony Hart was twenty-three, plain as suet, and lived with her mother up Orchard Hill. Tom suspected her recent church attendance might be part of a net cast wide in a husband-hunting strategy—decent blokes went to church, didn't they?—but as long as he wasn't the fox in this instance, he didn't mind. He hoped Briony lasted on the PCC. Unattached men of marriageable age at church were often a scarce commodity; most of the unattached tended to be widowers, like John Copeland, or the never-married-and-not-bloody-likely types, like Roger Pattimore.

He worried a little that Mark Tucker, his new treasurer, might be the fox. Briony was swift to agree with anything he said, but Mark, bless his soul and his wife and child, remained sweetly oblivious to many and any a nuance—which reminded Tom of the task that Violet Tucker had set for him.

Roger was still squirming in his chair as if imagining his adipose frame hurtling through space over Devon's patchwork fields, but Tom thought he might be persuaded to jump, or perhaps they might each goad the other. He hadn't quite realised when he explored the possibility of a parachute jump as a charity fund-raiser that it might involve him—Tom Livingstone Christmas—stepping out into thin air, thousands of feet above the ground—a notion that made him gulp with alarm when Jamie Allan, the charity's organiser, explained it over the phone. Still, he had to put a brave face on it. It *was* a good idea. If only they could get enough people in the village to agree to jump and sign up lots and lots of sponsors.

Often, particularly when matters were trivial, the members of the PCC would split into two violently opposing camps, emotions would run high, and opinions would fall either side of an imagined Maginot Line. Tom would feel his face stiffening into a mask of benevolent exasperation and the matter would be deferred until the next meeting when some subcommittee, struck in the heat of the moment, would report. At least the church roof engendered little controversy. The last quinquennial report had stated baldly that the roof of St. Nicholas's was in bad nick and had to be repaired and no argument, lest they want rainwater dripping on their heads in the middle of Communion. There was none. The only argument was how it would be afforded. The cost, according to the estimate, pressed one hundred thousand pounds. Applications had been made for grants from English Heritage and the National Churches Trust, but the rest of the money they would have to find on their own. There were the usual stratagems—the bring-and-buy, the coffee mornings, the carboot sales, the jumble sales, the May Fayre—and all had been scheduled for the forthcoming months, but a sponsored parachuting looked a novelty that would draw more people, particularly younger ones, perhaps garner some publicity, and generally make a fun day of it for Thornfordites. Something about the spectacle of it persuaded them, at least all who made it to the PCC meeting. Only Karla demurred from this new scheme, which surprised Tom not a whit. Defending the traditions of the village, including its fund-raising customs, was Karla's bailiwick. Jumping from airplanes wasn't one of them.

"Then what is the role of the . . . what are they called?"

"The Leaping Lords," Tom supplied.

Karla clicked her tongue in dismay. "What is their role in this?" She replaced her spectacles on the bridge of her nose. "And are they life peers or hereditary peers? Some of the life peers are the worst sort. Trades union hacks and so forth."

"They'll have their own sponsors, of course, and they put on a show—formations in the sky and suchlike." Tom answered the first question first. "I'm not sure how they achieved their titles." *Can it possibly matter?*

"I trust none of the Lords Spiritual are engaged in such foolishness."

Tom couldn't help his mind's eye witnessing Bishop Tim hurtling through the air, one hand steadying his mitre, the other holding down his cassock. A smile teased at the corners of his mouth. "I don't know," he replied. "It would be rather fun, I think."

Karla peered at him disapprovingly, then grumped, "Well, I can see I'm outvoted on this. Mr. Chairman," she continued—she insisted on addressing him thus at PCC meetings—"I would move that we erect a thermometer at the north porch so those coming to services can see how much money is being raised—*however* we raise it," she added sourly.

"No!" The word was out of Tom's mouth before he could think.

"No?" Karla raised an inquisitorial eyebrow.

All the reasons why setting a twelve-foot tongue of plywood up the side of St. Nicholas's with an upturned red plastic bowl for a reservoir, guttering up the middle for a capillary tube, and gradations calibrated in thousands of pounds up the side was not acceptable frog-marched through Tom's cerebrum: They looked bloody hideous; they attracted vandals; and they soon became an object of derision, particularly when fund-raising optimism went pear-shaped, as it sometimes did, and red paint no more climbed the capillary. Thermometers were sad. They were boring. And he wasn't having it. But he feared it was the very trivial issue that would bog down the meeting.

"Insurance," he declared impulsively, pulling a metaphorical rabbit out of a hat. "We'd have to insure it—the thermometer."

"Why?" Karla frowned.

"Theft, fire, termites—"

"Don't be silly, Mr. Chairman. We don't have termites in England."

"Yes we do," Fred interjected, picking the raisins out of his biscuit. "Lady had 'em in North Devon a while back. Ate her entire porch."

"I suppose," Mark reflected, "if fund-*raising* is our goal, then perhaps we best not be spending money unnecessarily. There would be cost for wood, paint—"

"But *insurance?*" Karla fumed.

"I can look into it," Mark offered.

"I'd suggest," Roger said between bites of his biscuit, "we defer this to our next meeting. We don't have quite a full complement here tonight, so we might want to have other views before we proceed. Besides, should we be fortunate to get money from English Heritage or the like, then we could start the thermometer off with a super-high temperature, couldn't we?"

Mercifully, after some mutterings yea or nay, that held the day. Tom said a silent prayer of gratitude for things deferred, and thought as he glanced around the table: *They aren't such a bad lot, really.* A charity parachute jump took a bit of chivvying, but they all came around in the end, save for Karla, and most of them—very surprisingly—were willing to at least entertain the notion of leaping from an airplane themselves, if it served the church's needs—though on a winter's eve, nestled in the Old School Room, the summer looked a long way off, and perhaps they all wanted to appear enormously plucky, he among them, even if they weren't.

Unbidden, a vision of himself plunging into the cold air from the door of an airplane flashed like a diamond in his brain, and he took a sudden gulp of air. Briony flicked a glance at him, smiled, and resumed her merry typing. Indeed Briony's fingers never seemed to leave the keyboard, and he wondered if she minuted absolutely everything—*Vicar takes sharp breath*—and only hacked and pruned later. As she couldn't enter his thoughts, she couldn't write, *Vicar notes room is faintly redolent of last occupants,* which his nose told him it was. In good weather, on weekday mornings when it was used as a crèche, the Old School Room might smell of little children, of milk and sun-warmed hair; in bad weather, on weekend afternoons, when it was used for meetings of the camera club or the chess club, it might smell of damp wool, dogs, and an illicit cigarette or two. This evening, the Old School Room's aroma hinted of glue and microwaved popcorn and talcum powder. Scrapbooking, the art of preserving family history in a scrapbook, had lately caught the fancy of some villagers, and the Thornford Scrappers, as they called themselves, commandeered the Old School Room one afternoon a month for their cutting and pasting and drawing. The detritus of their activity rested by a dangerous-looking paper trimmer on a table by the wall over which was placed a DO NOT REMOVE! sign: scissors, pens, rubber stamps, stencils, inking tools, and various kinds and colours of papers and card stock. It was the last items that recalled Tom's mind to the morning's encounter with Victor Kaif and that sheaf of lavender paper, a stain against the white snow of the memorial garden.

It was, he was certain, precisely the colour of the note Madrun had received asking her to contribute berry tartlets to the Burns Supper. After their conversation in her rooms, she had gone for her coat hanging in the vestibule and found it; she had indeed used the back of it as a grocery list.

The coincidence of colours was, at the very least, a bit startling. Still, he thought, turning to view again the papers on the table of the Old School Room, the lavender might be a stock colour, one that the Thornford Scrappers, too, would count among their items.

He thought back to his encounter with Victor. He had left the Daintreys with a wisp of suspicion about Will's death clinging like a vapour trail to his more ordinary ruminations—his overdue contributions to the next issue of the parish magazine, his Sunday sermon, writing the service sheets, preparation for the PCC meeting, pastoral visits to come. Bother Florence Daintrey—again!—for putting cheerless thoughts in his head. It was a small matter, surely, this inviting Madrun to contribute a sweet to the Burns Supper. It was someone's whim, an off chance, the note composed in haste, the signature forgotten, and quickly popped through the vicarage's letter slot on a flying visit in the midst of other quotidian tasks.

But was it *Victor's* whim? The coloured paper suggested it might be so. But Victor didn't strike him as a man who would trouble himself with the minutiae of a banquet menu, particularly when he wasn't charged with its planning.

And now, as the PCC members shuffled to the next item on the agenda, he wondered if he *should* have asked Victor if he had requested berry tartlets from Madrun. The bush telegraph was swift, but it wasn't always thorough: Nothing in Victor's manner or conversation suggested that word of Madrun's folly had come his way. If he introduced it, referencing the stationery and its distinctive colour, mightn't he seem accusatory, particularly if Victor queried why he was asking? And would it have been effective? Victor could simply have lied.

Tom sighed. He was feeling a bit ineffective, helpless before the unhappiness that had slipped into his household. Madrun wore a brave face, but her conversation—usually voluble and opinionated—had fallen to low ebb at breakfast and at lunch, soliciting enquiring glances from Miranda. When he returned to the vicarage after his visit to the Daintreys, he had asked to look again at the unsigned note she had received and was troubled to see what hadn't met his eyes the first time he'd looked at it.

Then, the text alone had held his attention. Now it was the paper itself. The colour appeared to be the same as Victor's stationery, yes, but could he really trust his colour memory? Soon after he and Lisbeth arrived in Bristol, in a flurry of new-home excitement, they had repainted their bathroom. It had been an ancient shade of turquoise, peeling badly, and Miranda, at age three, was wont to put paint flakes in her mouth. But the new light, creamy neutral—called, bizarrely, "Oak Smoke"—that dried on the walls was not, in Lisbeth's insistence, the same as the Oak Smoke promised by the paint chart. He, splattered and weary, couldn't see the difference—it *looked* sort of beigy, neutrally, whatever—until Lisbeth fetched the chart. The difference was subtle, but enough to dissatisfy his perspicacious wife. Back to the paint shop they trotted.

The more troubling aspect of the mystery note, however, began with its dimensions. The paper had the width of standard commercial bond, but not the height. A portion, a top piece—or perhaps a bottom—had been trimmed, most likely by someone scoring the paper against a sharp edge, a ruler perhaps. The effect was not crude: The edge wasn't ragged, but neither was it crisp, as it would be if cut by machine—or even by a paper trimmer like the one on the Old School Room shelf. Was the sheet a bit of old discard? he wondered. Or—more worrying—had a strip of it deliberately been removed? The portion, say, with the printed letterhead?

Wordlessly, he had handed the paper back to Madrun. She had regarded him over the rims of her spectacles with not a little expec-

tation and curiosity, but he could only offer her a noncommittal
shrug. All he had was speculation, and it was thin and cursory, and
might well be without foundation. He didn't want any of his dark
musings speeding along the bush telegraph and causing needless
insult and injury. That he couldn't confide his speculations to his
housekeeper brought him no joy. She was the only other adult in his
household (*how he missed Lisbeth!*) and a font of information—and
wisdom—about the village, but he was uncertain of her abilities in
the great circumspection challenge. Perhaps, he thought, it was his
own fault. When he had asked her kindly but very firmly in the past
to keep something to herself, she had done. When he had been less
direct, she hadn't. And in an instance when it never occurred to him
to ask her to keep mum, as it had the day before when he had confided to her Màiri's information, and assumed she would be too
shattered to share it, she had indeed shared it—with Judith Ingley,
who had promptly passed it along to the Daintreys. Had Madrun
not thought it would go farther? And did she know—he watched
Fred inspect another raisin biscuit—that word of the taxine poisoning had got about? Did she not think about who would condemn
her, who would doubt her, who would wonder how she could have
made such a fatal mistake?

The tongue is a fire, he recalled the apostle James saying. *For every
kind of beasts, and of birds, and of serpents, and of things in the sea, is
tamed, and hath been tamed of mankind.*

But the tongue can no man tame, James continued. *It is an unruly
evil, full of deadly poison.*

Tom's eyes wandered to the ceiling. A bright centre light flooded
the room, casting short, sharp cruel shadows on the figures around
the table. He turned his head towards the two uncurtained mul-
lioned windows overlooking Church Walk, stark black lozenges
against the night fracturing and distorting the movements of their
heads and shoulders, as in a fun-house mirror. The air seemed close,
entrapping. It had been cool when they'd first gathered. Now, gusted

by palpable jets of heat from an electric heater rotating with a tiny mosquito whine, the air felt sultry. Yet despite this, he could feel his skin drawing into gooseflesh. A harbinger of something? Cold or flu. No, he thought. It was what awaited. For days, pummelled by snow and ice, Thornford had been suspended in a limbo of time, very much at the mercy of events beyond any human agency. With no incessant demands of school and work, most villagers had spent stolen days in paradise. For a few, however, the days spent were in hell. But the snowploughs had opened the lanes to Thornford. Through the afternoon barometers rose. The weather vane atop Thorn Court Hotel's tower veered towards the southwest. In his study that afternoon, beginning work on his Sunday sermon, he had heard the snow slithering from the roof with a rushing sound, and as he walked to the Old School House in the dark he could hear, though not see, rivulets of water trick along the cobbles. The snow was melting. This freakish episode in the village's history was ending. Thornford would return to its normal rhythms, but for this: After supper, as he was about to leave the vicarage, a phone call came through from Màiri White. *Whatever can this be about,* he thought with a frisson of pleasure, taking the receiver from Madrun, who cast him a gelid eye. But it was no bid to chat. Màiri was between Totnes Police Station and her car and had but a moment to pass along a bit of information: An inquest into Will Moir's death was set for Thursday morning at ten o'clock.

CHAPTER FIFTEEN

Violet tells me you've taken to writing." Tom eased into the subject as he eased his hands into the sink and groped for the washcloth. Only he and Mark remained in the Old School Room, "New Men" doing the tidying and washing-up in the tiny kitchen at the back.

"Yes." Mark stepped behind him and placed more used plates on the counter. "Shouldn't the Scrappers put away their things before they leave? The kids will be back here in the morning. There's scissors lying about and that paper cutter . . ."

"I think they got lost in what they were doing and didn't notice when it was time to get home and put a meal on. Ruth Brody was here when I came in." Ruth supervised the crèche. "She said she'd be here early to lock the Scrappers' things away. Anyway, tell me about your writing."

"Oh, that. Well, I took a creative writing course in town last spring, which was really great fun, and so I've been having a bash at writing a novel. I'm really enjoying it."

"What are you working on?" Tom lifted a plate from the warm, soapy water and rinsed it under the cold faucet. He felt a sudden nostalgic pang for washing-up conversation with Lisbeth. Typically, she washed, he dried. Neither pressed to install a dishwasher; each too much savoured the snatched time, the shared task, the cosy domesticity, at times even the forced sequestering that fostered bouts of problem-airing.

"Well," Mark replied, "it's a story about boy wizard who's an orphan and goes to this marvellous, magical school for . . . well, other wizards."

"I see. Interesting." Tom put the plate on the draining board. "And do you have a name for the boy wizard?"

"I was thinking perhaps 'Harvey Porter.' "

"Mmm, yes," Tom murmured. "I see. And the school?"

"For some reason 'Pigblisters' popped into my head." Mark reached for a tea towel. "I don't know quite why. Fun, I thought."

Tom swished the cloth around a second plate, lifted its soapy surface to his eyes, and affected to look for bits of food still adhering. He took a fortifying breath. He knew all about Harvey Porter and Pigblisters—and Clytemnestra Tranger and the Bumblebore family, too. Violet Tucker had told him. She had it firmly in her head that Mark was prepared to chuck his job and plunge into a grafter's life of writing fiction for a living—of all the ridiculous things, she added.

Tom could hardly countenance the idea. Mark seemed born to figures, not to words. Since stepping in as PCC treasurer in the summer, he had worked wonders with the accounting, introducing new systems and streamlining old. The previous treasurer had been a long-retired banker, accomplished in accounting certainly, but compromised in his abilities, in part by his advanced age (he had served in the Second World War) and in part by some very nasty events in the village. Mark, too, was busy pursuing moneys belonging to St. Nicholas's from the illegal sale of a valuable Guercino painting purloined from the Lady chapel during a previous incumbency. He was really very good. Tom would hate to lose him from the church council, and told Violet so. She pleaded with him to talk to her husband, and he agreed, in principle, but only to feel him out: It was not his place to advocate for one spouse over another. And besides, he was loath to puncture another man's dreams, however impossible their realisation might seem in the beginning. He knew that Dosh, who adopted him when his first adoptive parents died in a plane crash, was hardly chuffed when he decided to pursue a career in magic, and that Kate, her partner, was less than thrilled when he found his true calling in the Church—but each in her own way managed to conquer her misgivings.

"You know," he said, giving the plate a second wash. "It sounds a little, just a tad—don't you think?—like Harry Potter?"

"Funny, that's what Violet said, but it's really quite different."

"Mmm. Have you read the Harry Potter books?"

"No, have you?" Mark picked up the plate and frowned as water dripped on his shoes.

"Bits. Miranda has read some of them, though she prefers Alice Roy—the French version of Nancy Drew."

"I've seen the Potter films. We have some of the DVDs."

"You don't think, Mark, you might be infringing, just a bit, just a touch, perhaps just a hair, on J. K. Rowling's territory?"

"The author? But she's richer than the Queen!"

"Yes, but I'm not sure getting rich was her ambition. She just wanted to write her story, and all the lolly sort of happened along." He turned his head to look at Mark, who was drying the plate with exceptional thoroughness, his plain face concentrated over the task. Tom tried to suppress a smile. Mark really was a bit of an anorak, naïve, awkward, and a bit obsessive, puppyishly eager to muck into any task. Perhaps with diligence, he could accomplish the feat of writing a novel. He had learned the bagpipes on his own, had he not? The only thing the boy—and for some reason, though only about a dozen years separated them, he couldn't help thinking of Mark as a boy—seemed to lack was a sort of individuated imagination. "You're not keen on writing as a get-rich-quick scheme, are you?"

Mark's eyes widened. "Oh! No, golly, I couldn't imagine . . . " His voice trailed off as he slipped the clean plate onto the wall rack. "It would be nice, though."

Silence descended a moment. As he plunged his hands once again into the sink, Tom glanced into the window, which looked into a courtyard shared with the Church House Inn and the verger's cottage (empty for the time being), and saw his own face, and Mark's, darkly reflected.

Mark's face seemed to brighten: "I could pay for the church roof myself! That would be something, wouldn't it."

"Still . . . "

"She's not litigious, is she?"

"Miss Rowling? I have no idea. But I think I'm safe in saying the publishers may sort of push away anything *too* much like hers with a long stick."

"So, then, do you think perhaps I should give up the idea of writing?"

"No, no, I didn't mean that. I just think it might be best if you— I don't know—*hone* your ideas a little more. Do have another one?"

"Gosh, yes, heaps."

"Well . . . ?"

"Let's think. Oh! How about this one. I'm sure it's a winner!" Tom looked over at Mark as he dug his chin into his neck and set his features into a serious frown. "Set against the background of the Civil War . . . ," he said in a strained basso profundo.

"You sound that fellow that does all the voice-overs on film trailers."

"Yes! Set against the background of the Civil War . . ." Mark rain-barrel-bottomed again. "Gosh, that hurts. Anyway"—he resumed his normal timbre—"you'll like this one. It begins at a manor house outside of London somewhere. Hampshire should do—one of the Home Counties—and the heroine is this vivacious young woman whom all the men fancy absolutely rotten. She really could have the pick of the litter—they're fine fellows, upper-crusty, you know—but she's very set on this chap who has a big house in the next parish. He's actually a bit wet, so it's hard to know why she's so keen on him." He paused. "Difficult to know a woman's mind sometimes, isn't it?"

"Well, that will be one of your challenges writing the story, won't it."

"Yes, I expect so. Anyway, this chap is engaged to his cousin—bit racy, don't you think, marrying your cousin—?"

"Yes, I suppose . . ."

"—but there's this *other* guy—a dashing Cavalier—who really really fancies our heroine. Are you following?"

"Er . . . yes. Sort of one of those romantic triangles." Although— he paused in his chore—something vaguely familiar about this triangle was beginning to tease at him.

"Exactly!" Mark whipped his tea towel into a twist and flicked it into the air. "So our heroine—"

"Does she have a name?"

"Well, I thought she could be Irish, or part Irish."

"Would there have been many Irish with manor houses in Hampshire in the seventeenth century?"

Mark paused as he untangled his towel. "Perhaps not. I can always change that. It's not really that important. Anyway, I've been calling her Pinkie O'Shea. What do you think?"

"That is very Irish. The last name at any rate."

"Pinkie Stewart?"

"Scottish."

"Pinkie Jones, then."

"It doesn't matter." Tom rubbed the next plate a little impatiently. "You can call it a placeholder and decide later. Tell me more. Go on."

"Well, let's see. Pinkie's a Royalist—"

"An *Irish* Royalist?"

"Yes, I can see the Irish bit isn't going to work. Anyway, Pinkie goes up to London and is more or less stuck there after a time as the city is run over by Cromwell and all these disagreeable Roundheads. She yearns to go back to the safety of Bailemór—that's the name of the big house in Hampshire—but . . . remember the wet fellow? Well, he married his cousin then went off to join the Royalist forces, and Pinkie ends up caring for this cousin and delivering her baby for her. It's all very dramatic."

"Yes." Tom drew out the word thoughtfully.

"They think they'll never get out of London, and there's this terrible fire—"

"But the Great Fire of London was in 1666, *after* the Restoration."

"This is another terrible fire, an earlier one. It's fiction, Tom."

"Of course, sorry."

"Anyway, as the flames lick their terraced house in Chelsea, the dashing Cavalier comes along and rescues them and smuggles them out of London, though he does leave them halfway—somewhere outside Basingstoke, say—which isn't quite on, but he has his reasons. He's still enormously attracted to Pinkie, but she doesn't give a toss. She's still in love with the wet chap who's married."

The penny dropped. "Ashley?" Tom said tentatively.

"The wet chap? That could be his name, I suppose. I hadn't settled on one."

"And then," Tom continued, swiftly picking up the story, "after the Civil War, after Charles II is crowned king, does Pinkie return to London, become a wealthy businesswoman, and marry the Cavalier, whom she still doesn't love, and then, in the end, after much agony and miscommunication, she realises she does love him, but it's too late . . . ?"

"Yes! More or less. How did you guess?"

Tom looked up to see Mark's reflection move into the main room and pick up some of the coffee cups. "You haven't read the novel *Gone with the Wind* by any chance?" he called over his shoulder.

"I've seen the film."

"Ah. Hmm. I wonder, though, if your story doesn't bear a certain . . . likeness."

"But that one's set in the American Civil War. Mine's the English Civil War."

"Still . . ."

"Oh, I suppose." Mark was back and placing the used cups on the counter. "But I thought it would be all right. I'm told artists sometimes do such things now. I heard Colm once say in music it was called 'riffing.' Or was it 'sampling'?"

" 'Homage,' perhaps?" Tom dropped some of the cups in the dishwater and squirted in some more Fairy Liquid. "Well, it . . . could work, I suppose. It's very ambitious, though, don't you think? Have you thought of starting with something, you know, less . . . epic?" He swirled the dishcloth inside the cup. "Something more here and now. 'Write what you know.' Isn't that what they tell you in these writing courses?"

"Yes, the instructor did say something along those lines. But what do I know?" His tone turned glum. "I live in a village. I work in town . . ."

"You have a lovely wife and a sweet little baby . . ."

"And another one on the way."

"Really? That's brilliant!" Tom turned to him. "Congratulations. You must be enormously pleased."

"Over the moon." Mark's face flushed suddenly—with pride, Tom thought at first, but he heard a catch in the younger man's voice.

"And Violet is well? Happy? No complications? Sure?"

Mark's head made appropriate bobbings.

"You'll cope, you know," Tom said gently. "You do. Look, you've already had experience."

"I know. But Violet's only just told me. I suppose I'm feeling a little overwhelmed by it all. Ruby's barely two."

"There you go. That's the sort of thing you could write about." *When you have a minute between feedings and nappy changes.*

"But, Tom, all sorts have babies and such."

"Yes, but that's the very stuff of life—the kind of domestic particulars and local doings Jane Austen wrote about—from Hampshire, by the way, the very county your Pinkie O'Shea comes from."

"Isn't Austen the one who writes about all those husband-hunting sisters?"

"*Pride and Prejudice,* you mean?"

"I watched a bit on television. Violet was devoted to it."

"Lisbeth loved Jane Austen. Though *Emma* was her favourite." Tom stared unseeingly at his reflection in the glass. He'd suddenly thought of poor Miss Bates, the kindhearted spinster in the novel, worried that word should get to the wrong ears that her apples were but twice-baked, not thrice-baked. "You might have something incidental, something like a woman in the village becoming deeply troubled when her Yorkshire pudding stubbornly refuses to rise."

Mark frowned. "Like Mrs. Prowse's?"

"Well, that's just a for-instance. It could be anything, really."

"Or," Mark said after they worked silently for a moment, "someone in the village dies under mysterious circumstances."

"Or that, yes."

"Like Will."

Tom started. "Do you think the circumstances of Will's death mysterious?"

"I didn't at the time, but . . ."

"You've heard the rumours about the tartlets, then."

"Oh, yes. I guess most of the village knows by now. Sorry." He shot Tom a rueful look.

"No one said anything this evening. Usually—at least at the beginning of the meetings—everything is discussed but the points on the agenda."

"I think everyone's a little frightened that Karla might bite our heads off if we talk about Mrs. Prowse that way."

"True." Karla Skynner was Madrun's great friend in the village. The same age, they had grown up together, gone to the same school; neither had ever married. "Anyway." Tom landed another wet cup on the draining board. "Your story. A village, a mysterious death. How might it have happened? Means?"

"Poison?"

"Well, yes, I suppose." Tom sighed. Mark's imagination didn't really seem to fly above the already at-hand, such as Saturday's tragedy. "Motive?"

"Let's think. Money. That's always a good one, isn't it? Say, a wife kills her husband to get her hands on all the insurance money."

Tom flicked Mark a sharp glance. Was this at-hand, too? "What brought that to mind?"

Mark seemed to stare through him. Slowly, a rising crimson tide seeped into his face. "I must have seen it in a film."

"Which film?"

"I don't know. I can't remember."

Tom turned back to this task. "Well, it's none of my concern."

"You think I didn't make that up?"

Tom shrugged. He didn't wish to hurt Mark's feelings, but none of his ideas so far would handily illustrate a dictionary definition of *sui generis*.

"I didn't mean to suggest . . . ," Mark began awkwardly, then stopped. He pushed his glasses up the bridge of his nose. "And it never occurred to me until a moment ago . . . "

"What didn't occur to you?"

"And it's probably nothing anyway. I'm *sure* it's nothing—absolutely nothing."

"Well, then—"

"Tom, I know you're the soul of discretion, so I say this knowing you'd never say a word to anyone, but the thing is—gosh, I feel awful saying this—Will purchased some additional life insurance—for quite a sum—not that long ago."

"How would you come to know that?"

Mark grimaced. "Someone told me. An insurance broker. You know the building I work in . . . ?"

Tom did. It was a three-storey, Wedgewood-blue structure in the High Street in Totnes, knocked together from two former eighteenth-century merchants' houses. Tucker, Tucker & Tucker occupied the ground floor, and he knew a dance studio occupied the top. Who was piggy in the middle suffering the noise of tapping feet, he didn't know. Mark told him: It was the Mayhew Group, a firm of insurance agents.

"But ought insurance people to be so indiscreet?"

"No, never. Well, hardly ever. But Elk—Elkanah—Mayhew is a good mate of mine; went to uni together, and he's a piper with the Thistle But Mostly Rose. You would have met him Saturday if the weather hadn't been so awful. Anyway, I'd run up to fetch him for a Spinning class before—"

"Spinning?"

"Indoor cycling. We go a couple of times a week before lunch. Anyway, Elk was just showing Will out the door. I guess I was a bit surprised to see Will there. Elk told me after, I expect because he was rather surprised that Will had taken out a policy for such a large sum."

"For what sum?" Tom couldn't help asking.

"Half a million pounds."

The Vicarage

Thornford Regis TC9 6QX

Dear Mum,

It was lovely to get your note yesterday. It quite bucked me up.
Mr. Christmas is quite ~~adaman~~ sure I have nothing to worry
about really. The inquest opens in the v. hall later this morning,
but Mr. C says there is no reason for me to attend, as he is sure it
will be only a preliminary sort of thing and likely won't last half
an hour. I was quite relieved by this, but when I went to the post
office yesterday, Karla said of course it's only preliminary as the
coroner will be wanting the police to get on with their enquiries and that they'll reconvene later once they know a thing or
two. They're going to treat it as a suspicious death, she said, and
I wish she hadn't used those exact words. Having our good
Prowse name attached to a "suspicious death" makes me feel very
downcast. Jago was peevish with me yesterday on the phone
wondering why I don't just buy my soft fruit at Sainsbury's or
Morrisons or even Pattimore's like everyone else, which of course

I do! But I can't abide the waste of all the local ~~edable~~ edible wild foods. Besides it was Dad who started me on this when he showed me his secret spot to find morels all those years ago—you know where it is, but I daren't write it down lest someone besides you and Aunt Gwen should read this letter! How Mr. James-Douglas loved my braised chicken with morels and leeks! Anyway, Kerra must have heard Jago carrying on on the phone, so she came around to the vicarage yesterday for a visit and we had a nice cup of tea in the kitchen. Will Moir's death has shaken her too, I'm sure, and I worry that she is blaming herself for what happened, as she was serving the meal. I asked Kerra if Molly said anything about the pastries I sent over with Mr. Christmas that night, as I can't think who might have sent me that note and Molly seems likely as she was the cook for the Burns Supper, but Kerra said both of them were so run off their feet that they hardly talked about anything other than getting the ~~foot~~ food served. I asked who laid out my tartlets and Kerra said Molly put one tartlet on each plate with the cranachan, but because only half the Thistle But Mostly Rose reached the hotel in the storm, she put the leftovers on a silver platter, which Kerra put on the table if the men wanted extras. I must admit Kerra and I looked at each other and she wondered out loud if Molly might have tampered with the tartlets, as she is an odd sort of woman, really, and her husband is a ~~homo~~ homeopath and they use all sorts of poisons, but she has had terrible troubles lately with her son's death and all so I really shouldn't say this, but then neither of us could reckon how the wrong tartlet would have got into Will Moir's hands. Molly didn't tell Kerra to put THIS *plate in front of* THAT *man and when she put the platter down on the table as nice as you please, Molly didn't say, turn it this way or that way so that a particular tartlet would be near Will's hand. We are both very puzzled. I'm sorry her first experience serving at Thorn Court went poorly. I thought once it was renovated, it would be a much smarter place for Kerra to work part-time than at the Waterside, although if Nick Stanhope is set to hang about the hotel as he seems to be doing these days, then maybe it won't be. Kerra said Nick took a liberty with her right in front of her father that night, which Jago was not best pleased about, but then Nick had the cheek to try it on again with her when she came upon him in the serving pantry. You mustn't worry, Mum. Kerra has a strong will like her father and won't put with that sort of malarkey. She's up to her orange belt in ka-rate, she told me, and I think Nick Stanhope felt the benefit of it that night! Serves him right. He's one of those men who thinks he's God's gift and wants taking down a peg or two. Chip off the old block, says our houseguest, Judith, who knew Clive Stanhope when she was young, as the Frosts worked for the Stanhopes, as you remember, of course. My memories of Clive Stanhope are after he'd married that very nice Dorothy Lindsay and they'd had Caroline. Then there was some scandal about some other woman—can you remember her name? I can't—which sent them off to Australia for a "fresh start"? I think Clive's father died around the same time. Maybe Karla remembers. I shall ask her when I take this letter to post. Anyway, I was going to say, when I was at the post office yesterday and Karla was going on about Will's death being "suspicious," Enid Pattimore came in through the door, took one look at me, and went back out again, as if I were Typhoid Mary. Mum, I wouldn't say this to anybody else, but I was very hurt, though of course I didn't show it. I can't think the last time I felt so cut by someone. Enid has always bought my pastries at the May Fayre and the bring-and-buy bake sale and has eaten them at the Harvest Festival and all those times when Mr. James-Douglas was incumbent, she came with Roger to Sunday lunch at the vicarage, which I cooked! Karla said to pay her no mind as it's just her ~~hippocon hypocon~~ being so fixated on her health, Enid that is, and getting worse. I* suppose I shouldn't have talked about my worries about the yew-berries with Judith, but she could see I wasn't my usual self after my conversation with Mr. C, so I couldn't really NOT tell her, could I, Mum? Nice to have someone in the house who likes a good natter. I do miss Mr. J-D sometimes! Maybe Judith thought Florence Daintrey would keep it to herself, but she hasn't seen Florence in more than 40 years so she doesn't know what a cow she can be! Or maybe she forgot what village life is like. Anyway, Mr. C wasn't quite his usual sympathetic self when he returned from visiting the Daintreys on Tuesday. Hoisted on your own petard, he said to me, or something to that effect, which I thought was a bit unfair as some of the talk I've heard in the village has been useful to him in the past! He did relent and say it would all come out anyway, what with this inquest and all. Still, to be cut by one of my oldest friends! Anyway, and you'll be proud of me, Mum, after a few moments to gather my wits, I marched right across the road to Pattimore's to give Enid a piece of my mind, but she had shot upstairs and there was only Roger in the shop and he wasn't going to have his mother troubled. I did get out of him, though, that it wasn't ~~he him~~ he who sent me the note asking for some baking for the Burns Supper. He said the first he'd learned of it was when he and Mr. Christmas were walking up Pennycross to the hotel last Saturday. I asked him who was on the pipe band's menu-planning committee and he looked at me like I was mad. Of course, being men, they never think of these things. Apparently, at a band practice in November, someone said what do you fancy for your Burns Supper? and Nick Stanhope plumped for curry and they all agreed. I don't know why they didn't simply hire a private room at an Indian restaurant in Torquay, if it's curry they wanted, but Will had said they could have Thorn Court, and I suppose Molly was the logical choice as chef. My experience is most everybody loves curry, but no one much cooks it, not properly, unless they're Indian, or like

Molly who went a bit native when she married Victor who really isn't very Indian at all. They might have asked me as I make a very good curry now. Mr. J–D never cared for it, but after Mr. C moaned on a bit a few months back how he hadn't had curry in ages, I dug out the Madhur Jaffrey I'd bought at a book stall at the May Fayre years ago, and made a prawn ber-roni biran and rice dish, which he loved. Anyway, best I didn't do the curry for the Burns Supper as who knows what people would be saying about me now! Well, I mustn't dwell on this, must I. Worse things happen at sea, as Dad used to say. I'm so glad the weather is warming. The snow has made a good start at melting and Miranda's snowman in the back garden looks a bit past caring. No banana frown now! Bumble snatched it off the ground and thought it a great treat, though I'm not sure if bananas are suited to dogs. The good news is that the Wassail is going ahead after all Saturday. Miranda says now they can start making their lanterns for the lantern procession! Well, I should wrap this up, as there is breakfast to get on with, as usual. I think Judith is staying on with us a few more days, though the roads have been passable enough that a detective constable from town was able to get through to take a statement from Judith, as she was the first to find Will's body. Also, an estate agent from Leitchfield Turner is coming from Totnes tomorrow to show her the Tidy Dolly, which she is thinking of buying, but I'm not sure how keen she really is. If you're retired with a bit of money, why not just buy a cottage in the village, put your feet up, and smell the roses? I asked. I like to keep busy, Judith said, which I understand as I do too. And she has been busy, walking about the village, fetching her car from Thorn Court and driving around the countryside, and she's been busy on Mr. Christmas's computer, too, so I think she's trying to see if Thornford is the sort of place she'd like to stop in, life being circular, ending up in the place you started—a bit like you, Mum! Since she lost her husband a few

months back from Parkinson's, which must have been very hard,
she must still be in a bit of a state. Must go. The cats are pleased
that the snow is melting, as am I. We are all as well here as can
be hoped at the moment. I will be very glad when this day is
over, but I hope yours is good. Love to Aunt Gwen.

Much love,
Madrun

P.S. At least the weather won't keep Karla and me from Tenerife, but now I'm worried this inquest will!

P.P.S. Letitia Woolnough rides a mobility scooter, by the way. It's
a very distinguished black and it looks quite smart I think.

CHAPTER SIXTEEN

*B*loody hell, what did she do? *Stuff* those flaming pastries with whatever that poison is?" Nick struck a match against the wall of the village hall.

"Taxine," Mark supplied brightly.

"You watch it, mate." Jago leaned towards Nick, fists clenched. "That's my sister you're talking about. And she didn't bloody stuff anything with bloody anything. Who's to say *you* didn't stuff them with something? You kept going out for a pee."

"Get your own self stuffed, Jago." Nick flicked the match into a patch of snow. "If I wanted to kill a bloke, I wouldn't waste my time fucking about with poison."

"You bloody would, too, if you thought it would work."

"Gentlemen," Tom snapped before Nick opened his mouth to retort. "Enough! This is serious. Will's death is being treated as suspicious. The coroner said as much not five minutes ago."

Everyone stopped and flicked him a cheerless glance, then

looked away. With the preliminary hearing of the inquest into Will Moir's death completed, there was no compelling reason to stand about in the frosty air made acrid with the smell of Nick's cigarette smoke, yet none of the representative members of the Thistle But Mostly Rose seemed inclined to dash away to resume the rhythms of his day. For Tom, at least, the inconclusiveness of the morning's proceedings brought little surprise; it was the finer points of the testimony that left him disturbed and confounded—and, if truth be told, somewhat relieved.

He had arrived early to find Joyce Pike, the village hall custodian, struggling to unfold the ancient trestle table by herself. Silently—as Joyce was little given to conversation—he lent a hand, setting out the old wooden folding chairs so that the smaller of the building's two rooms resembled a court. Roger Pattimore, who had left his shop in the incapable hands of his mother, joined him in the task, but, as it happened, they underestimated the need for seating and by the time the coroner arrived, some ten minutes late and without apology, a number of villagers had only the back wall to lend their frames support. The air was thick with curiosity, but it was a curiosity left unsatisfied. The coroner, a well-upholstered woman with grey hair swept into a French twist and dark eyes behind wire-frame spectacles, moved briskly and with little formality through the proceedings, as though a much more attractive option—an early luncheon at the Ritz, perhaps—was in the offing. She acknowledged statements taken by police from Judith Ingley, witness to the death of the deceased, and from Adam Moir, who had made the official identification of his father's body at the morgue. What arrested Tom in the recitation of details to establish the facts of Will's death was the pathologist's evidence. The pathologist herself was fetching—svelte frame encased in a smart black two-piece suit, honey-blond hair falling over her shoulders—but Tom lent her his ears rather than his eyes.

According to cardiac blood samples taken at the time of autopsy,

Will died of acute taxine poisoning after ingesting an unknown quantity of plant material of *Taxus baccata*, the Latinate name for the yew. What the pathologist found more compelling and quite unusual was the evidence provided by an examination of the contents of Will's stomach. Though very few cases in her career had featured taxine poisoning, all had yielded up observable quantities of yew leaves or seeds in the stomach and duodenum. In Will's stomach, however, the yew residue was not detectable except by microscopic analysis, indicating that the taxine had been delivered to his system in finely fragmented form—crushed into particles or possibly mashed into a pulp. The poisonous plant material, she said, looking up from her notes for the first time and flicking a glance at the coroner, had been "pre-extracted." The word seemed faintly elliptical and a moment passed before its meaning—that the plant material had been processed—registered, but when it did, when most realised a deliberating intelligence, not bloody bad luck, lay behind Will's death, a small frisson of horror, like a jolt of electricity, passed through the room. But before anyone could even let out an involuntary gasp, the pathologist moved quickly to a generalisation with terrible implications: The decisive role in the process of poisoning was the form of ingestion. Yew leaves or seeds or bark by themselves brought a slower toxin release than pre-extracted plant material. The latter ensured that survival after poisoning was relatively unlikely and that death was relatively quick.

"Bless," Roger said, breaking the silence, "I can't wrap my head around it. I know the coroner's role is only to establish the cause of death, right? But if I understood what I heard, it means that someone at the Burns Supper deliberately poisoned Will. Yes?"

"I can't think it's anything else." Tom whispered a prayer.

After the pathologist's evidence was heard, the coroner adjourned the inquest for the police to make further enquiries. But for the final civilities, the hearing had taken all of twenty minutes.

"Metric still foxes me." Roger lowered his voice, glancing at

Nick, who had moved away to finish his cigarette. "That pathologist went on about . . . what was it?"

"Grams per kilogram of body weight," Mark supplied. "In Will's case, then . . . " He frowned in thought. ". . . A lethal dose would be between . . . fifty and a hundred grams of taxine."

"Which is what in imperial?"

"Oh, somewhere between two and four ounces."

"Bless, that seems like a lot! Sorry, Tom, you're thinking me callous."

"No." In truth, the conversation was a little disconcerting, but Mark's calculations proved illuminating. Surely one of Madrun's pastries weighed no more, and most likely less, and surely now no question lingered over her culpability in this tragic death.

"Although someone else could have added the taxine to the tartlets *after* they arrived at Thorn Court." Mark directed the remark to Tom.

"You're reading my mind."

"But then how would anyone ensure that Will took the right tartlet? Or the wrong tartlet? Or tartlet*s*?" An incredulous look descended over Mark's face. "Maybe the poison was intended for someone else."

"But who?" said Jago.

"Bless, and why?" Roger added.

"Taxine must be bitter," Mark mused. "Most poisons are. I've been doing some research."

The others smiled at him indulgently. Mark Tucker's literary ambitions weren't unknown in the village.

"Better to doctor the curry," Jago said. "You could disguise anything in all that spice. Well, at least our Madrun had no hand in that! Would you bloody look at *him*!" Jago jerked his head towards Nick as he tossed his cigarette away and loped after the pathologist exiting the village hall, her hair swimming becomingly over her black coat. "He doesn't half fancy his chances, does he."

They watched in silence as Nick detained the woman aiming her car starter at the door of a Mercedes. She appeared to be listening to Nick with some concentration.

"Perhaps he's asking some sort of technical question?" Mark offered.

"Pull the other one." Jago thrust his arms across his chest.

"I doubt she'd tell him anything of importance." Tom's eyes shifted from Nick's chatting up the pathologist to Judith exiting the hall with Old Bob, and shifted again, as a familiar red Astra parked next to a fat green Citroën van that could only belong to the coroner. Through the windscreen's smoky glass, he glimpsed two familiar figures. So had Jago.

"They're late," he said.

"Who?" Mark asked.

"The coppers."

"Detective Inspector Derek Bliss and Detective Sergeant Colin Blessing," Tom supplied. "Totnes CID."

"Well, I've got work to get back to." Jago turned up the collar of his jacket. "Caroline's car was towed in earlier this morning."

"Bless! Poor woman! What now?"

"Someone crashed into her."

"Oh, no!"

"On Saturday or Sunday, Roger. Where she'd parked it, no damage to her. Buggered the steering a bit, but nothing to worry about." Jago frowned. "Best we hold off band practice and the like for a while, yes?"

"Bless, I suppose we'll all be having those two to tea." Roger sighed as they watched the two policemen squeeze out of the Astra. "I don't know what possible use I can be, though."

"Nor I," said Mark.

"They won't have an easy time of it, I shouldn't think. All the evidence has likely gone into the bin, for one thing."

Roger wrapped his scarf tightly around his neck. "Molly was a fiend to clean up last Saturday. Perhaps she finds activity soothing, poor woman. I suppose neither she nor Victor was here this morning because attending another inquest so soon would be unbearable."

Tom had attended the inquest into the death of Harry Kaif, in September, and it had indeed been unbearable. The day had been exceptionally warm, the venue the same. The pathologist had not been the smart young woman currently being importuned by Nick Stanhope, but a middle-aged man with prominent ears, who read through his report emotionlessly. Few villagers bore witness in the stuffy room. There was no mystery, after all, no ambiguity, nothing to be curious about. Perhaps people felt they would do best to not attend the Kaifs' grief in this perfunctory exercise. Perhaps, too, Tom thought at the time, some felt the taint of guilt for their own absence of consideration to the boy who had found living too intolerable. Molly did not attend; she was at home, at Damara Cottage, sedated. Victor did, sitting stone-stiff next to a table where someone—Joyce?—had failed uncharacteristically to tidy a vase of wilting red roses, which released three or four petals, like drops of blood, in the lazy stir of air onto the table's white surface. Will had attended, slipping in as the proceeding began, slipping out just as it finished, acknowledging Tom with a pained expression. Events moved swiftly to adjournment, cause of death was undisputed; the small hall heard no lamentation, but the atmosphere seemed drenched desolation. Tom had been reminded too painfully of the inquest into his own wife's death, with its brisk, uncomforting ritual and its verdict of unlawful killing—a murder whose perpetrator had yet to be winnowed from the masses.

Mark interrupted his thoughts: "You said earlier that you were going into town."

"I have hospital visits this afternoon, and I'm driving Old Bob in for a medical appointment. I have a notion—if there's a minute—to take him to the optician in Fore Street."

"Eye trouble?" Roger frowned down at his zipper, which was being uncooperative.

"I'm willing to stand him some new frames."

"Bless, folk have been saying that for years, but you'll never get them off him."

"Why not?"

"Ah, Tom, those spectacles of his once belonged to Mrs. Prowse." Tom frowned.

"Old Mrs. Prowse, I should say. Madrun's mother. She was quite the looker in her day."

"You mean she and Old Bob had a . . . ?" Mark interjected, eyes twinkling with incredulity.

"Bless, I wouldn't really know," Roger retreated quickly. "I was much too young to notice. At any rate, he's very fond of those frames. He'd hardly be Old Bob without them. There!" He rolled the zip up. "Got it! Well, I'd best be off before Mother has one of her spells."

Tom and Mark watched him pass through the gate and turn into Pennycross Road, followed at a short distance by Nick, who turned in the direction of Thorn Cross. The pathologist backed her car out of its parking space.

"I'm sorry I blurted out that bit about Will's life insurance to you the other night." Mark made a face. "Will you say anything to those detectives, if they ask? I don't want to drop Caroline in it."

"It's hearsay, Mark, as far as you and I are concerned. I shouldn't worry anyway. They'll be digging through such things on their own, and won't need our help. I'm afraid some focus on Caroline is inevitable."

"Spouses potentially standing to benefit and all."

Tom grimaced.

"Your experience? Sorry, shouldn't ask."

"It's all right. In my case, it was simple proximity. When Lisbeth was killed I was in the same building—in St. Dunstan's Church. She was in the south porch. I was in the office. Bristol CID found that interesting—at least for a time."

"Opportunity."

"But no motive. They did dig around, though. It wasn't pleasant."

"Lucky for Caroline, she was in town last Saturday."

"Yes, that will help."

"I must go, too. My father will be wondering where I've got to. I was finally able to deposit Sunday's collection money at the bank, by the way." Mark pulled a pair of leather gloves from his pocket. "John looks grave," he added over his shoulder as he departed.

Tom watched John Copeland push through the doors of the village hall with Adam Moir, passing Bliss and Blessing with a frowning glance. John's open jacket revealed a three-piece of olive tweed and a tie loosened at his neck; Adam was more informally dressed, in jeans and waxed jacket.

"I'm so very sorry for this appalling consequence," Tom said to Adam, feeling, as he sometimes did, the very meagreness of words.

Adam stared at him mutely.

"He's a bit cut up," John answered for the younger man, putting one hand on his shoulder briefly. "We all are. I suppose no one's wanted to believe that this"—he gestured towards the village hall—"would be the result."

"How's your mother been?" Tom addressed Adam.

"Caroline's being very brave." John answered once again.

"I think she wants to meet with you." Adam's voice was thick with suppressed emotion. "I mean, because of the . . . "

"Yes, I know," Tom said gently. Now that the autopsy was complete and its results known, Will's body could be released from the hospital morgue and a funeral planned. "Tell her I'm happy to come tomorrow morning, if she would like. Or earlier. Anytime, really. Others will understand if I'm unavailable. This evening, perhaps."

"There's the men's group," John reminded him.

"Ah, yes." Tom had launched the St. Nicholas's Men's Group as a low-key way of spreading Christian fellowship. "Perhaps we ought to cancel, in the circumstances. What do you think?"

"Isn't Brian Plummer coming from Plymouth to talk about coaching Rugby League? It might be a welcome distraction." John frowned at the flat cap in his hand.

"Tomorrow's fine, Mr. Christmas. I'll tell Mum." Adam stepped towards a villager who had stopped to offer her condolences.

"Are you not busy at Noze?" Tom asked John conversationally while they waited.

"We were to have a German syndicate this week, but the snow put paid to that." He peered at the grey sky. "The weather's turned better than expected so the Americans won't cancel their shooting party. They're coming on Monday. They're already in London with their wives, probably obliged to shop, so I expect nothing will put them off coming down here."

Tom smiled. He regarded John's ruddy complexion. On Tuesday night, as he and Mark had stepped out of the Old School Room, he had glimpsed a quickly moving vehicle blaze for a second under the pub's single security light as it turned off Poynton Shute onto Pennycross Road. *Land Rover*, distinguishable for its boxy frame, had registered in his mind. Land Rovers were unremarkable transport in the country, but this one had a singular feature that even in the flash of light distinguished it: the badge of the earl of Duffield on the side, which marked it as one belonging to the Noze Lydiard Estate. That John had sent his regrets to the PCC meeting when in fact he had been in the village was disappointing, but it had triggered a niggle.

"John, a question, if you don't mind."

"Not at all."

"Have you ever sort of shot up in bed, suddenly awake, seemingly for no reason?"

John frowned. "Not . . . recently, that I can recall."

"Well, I did. Last night. And I realised something that had been swimming around in my unconscious suddenly decided to spring into my conscious, although I suppose it could have picked a more convenient time."

"Yes . . . ?"

"Anyway . . . " Tom took a breath. He'd no reason to doubt John's honesty before, and he felt a bit of a fool for asking. "Sunday morning you went to pick Caroline up in town, yes?"

"Yes."

"Well, the odd thing is, when I went up to Thorn Court after the service, your car, your Rover—at least I think it was yours—appeared to be sitting under a mound of snow and there were no tyre tracks running along the forecourt. So how . . . ?"

John cast him a vacant look. His brow furrowed, then enlightenment gleamed in his eyes. "Sorry, I must have given you the wrong impression Sunday. I went to Thorn Court *intending* to get the Rover to fetch Caroline, but Adam here . . . Adam?" He flicked a glance at the young man, who excused himself from what had turned into a group of condolence-givers. "Adam had already brought Caroline in from Noze and dropped her off. Sunday morning, Adam," he prompted.

"Yes, that's right," the younger man said. "I had one of the other estate vehicles and was able to drive Mum back. Her car got stuck in the snow."

"Sorry, Tom." John put his cap on his head. "I didn't mean to give the impression I was the hero of the hour."

"I see." Tom turned to Adam sympathetically. "Then you couldn't have known what happened."

"I don't understand."

"You—"

Tom saw Adam's eyes dart to his left, and he was suddenly conscious of a new figure at his elbow. "Judith. I'm sorry, I didn't see you. This is Adam Moir, Caroline's son. Adam, Judith Ingley. She lived in Thornford as a child."

Judith tilted her head and peered up at him. "I can see the resemblance to your father. I'm very sorry for your loss."

"Thank you." Adam smiled wanly.

"My apologies, I think I interrupted your conversation." Judith twined her scarf between her fingers.

"Oh, it's nothing, really," Tom responded. "I was saying Adam brought his mother in from Noze Lydiard on Sunday morning, but of course as there'd been all the trouble with the phones and such, neither of them was aware of what had happened—"

"Oh, I see what you mean." Adam flushed. "Yes, I dropped Mum off at the gate to the hotel—she . . . she wanted to get back to Ariel—and I drove straight back to Noze, never knowing. Of course, Mum called me later and so . . . " He faltered suddenly.

"And then I expect with all the new snow you couldn't get back to the village until the next day." Tom felt the boy's distress as if it were his own.

Adam blinked rapidly, but one tear escaped. "Sorry," he mumbled as he struggled to regain his composure. Tom felt his heart contract with pity. Adam was, in a way, blooded by this death, initiated into the millionfold congregation that suffered the shattering loss of a loved one—a parent, a spouse, a child, a lover—and was struggling with profound and terrible feelings. He glanced at Judith, who had lost her husband only months ago. She regarded Adam, studying him, almost clinically, Tom thought at first, until he noted her unfocused pupils, suggestive of thoughts straying to another realm. John, too, had lost his spouse—more than a decade earlier—but perhaps it was this span of time that coloured his reaction to Adam's shattered composure: No sympathy softened the edges of his broad features; rather there was an indrawing, a faint furrow to the brow, a slight narrowing of the eyes, a pinching of the lips. It was the expression of a man who sat in judgement and what he was seeing he did not like.

CHAPTER SEVENTEEN

Tom glanced at the gauge. The needle now dipped perilously into the red that meant "empty."

"I'd better stop for petrol," he said to Old Bob as his car reached the outskirts of the village. "Otherwise we may find ourselves hitch-hiking into Totnes."

"Did tha' a bit when I were a lad, puttin' me thumb out," Bob remarked, gesturing with his own digit. "Remember hitchhikin' all the way to Plymouth to see Beryl Davis sing. Folk would stop for you then. Not now, I don't think."

"People are more cautious now, it seems." Tom waited for a lorry to pass, then turned off Pennycross Road. He had ventured hitch-hiking in Europe when he had busked his magic act for a year or so after university at street cafés and local festivals, but had met with little success. People had soured on picking up strangers. Too bad, really.

"I remember—"

"Keep that thought," Tom interrupted slowing the car into the petrol bay of Thorn Cross Garage—or, rather, as the sign over the service bays proclaimed, TH RN CR SS GARAGE.

When no one came out to serve them, and thinking better of embarking on an impatient bout of honking, Tom stepped from the car and studied the filling pump, which, with no credit card slot, was clearly not intended for self-serve. He glanced around the yard and noted a flatbed lorry with what looked like a load of building materials on it, a half-red, half-butterscotch vintage Mini, an old motorcycle, several saloon cars of more recent vintage, a mini cab with its bonnet open, and nothing with a human form.

"Halloo," he called into the garage's service bay, a shadowy cave illuminated by a single naked bulb. Then, as his eyes adjusted, he noted a pair of dungaree-encased legs stretching out from under a car.

"Jago?"

The legs twitched. Tom heard a soft thud followed by a string of curses. The body of a stocky middle-aged man in a boilersuit rolled out on a wooden dolly. On his forehead was a spot of grease like a black bindi; in his hand was a pair of snips. He glared up at Tom, but his expression softened when he saw who it was.

"Sorry to trouble you." Tom reached in his pocket for his billfold. "Look, I'll fill it myself and leave you fifty pounds."

"No, don't do that." Jago rubbed his forehead, turning the grease spot into a black smudge. He scrambled off the dolly and yawned. "I need to stand up. I must have nodded off." He snatched a flannel from a hook by the door and rubbed at his hands.

"That looks like Caroline's car." Tom glanced at the hulk of a Subaru Estate as they passed from the darkness of the service bay into the light of the afternoon.

"It is. It's not in bad shape. Pound out the dents where the tractor hit it and it should be right as rain. I was just under, giving it an oil change. The Moirs have been a bit negligent lately with maintenance on their vehicles. And I can't say I've seen yours in here and you've lived here for nearly a year."

Tom pulled back the petrol tank cover as Jago lifted the hose from the pump. Something Thorn Cross Garage's owner said confused him. "A tractor? What was a tractor doing on the streets of Totnes?"

Jago inserted the hose, frowned. "I don't know. Is this a riddle? What *was* a tractor doing on the street of Totnes?"

"You said this morning that someone had hit Caroline's car where she parked it."

"That's right. She left it just off the A435 where Bursdon Road intersects."

"What? But that's barely halfway to town."

"I think she got stuck or reckoned she couldn't go on in that bloody weather Saturday and abandoned it. At any rate, she left it in the lane into Upper Coombe Farm, by a hedgerow, the AA guy told me. But by Monday, it was under a mound of snow and when Dave took his tractor out on Tuesday to do God-knows-what, he nicked its fender and bent it into the tyre."

"I just assumed someone had hit it in town. Then however did Caroline get to Totnes?"

"Walked?" Jago's eyes darted over the figures clicking on the petrol pump.

"I suppose she must have." Tom calculated the distance: It was at least a couple of miles. Not impossible.

"Or someone gave her a ride on the A435." Jago squeezed the pump handle. "Though walking might have been faster in Saturday's conditions."

"We were just talking about hitchhiking, Bob and I."

"Oh, have you got Old Bob with you?"

Tom bent to look into the car's interior. "Well, I did. Where's he got to?"

"Toilet, likely. He's diabetic, did you know? Makes him a frequent visitor." Jago replaced the hose. "Either you or my sister goes up to Exeter some Saturdays, yes?"

"Me this Saturday. Why?" Tom followed Jago across the pavement into a tiny office where the aroma of motor oil and car exhaust was particularly intense.

"Tamara's been wanting a certain pair of her shoes she forgot to take with her when she moved to Exeter."

"Did last weekend's concert go well?"

"Cancelled, wasn't it, what with all the snow."

"Cancelled?" Tom frowned. "I never thought to ask what happened. They must have all bunked in at Noze during the storm."

"Who? Caroline? With Tamara and Adam? Oh, I suppose." Jago took Tom's credit card.

"You didn't ask?"

"There comes a time when a father doesn't want to know where his daughter spends her nights. Or," he mumbled darkly, "with whom."

"Adam's not such a bad lad."

"Adam's a plonker."

Tom smiled. "Think you'd approve of any man your daughter went out with?"

"Like as not." Jago swiped the credit card with a certain ferocity. "The shoes?"

"I can take them up then. Have you got them here? I'll leave them in the car."

"Tamara works at Drake's Coffee House on Saturday mornings, though."

"Then that's perfect. I'm picking up some books at a shop on Cathedral Close, too. I can drop them off to her then."

Jago reached below the counter and pulled out a wrinkled Morrisons carrier bag. At that moment, somewhere behind the wall mounted with a rack of crisps, peanuts, and pork scratchings packets, a toilet flushed.

"I remember," Bob continued, as if there had been no interval of petrol-purchase, bladder-relief, and cheese-and-onion-crisp-buying, "when Bill Frost and me 'itchhiked up Tiverton way for . . ." His wrinkled face distorted at the effort of remembering. "Not sure why now. Anyway, this were near end of th' war, before Bill got wed. Petrol were rationed, so it were th' only way t'get about."

"Were you in the service?" Tom pulled back onto the main road.

"Might have been, by '44 we was eligible and wanted to join up, but they wanted us on the land, Bill and me. We worked the Stanhopes' farm in them days, before they sold it." Bob rattled the crisp packet in an effort to open it.

"Should you be eating those? Jago tells me you have diabetes."

"Don't matter."

The undertone made Tom glance at him sharply. "Bob . . . ?"

"As I were about to say, Father, weren't a lot of other lads about then, so many off t'war and all, that we had our pick, y'know. Of course, there were all these Yanks stationed here," he added darkly. "Tha' didn't help none. Anyway . . ."

Crisp packet opened, he proffered it to Tom, who slipped his hand in and pulled out a crisp unseen, keeping his eyes on the road, which cut past a few remaining Thornford cottages and into a funnel of hedgerows along Bursdon Road drab with winter.

"Anyway, Father, it were at Tiverton where Bill met Irene, who became 'is missus. She were from London. Her parents sent her to live with some great-aunt who were landlady of a pub. Thought she would be safer. Not sure she were." He chuckled.

"Strange how life-altering a chance meeting can be." Munching the crisp, Tom reflected on his own transformative experience: If he hadn't fallen off a punt into the Cam when he'd been at the vicar factory in Cambridge, if Lisbeth hadn't seen him flailing about—he being the only one at school *not* to earn his swimming certificate— and pulled him out; if he hadn't looked into her remarkable green-flecked eyes and worshipped the very bones of her from that very instant, wherever would he be today? Most likely not, he thought, glancing at Bob, driving through deepest Devon with an octogenarian wearing pink lady's spectacles.

"Have you spoken much with Judith Ingley . . . Frost that was?" Tom gave his tongue a taste and wondered how far past their sell-by date those crisps were. He glanced at Bob munching unconcernedly away, crumbs falling onto his jacket. "I saw you come out of the village hall with her this morning."

"No. Just t'say hello. She remembered me, though."

Tom pursed his lips in thought. They were coming to the junction of Bursdon Road and the A435 near where Caroline had abandoned her car Saturday evening, and he was curious to see the spot, but he also had a vital question for Bob that had been gnawing at him.

"When we were talking in the pub Sunday," he began, slowing the car, "you said Judith's father had died when he fell off Thorn Court's roof—"

"Aye."

"—but you seemed to suggest it was no accident."

"Aye, 'e were pushed."

"Who pushed him?" Tom stopped the car at the junction and glanced right.

Bob was silent a moment, gnashing at another crisp. The salty aroma of cheese and onion pervaded the car's interior. He brushed crumbs from his jacket and mumbled, "Can't zay for sure."

"You mean there was no police investigation, no charges, no trial? Surely at the very least it was manslaughter."

" 'Tweren't no proof, you see, Father. And I were only one who saw it."

"What did you see?"

"I were in the garden, near south wall, clippin' one of them box hedges. This were in summer—July I think it were, maybe August—and 'appened I looked up. I knew Bill were goin' up th' roof to fix the weathercock. I heard noises comin' from up there, but I paid no mind. But then, as I say, 'appened I looked up—don't know why, to look at one of them rooks maybe—when Bill were climbing the ladder by the tower, and I saw it."

"What exactly?"

"A stick of some sort comin' out th' tower window. It went—" Bob mimed a quick stabbing forward thrust with his gnarled hand. "Tipped the ladder, like."

"You mean . . . ?"

"Aye. Fell to the pavement. Died on the spot, Bill did. A blessing, that were."

"Good Lord!" Tom shuddered. "And you're sure it was no accident?"

"I'z can see it plain as day, Father."

"And you have no idea who would have acted so . . . criminally?"

Bob was silent another moment. "I 'ave me suspicions. Weren't any of staff. We all got on. And guests don't make sense. And it weren't old man Stanhope; 'e worked you hard, but he were fair . . . most times. 'Sides, front door of the hotel were open and 'e were at Bill's side right after." He crumpled the empty crisp packet into a tight ball. "No, I think it were old man Stanhope's boy."

"Clive? Caroline and Nick's father?"

"Aye. He were a bad'un, that lad."

"But still—"

"Bill 'ad rowed with him, not the day before. I know, I 'eard they voices when I were near th' toolshed. Clive came out. Never seen him look so fizzed."

"Do you know what they were rowing about?"

"I couldn't hear th' words proper, and Bill wouldn't say."

Tom imagined the immediate aftermath in those more deferential days nearly half a century ago: Arthur Stanhope, though having reinvented himself as a hotelier, still a man of substance and figure of consequence; Bob, a mere labourer, perhaps already evincing signs of the eccentricity that led to the incarnation on his left; the police tugging their forelocks—though perhaps that was overlarding the image. "Have you told no one this?"

"Thought to tell Father Giles a time or two. It's played on me mind over't years now and again, all this, y'see. But he weren't like you."

"Sorry?"

"He liked to talk. Bit of an old woman, Father Giles, if you don't mind me saying."

Tom suppressed a smile.

"Seein' young Judith—well, not so young now, is she?—brought back memories." Bob's voice faltered. "Bill were my best mate in them days. I didn't pay proper mind to 'is memory, did I? And I let myself . . ."

"Yes?"

Bob worried the crisp packet ball as he talked. "Old man Stanhope made life easier for me after tha', you see. I think he thought I knew something. Gave me freehold to my cottage when 'e died, for one thing."

"I see." Tom tried to keep the disappointment from his voice. *A wicked man accepts a bribe in secret to pervert the course of justice*—the Proverb flitted through his head. He glanced over at Bob, at the wrinkled lips surrounded by white stubble, at the skull *sans* bobble hat knobbly as a potato. Wicked, no. Uncertain, frightened, doubting, yes. Who of us didn't blind ourselves to what is right simply to ease life's burdens?

"And what of Judith?" Tom asked after a moment's silence. "Was she still living in Thornford when her father died?"

"She were, but she left soon after—up north to school, I think. Never saw her again after tha', until now."

"And I presume you didn't confide your . . . misgivings about her father's death to her at the time."

"She were so young, Father. 'Er whole life were ahead of her and Bill couldn't come back, could 'e?"

"What about now? Will you say anything to her?"

"Don't know."

Tom took a long breath. "Bob, do you think you may have wronged Judith?"

Bob was quiet awhile. "P'raps," he said at last. "In a way."

"A sin of omission rather than commission, I think. It's not too late to make reparations of a sort, if you're of a mind."

"Oh, Father, I don't know."

In truth, Tom wondered about the practical effect as they crossed the bridge over the Dart and entered Totnes: It was no hard fact that Clive Stanhope ended Bill Frost's life, but Arthur Stanhope's coddling of Bob seemed to give it the awful shimmer of truth. Would it liberate Judith Ingley in some fashion or simply burden her with an ancient, yet newfound, horror? All the protagonists were dead and buried; there was no hope of worldly justice now. But, he thought, God in heaven was wronged.

"I'll think about it, Father. P'raps best Judith not know. I'm not sure. What could she do now? Best she never know, p'raps."

But Tom couldn't help himself wondering as he turned into Coronation Road: Perhaps Judith did know. She had struck him as no fool from the first instance. Perhaps she had known all along.

CHAPTER EIGHTEEN

At The Happy Pair, a shop on the High Street in Totnes tucked between Oxfam and GoodGreens, run by a happy pair of elderly Fabians swaddled in corduroy, few of life's material wants and needs seemed absent. Tom found he could, for instance, if he wished, buy a mousetrap, clotted cream, dog biscuits, wrapping paper, gluten-free fettuccine, organic parsnips, Bruce Lee DVDs, baked beans, batteries, baby food, Royal Wedding tea towels (left over, at a knockdown price), ships (wooden model kits) and shoes (flip-flops) and—yes, really—sealing wax. It was next to that last item on a shelf of items tangentially related to the arts of communication that he espied a goodly supply of typewriter ribbons, which Madrun had asked him to fetch if he had any time left on his pay-and-display ticket after his hospital visits.

He did have time. Mrs. Hex, who had seemed to be convalescing well from her surgery, had been rushed into surgery that afternoon with internal bleeding. Mr. Johnson had, unbeknownst to him, been released that morning and taken away by his son to recuperate at his home near Buckfastleigh. The trip into town had not been the most useful expenditure of time. He had left Old Bob in the hospital's outpatient clinic, where he would be sure to be some little time, as the ailing, in the wake of the snowstorm, were stacked like cord-wood and the doctors were falling behind, and walked to the town centre troubled by the old man's disclosure. A crime unreported, a witness affected by guilt, a young woman quitting the village—chased by a shadow?—and never returning. And then, in the car, as he drove into the hospital parking lot, a new and unhappy revelation. Tom understood why Bob was telling him these things: The old man trusted his discretion, which was gratifying and humbling. And he understood that Judith's arrival in the village had stirred old memories. But why tell him, Tom, at all, now? Because, Bob said, blunt as a bag of dead bats, "I'z ain't long for this life, Father. I needs to get things off me chest." And there, in the car, in the pay-and-display outside Totnes Hospital, he told Tom that, as he put it, "Me kidneys are shot." Suddenly, the man's peculiar spectacle frames seemed inconsequential.

"Hello, Mr. Christmas." A shy voice broke into Tom's thoughts. "I'll just squeeze by you here."

The aisles in The Happy Pair were narrow and Briony Hart, for that's who was edging around his backside, reached for a packet of birthday candles on a shelf next to the one Tom had been staring at.

"What are you buying?" She opened the packet, which wasn't sealed, and looked in.

"My housekeeper needs a new typewriter ribbon." Tom plucked a second and third one from the rack. Why not? Unlike organic parsnips, they didn't go off.

"Oh," Briony said. "Do they need ribbons? How interesting. I've never seen a typewriter . . . outside of films."

Tom smiled weakly. It was all very well having someone as young as Briony on the PCC, but such folk could unthinkingly make you feel old at times.

"That reminds me," Briony continued, "I'll email you the council minutes this evening. I'm nearly finished."

"Lovely," Tom responded, though *no rush* would have done. Her predecessor took six weeks to decipher his scrawls. "How's everything at GoodGreens?" he asked, poking about his brain for a conversational gambit.

"Ooh!" Her voice fell to an excited whisper. "We've just had two detectives in."

"Whatever for?" Tom asked, though with sinking heart he could guess.

"About Mr. Moir's death, I think. Well, no one knows for sure. They asked to see Fatima, the manager—well, the real manager, since Mrs. Kaif hardly ever stops by." Briony regarded him expectantly.

"Oh, dear" seemed the most judicious response.

When Tom refrained from further enquiry, Briony continued in a soft voice, "Maybe they think Mrs. Kaif is involved."

"Briony," Tom responded gently, "they may simply be checking sources of—"

"*Taxus baccata*—taxine, I know. We use it in remedies for gout and rheumatism and some skin conditions and such, but all we have in the shop are tinctures, a few drops in water. They're prepared in Wiltshire where Mrs. Kaif's parents live, so there may be"— Briony's eyes widened—"barrels of it there, gosh! But still . . . as I said, Mrs. Kaif is hardly ever in the shop especially these days, you know, not just because of her catering business, but because, well . . . Anyway . . ." Her eyes darted past his shoulder, widened again, and her cheeks flared. "I'd best get back. It's Fatima's birthday. Gosh, I hope these are enough candles."

As she scuttled up the aisle, Tom turned to see the source of her alarm. Two men, large of size and navy of suit beneath coats of black leather, appeared to be bearing down on him, though, in fact, their eyes were busy scrutinising the laden shelves.

"Bugger it," barked the younger of the pair, Detective Inspector Bliss, distinguishable by his jutting nose and greying choirboy's fringe of hair, shouldered past him.

"Oh, hello, Vicar." The older, though junior-ranked Detective Sergeant Blessing, a man with skin pitted like a pavement, flicked him a glance of recognition.

"I thought you might have set up shop in Thornford." Tom plucked a bottle of Wite-Out from the shelf and gave a passing thought to its utility. Did Madrun concern herself with typos? Or did she have a lifetime's supply of Wite-Out tucked into a cupboard somewhere?

"Undecided." Blessing frowned at the items in Tom's hands. "I think you'll find buggy whips in the next aisle, if you're looking."

"They wouldn't keep typewriter supplies if there wasn't a need."

As Bliss continued up the aisle, Blessing swiped his finger over a boxed typewriter ribbon near the back of the shelf and displayed to Tom the result—a clot of dust. "Still, our investigation might go easier if people did use typewriters rather than computers, typewriters having more of a 'signature.'"

"Ah, I take it you've talked with Mrs. Prowse."

"We have indeed. Her pastries are legendary. And we've taken away the note she received for forensic examination. I'd ask you to come to the station to give us your dabs, sir, but"—Blessing shot him a mirthless smile—"they're on the national database, of course."

"Of course." Tom had had his fingerprints taken shortly after Lisbeth's death.

"For elimination purposes, of course."

"I'm sure."

"Not that a priest mightn't poison a parishioner."

"Name one outside of fiction," Tom said mildly as a passing

shopper, overhearing, glanced from his exposed clerical collar to his face with creeping horror.

"I'm sure if I look, I'll find one. Anyway, the inspector and I were looking to speak to you, too."

"I'll be back in Thornford later this afternoon."

"What about a quick word now? I'd suggest The Nosh Pit just up the street a bit. I think DI Bliss will be agreeable . . . once he finds what he's looking for."

"And what is he looking for?"

"Oh . . . some balm or other."

"Has he ever thought to try homeopathy for . . . what ails him?"

"I don't think that would find favour at the moment, do you, Vicar?"

The Nosh Pit was a Totnes institution, a paean to the town's countercultural reputation, with bead curtains, tables shaped like mushrooms, and artfully graffiti'd walls. Situated where the High Street curved past Castle Street, its front window afforded an advantageous view of the narrow, steep thoroughfare bordered by arcaded shops. By midafternoon, the winter skies were already darkening and the gold of the shop lights began to eclipse the pastels of the shop façades. Tom pressed his hands against the thick china of the cup and felt the heat seep through his skin as he watched Blessing scribble in a notebook.

"You must understand," Tom continued, lifting the cup to his mouth, "that everyone had had rather a lot to drink that evening."

"Even you, Mr. Christmas?" Bliss barked, shifting in his seat as if he would never find a comfortable position. The inspector had ordered a cup of hot water.

"I tried to be sensible, but I hadn't much to eat most of the day, so perhaps the scotch did affect me rather more than I thought. Still, I think I was reasonably clearheaded."

"Reasonably?"

"Well, it's difficult to assess. Yes, I know you think us all a pack of unreliable witnesses. Or you will, once you're done with us."

"Your words, Mr. Christmas, not mine."

The detectives had asked Tom to take them through the events of the evening. He had dutifully relayed his arrival with Roger Pattimore at Thorn Court, through pre-dinner drinks in the reception room, to his first glimpse of the private dining room.

"The table was originally set for twenty-odd, but because of the snowstorm only about half showed. So at table there were eleven pipers—"

"Can you give us their names?" Blessing asked.

"You mean you don't have them?"

"Weather's played havoc with our routines, too, sir. So, if you don't mind . . . "

"A few I'd not met before," Tom added when he'd completed the task. The evening now seemed like a disjointed series of tableaux. "And others I can't say I know well, but—"

"And who else was in the hotel?" Blessing looked up from his pad.

"Well, Molly Kaif, but you must know that as you were just at GoodGreens . . . "

Blessing lifted an eyebrow but said nothing.

" . . . and Kerra Prowse, who was serving. Jago Prowse's daughter."

"And that's everyone?"

"No, there was an unexpected . . . guest, I suppose you could say. Judith Ingley turned up in the storm from Stafford and thought mistakenly that Thorn Court would be open for business. She's been staying at the vicarage since. But I gather she's already given a statement to a DC."

Bliss grunted ambiguously. "And when did Mrs. Ingley arrive?"

"I'm not exactly sure. I found her in the reception room when I nipped out after the curry, and—" He glanced from one to the other; neither seemed surprised. "You know our Burns Supper was curry, do you?"

Blessing responded, "So far, we've had time to talk to your housekeeper and we've had time to pay a quick visit to Thorn Court's kitchen."

"Which I expect was scrubbed down as restaurant kitchens often are."

"You're an expert on restaurant kitchens?"

"I once worked on a cruise ship."

"As a priest?" Incredulity pushed Blessing's acne-pocked forehead into accordion folds.

"No, as a magician."

Blessing opened his mouth to respond, but Bliss cut him off with a sharp look. "There was curry left over and frozen, which we're having taken away for examination."

"The leftover haggis, neeps, and tatties being binned, I expect," Tom said, reasoning that such unloved comestibles had little chance of being reheated and eaten. "There was cranachan, too. Cream, oatmeal, raspberries," he explained.

"Binned as well." Bliss jerked in his chair.

"Does it matter?" Tom glanced to the windowpane, spotting now with driblets of rain. "Surely that taxine was administered to one particular plate or glass or cup and somehow got put in front of Will."

"Or a certain tart," Blessing murmured as he scribbled in his pad.

"You can't believe this is Mrs. Prowse's doing? You heard the pathologist this morning . . . or you must have read the report by now. The *quantity* of taxine Will ingested staggers the imagination."

Blessing shrugged.

"And besides," Tom continued with growing irritation, "how

would a particular pastry, doctored with poison or not, be directed to Will *specifically*? Surely," he insisted, "one of the other dishes must have contained the poison."

"All the food was served individually, yes?" Blessing looked up.

"Yes . . . well, no, not quite everything. The extra tartlets were put on a platter and laid on the table, and then there was a cheese course, but . . . " He considered. "The cheese and biscuits arrived after Will vanished, so . . . "

"Did Will take one of the extra tartlets from the platter?"

"No, but . . . "

Bliss regarded him through narrow slits. "But?"

"Well," Tom hesitated, remembering, "Will did have an extra one, but it was Nick's. Nick took it off his own plate and handed it to his brother-in-law, claiming to be too full."

He watched the two detectives exchange glances. Then Blessing resumed his scribbling as Bliss said, "At any rate, *most* of the food was served individually."

"Yes. Typical restaurant style. At Thorn Court, you probably noted there's a serving pantry between the kitchen and the private dining room. I presume Molly plated, say, four or six dishes, set them on a tray, then took them to the serving pantry. Kerra would then pick up the tray, go into the dining room, and serve the food while Molly plated the next batch in the kitchen."

Blessing lifted his pencil and peered into the middle distance. But it was Bliss who spoke: "Did the waitress serve the food in a particular order?"

Tom let his mind's eye rove over Saturday's menu. "If I remember correctly, Kerra served from the top down. I mean," he added, observing the detectives' puzzlement, "she served the end of the room farthest from the pantry first, then worked her way down one side, which means . . . " He found himself reluctant to acknowledge it: "Which means Will was likely served first. He was at the head of the table."

252 · C. C. BENISON

The two detectives glanced at each other. Bliss said, "Then when she arrived at Mr. Moir's seat, she would have taken the plate closest to her. The tray was . . . what shape?"

"Rectangular."

"Even better."

"I see." Blessing dropped his pad and pencil on his lap. "Miss Prowse is right-handed, yes?" Tom nodded, and the detective mimed lifting a tray, balancing it along his left arm, then serving from it. "The closest plate would be the one in the right corner of the tray nearest her body where she could most easily reach it with her right hand. If she were methodical, she would serve the same way every time."

Tom shook his head. "But it's such an awful risk. By some whim, Kerra might easily have taken the plate above or beside and someone other than Will would have died. Isn't there the possibility that Will was not the intended victim?"

Bliss shrugged. "Who was served second?"

"Kerra served the side of the table opposite me each time, which means . . . Roger Pattimore was the second man served. Good Lord, Roger wouldn't harm a fly and no one would want to harm him."

"Suggesting," Bliss remarked, "that someone might wish to harm William Moir?"

Tom felt himself treading in dangerous waters. As always, he felt constrained to balance the need for justice—in this case, getting to the truth of Will's premature death—with a need to protect his flock. "I've been vicar of Thornford less than a year, you understand, so I can't say I know the depths of the souls of everyone in the village, much less those of my congregation. Roger is one of my churchwardens, so I think I've come to know him reasonably well. Caroline Moir is a member of St. Nicholas's choir, so I see her at least once a week. Will I know rather less well. He didn't attend church with any regularity. Managing a hotel is time-consuming, for one thing."

"I'm not sure you've answered my question, Vicar."

"Well, I *don't* know," Tom insisted. "Will had, as one of my parishioners said to me recently, a rather large personality. He had many involvements in the community, some of which, I suppose, might have involved him in some sort of disagreement. He helped organise a fund-raising fun run for the church—that went well. But he was on the parish council and he acted with Thornford's amateur dramatic society and he coached the Under-fifteens at the Cricket Club—"

"Until that episode with that lad, the Kaifs' son." Bliss cut him off.

"That was very unfortunate, and Will regretted his outburst deeply."

"It would appear the boy took his life not long after."

"You're suggesting direct cause and effect?"

Bliss shrugged.

"Harry Kaif was a small, sensitive boy who was being bullied at school, and through the Internet." Tom glanced at a familiar figure emerging from the bank across the street. Caroline. "There's a shared responsibility for this tragedy," he added, watching her stop and fumble with a large envelope.

"But Mr. Moir's outburst might have tipped the balance."

Tom half watched Caroline pull some papers from the envelope, then turn and move away down the High Street. Of course, how could one possibly know what fervid imaginings troubled the boy's mind? There had been no suicide note. "I don't believe Victor Kaif saw it that way—at least in the end. Because I'm chaplain to the Thistle But Mostly Rose and Harry's death had caused a rift, I tried to bring about a reconciliation between Victor and Will. The meeting was difficult and painful, but I don't think when we were done that Victor still held Will somehow directly responsible."

"Still?"

Tom regretted the word choice. "It's not unreasonable that in his grief Victor would look for someone to scapegoat, and he did, at first, with Will. But I think he came to see that no single incident led to his son's death."

"And how did Mr. Moir account for his—'outburst,' as you call it?"

"Well . . . he couldn't, really."

"Was he prone to fits of anger?"

"Again, Sergeant, I've only been in the village a short time, so I can't properly say. I think Will could be forceful—if you've been a professional cricketer and coach, how could you not be?—but I'm not aware of similar public . . . explosions. I think the business with Harry Kaif had a shattering effect on him, really. He's been somewhat subdued, depressed perhaps, in the months since, dropped some of his activities. I gather the year before he did a star turn at the village hall in *Abigail's Party*—"

"I saw that," Bliss interrupted. "The wife dragged me. She likes theatre. Dress rehearsal for a heart attack, that play. Will's character had one."

"Not poisoned, though?" Blessing looked up.

Bliss shook his head.

"Anyway," Tom continued, draining his cup, "Will wasn't in the play this autumn and he resigned from the parish council . . ."

"You've . . . suggested Victor Kaif bore no ill will against Will Moir." Blessing read from his notes. "What of Mrs. Kaif?"

"I'm afraid I'm not party to her mind."

"She hasn't sought your priestly counsel?"

"No, not in any formal sense. The Kaifs only occasionally attend St. Nicholas's, although their daughter is in Sunday school and a friend of my daughter's."

"But being a mother, she was, I'm sure, knocked for six by her son's death."

"I don't think there's much doubt of that, Detective Inspector."

"Found the energy, though, to cook a three-course meal for more than twenty guests, didn't she."

"But it was sheer circumstance that led to Molly's presence. The band holds its Burns Supper at a different hotel or restaurant each January. This year it was Thorn Court's turn, but because the hotel is under renovation and the staff on hiatus, someone else was needed to cook the meal. Molly's a caterer and apparently has a reputation for her curries."

"And why curry at a Burns Supper?"

"Good heavens, Inspector, everyone loves curry. It's the national food of England."

Bliss frowned deeply.

"DI Bliss much prefers fish-and-chips," Blessing interjected, flicking a glance at his superior. "I think the question is, why curry at *this* Burns Supper? Who decided for curry? If you'd all fancied Chinese, who would have cooked your meal?"

"I get your point, Sergeant." Tom sighed. "It's all a question of opportunity. What better food to disguise a poison than a spicy curry? And who had the best access to that curry? The cook, of course. And who was the cook? Molly Kaif. But isn't it all a bit unsubtle? If she seriously wished to harm Will, wouldn't she take care *not* to make herself the obvious suspect?"

Not if Molly had lost the balance of her mind, Tom thought, worrying the edge of his fingernail as both detectives favoured him with noncommittal stares. He cast his mind over the previous Saturday evening, as if viewing it through the lens of a speeded-up movie. He said, "Gentlemen, you've a daunting task sorting out the Burns Supper. All the people, all the moving about the place—"

"You'd got us to the dining room earlier, sir, in your description," Blessing interrupted, flipping back in his pad, "twelve of you. And you all remained there for the course of the meal?"

"Well . . . no."

"No?"

"Let me see." Tom strained his memory. "Of course, there was the piping-in of the haggis, so after the soup course Victor left to fetch his bagpipes, as he was the designated piper—"

"Left . . . ?"

"Through the door to the corridor that leads to the lobby. There are two doors on the—let me think—east side of the dining room, one to the corridor, one to the serving pantry. I remember Nick Stanhope popping out for a pee early on, possibly before Victor went for his bagpipes, although—"

"Although?"

Tom felt as if he were shopping Nick to the police; worse, he was taking some guilty pleasure from it. "Although he took the serving pantry door." To Bliss's inquisitorial eyebrow, he added, "possibly by mistake. He was fairly legless early on.

"And then . . . I remember John Copeland going to fetch some antacid tablets, which would have been after the haggis course."

"But before the curry?"

Tom nodded. "I'm not sure about the movements of others down the table, though. Oh, and in the interests of full disclosure, there's me. I headed to the loo after the curry course."

"Yes?" Bliss appeared weirdly pleased.

"I have no trouble digesting curry." Tom glanced at Blessing, who was snapping back the pages of his notebook.

"Which would be when you say you encountered . . . Judith Ingley," the inspector said.

"Yes, I was crossing the lobby and glimpsed her in the reception room."

"So she had already checked in."

"No, no, I already said: Because of the renovating, Thorn Court wasn't taking guests. Mrs. Ingley didn't know that."

"Didn't check online or phone?"

Tom shrugged. "Country hotels aren't awash in guests after

Christmas, I wouldn't think. She probably assumed a room would be available."

Bliss's face twitched. Whether he was unconvinced or suffering the agonies of irritable bowel, Tom couldn't tell.

"So," Blessing said, taking a cue from his superior, "you came upon her in the reception room—"

"Yes, she said she had tried the desk, but as we were all in the dining room and being quite noisy, she couldn't make herself heard."

Blessing paused, took a sip of coffee, then looked past Tom down the High Street, which seemed to be drawing in on itself in the growing gloom.

"Then you don't know how long she had been in the hotel before you found her, do you?" He returned his eyes to Tom's.

Tom thought back to the figure he had encountered in Thorn Court's reception room. Judith had not removed her jacket, but that meant little as the fire was embers by that time and the room had cooled, and her cheeks had a rosiness to them, as if she had just slipped in from the outdoors, but then they remained rosy through the rest of the evening and all the days after, an effect of her makeup—or makeup itself.

"No," he replied slowly, "I suppose I don't."

CHAPTER NINETEEN

By about the fifty-seventh slide—this one of the Reverend Hugh Beeson, vicar of St. Barnabas in the village of Noze Lydiard, all seventeen stone of him, emerging from what appeared to be a concrete tepee in a place called Holbrook, in Arizona—Tom's eyelids were feeling the wrench of gravity. It had been very kind of Hugh to come to Thornford to fill in as guest speaker at the St. Nicholas's Men's Group—though, Tom thought, squeezing the tiny muscles around his eyes in an effort to keep his lids from descending, perhaps he was being kind in thinking that Hugh was being kind. After Tom had mentioned on the phone only hours before his disappointment that Brian Plummer, the well-known Rugby League coach, had to cancel his appearance last-minute due to something that sounded like little more than a tummyache, his colleague in the neighbouring benefice had fairly leapt at the opportunity to come and show his pictures, now ten years old, of the journey he and his wife had taken down Route 66, a highway in America that, according to a song he'd blasted out of a CD player to open his presentation, "wound from Chicago to LA." Hugh, Tom suspected, was happy for any opportunity to display the flowerings of his great avocational enthusiasm.

Which was motorcycles. Hugh adored them, in a fashion that struck Tom as faintly idolatrous, but then Hugh wasn't a lone figure in this mania. There was a little clack of priests in England who received press attention for their affectation and who parlayed their helmeted, leather-clad presence, singly or collectively, into charitable fund-raising deeds. This was a good thing, though. And, he supposed, Hugh's enthusiasm was a useful thing, as well. Tom counted himself fortunate to have only two churches in his benefice. Hugh had four—four small congregations scattered about the countryside, which meant Sunday-morning services were a bit of a tear. What more efficient way to get from St. A to St. B then by skirting through and around traffic on a marvelous rocket machine? The Holy Hog, Hugh called it.

Hugh had been an almost alarming sight sauntering into the Church House Inn on a winter's eve, squeezed into black leather, helmet in the crook of his arm like a severed head, until he pulled the snaps back from his bulging neck to reveal his straining clerical collar. But this walking medicine ball could relieve the regular punters slumped in their chairs of their dull conversation. Tom had fetched him to the pub's upper reception room where grub was laid on, and a screen, like a stiff white flag, was scrolled into place in front of a projector, a device now as quaint as a typewriter, miraculously unearthed by Joyce Pike in the recesses below the stage of the village hall.

Hugh shucked his leathers and entertained with brio, taking them through the stations of this modernist, unsanctified pilgrimage. Spicing the show and keeping the men alert was the presence in nearly half the photographs of Mrs. Beeson, the second Mrs. Beeson, as it happened, a woman fifteen years Hugh's junior and gamer than Vicar's Wife Mark I to suffer the skin-searing, hair-flattening effects of a two-thousand-mile cross-country tour from motorcycle sidecar. As the Beesons travelled from cool, grey Chicago to the sun-drenched climate of the American Southwest, Mrs. Beeson seemed to shed layers of clothing—*there's Holly at Cadillac Ranch*—revealing a figure remarkable for shapes and curves somehow stifled in England. Tom had met Holly, of course. Ten years had passed since these projected photos, but she appeared little changed today, her heart-shaped face still smooth as a doll's, her breasts, he suspected, still voluptuous somewhere under the sensible cardies she wore at the vicarage in Noze Lydiard. She was a bright thing, to boot, an accomplished artist who taught theatre design—and Tom, glancing with drooping lids from the bright screen to the shadow enveloping the bearded, rotund figure working the projector, couldn't staunch a prickle of envy. *You've done well, you old goat.*

But even the vixen charms of a younger Mrs. Beeson—*there's Holly at London Bridge, Lake Havasu*—couldn't keep Tom's mind from going walkabout. The room was thick with warm air, dark but for the jewel glow of sky and tree on the screen; the pint of Vicar's Ruin had glided nicely into his veins and now breached his cerebral cortex. Kingman, Barstow, San Bernardino were all very pleasant, but he found himself drifting to a place nearer to hand, to The Nosh Pit in Totnes, where Detective Inspector Bliss and Detective Sergeant Blessing had planted their bottoms and held him prisoner to a mushroom-shaped table and a rather decent cup of coffee. Perhaps it was Hugh's mention of a bout of food poisoning at a diner in Albuquerque that recalled Tom to the earlier conversation.

"A woman's weapon, poison, don't you think, sir?"

Tom had looked up from his coffee, wondering at being asked to speculate, but saw that Blessing was addressing his superior, who merely grunted in response and said to Tom, "According to the report we received, Mr. Moir's body was found in Thorn Court's tower. Do you know why he would have gone up there?"

"I'm afraid I don't. It seems an odd thing to do, and I've thought about it since. I can only speculate that he felt ill and didn't want to trouble us—his guests. People who feel unwell often fall into a kind of denial. Shame and embarrassment can be powerful forces, Inspector."

Bliss looked unconvinced. "But why the tower? The hotel is full of bedrooms if he wanted to lie down, and the Moirs' residence is right next door."

"We realised at one point that he couldn't have gone next door. One of us—John Copeland—looked out and saw no footprints."

"Fresh snow could have covered them."

"Not that quickly, I don't think."

"Another question is *when* he went up the tower. He didn't leave in the middle of the meal." Blessing flipped back in his notebook. "You had your sweet, complete—" He paused to lend emphasis. "—with berry tartlets."

"The programme was to include various toasts and speeches, and some bagpipe music, too, I think." Tom sipped his coffee. "But after the meal, we broke away to get some air and so forth. Some of us went into the lobby or the reception room. After about fifteen minutes we reassembled in the private dining room."

"And no Will Moir."

"No." Tom paused. "We waited for a bit, but then his continued absence seemed strange—at first—and then worrying. So after a time, we sent out a search party."

"Then Mr. Moir was out of everyone's—presumably everyone's—sight for . . . ?"

"More than half an hour, I would say. Perhaps forty minutes."

Bliss squinted at the ceiling. "And in that time, he never tried to come downstairs, never sought help, never declared he felt unwell—Odd."

"Sir," Blessing interrupted, "his precise time of death can't be pinned down. He may have only reached the tower when he collapsed, and couldn't move to get help."

Bliss appeared to consider this. "The search party consisted of whom?"

"Besides me, Mark Tucker and Roger Pattimore . . . and Judith Ingley. It was Judith who found Will's body, which I think you know."

"I'd wondered about that. You'd only known her an hour and yet she was already part of a search party."

"Mrs. Ingley is a nurse," Tom explained. "We thought—without saying it, of course—that she might prove useful. You see, Inspector, when she first arrived, I brought Will out to the lobby to meet her to let her know that there was no room in the inn, so to speak, and she thought he looked a little unwell then."

"And this is *after* the curry course." Blessing looked at his notes. Tom nodded.

"And what made her think of the tower, do you suppose?"

"We had eliminated all the other possibilities, so she went up."

"*She* went up. Alone?"

"I know what you're thinking, Inspector, but we didn't send her up. She had gone up on her own before we three arrived at the bottom of the stairs."

"But you did go up."

"Yes."

"And . . ."

"Well, Inspector." Tom felt a surge of sadness. "In the low light, you might have thought Will was resting."

"Presuming the body hadn't been moved," Blessing muttered.

"Judith is a small elderly woman and Will was not a small man," Tom remarked, adding, "But she told us she did arrange the body."

Tom's body gave an involuntary jerk. His eyes snapped open and he blinked to readjust his sight to the glowing screen and its new images. Yes, there was Holly, in sunglasses, waving to the camera in front of Grauman's Chinese Theatre on Hollywood Boulevard. And there she was again in front a bronze statue of Bugs Bunny on the Warner Bros. lot. And there were the two of them—both waving this time—as an attendant strapped them into the seat of a Ferris wheel. This, explained Hugh, was Santa Monica Pier, the real and symbolic end of Route 66. Tom attempted to suppress a yawn, but someone turned on the coach lamps ringing the paneled room at that very moment, catching him with his mouth stretched wider than the west door of St. Nicholas's.

"I trust I haven't bored you, Tom," Hugh remarked as he switched the projector.

"Not at all," Tom white-lied, aware that he had missed most of Arizona and California. Or was it New Mexico and California? He gulped back another yawn. "It was most illuminating."

Tom rose from his chair, thanked Hugh, and called for a round of applause.

"I do apologise, Hugh," he said a few moments later after Hugh had answered a few questions from the audience, "I think I nodded off for a bit. It's been a long day. Have you thought of scanning your slides into a PowerPoint presentation?"

"I have, and that way I wouldn't have to cart that ghetto blaster with me for the musical accompaniment, but finding the time is always the trick. It was only chance I had this evening free."

"Well, thank you for coming on a winter's night."

"How is your men's group coming along?" Hugh had a trimmed greying goatee beard, which he stroked reflexively as if it were an attached pet.

Tom watched the strong fingers ply the hairs. "I'm not sure how successful I am in integrating the Christian message, but at least we're building fellowship."

"Old Giles rather let his mission work slip in his last years." Hugh broke off his stroking and cut the light on the machine, which continued to whine as it cooled.

"We've had several outings in the autumn," Tom continued, "a guided walk to Buckland Beacon, and some of us kayaked the Dart. Haven't I mentioned this?"

"Ah, yes, I remember you saying something about that at the last deanery supper. Not fond of water, I seem to recall." He eyed Tom with a half grin.

"Falling in, I'm not fond of. I can't swim."

"But that's how you met your wife. I remember that story."

"Fortunately, the kayak didn't tip."

"You're a brave bugger, you are, Father Christmas."

"And for my next trick"—Tom executed a stage gesture—"I'm going to see if I can get this lot to jump out of an airplane."

"I believe the notion, Tom, is to increase the flock, not cull it."

"I'm jumping with them."

"The Church frowns on taking one's life."

"It's to raise funds for a new roof for St. Nick's."

"St. Barnabas's is in want of a new boiler and I don't think I can face another bring-and-buy. Any chance of piggybacking?"

"None." Tom's grin edged higher. "I'm feeling inordinately uncharitable in this instance."

"Then this is the last time I favour you with my holiday snaps."

Tom laughed. "Stay on and have another drink with us."

Hugh's eyes travelled to a corner of the room where several of the men were gathered in a conversational knot by a framed set of Hogarthian engravings. "Best not."

Tom followed the direction of Hugh's gaze. "Drink-driving?" he asked, but he sensed the reason lay elsewhere.

"It's been some time since I've seen John Copeland," Hugh said after a pause.

"But he lives at Noze," Tom protested, mildly startled.

"On the estate, not in the village."

"Still . . ."

"Did you not know he was married to my sister?"

"Good heavens, no. I had no idea. Then . . . oh!" The fate of the woman in question dawned on him. "I'm so sorry. She can't have been very old."

"Regina wasn't yet thirty-five. Much too young. Did you know?"

"Yes, John did tell me once."

Hugh's lips thinned to an uncompromising line as his glance returned again to John. "I'm afraid I've never been able to quite forgive him. Despite the commands of my faith."

Tom noted that John's gaze had turned their way and felt a prickle of guilt along his spine. "Sounds fraught," he murmured, watching Hugh edge the carousel back into a frayed cardboard box.

"I've said too much as it is, Tom, and I really must be getting back to Holly." Hugh grabbed for his CD player, as if suddenly impatient to leave. "I expect I'll see you again at the next deanery meeting, rescheduled for . . . when is it?"

"Wednesday week."

"Right."

"Thanks again."

"I'll get kitted up in the loo." Hugh reached for his outerwear. "Me squeezing into these leathers is not the most edifying of sights."

Tom beamed at him and thought that this was likely so.

Tom squinted at the spiderweb of circles on the board, concentrated his attention, inhaled, then, as he exhaled, launched the last of his three darts. He laughed in surprise as it embedded itself in the bull's ring. He was usually rubbish at the game.

"I didn't realise that it was Hugh's sister you'd been married to," he remarked to John as he went to pull his darts from the board and chalk up his score.

"I thought my ears were ringing." John stepped up to the line on the floor and frowned at the board. The two had moved from the upper room to a corner of the bar below. Most of the others of the St. Nicholas's Men's Group had left for home and hearth; a few lingered for a final half to observe the pub quiz, in progress; John had suggested darts to Tom, an alert that something was on his mind. John never lingered; there was often some evening chore at Noze. Tom had never seen John play darts in the Church House Inn at all.

John's second and third darts hit the double-twenty section. "What did he have to say?"

"Hugh? Not much, really." Tom lined up for his turn while John fetched his darts and recorded his score. "Other than mentioning your kinship by marriage."

John's face darkened. "Did he tell you that I killed my wife?"

Tom's hand fell to his side. He felt the dart spike his thigh. "No, he did not," he responded, surprise lost in a flash of pain. "I suppose I should ask if you did, but I expect *if* you did, you would be a guest of Her Majesty somewhere, not here with me playing 501."

"If Hugh had had his druthers, I'm sure I would be locked away. Are you all right?"

"I'm fine." Tom rubbed at his trousers where the dart had pierced. "I'd understood she'd been taken by cancer."

"That's what I tell folk. Regina was in stage three breast cancer, but her treatment was not going well, and the prognosis was poor. She would have died of cancer before long, though Hugh refused to believe it. No, she died accidentally."

"I'm sorry to hear that." Tom lifted the dart, but his eyes strayed from the board to John. "Then why would Hugh—?"

"Because her body was found at the bottom of the stairs in the castle ruin at Noze."

Tom frowned. "Are you suggesting that it wasn't an accident?"

"I'm sure she didn't intend to die in that way. Are you going to throw that dart?"

"Then she intended to die another way?"

"Regina had no intention of dying at all, if she could help it. She feared death—she didn't have her brother's Christian faith, nor mine—but she was emotionally troubled. Was all through our marriage. She attempted a few times to take her own life, but without success. One time I found her unconscious with a near-empty bottle of her antidepressants on the bedside table. Another time she tried a paracetamol overdose. There was a consulting psychiatrist at the hospital who took me aside and said—well, she put it in some fancy language, but the rub is, Regina never intended to kill herself. She knew when I would likely be back and timed her attempts so she would be caught in time—rescued."

"More cry for help than anything, I expect." Tom raised a second dart. "Still, that's a hard way to live, John. For you, I mean."

"She was a bright thing when we married," John said as Tom's dart missed the board altogether. "I had no idea the sorts of moods she could fall into—the anxiety, the depression, the anger. Her family knew, Hugh knew—I think they were secretly glad to hand her off to someone.

"She never really took to country ways," he continued. "The Beesons were Londoners. I met Regina through Hugh who was vicar at a church near the Encombe estate in Dorset where I was an under-gamekeeper. I think Regina thought she was marrying that fellow—what's his name?—from that book, you know . . ."

"What book?" Tom raised his third dart. He inhaled and exhaled twice to steady his hand.

"There was great fuss about it way back. I can't think of the name."

"Oh, you must mean *Lady Chatterley's Lover*." He launched the dart, which, perversely but satisfyingly, sank dead centre. "She thought you were Mellors?" Tom tried to keep the scepticism from his voice. He had a vague recollection of Lawrence's novel, having read it as a teenager mostly for the bits presumed salacious. Mellors was a sort of demon lover, but aloof and gruff, tall and lean, with fair hair if he remembered correctly. The woman, Lady Chatterley, whatever her first name was, was faithful and dutiful and a bit dull, he thought—until she met the gamekeeper. Of course, the John Copeland before him at the dartboard was close to fifty, no longer a young man, though still handsome in a fleshier bullish way. But twenty-odd years earlier, he might have filled the contours of a highly developed romantic imagination. He said as much, thinking he was choosing a diplomatic response until John cast him a dark frown.

"I mean in terms of class," he hastened to explain as he went to pick up his darts. "Mellors was supposed to be working-class and Lady Chatterley some sort of minor aristocracy. I don't think that applies here."

"Not unentirely." John stepped up to the line and peered at the dartboard. "The Beesons think they're a cut above. Hugh is High Church, as you know, though you wouldn't think so with all this rough motorcycle show of his. Had us marry at St. Margaret's, Westminster, no less." He launched the dart, which scored another double twenty. "Still, things seemed all right at the beginning, even though no child happened along. I thought we'd have kids right off. Anyway, after a time, cracks began to show. If I were out for hours at night lamping, she'd think I was with another woman, for instance—that sort of thing. Accuse me of all sorts. There's not much romantic about gamekeeping, Tom. Maybe you don't know, being a townie yourself."

"I think I can guess."

"It's bloody hard work—and it's not easy on wives, I'll admit that. Meals at all hours, wet dirty clothes for the wash all the time, never time to go into town for a meal or a film, night work, as I said. I thought things would get better when I was hired soon after as gamekeeper and shoot manager at Noze. I could delegate, at least. There was a lad before Adam came on. But . . . " He raised his second dart. "And I'm not always easy to live with—I admit that, too. If the wind's wrong on a shoot day, it can put you in a foul temper."

Tom paused to wave good-bye to two departing members of the men's group, who regarded them curiously. "Then how," he said, dropping his voice as John's dart scored a triple eighteen, "did your wife come to be found at the bottom of the stairs at Noze Lydiard Castle?"

"We had had an argument. I can't remember what it was about now. Something silly. Regina's illness seemed to make her even more moody. Despairing one moment, euphoric the next. Hateful, then begging forgiveness. She was frantic I was going to abandon her. And usually during these episodes, I would go out and work on the estate and be back in a few hours when she had calmed down. But this particular day—it was a Sunday afternoon in November, the middle of the shooting season—instead of even just going for a walk or going out to one of the outbuildings to play my pipes, I took the car into Torquay." He threw his next dart with sudden ferocity; it hit the wire and fell to the floor. His face reddened. "It was an impulse. I was worn out.

"Before I walked out the door, she said she was going to jump off St. Hilda's tower if I hadn't returned by supper." John paused, then went to retrieve his darts. "Even though the castle is closed in winter, we had a set of keys to the grounds. But she had cried wolf too many times. I didn't believe her, and the castle is a good walk away, and she was still weak from her last round of chemotherapy.

"One of the lads patrolling the castle grounds found her at the base of the stairs up to the tower the next morning."

Tom said a swift and silent prayer for the soul of Regina Copeland. "John, I'm sure you did everything you could do."

John was silent a moment, rolling the darts in his fingers. "That wasn't Hugh's view."

"Yes?"

"The circumstances were . . . different, I didn't disagree with Hugh there. Regina had had these . . . melodramatic episodes in the past, as I said, but always ensuring—consciously or unconsciously, I don't know—that she would be rescued. And she always did these things at home. But threatening to jump off the castle tower was strange—I should have paid attention. And then her doing it. It's a half-mile walk. It was November. It was cold and mizzly, getting on for dark by four." John shook his head, as if to shake off a memory. "Hugh blamed me for not being home, for not getting home in time, for not allowing myself to be emotionally blackmailed, again. Worse, he got it into his head that it was no accident."

"You don't mean . . . "

"Yes, he suggested to police that I may have pushed her down the stairs."

Startled, Tom turned his attention from the dartboard. "But you were in Torquay, were you not? How could you be involved?"

"Tom, it takes less than half an hour to drive from Torquay to Noze. I could have driven home and been back to Torquay in short order."

"But—good heavens—surely someone in Torquay would have been able to identify you. Put you *in* Torquay at the time of your wife's death."

"An alibi."

"Yes."

"I did have an alibi." John paused and lifted a dart. "And I didn't."

Tom stepped from the pub into the cold, bitter air and glanced upwards as he held the door ajar for John. The night sky, pricked with stars, decanted into the coal blackness of the village, punctuated by squares of window light here and there winding up the hills. The hour was late. He didn't need his watch to tell him so: He could read the story in the arrangement of illuminated windows in the vicarage, a shadow looming past the low stone wall across Church Walk. Three gold squares below the roof proclaimed Madrun's waking presence in her private flat, but no light escaped from the floor below, where his daughter slept. Not for the first time, and certainly not for the last, he felt a stab of regret for his evening absences from Miranda's bedtime routine, but he could do nothing but let the feeling pass and thank God for his wise child's understanding. He looked to the windows of the ground floor where light behind sheer curtains cast a glow over a remnant snowdrift half covering the rose-bushes below the sill—a lamp in the sitting room for the master's return. Judith, he presumed, had gone to bed—but no, for as he and John descended the few stairs to the cobbles of Church Walk and turned towards Poynton Shute, Judith emerged into the circle of light afforded by the pub's security lamp, shining her torch in front of her.

"You're out late," Tom called to her.

"Visiting old friends," Judith called back, shining her torch on them, one to the other. "Are you coming?"

"Shortly. Go on ahead. We have a . . . something we have to do first."

"Oh, Mr. Copeland, I thought I might pay a visit to Noze Lydiard." She moved under the light.

"I'm afraid the castle is closed to visitors in the winter."

"That's all right. I visited it many times when I was a girl. What I meant was the estate, where you work."

"Well . . ."

"I've never been on a shooting estate, you see. There wasn't one at Noze when I was young."

"I'm not sure there would be much of interest to a . . . a . . . "

"To a woman?" Judith peered up at him, then glanced at Tom as if seeking an ally.

"Well . . ." John frowned, clearly discomfited. "We have an American syndicate coming on Monday and we're booked through to the end of the season."

"Then Sunday—afternoon? Lovely. I'll see you then, if I don't see you in church earlier."

Judith waved and continued towards the vicarage gate.

"Sorry," Tom murmured, feeling the need to apologise for his guest's behaviour.

"Bloody cheek."

"You could have said no."

"She caught me off guard."

"Well, best we don't go to the vicarage to talk. Let's go into the church for a minute." He felt in the pocket of his Barbour. "I've got the copy keys. Fred will have closed up hours ago. Have you got your torch?"

"Any word on a new verger?" John pulled the instrument from his coat pocket and switched it on, sending a beam of light along the cobbles.

"If you had been at the PCC meeting Tuesday evening, you'd know."

"I'm very sorry. I had something that needed doing."

Tom regretted his waspish tone. "It's all right. Briony tells me she's about finished the minutes, so you should have a copy emailed before long. Anyway, no, we're no further in attracting a new verger. I miss Sebastian," he added, referring to the previous incumbent. "He somehow fit the contours of the role. Fred means well. I can't fault him too much, but he does lack a certain . . . something. He's absolutely swimming in the verger's gown, and I'm not sure it's worth the expense having a new one fitted for him."

"At least he doesn't pinch the church silver."

"No, that's a blessing."

Fred Pike, village handyman, sexton, and general all-round good egg, was also the village kleptomaniac, a bent Thornfordites forgave and accommodated by trading back the purloined objects or selling them at fund-raising events for the church.

The two walked on in silence through the lych-gate and scrunched down the pea shingle path towards St. Nicholas's north porch. With the end of the pub quiz—with the prize-giving attended by much cheering—conversation in the Church House Inn had fallen swiftly to a sedate murmur, no damper to private and candid conversation. They had said their good-byes to Eric Swan, the landlord.

John aimed his torch on the ancient lock of the north door; Tom turned the key and pushed the great slab of oak open into the dark, then, groping, pushed the interior door into the charcoal gloom of the nave where column, wall, and pew blended into a single dormant mass. The air was glacial cold, an amalgam of ice and dust. When he had said his evening office in the chancel at six thirty he hadn't bothered to switch on the heating system.

"The vestry would be best," he said to John, who aimed his torch along the flagstones of the ancient floor. "There's the old space heater in there."

Unconcerned with aesthetics had been the moderniser who had installed fluorescent light in the vestry ceiling. The three bars flicked and buzzed after Tom pressed the switch, then cast a shocking glare over the lime-washed walls, garishly bleaching the tiny room's detritus: the litter of papers and old magazines, the stacks of frayed hymnals, the jumble of cleaning supplies, the boxes of candles, the bursting of clerical clothing peeking from a full corner closet. Under its pitiless blue-white brilliance, too, skin appeared pale and grey. Tom could see the unflattering effect on his own face in the clouded old wood-frame mirror over the vestry table before he crouched to activate the heater, then again in John's when he turned to face him. They stood, as even the single chair in the vestry supported a tower of books.

"I was telling you in the pub," John began, "that I had an alibi for the time of my wife's death. And that I didn't."

Tom nodded, waited.

"I booked a room at the Imperial—"

"Yes."

"—and stayed over."

"Then . . ." Tom shrugged, puzzled, "you had a credit card receipt. A waiter remembered you from the dining room . . ."

John shook his head. "I was only in the bar for a while. You see . . . I met a woman."

"Ah." Tom leaned his back into the edge of the vestry table. "I think I get the picture, John. But then wouldn't she be your alibi?"

"I only had her Christian name, you see, and even that, it turns out, wasn't real. She was in Torquay for a conference."

"Well, I suppose I should make some priestly remarks about infidelity, but . . . I must say, John, you work fast."

"It wasn't me who worked fast," John protested. "She was the one who invited me to *her* room."

" 'No thank you' is always an option."

"I lost my head. I know it was wrong, but after years of misery living with Regina . . . and she was beautiful, a stunner. "

"You're saying this woman couldn't be found."

"No, she couldn't. There were hundreds at the conference. The Imperial is enormous. Big staff. Lots of guests milling about. You know, you've been there, I'm sure."

"Aren't there security cameras in the halls?"

"This is nearly a dozen years ago. Security was less of a concern."

"Or CCTV clocking you leaving the parking area?"

John shrugged. "I think the police thought my involvement in Regina's death was a bit of a half-baked idea. They were only being goaded by Hugh."

"There was an inquest, of course. What was the ruling?"

John looked away. "The coroner ruled an open verdict."

Which meant, Tom considered, that insufficient evidence had

been found for suicide or accident or unlawful killing. In the eyes of the law, John was not yet free and clear of culpability. He took a full breath and said, "I can understand how distressing it can be to go through this sort of process." Tom gave a passing thought to the aftermath of his own wife's murder—the questions, the suspicions—and felt again a shiver of distaste. "I suppose it got in the papers."

"Some. The legend that Noze Lydiard Castle is haunted by ghosts who lure people to St. Hilda's tower and to their death didn't help."

"I can imagine. You said earlier that your wife's death bore some relation to—"

"It has to do with my alibi. You see, years later—five years, to be precise—I happened to meet the woman I'd been with that night."

"Yes . . . ?"

"It was at Upper Coombe Farm where Dave Shapley has his barbecues for the band in the summer. Will Moir had joined the Thistle But Mostly Rose that spring and since the invitation included wives or partners, he came with his wife." He paused. "Caroline Moir was the woman I'd been with."

Tom allowed an affect of surprise to play over his features, but he supposed he wasn't very convincing, for John folded his arms and said, "You don't seem . . . shocked."

"I am a little," Tom allowed. He didn't wish to say he knew the Moirs had had at least one significant bad patch in their marriage. Was this Torquay episode cause or effect? "But it hasn't escaped the notice of some of the women in the church that you appear to have a soft spot for Caroline."

John looked off towards the lancet window, his silence assent.

"Did you ask Caroline to confirm to authorities that you couldn't have driven back to Noze that night and pushed your wife down the castle stairs?"

"No, I didn't. How could I involve her in something so sordid?"

"Then . . . ?"

"There's something more, Tom." John twisted the cap in his hands. "Ariel is my child."

Tom started. "What *are* you talking about?"

"She is. I know it. Think about her. Think about what she looks like."

Tom wished to resist this speculation, but, unbidden, Ariel Moir's face shimmered into consciousness. He had seen her at play with Miranda many times, and in the company of Will or Caroline many times, too. Yes, it was true, Ariel did not appear, like her brother, Adam, to be a variation on the familial theme of litheness and blondness. Yes, she was dark-haired and sturdy-bodied. Yes, possibly, she could be a tiny female edition of the dark, sturdy-bodied, ruddy-faced man before him, but only possibly, where folk were swimming in the same crammed Anglo-Saxon-Celtic gene pool.

"But, John, all children don't look a match to their parents. Would you say Miranda is my spitting image? She looks more iden-tifiably like her mother, but I am as assured as any man can be that I am her father. What on earth has put this idea into your head?"

"Being at the vicarage Sunday confirmed it for me. Sitting at breakfast with Ariel. But I've wondered before, when I've glimpsed her with Caroline bringing her to Sunday school. It's there! It's in her face, in her gestures. I'm her father."

"You're *not* her father, John. It doesn't matter if you made some . . . genetic contribution. By law, a woman's husband is the fa-ther of her child. Will Moir is Ariel's father."

"But Will is dead."

The words fell between them like a sword.

"That changes nothing," Tom countered heatedly. The nasty thought that John had rid himself of Will in order to claim his woman and his child tore across his consciousness. "Will's death doesn't provide you with a claim to his child. It's outrageous to trou-ble Caroline with this—now, with Will not even buried. Don't tell me you've actually broached this with Caroline? Oh, Lord, you have. I can read it in your face."

"I'm thinking of Ariel," John protested, his face reddening again.

"That's why you weren't at Tuesday's meeting, yes? You were at Thorn Court with Caroline. How can you say you're thinking of Ariel? Any sort of inkling of this—at this time—would hurt and confuse the girl terribly. John, have you lost your mind?"

"What would happen if something happened to Caroline?"

"What *could* happen to Caroline? She's still a young woman."

"And Will was a reasonably young man."

"He was a healthy young man until someone poisoned him, John."

"What would happen if something happened to Caroline?" John persisted. "Who would take care of Ariel?"

"But it's none of your business."

"But who?"

Tom released an exasperated sigh. He knew Will had no living parents, no siblings. But Caroline wasn't bereft.

"Caroline's mother," he said.

"She's elderly and living on the other side of the world."

"There's Nick."

"Would you be happy seeing a court award Ariel to Nick Stanhope's care?"

"Adam."

"He's barely out of childhood himself. Too immature to raise a child."

"You work with him."

"That's how I know."

"John, I'll grant you the possibility that something could remove Caroline from the picture. Something could take any of us, couldn't it? We could be hit by a car speeding down a lane. But I can't grant the probability. I'm not sure what you want me to do."

"My hope is that Caroline will tell you it's true."

"That you're Ariel's father? Which, I take, she didn't countenance Tuesday."

"Yes."

"But to what end, John?"

"So that Ariel will be safe."

"That seems both vague and fraught."

"I can't say more."

"Besides the inappropriateness of mentioning any of this conversation to Caroline, it's the urgency that eludes me."

"I'm afraid, Tom, it doesn't elude me."

The Vicarage

Thornford Regis TC9 6QX

16 JANUARY

Dear Mum,
It was so lovely to get another letter from you. I know how hard
it is for you to put pen to paper what with your arthritis and all,
but your words cheered me so. Yes, I did flush the yewberries
down the loo. There were about six quarts of them left in the big
freezer. I thought no matter what was to come from the inquest I
best not keep such things at the vicarage. I began to worry that
Miranda might root through the freezer one day and something
dreadful happen, though of course it wouldn't because I am so
careful, but still, I wouldn't want to go through what I've gone
through this week all over again. No sooner had Mr. Christmas
left for town yesterday afternoon when the two detectives from
Totnes arrived at the vicarage to talk to me about my baking
and other things. They were the same two who parked them-
selves in the village last spring after poor Sybella Parry was
found dead in that huge drum in the village hall, one of them

named Blessing, who it turns out is a younger brother of the Sandra Blessing I went to school with and now does something at the Dartmoor National Park Authority. I got the sense that they weren't best pleased that I had got rid of the berries, but I told them they wouldn't have found a single seed in any of them. They wondered what I did with the seeds after I picked them and prepared them for freezing and I told them that they went down the loo, too. Had I ever ground the seeds into a mash or dried them and made them into a powder or such, they asked, and of course I said no because of what possible use could that be, though it did occur to me afterwards perhaps ground yew seeds might prove useful against mice, although we have Powell and Gloria guarding the vicarage against vermin so really it would be a waste of time. The reason they asked is that at the inquest yesterday morning, the ~~pith~~ pathologist said poor Will Moir had rather a lot of yew poison in him. (There's a proper name for it, but I can't remember.) I didn't go to the inquest, as I said I wouldn't, but Mr. Christmas did and came back and told me about it as I was making lunch (a very nice omelet). Terrible to say in a way, but I felt relieved. No one could possibly believe I would leave a whole lot of the bad bits of the berry in my pastry, I thought, and said so to Mr. C and he agreed with me, though I had a wobble when the detectives came later and looked at me as if I had deliberately put a whole lot of the bad bits in my pastry and began asking me questions about my "relationship" with the Moirs, as if I had one. I told them they were a very handsome couple and a great asset to the village and that I knew of no one who wished them any harm. They took away the note I told you about, the one asking me to send some pastries over to the Burns Supper, slipped it into a little plastic bag like the ones I use for Miranda's sandwiches for school. I told them I hadn't a clue who'd sent it. I was glad when they left. I told myself I mustn't worry and Mr. Christmas says I mustn't worry, but I still feel a

*bit shattered, truth be told. After Mr. C gave me the news of the
inquest I thought perhaps I would go ahead and contribute
something to the baking stall at tomorrow's Wassail, but after the
police left, I thought better of it, as perhaps it might not be
bought. I shall attend the Wassail, though, Mum. I'm not having
people wondering why I'm not there, as I am every year. Besides,
it will be Miranda's first Wassail and she is so looking forward
to it, and I suggested to Judith—our guest, as I've
mentioned—that she might enjoy it and she said she was keen to
go, as she remembered it when she was a girl. Yesterday, after the
police left, I went with Judith to the Tidy Dolly, which she is
thinking of buying. What with all the snow, it's taken this long
for an estate agent from Leitchfield Turner to make herself
available! Anyway, the agent who was named Gillian was
really quite chatty. She knew all kinds of things about Thornford. I'm not sure how interested Judith is really about taking on
the tearoom, but she had some firm questions for Gillian about
how much trade the tearoom gets and would have to look at the
books and of course the economy isn't up to much these days, and
who knows if there will be fewer coach tours this summer, but
Gillian was very "positive" as these estate agents always are and
pointed out that as many as 20 new cottages were going up in
the heart of the village before very long, meaning perhaps 60 or
80 more folk living and trading in the village, which would
boost trade at the Tidy Dolly. I knew she meant Thorn Court
and said it was just an old rumour that someone wanted to buy
the land and turn it into housing, but she said she had heard
that with Will Moir passed away, the widow was selling. I said
I didn't think so as Caroline so loves the place she spent her childhood in, but Gillian said one of the investors was owed a lot of
money and wanted it back and the only way to get it was to sell.
That could only be Nick Stanhope, I thought, as I've heard from
Tamara who had heard it from Adam Moir that Nick put*

money into Thorn Court when the Moirs bought it, though it wouldn't surprise me he wanted the money back as I hear he has debts of his own. I thought to myself that surely money troubles would at least be behind Caroline now, as Will must be insured in some fashion, and Nick could probably have his money if he were so keen to have it. I asked if the investor were Nick Stanhope and she said yes. She said she knows folk at Moorgate Properties who told her Nick is angling to be an exclusive supplier of security systems to the new homes they're building all over south Devon. I thought that was a bit rich, Nick cosying up to a company that wants to do his sister out of her home. Judith said nothing about the Stanhopes would surprise her and that they all had a streak of ruthlessness about them. What's bred in the bone comes out in the flesh, she said. I don't think Judith is very fond of the Stanhopes. The other day she told me a story her father told her about Caroline's ~~grandfather~~ great-grandfather Rupert going about the village on his horse and setting his whip on folk who got in his way. Do you know any of this, Mum? Of course you wouldn't. This was before the Great War. But then there are stories about Caroline's father and women who weren't his wife, aren't there? And old Arthur Stanhope ran roughshod over his staff, they used to say, so maybe there's some truth to it, though I think Caroline Moir is really quite lovely. Judith went up to Thorn Court yesterday evening saying she was going to pay her respects to Caroline, which I thought was a bit odd as Judith had left Thornford before Caroline was born, but then Judith's family worked for the Stanhopes for generations. Anyway, I had gone up to bed before she returned, so I assume they had a good natter. I haven't faced Caroline myself. I did send a casserole up with Mr. Christmas earlier in the week, but I didn't know then how Will had died, so now I can't help thinking how ~~inapropr inapproppr~~ poor a gesture that was. Karla is quite ~~adi-~~

~~man~~ *firm that I'm guilty of nothing more than not questioning anonymouse requests for baking contributions, which of course I will do in the future. Anyway, I believe Mr. C is going up to Thorn Court this morning to discuss funeral arrangements with Caroline, so perhaps he'll know better the state of her mind in the wake of this unhappy event, which reminds me that I must give him Becca Kaif's torch to take back, as I found it under the sofa when I was hoovering the carpet yesterday. I'm not sure if I ought to go to the funeral, though I always find funerals so soothing. Bit of odd news, Mum, before I sign off. I went through the churchyard yesterday morning to take your letter to the post office. You don't very often see anyone there on a weekday morning in winter other than Fred on occasion, digging a grave or tidying the grass, but I noticed this tall woman in a long black fur coat near the bottom of the graveyard where Sybella was buried last year. You remember Oona Blanc, Colm Parry's ex-wife, the model, who disgraced herself at her own daughter's funeral last spring? I didn't think women like that got up before noon and what on earth would she be doing down here in January? She was wearing sunglasses, and who wears sunglasses on the sorts of grey days we get in winter unless they're famous? But no one believed me at the post office. "Is there a great ruddy limousine parked out on Church Walk?" old Mr. Snell said, as if models only get about in limousines, silly man, but even Karla said Oona'd have to have dropped from the sky not to be noted coming into the village, which is probably true, though Mr. C said some type of sports car nearly ran Roger and him over in Pennycross Road Saturday night. I went back to the vicarage down Poynton Shute and looked at the registration marks on the number plates to see if any were from London, but there wasn't a one, so I suppose I could be wrong. I must say, Mum, I haven't had the best week, what with more flat Yorkshires, folk going off my*

lovely food, and now them thinking I'm ~~having hattoocin halu-~~
~~tinn~~ going mad. Anyway, as you always say, this too shall pass.
Must get on with things now. We're all otherwise well here, cats
included, and Bumble, and I hope you are, too. Love to Aunt
Gwen.

Much love,
Madrun

CHAPTER TWENTY

*H*ave you got a minute? Come and see the Wassail lanterns the children have made." Eileen Lennox, head teacher at Thornford Regis C of E Primary, dabbed at her eyes while Tom repacked his old leather magic bag.

"That last trick was really marvellous," she gushed, her hand pressed against the large floppy bow at the neck of her blouse. "And so true. Goodness, I must look a mess."

"You look fine."

Tom had heard from Miranda that Mrs. Lennox seemed to find many things tear-worthy these days and wondered if she was going through a bad patch of some nature. In truth, her mascara was smudged and her lipstick, a rather vibrant red, seemed to have skidded past the usual boundaries. Perhaps, he thought, busy woman that she was, she applied makeup in the car—she lived north of the village—an uncertain task on a grey winter morning.

"Each snowflake that comes down from above is unique and

beautiful, just as each of you is unique and beautiful," she intoned, paraphrasing part of Tom's closing remarks to the Friday-morning school assembly of the Tigers and Leopards, Years Three through Six, respectively. Somehow, from Mrs. Lennox's lips, his words sounded slightly insipid and he wondered if he should revise them before he performed that particular trick again in front of school-children. "However do you do it?"

"The snow trick?" Tom closed the clasp on his bag.

"Yes."

"I'm afraid I can't say, Mrs. Lennox. I'm still a member of The Magic Circle in London and they would have my guts for you-know-what if I spilled the beans." In fact, the snow trick was fairly simple, a combination of special paper, water, and sleight of hand, but it produced a lovely, gasp-making finale to a performance, as a simple cutout paper doily snowflake transmogrified into a shower of snow.

"I see, yes," Mrs. Lennox responded. "My husband is a member of the Paignton Rotary and they would have his viscera, too, if he revealed anything of what they get up to." Mention of her husband seemed to put some starch into her persona. She took a final dab at her eyes, then focused on his. A news story of some Rotary members misbehaving with a stripper at a club in Torquay flitted through Tom's mind, and the look he exchanged with Mrs. Lennox signaled realisation of a common thought.

"Anyway," Tom said quickly, gesturing to the floor, which was littered with a confetti blizzard of white paper. "I am sorry for the mess."

"It's nothing. Well worth it." She led him from the school hall, which had been exited by the students five minutes earlier. "And apropos given the weather we've had the past week."

"That's what put it into my mind."

"I hope we don't see snow like that again for a good long time. It played havoc with our scheduling. Lantern-making was to have been Sunday afternoon, with Nancy Ablett, our itinerant primary art teacher, at the Old School House."

"Yes, I know. Miranda was disappointed."

"Anyway," Mrs. Lennox continued, "Ms. Ablett was able to come yesterday afternoon. There's just some finishing touches to do, and the children all take them home this afternoon and have them in time for the Wassail tomorrow."

Long trestle tables formed a square within the square of the light-filled teaching room, itself a modern extension of the Victorian stone building that housed Thornford Regis Primary. Rising above the detritus of paper and paste and scissors and tape on the tables were skeletal frameworks of wicker or willow in shapes both wondrously abstract and ponderously specific, some clothed in translucent paper and embellished with paint or ink or trimmed with strips of coloured paper or stickers or stars or moons, or pricked with tiny holes in flowery patterns.

"They're splendid," Tom remarked, plucking one, a vibrant aquamarine-blue fish with comically oversized fins, from the table nearest him and letting it dangle in the air off its carrying pole. "Though this one has spots." It did, small purple circles dotted all over its paper skin. "A fish with measles?"

"I think it's supposed to be a shark." Mrs. Lennox frowned at the thing. "But with spots, as you say."

"Which one is Miranda's, I wonder?"

She glanced around the tables. "I do know, but I think I should let her surprise you later."

"Fair enough." Tom gently returned the shark and continued his inspection of the others. "And are they safe?"

"Installing little battery torchlights has been considered," she replied, "but everyone seems to love the candles. More atmospheric, I suppose. See"—she lifted one, an unexceptional pink ball, for examination—"the votive candles are secured very firmly to the frame with string and glue. We've never had an accident, knock on wood, and heaven knows it more often than not rains at Wassail, so water is more of a concern than fire."

Tom was silent a moment, passing his eyes over the shapes along the tables.

"I expect you think this is all rather pagan," Mrs. Lennox remarked, following his glance.

"What?"

"I say, I expect you think this is all rather pagan. You were frowning."

"Was I? Oh! Well, yes, it is rather pagan. But I don't expect Thornfordites to suddenly start worshipping Woden, so I'm not too bothered. No, I was noticing a certain . . . colour theme running through the lanterns."

"Oh, yes, the violet, or lavender perhaps, for the trim or decoration. It does seem to be this season's thing! Whether it's crayons or jumpers, not a year goes by that the girls don't have to have something in a certain colour, although I expect Garner Tait put the purple spots on his shark to tease the girls. See, the girls' ones tend to be bells or stars or hearts." She lifted one of the hearts, ivory in shade, crudely shaped, covered with smaller purple hearts. "Hearts . . . " She shook her head. "Wait until they find theirs broken."

Tom frowned at her and wondered if he should ask a leading question, then thought better of it. He had another pressing appointment this morning.

"Who's responsible for the supplies, for the lanterns?" he asked instead, lifting a piece of the purple paper.

"Ms. Ablett comes with the tissue paper and willow sticks. But the children are encouraged to come with anything they like for decoration."

"Do you know who brought this in?" Tom rubbed the paper between two fingers. "It's really just notepaper, I think. Not construction paper."

Mrs. Lennox's brow furrowed. "I'm not sure. Why? Is it important?"

"No." Tom tossed off the response, but he was beginning to think it might be.

"Actually, I have a notion it might have been Ariel Moir. I can see her—" She squinted as if reviewing the children filing in in the morning. "—carrying a small sheaf."

"Ariel? How odd."

"Is it?"

"Oh . . ." Tom groped for a satisfying response. "I'm just . . . thinking Caroline might have kept her from school."

"She wasn't here Wednesday when school reopened, but she did return yesterday, I expect in part for the lantern-making. Such an awful business! I'm sure Mrs. Moir wants to restore some normalcy for Ariel—well, as much as it can be restored, poor child. We sat the children down and had a little discussion about Mr. Moir's death, so they would be prepared, but I must say some of them are still a little tentative. Your Miranda is very good with Ariel, though."

"Well, as you may know, it's something she's gone though herself."

"Yes, I had heard." Mrs. Lennox blessed him with a sympathetic smile.

A red Astra crossed Tom's field of vision as he stepped from the path up to Thorn Court and onto the level black asphalt of the hotel's forecourt. DI Bliss was visible in the passenger seat; he turned his head at that moment, presenting Tom with squinting eyelids in the frame of the window, but he signalled no awareness of his presence. Tom watched the car disappear through the gates and begin the climb up Pennycross Road and out of the village and recalled for one piercing moment his own sufferance of police intrusion in the midst of crashing grief, the dread at seeing once more the CID, the jolt at hearing yet again their voices on the telephone. He felt curiously allied with Caroline, a woman whose spouse, too, had died suddenly and without warning, who was left with a young daughter to bring up on her own, and who, he suspected, was now, for the police, a person of interest, as he himself had been in the days after Lisbeth's death. And yet there was no answer at the door to the Annex; nor could he find Caroline when he went next door and wandered through Thorn Court's empty reception rooms. Hammering and crashing from the floor above sent him upstairs, but a boilersuited, plaster-covered worker there could only shrug at his enquiry for the mistress of the house. Finally, he found Caroline outside, tucked into a corner of the converted stables, in huddled conversation with a large, balding man in a yellow safety vest. A flexible ductwork like a great loopy noodle led from one of the upper-storey windows to the flatbed of a truck; above it clouds of grey dust rose and fell to the tempo of cascading bits of plaster and lathe and carpeting. The parking area contained a number of vans with their purposes emblazoned on them—TAVERNER AND SONS BUILDERS, JTL PLUMBING, further evidence that the hotel renovations had resumed in earnest.

"I'll get right on it, Mrs. Moir," Tom could hear the foreman say as he approached. He noted with amusement the man's beefy hand sweep towards his forehead, almost as if he were to grasp a forelock and tug it, though hairs were few on the man's bulldog head.

After glimpsing Tom and dismissing the foreman, Caroline said, "I'm so sorry, I've been delayed this morning." She shifted the sleeve of her puffa jacket and glanced at her watch. "I knew you were coming at ten thirty."

"You had visitors. I saw them leaving."

"I don't know what the police think I can tell them." Caroline said it with some heat in her voice, leading him back towards Thorn Court's front entrance. "I wasn't here Saturday evening. And I didn't cook the meal. Can't they understand how awful this is for me?"

"They must go through their routines, I expect. You mustn't take it personally."

"I don't know how else to take it."

"Well, I mean as a personal attack." Though saying it, he realised how at times the detectives from Bristol CID had made him feel their questions were exactly that, informed by some inexplicable animus. "I'm sure they'll come to some resolution before very long."

Tom could feel her body tense alongside his. In her eyes, he thought he could read a wariness—worse, a flicker of fear—before she turned her head away; the glimpse troubled and confounded him. She led him through the lobby and around the front desk to the hotel office.

"It's warmer here," she said unnecessarily. "The heat's at bare minimum in the rest of the hotel. Take a seat."

Tom chose one of the well-worn burgundy leather armchairs facing a mahogany pedal desk of late-Victorian vintage, not unlike his own in the vicarage study, and nearest a hissing gas fire set into the recess of a fireplace along one wall. Though small and window-less, the room, with its cream walls and minimal decoration, felt cosy, more like a sanctuary-retreat than the busy office of a country hotel, despite the computer, the printer, the photocopier, and the other apparatus of the modern age. A couch against one wall, cov-ered in the same aged leather as the armchairs and festooned in sagging silk pillows, suggested decades of surreptitious naps—somehow, Tom sized the concavity, by some male figure. The room felt clubby and masculine, missing only the tabaccanalia of an earlier era, though one corner contained a narrow gun cabinet containing, he counted, four shotguns.

"Do you shoot?" he asked wonderingly.

"I can, actually. My father taught me in Australia. But I don't. Those were my grandfather's." She gestured towards the cabinet. "My father carted those to Australia, then brought them back. Nick and I shared the collection when he died. Will takes—took—one of them out once a year to shoot it at the Wassail, and that's the extent of it."

Still wondering at the room's provenance, Tom found his eyes travelling up the wall over the couch with its row of framed prints to a decorative ceiling rose, which, instead of being centred and pricked with some light fixture, was within inches of the coving, its central hole plugged.

"I don't know why my grandfather didn't have that removed," Caroline said, following his glance as she sat behind the desk. "You can see how the room once was." She gestured towards the artwork on the wall, which Tom, on closer inspection, could see were architectural renderings of Thorn Court when it was a private home. The foyer then was the smaller room, much so; the office, where they were seated, the larger.

"I don't think they bothered to move the furniture when they moved the wall. The desk and sofa are impossible to get through the door. The gun cabinet is built in. Even Van Haute, the hoteliers my father sold Thorn Court to, never tried." Caroline shifted absently through the stack of post in a tray. "Still, it's lovely to have Grandfather's things so close to hand."

"You were fond of your grandfather, I remember you saying when we last talked."

"Yes." Caroline glanced at him. "He was lovely to me, at any rate. I was his only grandchild—at the time. Nick, of course, was born some time after he'd died. I think grandparents often have fonder relationships with their grandchildren than their children, don't you? They must work all the fright and worry from their systems. I know my father and grandfather did not rub along too well together, to say the least." Her smile was mirthless. "And I'm sure some of the older villagers might take a different view of my grandfather. He was a businessman after all. When you're in business, sometimes you have to do unpalatable things."

"I wonder what we shall be like as grandparents?" Tom opened his jacket.

"One has to get through parenting first."

"Yes, that's true. You do have Adam on his way, though." He smiled. "You may be a grandmother sooner than you know . . . or wish." He was jolted to see Caroline's face shudder suddenly, as if a cold wind had blasted it. "I'm so sorry. That was gauche. I didn't mean to suggest . . . of course Adam is very young . . . "

"He's twenty."

"And Tamara is very set on getting her education, so I don't think—"

"I'm not being a snob, Tom." She looked at him, apology in her eyes. "I don't care that her father runs a garage. I run a hotel. I'm not sure there's a great difference. My grandfather would be appalled to know his great-grandson was an underkeeper, but it's a different world. For heaven's sake, a prince of England married a party planner's daughter."

"Then?"

"I—" She faltered. "Sometimes . . . girls, women get it into their heads—you probably don't know this, being a man—to have a baby, to get pregnant, regardless of the consequences."

"I suppose." Tom frowned, confused. "I tend to associate that with naïve teenage girls, though. Young teens. Tamara is nineteen, but she's a very smart young woman, from what I can tell, who is very much set on her education. A baby would be the last thing on her mind, surely. You would know better, of course. You've seen them together."

"Tom, it's something else. It's . . . " She stopped, seeming to rein in some strong emotion.

"Good heavens, what? Caroline, you look absolutely shaken. I'm sure Tamara's no trouble. She's going to be, I think, some sort of environmentalist. She's quite single-minded—"

"Like her aunt?"

"Oh, surely . . . !"

"I'm sorry, I'm overwrought."

"Mrs. Prowse is keeping a stiff upper lip, but I think she's quite upset to think she may be accused—"

"Tom, you must tell her that I hold her responsible in no way. Really. The idea is too outlandish."

"Well, I'm sure Madrun will be greatly relieved to hear it. But I don't understand your concern about Tamara and Adam."

Caroline's expression remained drawn. "I'm sure in many ways Tamara would be a fine match for my . . . well, somewhat immature son, but . . . Oh, look, I shouldn't be concerning myself about their relationship. Not now, not when Adam has just lost his father. He's too young to have lost his father. Will wasn't much older when he lost his mother."

"You're too young to have lost your husband," Tom said gently.

"And you're too young to have lost your wife."

"But your suffering is fresh, Caroline, raw."

"I'm finding the waiting almost unbearable, Tom. At least with Daddy's funeral, there was only a three-day wait. But with the snow and the inquest, and now the police, and my mother—she won't arrive from Sydney until Monday and I should give her a day to rest . . . " She sighed. "We must get on with it, mustn't we?"

"I find it helps in healing. Do you know Will's wishes?"

"He had them written down. I thought there might be a copy in the Annex, but I couldn't find it, so I retrieved the papers from the bank."

"Yesterday? I saw you pop out of Barclays and go down the High Street."

"Oh, did you? Sorry, if I went right by you without saying hello."

"I saw you from The Nosh Pit's window. I was having a coffee." He decided not to say with whom. "You looked rather upset."

The computer chimed softly. Caroline glanced unseeingly at the screen. "I . . . yes . . . well, it's all these final things, you know, the will, other papers . . . I went to Thompson's . . ."

"Yes, their director called me late yesterday."

"I made the presumption that you would take the funeral. I should have consulted you first—"

"Nonsense." Tom waved his hand dismissively. "Tuesday? Will your mother have time to recover from the time change?"

Caroline nodded. "Adam would prefer a green funeral. I understand his concerns, but it's not his father's wish. I told him that. Here . . ." She pulled a sheet of paper from a file and handed it to him. "This has hymn suggestions. Of course Will would like the pipe band to . . ." Her voice broke. "I'm sorry."

"I understand." Tom waited for Caroline to recover her composure, then passed his eyes over the text, which was handwritten, and unexpectedly careful, clear, and legible—somehow he imagined Will dashing off instructions in short, swift strokes—to the paper itself. Again, that colour, that pale shade of purple—it seemed to be everywhere.

"This looks fine," he said. For hymns, Will chose "For All the Saints," "Who Would True Valour See," and "Guide Me, O Thou Great Redeemer." His wishes were quite precise. "It was thoughtful of Will to have had this at the ready. Many don't until they're much older. If at all."

"Yes," Caroline responded slowly, as if taken from some private thought, "it does . . . help, doesn't it?"

"This is quite recently written, too, is it not? Something about the paper . . ."

"It must be recent." Caroline frowned, as Tom set the sheet on the desk. "It looks like part of the stationery samples I got from Farbarton's in the High Street the other week. We were considering new letterhead, brochures, cards, and suchlike to go with the renovations. A new look."

They both stared at the paper a moment, Tom pricked by the

peculiar notion that Will had some premonition his life was drawing to a close. And yet how could that be when his end was wrought—most cruelly, most unexpectedly—by some outside agency? Is it possible, he wondered, to truly sense nemesis in your midst and feel helplessly pulled under, arranging last things your only recourse? He looked to Caroline, trying to gauge her thoughts, but her expression remained shuttered; only her hollow, bruised eyes hinted of the suffering of the last days. Both their hands reached for the sheet of paper at the same time, Tom, the nearer, gripping it first, then tugging against Caroline's pulling.

"Shall I take this with me?" he asked.

For a second they seemed to contend over possession, then Caroline dropped her hand. "Of course, you must," she said. "But—"

"I will return it. It's just so I won't forget the details. I'll need to let Colm know about the music."

"Why don't I make you a photocopy?"

A muffled shout from the lobby shifted their attention. A flash of pique crossed Caroline's face as she rose, opened the door, and stepped from the office. A rustle of paper and a young male-voiced enquiry of Caroline if she was Mrs. Moir reached Tom's ears, before she returned half hidden by an enormous paper cone.

"Goodness!" Tom exclaimed.

"I wish people wouldn't send flowers."

"Who are they from?"

Caroline shifted the cone to the crook of her arm and tugged a small sellotaped envelope. "Here," she said, handing the package to Tom as she peeled back the envelope's flap. Tom dropped the cone between his seated knees, catching a moist hint of hothouse blooms through the wrapping paper, and watched Caroline's face tighten as she pulled out a small card and read it.

"Oh, for God's sake." The dismay in her voice was palpable.

"Dare I ask?"

"John Copeland." She took the package from Tom and tore the paper along the top. "They're roses—pink roses."

Tom frowned. "I suppose it's an understatement to say roses are an odd choice." He watched her toss the package onto the desk, then reread the card.

"May I?" Tom asked.

Caroline hesitated, moved to pass the card over, then reconsidered. "No, I don't think so. Sorry, Tom. It's too . . ." Her mouth formed a grim line as she slipped the card into her trouser pocket, but a certain intelligence passed between them, and in the flicker of her eyes Tom saw a fresh anxiety.

"Caroline, John isn't . . . bothering you in some fashion, is he?"

She looked away. "No . . . not really. No. Well, not until this. I've been a widow for less than a week, for heaven's sake. I suppose I should be grateful they're not red." The anxiety in her eyes lingered, now glossed with a lie: She *was* bothered. "He's told you, hasn't he?"

"I'm not sure—"

"He has told you. He's told you *something*."

"Caroline, you put me in a difficult position. People do tend to tell me things that they mightn't tell anyone else." His hand stole towards his clerical collar. "It seems to come with the job."

"I think it has more to do with your kindly face."

"In either case, I feel duty-bound to keep my counsel."

Caroline resumed her seat. She regarded her computer screen and tapped aggressively on the keyboard for a moment as if needing the time to think. "Then I will tell you, knowing that you're duty-bound to keep your counsel—" Her face reddened. "—that what John has told you is true—"

"Caroline—"

"That I knew him before I returned to Thornford to live."

"Caroline, you needn't—"

"That I met John at a hotel in Torquay ten . . . more! years ago, that we slept together, and that Ariel is his child—his *biological* child."

Tom felt cuffed by the force of her fury. He struggled for a response. "Which you have not admitted to John—"

"Which I bloody won't! Ariel is *my* child. Mine and Will's. I can't be having this sort of contention in my life. Not now! Now with so much else to bear!"

"I know, Caroline," Tom said soothingly. "I think perhaps John has become animated by the possibility of a child—his child. He had an unhappy marriage, a childless one. He leads a sort of life of routine—"

"He has that woman, what's her name? Helen somebody, who caters the shooting lunches—"

"But—"

"*And* he has my son living on the estate."

"John isn't the most subtle of men, I suppose, but I don't think he intends to—"

"He can make no claim!"

"I was going to say, I don't think he intends to intrude on your life." Although saying it he wondered if it were true. In the vestry the night before, John had been, at best, ambiguous about his intentions.

Caroline shot him a hard glance. "I'm not convinced. I can feel his eyes on me in the procession on Sunday. I have done since we moved here. I can feel his attention on me at those bloody pipe band barbecues or any other time village events conspire to bring us to the same place."

"You are an attractive woman, Caroline."

"I'm not sure that's something I want to hear at this time, Tom."

"I merely meant that perhaps he feels there's something lacking—"

"There *is* that Helen."

"We don't know the nature of their . . . Sorry, I can't seem to say the right thing."

"It's called 'holding a torch,' Tom. And John's held it far too long for it to be healthy."

Tom glanced at the spray of roses, hothouse creations with heavy pink heads, forced to short life, doomed to quick death—a gift he recognised as a masculine gesture obvious and unimaginative and, in this instance, ill judged and exceedingly ill timed. What did pink symbolise? Admiration, perhaps? Gratitude? Sentiments less intense than love, he considered, as a silence descended on the room and a muffled clatter from the workmen above filled the void. He didn't credit John with subtlety; some wise florist likely talked him out of red roses.

"Did Will know?" Tom asked after a moment.

Caroline appeared to soften as she considered his question. "Yes," she said at last. "Yes, if you mean did he know that Ariel was not his. But, no, he knew nothing about John, and if he guessed, he never said. Not to me, and I can't imagine he would have told anyone else."

Tom felt a surge of tenderness and pity for Will, for the loss of this decent man. "You alluded at the marriage preparation class that your marriage did go through a sticky patch."

"That was the time. It was worse than sticky. I learned that Will—" She stopped herself suddenly, a look of horror creeping in her eyes.

"You needn't tell me more." Tom swiftly lifted his palms in a gesture of interdiction. He didn't really wish to know, but he could imagine: Perhaps Will had not been so decent, had had an indiscretion, too, and so Caroline, willfully, vengefully, had had hers, but with manifest consequence. It was not unknown. Such rancorous antics had slipped into his own mind, too, in the dark dispiriting days after he had plucked the photograph of Lisbeth clutched in the

arms of some "dark stranger" off his desk at St. Dunstan's. Blind-
sided by the picture's innuendo, trust splintered, he felt himself staggering through the next fortnight, though he fought to present a
reasonable facsimile of a dedicated vicar in his parish and attentive
father of a six-year-old. He felt a fraud as a pastoral counselor, the
clever dick who blithely advised troubled couples to air their hurts
with candour and love, and a fake as a hitherto uxorious husband,
turning away from shared intimacies until finally, with no evening
meeting to excuse his absence, with Miranda at her grandparents in
London and Ghislaine out on a date, Lisbeth corralled him to the
kitchen to do the washing-up and demanded to know what in sodding hell had got up his nose lately. With disquiet, Tom put down
the plate he was drying, pulled from his trouser pocket the picture,
now much creased, and held it up for her inspection. Lisbeth glanced
at it, glanced at him, and then again at the photograph. "Thank
you," she said coldly, returning her rubber-gloved hand to the water.
"It might do as evidence, should I need it."

"For what?" was all Tom, confounded by her aplomb, could say.

"Listen to me, Father Christmas." An appellation she used only
in two moods: ardour or anger. "What do you think is going on in
that picture?"

"It looks like you're making love to a man who is not your husband!"

"I'm being *assaulted* by a man who is not my husband! If your
private detective—"

"I didn't—"

"—had snapped a picture two seconds later, it would have been
of me pushing him over the bonnet of his car!" She paused, her voice
rimed with disgust. "He's a pharmaceutical rep from OndaFöretag.
They're bloody nuisances most of the time. I'm against accepting
any gifts, large or small, from these people, *as you know*, but I agreed
to lunch with him . . . Julian . . . I'm not sure why, really. He was
new, awfully persistent and—" She turned back to Tom with dismay.

"I'll confess, not hard on the eyes, so I thought, all right, this once. I didn't know he had a screw loose. I've made a formal complaint, and with any justice he'll be peddling pots and pans in Cumbria."

Appraising candour in those wonderful green-flecked eyes, Tom felt a full measure of relief flood over him. But of course wounds don't magically seal over. Each worried that the other had masked distress. Each wondered what spawned this wary-chary episode. Embarrassment? Worry? Sheer workaday exhaustion? But as First Corinthians would have loved keeping no record of wrongs, they sprinted to the bedroom to wipe the slate clean. It was only afterwards in bed that their thoughts flowed towards the riddle of the photographer's motive and identity. Tom could not bear to even paraphrase the ugly words of the accompanying poison-pen letter, and so—perhaps unwisely (he could never know)—he kept its existence from Lisbeth. Their marriage had only wobbled. Will and Caroline's had foundered. Laudable was that it had not been irrevocably shattered. Will might have shunned his wife, disowned the child forming inside her, and started a new life with someone else, but he had made the generous choice, sacrificing pride for love.

"The important part was that you were able to forgive each other, yes?" Tom asked Caroline.

She nodded.

"And you were happy in your marriage? You always seemed happy. Many have remarked to me what a loving couple you always appeared."

"Yes." Caroline blinked, her eyes glistening. "Yes, we were happy."

"Then that's all that matters."

CHAPTER TWENTY-ONE

*P*aying a pastoral visit, Vicar?"

"Not really. I'm returning this." Tom pulled a small torch from his jacket pocket to show to DI Bliss. "Molly's daughter must have left it at our place last weekend. My housekeeper found it rolled under the sofa this morning."

"Pity. I think you'll find that Mrs. Kaif is in want of a pastoral visit, or something along that line."

"I'm confused."

"Welcome to our world."

"I'm not sure that enlightens."

"Mrs. Kaif has confessed to poisoning Will Moir."

"*What!* But how . . . then why . . ." Tom stumbled over his words. He glanced sharply at Damara Cottage, past the arresting swirl of colour, flowers, and doodles emblazoned on the cob exterior to the front window where Molly Kaif stood, the pulled-back curtain in her hand.

"If you're asking why we aren't escorting her to Totnes station to further help us with our enquiries, all I can say is, we're giving it a bloody good think. A quick resolution to Mr. Moir's untimely death would certainly make our lives easier. Then we could get back to the important work of tracking down lead-roof thieves."

"Are you sure you should be telling me this?"

"That we are telling you this is an indication of how seriously we're taking Mrs. Kaif's confession."

"I'm detecting equivocation."

Bliss grunted ambiguously. "Coppers we may be, but we do know Mrs. Kaif has been in some distress since the death of her son. On the other hand—"

"On the other hand, motive, means, and opportunity," Blessing interrupted grimly.

Tom looked from one to the other. "Do I understand you two to have divergent views?"

"We are as of one mind, are we not, Sergeant?"

"Yes, sir."

"And of course, Vicar, we rely utterly, as always, on your complete discretion."

Tom watched them retreat to their car, tucked next to the gate to Damara Cottage, wondering a little at Bliss's candour, chattiness, and, possibly, compassion. Perhaps his bowels were in decent running order this morning.

"And a word of warning, Vicar." Bliss turned as he fit his key into the car lock.

"Yes?"

"Avoid the tea."

"Tea, Vicar?" Molly led him down the corridor to the kitchen, which, unlike Damara Cottage's riotous exterior (censured by the parish council for insensitive use of masonry paint colours), exercised a little decorative restraint. He had intended only to hand over Becca's torch, but his hostess had seemed intent on having him in, going so far as to take his hand and almost pull him over the doorsill.

"Well . . ."

"I brewed it for my two . . . visitors. It isn't fully steeped, if you're wondering. It benefits from a long stew."

"Then I guess a cup wouldn't go amiss."

Tom watched her lift the cosy, knitted patchwork with an orange bobble top, from a large grey earthenware teapot on the kitchen sideboard, which was painted a bright sunshine yellow. The kitchen walls, he noted, as they blazed against his retinas, were tomato red, the cabinetry sky blue, and the slate floor a mossy green, giving the space a peculiar fun-house feel. Molly, dressed in Sunday's rust jeans, a paisley shawl tossed over a black turtleneck, seemed taut, almost vibrating, as if barely able to contain some neat little triumph. The teapot shook as she lifted it and poured the liquid, which was as grey as its container, into a mug emblazoned with a stylised lion she had chosen from a wooden tree.

"You're a Leo, yes?" She frowned, handing him his tea.

Tom's mind pinged about for a confused second or two. "Oh, you mean astrologically. How did you know?"

"I put out a call to the universe."

"Ah! Well, the universe answered correctly." Tom raised the mug and was assaulted by the aroma rising with the steam. "Good that the universe is so forthcoming." He let the mug hover before his lips. "I pray to God daily, but find the line is often engaged. Still—" He gulped as the edge of the mug hit his lips. "—I don't give up. Goodness!" The hot liquid thrashed against his startled taste buds. "That's . . . different."

His kidneys had had thorough flushings of tea in his time, in church halls and at parishioners' homes, at meetings of the After-

noon Club, Friendship Club, Garden Club, Art Club, Mothers'
Union, and Women's Institute, in hospital waiting rooms and at funeral receptions. He had drunk black tea and green tea and white
tea, and concoctions of herbs and grains and flowers and fruit, but
never anything quite like this. The taste was compounded of damp
grass, prawn casings, and iron filings with boiled liver notes and a
dishwater finish. Nasty, in a word. The very haggis of teas.

"It's rhubarb-celeriac-barley infusion. It's good for digestion. I
brewed it for Detective Inspector Bliss, though he had very little. I
can tell he has some sort of elimination trouble."

"Really?" Tom replied noncommittally, wondering if DI Bliss's
irritable bowel was public knowledge or if Molly indeed had an in-
tuitive sense of others' well-being, born perhaps of having naturopaths for parents or a homeopath for a husband. (Or—the horrible
thought dashed across his mind—was Bliss slumped dead on the
dashboard of his car at this very minute?)

"I saw you talking with them."

"Bliss and Blessing? Yes, I do seem to run into them now and
again, hither and yon."

She pushed her curtain of red hair over her shoulder and gave
her head a finishing shake. "Come through to the dining room. I'm
nearly done with the crowns."

"Crowns?" Carrying his tea, Tom followed her to a room dominated by a round kaleidoscopic mural with mythical creatures that
seemed to be feasting on the gap that was the fireplace.

"For the Wassail. For the king and queen."

"You mean the Wassail crowns aren't permanent fixtures, like the
ones in the Tower?" He glanced from the startling artwork to two
golden cardboard circlets set amid an untidiness of crafts materials
on a large round table, each with neatly trimmed cross pattées and
fleurs-de-lis.

"The kids like to keep theirs, so we make new ones each year. Or
someone does. My turn this year on the mothers' rota." Molly

reached into a mound of greenery so glossy it could only be plastic, plucked out a seemingly endless strand of ivy, and wrapped it around the base of one of the crowns. As she took up her scissors, Tom noted the crown's interior, lined with paper of another colour. *It's that same bloody variant of purple,* he thought, watching Molly as she snipped the vine to fit. He looked at her concentrating on her task fastening the vine with dabs of glue, wondering if the two detectives had interviewed her in this room. He could only presume they hadn't—or were colour-blind.

"My Harry was Wassail king four years ago." Molly replaced the glue bottle on the table. "The picture's on the sideboard. Have a look, if you like."

Tom spotted the photo amid a nest of framed pictures. "Is that Amber Sherwill?" he asked, parking his mug of tea to lift the photo and examine it.

"Yes. She was queen that year."

Amber had been in Tom's confirmation class the previous spring, and he had despaired of her evident boredom and garbled syntax. But at Harry's funeral in September, she had somehow cast off her chavvy mien and spoken of her friendship with the dead boy with surprising eloquence. He looked at their sweet young faces under crowns not unlike the ones Molly was finishing, their cheeks blushed with cold, glowing in the golden light of a lantern in Harry's hand. Amber's eyes gazed slightly askance at the jug of cider in her hand, the sacrament of the Wassail, but Harry was captured in a moment of tender regard for his friend, startlingly almost the expression of a lover, if they had been of the age of lovers, in a last year before the agonies of adolescence would begin. Harry looked most like his mother, twinkle-nosed and small-chinned, though with his father's deep brown, watchful eyes. His was an elfin face, and it remained so; he was not blooming to manhood in the few months Tom was acquainted with him, the way

Amber, though a year younger, was to womanhood with a plurality of curves.

Tom looked past the frame to see Molly studying him. In her eyes, he saw a mixture of entreaty and pain, but, more disconcerting, a flash of defiance. "He was a beautiful little boy" was all he could think to say, suddenly pierced by the thought of Miranda spoken of in the past tense.

"He liked to dress up in those days." Molly snatched the frame from him. "Capes, hats, robes, costumes." She frowned. "By the way," she said, gesturing impatiently to his untouched tea, "did they tell you I poisoned Will? Those detectives?" As he dutifully lifted the mug to his lips, she continued, "Well, I did."

Tom allowed a little time to pass. "Molly," he responded after a tentative sip and passing thought to pouring it onto the plants in the window, "you must know that's not wise. They could take you at your word and charge you. Or at the very least they could have you for wasting police time."

Molly made a dismissive noise through her nose as she snipped another length of plastic ivy. "Shall I tell you how I did it?"

"Did you tell the detectives how you did it?"

"Tweedlebliss and Tweedleblessing? No, I didn't tell them. I told them they would have to figure it out for themselves and when they did—if they can!—they could come and handcuff me or whatever it is they do." She flashed him an oddly coquettish smile. "I might tell you, though."

"Molly, if you tell me, then I'm duty-bound to go to the police. Will's death can't go unpunished."

"Oh, can't it!" Molly's voice rose as she slapped the scissors onto the table next to the photograph. "Well, Harry's death went unpunished, didn't it. *Didn't it!*"

"Molly, don't you think perhaps you're trying to punish yourself?"

"That's what Celia says."

"Yes, you said you'd been seeing Celia."

"She's very kindly been giving me the benefit of her wisdom. She thinks I may be engaging in unwise strategies. I think *strategies* was the word." Molly trailed the length of ivy around the crown.

"But mightn't bear-baiting Detectives Bliss and Blessing be an unwise strategy?"

"It's not unwise if it's true."

"But it's not true."

"Well! Then perhaps I won't tell you how I did it."

"Yes, please don't."

"But you're a priest. Don't you have to listen to me?"

"No. I do not, Molly. I would only hear your confession under certain conditions, and one of those conditions would be that you go to the police. Anyway, I don't believe you poisoned Will."

"Why not? I've the best motive in the village. I'm sure half of everybody thinks I did it anyway, poor mad Molly. Why wouldn't they think such a thing? I cooked the meal. As soon as Victor said the Thistle But Mostly Rose craved curry, I thought, this is my chance to avenge the death of my sweet little boy."

"Then, Molly, you're telling me pretending not to tell me. You're being perfectly obvious. You tampered with the curry."

"Perhaps I did. It's the perfect food to disguise a poison, don't you think? So hot and spicy. Or I might have put it in the cranachan, with those sweet berries, or even the haggis—"

"But you didn't serve any of the food. Kerra did."

"Untrue. I helped serve the curry."

Tom was jolted by the memory. "So you did. But, *but*," he added, "Kerra served Will. How could you possibly ensure that Kerra would serve Will a poisoned dish of anything?"

She shrugged. "That's the genius of my scheme, isn't it? That's what those clever dicks will have to discover for themselves. Not that they'll ever be able to—"

"Molly, you're talking nonsense—and you're courting disaster. You have a husband and a child to think about."

"Oh, Vic doesn't care. He'd like to be shot of me, I expect."

"I'm sure that's not true. But Becca certainly needs you. You're her mother."

Molly grew silent. He was dismayed at having to remind someone of the feelings of others, especially loved ones; he recalled Miranda saying Molly often forgot to fetch Becca from her piano lessons outside of the village. He looked past Molly's shoulder out the window into the Kaifs' back garden, brown and bare in the January light, towards the property's border, a yew hedge, and wondered if it were possible. Might she have done this horrible, foolish thing after all? By making a claim so outrageous, one that she believed people—even the police—would dismiss, was she diverting attention from her genuine offence?

"Molly," he began, setting the tea down, "you might also have put the poison in Mrs. Prowse's yewberry tartlets, mightn't you?"

"Yes, I might have."

"In fact, the tartlets were ideal, as everyone would think Mrs. Prowse's pastries would be to blame."

"Well, I thought it might be a useful little diversionary tactic." Molly smiled conspiratorially.

"And did you not think how this might alarm Mrs. Prowse? I know she puts on a brave face, but I think she feels as though half the village regards her with some misgiving. And do you not see how unfair it was to draw her into this? She had no animosity towards Will Moir."

Molly remained silent a moment, her mouth a thin, unhappy slit. "Well, actually"—she pushed back her hair with an impatient gesture—"I *didn't* ask Madrun to send over any of her sodding tartlets. I don't know why they were there. Roger handed them to me while I was simmering the haggis. I thought I might as well put them out on the plates with the cranachan, since we didn't have shortbread or the like. Berry tartlets with cranachan seemed a bit redundant, but . . . "

"You're sure you didn't ask Madrun to contribute some of her baking?"

"Yes, of course."

Tom stared at her profile. She looked down, fiddling with the ivy around the second crown. He had no idea if or when she was lying. But there was one way to find out, though he would have to disclose information known only to him, Madrun, the police, and—oh, surely—Will's killer.

"I ask," he said, "because Mrs. Prowse received an unsigned note last week asking her to send some of her yewberry pastries to Thorn Court for the Burns Supper."

"Yes?"

"It was written on paper the same colour as the one you used to line those two crowns."

Molly blinked, first with consternation, then with dawning apprehension. "But Victor brought that paper home."

CHAPTER TWENTY-TWO

*T*om? Vicar?"

Tom focused on the face in front of him, at the red fox-tail eyebrows in interrogatory lift, at the large, ruddy face with its anchoring goatee, a pruning of his former full beard, streaked with incipient hairs of white.

"Yes?"

"Down a rabbit hole, were you?" Eric Swan, the Church House Inn's licensee, regarded him askance. "I was wondering if it were the usual you were after."

The notion of a large brandy flitted through Tom's mind, but as the sight of the parish priest pouring spirits down his throat middayish might spark undue prattle in the village, he gave Eric an assenting nod to a libation more modest and predictable. He had indeed been down a rabbit hole, of sorts, having left Damara Cottage, thinking, as Alice had, that it would be so nice if something made sense for a change. Molly's confession was surely nonsense, the outburst of an angry, grieving, attention-seeking woman. Even the police seemed unwilling to countenance this, at least for the time being. But was Molly adept at some sort of double bluff?

"Busy day?" he asked, hoping for the distraction of ordinary conversation as Eric placed a half of Vicar's Ruin in front of him.

"Well, might be busier if we had another natural disaster."

"Instead of a human one?"

"Will's death's still testing your mettle, I see. At least," Eric continued, pulling a folded newspaper from below the bar and twisting it round in front of Tom with a flourish, "it's only getting local notice." He plunked a pudgy finger onto the relevant column. "Not that Will wouldn't deserve national attention, of course."

Tom favoured Eric with a censorious lift of eyebrow. The murder in the spring of Sybella Parry, the nineteen-year-old daughter of St. Nicholas's choirmaster, Colm Parry, had attracted the national press in part because the victim, her body found entombed in a Japanese taiko drum in the village hall, was crowned with the aura of secondhand celebrity: Colm had been a pop star of middling fame once upon a time and his ex-wife, Sybella's mother, a model of more than middling fame, though now more renowned for disgracing herself in public in one fashion or another. Unfortunately, the circus allure pulled in the punters, which sickened Tom, and topped up the Church House Inn's till, which, at the very least, filled Eric with mixed emotions.

"And I say 'national attention' "—Eric held up his hands in mock surrender—"because Will was a fine fellow."

Tom let his eyebrow fall and his eyes drop to the passage in the *South Devon Herald.* Page three, top, was a squib with the headline in a type size several picas shy of shock-horror: MOIR INQUEST OPENED, ADJOURNED.

"By the way, those coppers were in here earlier, grumpy as hell."

Tom glanced up from the reportage, which was cursory, a distillation of whowhatwherewhenwhy. "I'm not surprised. I can't imagine how they'll come to a resolution. I can't figure how the poison got into Will's food. Or when it did."

"Or why it did?"

"Well . . ."

"Nick Stanhope was in here earlier with those property developer blokes."

"Interesting conversational transition."

"Is it?"

"Okay, then how do you know they're developers?"

"Seen them before, haven't I. They've been sniffing around Thornford for years." Eric picked up the bar towel and began absently wiping at the ring of moisture Tom's glass had left. "Belinda says they always look like they're measuring the village for curtains."

"Roger mentioned overhearing a couple of men in his shop speculating about turning Thorn Court into housing."

"That's probably them, then. Moorgate Properties."

"Will was very much against *any* new development. And Caroline would never bend to a scheme to sell Thorn Court and see it torn down. She's enormously sentimental about the place."

"But Nick isn't, is he?"

"How do you know?"

"I *know*. This boozer is the very nerve centre of the village."

"I thought the post office was the nerve centre."

"Depends on your sex—or gender, as I was corrected by my wife not long ago. This is the blokes' nerve centre. Look." Eric lowered his voice. "My sources—"

"Your *sources*?"

"All right, my great flapping ears have picked up that Nick has a little gambling problem. Owes a bob or two to some shady characters in Torquay."

Tom regarded the publican with interest. The conversation overheard between Caroline and Nick earlier in the week flitted through his mind. *Look, Caro, I need some bloody money and I need it soon, do you understand? It's a matter of life and death!* Caroline had dismissed her brother's melodrama, and so had Tom, really. But then Màiri had hinted that something not quite kosher about Nick had the power to scupper her chances of being accepted for training to be a full police officer.

"Put it this way," Eric continued. "With Will out of the picture, Nick benefits. Most of the business folk in the village know that Nick loaned money out of his inheritance for his sister and Will to buy Thorn Court. Either he gets paid back out of the insurance money—there has to be insurance money—or he bullies Caroline into selling the hotel to someone like Moorgate Properties."

"I don't think Caroline is easily bullied." Tom's eyes wandered over at the chalkboard on the wall by the bar with its list of lunch specials, then wandered back. "And I somehow can't imagine—"

"Nick doing the deed?" Eric smiled. "That's what I said to Belinda. Something womanish about poisoning someone, I said, and she tore a strip off me for that."

"You're not the only one to make that observation."

"Somehow I imagine Nick with a shotgun."

"Hardly subtle. You'd have to be at least a bit subtle to take someone's life and make it either look like an accident or appear so confusing that the court throws up its hands in despair."

"Nick's hardly subtle, from what I've seen."

"Unless desperation drives you to subtlety. What an odd idea," Tom reflected. "Usually desperation drives folk to some blunt action."

"Are you ordering something to eat?"

Jerked from his thoughts, Tom's mind went to the vicarage refrigerator, crammed with victuals, some of them still left over from Christmas.

"Your Madrun not on the job this dinner hour, then?" Eric ran a towel over a glass and placed it on an overhead rack.

"She's gone to town—Torquay, I think. Something about needing new clothes for her holiday in Tenerife." Tom caught the flash of amusement light up Eric's blue eyes and understood its source.

Eric shot him a semi-apologetic grin. "Coppers might not be best pleased if she leaves the country."

"Mrs. P has no argument with the Moirs," Tom protested. "She was devastated when I told her about the taxine."

"But the Stanhopes used to swank about this village in days past, they say. Who knows if they didn't run roughshod over the Prowses?"

"Now you're talking nonsense." Tom noted the twinkle in Eric's eye.

"I thought that might wind you up." Eric stroked his goatee. "But seriously, Tom, those two coppers are going to have to come up with something for their lords and masters. Prove they're on the job and all. By the way, your houseguest was here taking her lunch."

"Oh, yes?" Tom regarded Eric blankly, then shrugged. "Well, what with Mrs. Prowse being in town . . . "

"She was having a good long natter with Old Bob."

"Really?" Tom realised, too late, that his voice held too much curiosity.

Eric responded predictably: "Something going on?"

"Not really," Tom retreated. "Mrs. Ingley is, I suppose, just re-connecting with old friends in the village."

"She's been with you awhile. After three days—well, you know, fish and relatives begin to . . . "

"She's neither fish nor relative. Anyway, she's been no trouble. Keeps to herself to a certain extent. I think her plan is to leave early next week. She wants to attend tomorrow's Wassail and she's having a meal or something with John Copeland on Sunday. I'm not sure if she intends to buy the Tidy Dolly or not, though."

"Funny not paying a visit for fifty years. Stafford's not so far. You'd think you'd come and put a few blooms on your parents' grave once in a while, wouldn't you?"

"Yes, I suppose." Tom gave a passing thought to the last time he'd put flowers on Lisbeth's grave.

"Actually," Eric continued, "you'd think if you arrived after fifty years, you'd get to your parents' grave in short order."

"You wouldn't have seen it for the snow a few days ago, Eric."

"Anyway, she's doing her duty this afternoon."

Tom raised an enquiring eyebrow.

"She said. We had brief chat when she blew in. Got a holly wreath and all. By the way, she's won no favour with one person in the village—your houseguest, I mean. Though Nick doesn't live in Thornford, does he? God knows he's been here a lot lately—"

"Eric . . . ?"

"Sorry. Any road, when Mrs. Ingley left, Nick jumped up from his meeting with those two Moorgate blokes and chased after her. I could see him out the window giving her a right rollicking. Couldn't hear anything, though."

"Was there some provocation?"

Eric shrugged. "She didn't look bothered. I thought to go out and take Nick by the scruff, but it appeared Judith was giving as good as she got."

Tom frowned. "Did the police witness this?"

"They'd only popped in for a swift half. They were gone before either Nick or Mrs. Ingley arrived. Now, are you noshing or not? Steak and kidney pie is on special—Belinda's mother's recipe, as it happens."

Tom felt his stomach growl at the mention, but the ale had fueled another desire. "Sounds delicious," he said, raising his glass high to drain it, "but I have something I need to attend to."

Crossing St. Nicholas's chilled nave from the north porch, Tom glanced up at the memorial window erected in the south aisle in memory of Rupert Stanhope, Caroline and Nick's great-grandfather, who had perished in 1916 in the Battle of the Somme, a young man leaving his child bride and baby boy, Arthur, to manage the family holdings. The window, glowing faintly in the winter light, depicted a rich man dispensing alms, a pious and, Tom wondered, perhaps deceptive choice of subject, the attitude in which the rich liked to see themselves rendered. Perhaps the Stanhopes had been a font of charity in the village (he would have to find out), but perhaps the Great War and its sacrifices had altered the family as it had transformed society, hardened it to new realities. Arthur—Caroline and Nick's grandfather—grew up to reshape the private idyll of Thorn Court into a commercial enterprise. He spawned Clive Stanhope, who probably deserved the epithet *black sheep,* but somehow evaded scrutiny. Tom thought, too, of those who had laboured for them, thought about the bitterness of servants of times past, their helpless rage, in the days of deference to one's presumed betters.

He pushed open the heavy oak south door and felt the icy air brush his cheeks. The churchyard was bathed in the pale metallic light of a midwinter afternoon. He could see past the bare branches of the copper beeches to the still-frozen millpond and past that to a stark tracery of denuded trees on the far side, punctuated by dark green conifers rising like sentinels into a wavering wreath of mist. Except for rooks cawing, all was calm, the graveyard empty of life but for a small, still figure, wrapped in pink, near the bottom of the southeast terrace, a little distance from the rag stone wall, edged by sloping drifts of snow, that marked the boundary with the vicarage garden. Tom hesitated on the stoop, composing himself for the interview ahead, then stepped onto the pea shingle path.

"I hope I'm not intruding," he murmured to Judith when he reached her side.

"Not at all." She glanced at him sharply with her shrewd button eyes and returned her attention to the gravestone, touched here and there with green lichen, rising like a spectral shaft from a patch of snow. "You've come at a good time."

Tom noted the holly wreath, still in her hands, waiting to be set against the marker. Unprompted, he stooped and scraped away the snow from the base of the marker, feeling the bitter cold sear his uncovered hands.

"Thank you," Judith said.

"Shall we have a prayer?"

Judith nodded and set the wreath down on the mottling of dead black leaves as Tom said a short prayer for the souls of William George Frost and Irene Lynne Frost. After a minute, he stole a glance at Judith, hoping to adjudicate her mood. But in profile, her expression yielded little. The curve of her mouth was set in a contemplative frown; her eyes remained dry, though her cheeks were reddened, whether by icy air or emotion, it was impossible to tell.

"Your mother died very young," he remarked, glancing at the date carved into the stone, bare weeks after victory had been declared in Europe.

He thought he knew how and wasn't surprised when Judith said, "She died in childbirth—mine, as it happened."

"I'm so sorry."

"A home birth," she continued. "Unfortunately, the midwife was otherwise occupied."

"With what?"

"Another birth in the village—at Thorn Court, as it happened. By coincidence, Clive—Caroline's father—was born the same day, the same hour—"

"Good heavens! And resources being stretched in wartime, of course."

"I'm not sure they were stretched, as such, Tom." Judith's frown deepened. "I think a rich man's wife simply commanded attention in a way that wouldn't be acceptable today."

Tom drew in a breath of icy air. He had no balm for this tragedy or for the injustice behind it.

"How did you know I was here?" Judith asked, turning to him abruptly.

"Eric mentioned it. The landlord at the pub. He said you'd been lunching with Old Bob."

"That doesn't explain—"

"He also said he thought Nick Stanhope had been abusive with you. He happened to witness the two of you out the pub window. I thought I would come to see you were all right."

"I'm fine. I managed a care home for many years. When you have patients with various forms of dementia, you get quite used to abusive talk. Nick Stanhope's threats are nothing to me."

"Threats?" Tom felt a chill that wasn't airborne. "Judith, are you certain?"

She studied him a moment with her assessing eyes and again abruptly changed the subject. "Madrun tells me you're adopted—or twice adopted, in some fashion."

"Yes," Tom replied, startled, reluctant to let go his concerns. "Twice adopted, twice blessed." He couldn't help smiling at the adage, one belonging to the Reverend Canon Christopher Holds-worth, rector of St. George's in Gravesend, where he grew up. "My adoptive mother, my first adoptive mother, was a singer named Mary Caroll who died—"

"Yes, I remembered the name after Madrun mentioned it. A plane crash out of Stockholm, right after winning the Eurovision Song Contest. I'm sorry."

"I was a baby. I have no memory. I only have pictures."

"And you don't know who your natural parents were?"

"No. My adoptive father's sister took me in, I guess you could say. She and her partner raised me."

"And you were never curious about your birth parents?"

"No, that wouldn't be true. There were moments of great curios-ity, particularly when I was a teenager, and if I was in some sort of scrape with Dosh or Kate—my parents—I would think, *Well, I'll bloody go find my* real *parents!* But on the whole, I had a happy child-hood. I was raised by two lovely, loving women." He smiled at Judith. "They made me the man I am. I've often felt I would be hurting them somehow, by seeking out my birth parents."

"I see."

"The only time I gave it serious consideration was after I married and we were planning a child. I wondered if there might be some genetic time bomb ticking away in the background, but . . . well, my wife said, let's be glad for what God gives us and not worry." Tom glanced up at the dull sky, his attention drawn by a circling rook. "Lisbeth would have risen to it, if there had been an extraordinary challenge. Fortunately, Miranda is a challenging child in her own way, as children are."

"You must miss your wife."

"Terribly. Very much." The words always sounded so banal. "I miss being married," he added. "But you lost your husband only a few months ago."

"Yes, but he wasn't cut down in his prime as was . . . Sorry, Vicar, I didn't mean to be so blunt. Trevor was ten years older than I, and for the last twelve years he suffered terribly from Parkinson's. I feel I lost him years ago. His end was a mercy, really."

"But you have a son."

"Yes, I have a son." Judith glanced again at her parents' gravestone. "I've been thinking about nature and nurture, you see. That's why I asked you about your parents—your many parents. You say your adoptive mothers made you the man you are, but are you sure? You seem to me a man of compassion and good humour—mightn't those be legacies of your birth mother or father, just like the colour of your hair or the shape of your eyes?"

"Well, of course, I can't know for certain, but I think if nature and nurture were running the course at Cheltenham, I'd more likely put my money on nurture. It's the optimist's view, I suppose." He wrapped his own scarf tighter. "I have a sense you disagree."

"When I was younger I would have been inclined to your views, but I'm not so sure now. Watching families when they visited the care home, I could see the same . . . traits on display, from grandparent to grandchild, like little mirrors reflecting one another."

"Mightn't that be nurture as much as nature?"

"Possibly."

"John Copeland, whom you met, is adopted. So was Will, I understand. I wonder if they are reflections of their natural parents or their adoptive parents?"

"I wonder." Judith twisted her mouth in thought. "A better example might be Nick Stanhope. He's aggressive, inconsiderate, belligerent, probably reckless, perhaps conscienceless, but"—her eyes crinkled as she smiled up at him—"I'm not so past it that I can't see he wouldn't be attractive to women—young women."

Tom grunted, thinking of Màiri White and her comparable musings. "Nature or nurture?"

"He's very much like his father was."

"You knew Clive Stanhope well enough, I presume."

"My father and I lived over the old stables, now the garage, if you recall me saying." She glanced at her parents' gravestone. "And of course we were the same age—almost to the hour. Clive was likewise brash and self-involved and yet, I must say, attractive. Does Nick, then, come to his essential qualities by nature or by nurture?" She turned her attention back to him, regarding him candidly. "He is the son of a murderer, after all."

Tom was silent.

"You do know this," Judith persisted, peering at him. "Of course you do. I can see it in your eyes. Bob Cogger told you when you took him to town the other day."

"Old Bob?"

"He wasn't old fifty years ago. He has a last name," she added dryly.

"Did you know in those days how your father—"

Judith cut him off sharply. "I certainly suspected something. My father was meticulous, careful, cautious. He wouldn't take risks—not when he was the only parent to me. He would have assured himself that ladder was secure on Thorn Court's roof when he went up the tower. It's impossible that it was an accident!"

"And you didn't voice your doubts?"

"No." Her expression was stony. "The shock at first, I suppose. Then . . . it's all a blur now. I was barely eighteen. Arthur Stanhope was my father's employer. My family had worked for the Stanhopes for several generations. Arthur was an intimidating presence. I'm sure he had a quiet word with the local constabulary. There must have been an inquest, but I don't recall. 'Accident' or 'misadventure' was the probable ruling. It would have taken Bob to come forward and say what he had seen, but he . . . "

"Was persuaded otherwise."

"I don't blame him. He was almost in tears at the pub earlier talking about this, and I do know his prognosis. Chronic renal failure. It's not good." She absently brushed at a bit of lichen on the gravestone. "Anyway, Bob wasn't the only one. I had applied to take up nursing on school-leaving, which my father would have been hard-pressed to afford, but Mr. Stanhope—Arthur—offered to pay for my training. I wanted desperately to get away and make a new life anyway, so . . . in the end, Arthur Stanhope bought my silence, too, didn't he? Although I suppose I didn't recognise it as such at the time."

Tom studied her a moment, trying to imagine the young, frightened girl who was now this elderly, self-assured woman. "What led you to think Clive Stanhope was responsible for your father's death?"

"His shadow," she intoned.

"Shadow?"

"Clive's. I saw it—on the stairs leading to the tower. Sorry, Vicar, I don't mean to be melodramatic. In those days, at weekends or between terms at school, I worked as a chambermaid at Thorn Court—it had been a hotel for only a few years. I was changing the linen in a bedroom facing the forecourt, one of the grander rooms with a bay window, when my father fell. I heard a crash above me, then I saw his body plummet before my very eyes. I heard the scream." She shut her eyes momentarily, as if to ward off the pain of the memory. "I flew from the room and as I reached the stairs I glimpsed Clive's shadow against the wall of the staircase up to the tower. You've been up with me—there's a window on each side of the lower part of the tower. It was quite early in the morning, a bright day in summer, and the low sun created a shadow of Clive coming down the stair. I knew it was him, the way you know some- one from the back of a head or an idiosyncratic gait seen at a dis- tance. I even called out to him, 'Clive, come quick!' "

"And he didn't come."

"No. He later claimed to have been nowhere near the tower. But I knew he had—or, rather, it came back to me sometime later that he surely had been, and that he was lying."

"But why would he do something so cruel, so criminal?"

Judith shivered visibly.

"Would you like to go inside somewhere?" Tom offered. "We can go to the vicarage or back to the pub."

Judith drew her scarf tighter around her neck. "I'm fine, really. Coming to Thornford has stirred many memories, the strongest ones not happy ones necessarily. You're kind to endure my company for so long. I feel I may have outstayed my welcome."

"You've been no trouble at all."

"I expect you'd like an answer to your question."

"You're under no obligation."

"I think you disappoint a few folk in the village, Tom."

"Oh, really? Why?"

"Because you're not keen to gossip." She smiled up at him.

"I suppose I am a dull fellow that way. But I very much dislike tittletattle. *The words of a talebearer are as wounds,* says the Proverb. Unless the information is true and more—honourable in some fashion—I'm inclined to turn my ear away. However, I must confess"—he smiled back—"I have my eyes and ears in the village. Mrs. Prowse is a font of knowledge and is rarely disinclined to speak her mind when she feels moved to do so. Miranda, too, usually keeps me abreast of this and that. So really, they both let me remain on my high horse."

Judith laughed. "You always refer to Madrun as 'Mrs. Prowse.' Very old-fashioned. Harks back to the day when cooks and house-keepers were always 'Mrs.' no matter what their marital status."

"That seems to be the footing we got onto, but I don't think she ever addressed the previous incumbents with anything less than the proper honorific, and she expects the same in return. Oddly, I prefer it. Although I do use the occasional 'Mrs. P' out of earshot."

"Well, I shall tell you what I have not told your Mrs. P, as she is, as you suggest, terribly inquisitive and unlikely to keep it to herself. At the time of my father's death, I was pregnant . . . "

"Yes?"

" . . . with Clive's baby." She regarded him. "Are you shocked?"

"No. A little surprised, perhaps."

"That's because you're more than a generation younger than I. Attitudes changed so rapidly. When I was a teenager, pregnancy out of wedlock was still a disgrace. I dreaded telling my father, but finally I had to, before I began to show. The ignorance in those days was appalling. No advice bureaus, no discussion of birth control, no options but to give the baby up or have a backstreet abortion. If my mother had been alive, perhaps it all would have been handled differently. But my father had his own views, masculine, protective ones, I daresay. He believed I had been seduced, raped—I could hardly make my poor father believe that I had been more than willing."

Judith paused to glance at the gravestone. "My father was a very kindly man. Never raised his voice—at least not in my hearing—but that day, I could see it come over him, a kind of cold rage. I don't know quite what he did, but he must have put the fear of God into

Clive somehow. The next day Clive would have nothing to do with me."

"You hadn't told Clive first about the pregnancy."

"No. I . . . I suppose I had some vague romantic fantasies of marrying him, but I knew it would never be on. I was . . . well, not really the right sort, was I? A servant girl, you might say—all very Barbara Cartland if it had worked out—and, really, I'm not sure I really fancied being anyone's wife at that stage in my life." She paused. "Anyway, I suspect Clive had never been spoken to like that before, even by his own father who stood for no nonsense."

"But, Judith, to do what he did!"

"Impulsive, arrogant, thoughtless—that was Clive's nature. All the Stanhopes have the taint, I think. I doubt Clive made any plan to do it. He simply seized the opportunity when he saw my father on Thorn Court's roof. He stupidly thought if he could eliminate my father at that moment, *his* father wouldn't find out. Which was ridiculous, as my condition would eventually become evident and questions would be asked."

Tom frowned. "Arthur Stanhope must have learned the truth, somehow."

"Arthur was formidable, but I can't believe my father didn't address him with the truth of my condition. I don't know for certain, however. You must remember, all this happened within a couple of days. The subject was so painful and embarrassing for both my father and me that we didn't speak of it. But I felt the old man—Arthur's—eyes on me in that time and then, afterwards, when he insisted on paying for my nursing training . . . " She paused. "Either my father told him about my delicate condition, as they said in those days, or he suspected something and beat the truth out of Clive, which he was quite capable of doing. At any rate, ten days after my father's funeral, at this very church"—she glanced over towards the Norman tower—"I was gone, enrolled at St. James's in Leeds, never to return. Arthur must have pulled a few strings. I hadn't even ap-

326 · C. C. BENISON

plied there, but I think Leeds was the farthest place Arthur might
have had connections with.

"I heard little of Thornford after that. We Frosts were a small
family—both my parents, unusual for the day, were only children. I
had no cousins. A few school chums wrote a bit, but I'm afraid I was
a poor correspondent. I did get word in a letter a few years later that
Clive had married Dorothy, the daughter of a vicar in a nearby
parish—a more genteel alliance, I suppose. I knew who she was, an
insipid girl, I thought, but of suitable breeding. I'm sure the old man
kept Clive on a short leash for all the years till he died. I expect Arthur was barely cold before Clive sold the hotel and ran off to Australia."

"Tough years for you, a single mother—particularly in those unforgiving days." Tom gave a passing thought, as he had many times
in his life, to the nameless woman who was his birth mother.

"Saint James's was very forward-thinking for its time and accommodating to my situation." Judith seemed to choose her words
carefully. "And I met a wonderful man—a young administrator at
the hospital—within a year and married him. We had nearly fifty
years together, though the last ten, of course, were not what I would
have wished."

Tom stared unseeing at the Frost gravestone, its base mottled
with dead dark leaves. Judith had shaken the dust from her feet
when she left Thornford and had not looked back. She had em-
braced her new life, her child, her husband, her career. But her husband was dead, her son was on the other side of the world, and she
was soon to retire from her life's work. He could understand that in
the wake of a loved one's death, in the midst of grief, the mind
might rake through the coals in search of diamond-hardened memories. But that didn't satisfy the question he was burning to ask.

"Vicar? A penny . . . ?"

Tom bit his lip. "Judith, I hope you'll forgive the provocation, but
I don't really believe you came to Thornford last Saturday on a

whim, on a notion to buy a little business or see what had become of your former home. The weather that day wasn't a complete surprise. The forecast had been for an unusual amount of snow for almost all of England—which I think would discourage most people from taking to the roads. But you did, and not only did you, you very determinedly persevered down choked roads and through poor visibility, until you landed up at Thorn Court."

"I'm a determined woman."

"I believe you are. But are you willing to tell me why—in this instance?"

He watched her features shift as she seemed to struggle for a response. Then she released a tiny sigh. "I came for the Burns Supper."

"How would you have known there was a Burns Supper at Thorn Court last Saturday?"

"Tom, really." She shot him a withering glance. "The Thistle But Mostly Rose South Devon Pipe Band has a website—a rather comprehensive one, I might add. The supper was posted."

"But it was an exclusive event—by invitation only."

"Yes, I know, but I didn't think you gentlemen would be ungracious. And you weren't."

"I'm afraid I'm still very puzzled."

"It's simple, Tom. I wanted, as the young people would say these days, to 'crash' the event."

"But why?"

"Tom, I've told you things this afternoon that only my husband ever heard from my lips. But why I appeared at your Burns Supper, I can't tell you. At least, not quite yet."

The Vicarage

Thornford Regis TC9 6QX

Dear Mum,

I'm pleased to say I haven't lost my mind after all. I thought I saw Oona Blanc in the churchyard Thursday and everyone at the post office said I'd gone round the twist, but I was in Torquay yesterday shopping at Debenhams for some new beach shorts for Tenerife, when who did I spot also shopping for clothes, but Herself! Of course, I had to be sure. It seemed odd that she was alone. I always think people the likes of her travel around in great crowds. That's the way it looks on TV. And it was hard to believe she was shopping in anything less than a Harvey Nick's, but I guess you have to make do when you're down among us rough folk in the West Country. Of course she was wearing very large sunglasses, which made everyone look at her, though I'm not sure how many recognised her. Anyway, I went up to her, bold as brass, and asked if she were Oona Blanc. She made an odd noise, which I took as a yes, so then I asked her if she was still seeing that nice young man who accompanied her to Sybella's funeral last year, though I didn't specifically mention the funeral, as I thought it would be too upsetting, and she said something very rude to me, which I shan't type, but anyway, there you have it, and when I go down to post this letter, I'll be sure to tell those in the queue that I SPOKE *to Oona and that if she's visiting Torquay then she very well could have visited Thornford on Thursday, though I still can't think what would bring her to Devon at this time of year. I've looked through the papers and can't see any notice of a fashion show or the like. Anyway, I felt quite confirmed that this week's worry wasn't making me see things so I decided that I would contribute something to the baking stall at the Wassail after all—Cornish fairings, I thought, as they involve no fruit at all, which should reassure everyone, not that they need reassuring, and of course it's all for a good cause, the school and the Scouts troop. They turned out ~~magif mafni~~ splendidly, which was a great relief as my collapsed Yorkshires have been playing on my mind at bit, as I wonder if their fallen state was somehow a ~~hardinger harbinder~~ sign of worse to come. After all, the Moirs were here for their Sunday lunch and then six days later Will is dead! I did mention this to Mr. Christmas, but he took the view that the world doesn't work that way, which I expect is true. Certainly, I* HOPE *it's true, otherwise I shall worry every time something comes out of the Aga in an unpresentable state, not that that happens very often I must say. I'm glad so much of the snow has gone. It looked a bit touch-and-go there for a while as to whether the Wassail might be cancelled, as kiddies having to tramp about in snow wouldn't work very well, would it? The vicarage garden still has drifts against the east wall, which makes me wonder if the rosesbushes there will be damaged and of course the girls' snowman is now nothing more than a lump. I think various creatures have made off with the apple eyes and carrot nose. Bumble still barks at it. It must have the*

scent of the children. Anyway, I think everyone is looking forward to the Wassail, at least as a diversion from last weekend's
unhappy event up at Thorn Court. I told you Tamara is coming
down from Exeter to perform with Shanks Pony. I play their
CD when I'm up here sewing this and that, like the costumes for
the play at the v. hall, though I expect Shanks Pony won't last
much longer, as they're all going about their separate ways now. I
expect Tamara will have Adam Moir in tow. He has been one of
the Guns the last years at the Wassail, though I wonder if he will
again this year? It may not be the best thing to take a role at a
social event so soon after a death in the family, but then perhaps
instead of her mother he'll accompany Ariel, who I know was so
looking forward to the Wassail. Miranda came home from school
yesterday with the lantern she's made. It's shaped like a church
bell, quite wonderful. She was probably thinking of her father.
I'm sure it will be the best lantern there. Anyway, I expect all
shall go well at this year's Wassail, although the shotguns firing
to chase away the evil spirits and wake the trees never fail to
make me jump. There's rain in the forecast, but it shouldn't start
until later this evening, so with luck we'll be high and dry for
the festivities. I think our houseguest is leaving for home Monday. She's been good company, though she does ask me questions
more than answer mine. I'm not really sure how keen she is to
buy the Tidy Dolly or whether to relocate to Thornford in her retirement or not. Anyway, I won't be serving beef for Sunday
lunch, as I don't think I want to get back up on that horse quite
yet, not after 2 Yorkshire failures in a row. I'm planning roast
chicken instead, even if it means having poultry so soon after
Christmas. I got a lovely bird at the farm shop at Thorn Barton
which I'll do with rosemary and lemon potatoes, which is Greek,
isn't it? But I suppose I'm ~~antetici~~ looking forward to my winter
vacation though of course Tenerife is part of Spain. Anyway,
must get on, Mum. Mr. Christmas is driving Miranda to Ex-

eter this morning, as he has no weddings this Saturday, and he'll want to visit with his sister-in-law. Poor woman. I never know quite what to say to Mrs. Hennis if it's me taking Miranda to Exeter, but I think she's adjusting to her changed circumstances. We're all otherwise well here, cats and Bumble included, and I hope you are, too. Love to Aunt Gwen.

Much love,
Madrun

P.S. What about a RED mobility scooter? That would be more your colour, I think.

CHAPTER TWENTY-THREE

Animal, végétal ou minéral?"

"Végétal."

"Est-ce plus grand que ma tête?"

"Non."

"Est-ce . . ." Tom groped around in the atrophied French-language wrinkle of his brain as he pulled his car onto the A380 outside Pennycross St. Paul. *". . . une chose unique au monde?"*

"Non."

"Est-ce . . . darling, *pourrions-nous . . . commuter . . . commuter?"*

"Oui. Change? Switch?"

"Oui . . . pourrions-nous commuter à l'anglais. Tu sais que mon français n'est pas très bon."

Miranda sighed. "Okay."

"Bon! Or 'good!,' rather. Let's see . . ." Tom was relieved not to have to press on with Twenty Questions in his ill-taught and

ill-learned school French. "Vegetable, smaller than my head, and not a unique thing—so a category of things. Could I buy it somewhere?"

Miranda paused imperceptibly, then replied, "No."

"Is it found in England?"

"Yes."

"Is it found in this car?"

"No."

Tom tapped his fingernails along the steering wheel with a little impatience—not at the game. Twenty Questions on longish car trips with his daughter was a favoured pastime. More impatient-making was the traffic. They'd had a slightly late start, Miranda and he: Miranda to have her dark, now long, hair put in Dutch braids, for some reason that seemed vital to the three females occupying the vicarage; he because the archdeacon had called him when he'd returned from Morning Prayer with a question that seemed to need an immediate answer. Barring roadworks or breakdown, they should reach Exeter in just under an hour, sufficient time to unite Miranda with her Aunt Julia outside the synagogue.

"Does it smell?"

"No."

"Is it round?"

Tom glanced at Miranda when no reply came immediately. She was squinting, as if trying to visualise whatever the mysterious thing was. "No."

"Aha! Then is it . . . oh, what can the word be? Ellipsoid . . . or spheroid, like a rugby ball?"

"Yes."

"Is it a rugby ball?"

"No. Besides"—Miranda was counting questions asked thus far on her fingers—"aren't rugby balls made from leather? That would be animal."

"And rubber. Mineral."

"But rubber is made from trees. So vegetable."

"That's right. Well done, you. Besides, you can buy a rugby ball in a shop, and you said whatever it is can't be bought."

"You have ten questions left, Daddy."

Tom spotted a gap through the trundling cars and zipped into the speedier fast lane with a satisfied grunt, settling in for uninterrupted passage. The landscape outside the window, winter-drab, a study in denuded trees and lingering patches of snow, offered little cheer, but cocooned inside the car, with the heater's warm fug and Miranda's bright conversation, all felt well with the world.

"All right, something rugby-ball-ish. Is it smaller than a rugby ball?"

"Yes."

"Of course, I'd asked before if it were smaller than my head, so that was a wasted question, since a rugby ball is bigger. Does it, then, have something to do with sport?"

"No."

"Hmm. Is it . . . useful?"

When Miranda didn't answer with her usual swift assurance, he glanced over to see her biting her lip in thought. After a moment, she turned to him, a faintly troubled cast to her features.

"I can't answer."

Tom frowned and dropped his voice to the spooky range he sometimes used when he'd been The Great Krimboni. "How mysterious." He paused to set the windscreen wipers to intermittent as a smattering of rain hit the windows. "Is it usually found in the home?"

"No."

"Is it usually found out of doors?"

"Yes."

"Would we find it in our garden?"

"Mmm . . . no."

"Ah! Then might we find it in some other garden in the village?"

"Yes."

Tom let all Miranda's responses pass through his brainbox. Smaller than his head, spheroid, found in a garden, yet without an aroma. So not a flower. And some ambiguity about its utility? An actual fruit or vegetable? But mightn't one eat such a thing? That seemed to have utility. "Is it decorative?"

"Yes."

"Is it a . . . marrow?" He thought of the vegetables that folk brought to decorate the church for the Harvest Festival.

"No. One more, Daddy."

"Could I eat it?"

It was the look she shot him that gave him the clue. Solemnity freighted her dark eyes.

"I can't answer," she replied.

He returned his attention to the road. "Is it smaller than the end of my thumb?"

"Yes."

"Is it usually red?"

"Yes."

Tom's heart sank. "Is it . . . a yewberry?"

"Yes."

The need to merge into a single lane for the sake of some road-works diverted his attention for the moment it took to slow and join the long queue of cars, but when he turned back to Miranda he could see that she was downcast.

"I'm so sorry all this has happened, darling. Are you very upset?"

"I think Ariel doesn't like me."

"Oh." Tom took a fathoming moment. "I'm sure she doesn't hate you. She's just . . . " It was hard to find the right word. " . . . confused. It's because of Mrs. Prowse, isn't it?"

"Ariel thinks—"

"Do you?"

"No!"

"That's good. I know our Mrs. P has her friends and foes in the village, but she has no malice—well, certainly not to the degree of . . . you know. Besides, if I had the least concern that she might have . . . you can be sure we'd be making new living arrangements."

"But was it an accident, Daddy?"

"It doesn't seem so."

"Then who . . . ?"

"I don't know. I wish I did. It's all very, very puzzling." A certain question had slipped into his mind, as questions do, seemingly unbidden, but, really, provoked by the past. "You asked me the other week if you could have a sleepover with Ariel and Becca and Emily, and I said you could as long as it was fine with Mrs. Prowse, remember?"

"Yes."

"But I seem to recall when we were at Bristol your going to a sleepover—do you remember?—and your not liking it very much. You said you thought it was . . . gross. I think the people's house smelled a bit. So was last Saturday's sleepover your idea or . . . ?"

"It was Ariel's, Daddy. She said it would be fun, but we couldn't have it at Becca's because . . . well, because."

"Yes, I understand." The atmosphere at Damara Cottage was too sad.

"And we couldn't at Emily's."

"No room at the inn."

"And Ariel's is having stuff done to it. And we have lots of room, so . . . " She frowned at him. "Why?"

"Oh . . . " He didn't know whether he should speculate on such things with his daughter out loud, but found himself doing so anyway. "It just all seems so . . . well timed, somehow. Ariel stays over at our house. Mrs. Moir goes into town. If the sleepover was Ariel's notion, Caroline might have skipped the concert and held the sleepover at the Annex. 'Stuff' isn't being done to the Annex, and it's big enough for four for a sleepover. I know Caroline said she wanted to leave us men well alone because . . . well, because . . . "

"Because?"

"Because we mightn't be on our best behaviour."

"Like the boys at school when they're in a group. They're *terrible*."

"Well, a bit like that. Only with a lot of drink added."

Miranda twisted under her seat belt to regard him speculatively.

"I was good as gold," Tom added hastily.

"Daddy, do you think Ariel didn't think of the sleepover all by herself?"

"Well . . ." He really didn't wish to reflect out loud on suggestibility of children. "I don't know. It was just a thought rattling around in my head."

"Alice would say if logic doesn't work, '*tu dois écouter ton intuition.*'"

"Alice Roy?"

"*Oui.*"

"Good old Alice."

"Maybe I could ask Ariel at the Wassail, if she still doesn't want to talk to me."

"Didn't she talk to you at school yesterday?"

"No."

"Leave it be for the time being, darling. Everything will right itself eventually." Though he wasn't sure he believed it. For a moment, they motored along, father and daughter, in companionable silence. They were beginning the ascent of Haldon Hill where crusts of snow still edged the motorway. Passing through a patch of shifting mist, Miranda asked a question that so startled Tom he almost braked.

"Daddy, what's mercy killing?"

Unwisely, he allowed himself a few breaths without answering, which set Miranda to repeat the question in a more querulous voice. "Daddy?"

"Well, darling," he began, affecting an even tone, "what makes you ask that question?"

"I saw it on your computer."

"What! When?"

"Yesterday. Before supper. I was looking up 'mercury' for Mrs. Lennox's class because it's science week next week and it came up as soon as I started typing *m* and *e*."

"I can't recall looking that up."

"It wasn't you, Daddy. It was Mrs. Ingley. She didn't sign out when she was using your computer."

"Oh."

"I wasn't snooping!"

"That's all right, darling. I know you didn't mean to. Perhaps Mrs. Ingley was simply rooting around the Internet, the way you do sometimes."

"But what is it? Mercy killing."

"Well . . . it's complicated. It means someone taking another person's life—deliberately—usually because that person has had a terrible injury that can't be mended or a terrible illness that can't be cured, and there seems no other way to end the suffering."

Miranda was silent, absently tugging at her braid, which she had pulled around her neck. "Are people allowed to do that?"

"No, they're not. It's against the law, though some people think the law should change, allowing it in certain circumstances or under certain conditions. When I was a curate in Kennington—this is just before you were born—an elderly man in the parish ended his wife's life by . . . it doesn't matter how—because she—"

"But how?"

"Oh, darling."

"I'm not a baby!"

Tom sighed, then white-lied. "A lot of pills," he said. It somehow seemed less vivid than the truth—Mr. Collins had smothered his wife with a pillow on their marital bed. "She had amyotrophic lateral sclerosis, which is very cruel. He might have got away with it, but he felt terrible remorse and went to the police and turned himself in. He was jailed for two years."

He flicked Miranda a glance. He could see her concentrated in thought.

"But when Dolan got really, really old, and couldn't walk— remember? We were visiting Grannie Dosh and Grannie Kate— they took him to be put down."

"I know, but animals can't tell us very well how much they hurt, and there's little we can do for them, so sometimes it's the only thing we can do. When animals suffer, they suffer mutely, but we humans are unique, aren't we? We're made in God's image. He gave us minds so that we would know, and think and make choices, didn't He? I know, as in Mr. Collins's case, he felt great compassion for his wife, but we don't sort out the problem of suffering by doing away with those who suffer. Mr. Collins might have asked for our help, but," Tom reflected, "perhaps we were remiss in not being more forward in offering help. I don't know . . . "

"Poor Daddy."

"Anyway, life is God's gift to us and it's not for us to end it."

"Someone ended Mummy's life. Was it God?"

The question, coming as it did unheralded, shook him. *Was it God?* Had God capriciously, unreasonably, cruelly, *wantonly* chosen—no, *forced*—the moment when Lisbeth's life should be snatched away? This though he knew God no more set the moment of our death than He micromanaged the trajectories of the dust motes in the universe. At play, as always, mysteriously co-existing with His sovereignty, was the free will of man—*a* man, in the case of Lisbeth's end.

He brushed Miranda's cheek with the back of his hand. "It wasn't God who took Mummy away from us, it was someone who offended God."

CHAPTER TWENTY-FOUR

The sight of Julia, a lone figure in a black wool coat with collar turned up into her dark hair, silhouetted against the entrance of the narrow lane, brought a little blood to Tom's cheeks and a small fillip to his heart. He could feel it beating now below his skin, but he could excuse high colour with reference to the saturating damp in the chill air rather than to the intricate feelings that his late wife's sister could rouse. She might have been Lisbeth waiting for him and Miranda, so closely did her posture—the arms folded just so, one foot in advance of the other, head bent—mimic Lisbeth's in moments of impatience. As he approached, Miranda in hand, and Julia's face lit with the delight of reconnection, he was seized yet again with the physical resemblance, the high cheekbones, the ink-black glossy eyes, the intelligent intensity of her expression, feeling as if he were approaching Lisbeth in a dream like those that still visited his sleeping hours and left him disconsolate when he rose to the waking world. And when he kissed her in greeting, the sensation was magnified.

"You're shivering," he exclaimed, drawing back to look at her before she bent to kiss Miranda. "Have you been waiting long? I hope we're not too late."

"No, and services never start on time anyway. Rabbi Mendelssohn isn't noted for his punctuality." Julia smiled and gestured towards the synagogue door, discreetly set between two Doric columns barely higher than a man's head. "Are you joining us?"

"Not this time, I'm sorry. I have some errands that I must do while I have the chance." He held up a carrier bag containing Tamara Prowse's shoes. "Lunch, of course?"

"At mine."

"Lovely." Julia had found a flat in a converted Regency building not far from the city centre. "I'll be back to fetch you both in an hour or so. Be good and God bless."

It had been he more than the sporadically observant Lisbeth, because his faith was so front and centre, who had worried about Miranda's religious education. There had been no disagreement that she wouldn't be baptised, that she would be raised as a Jew. "A person who is not baptised is equally loved by God," he had told his puzzled daughter when she was five and attended the baptism of a preschool friend's baby brother at St. Dunstan's, where Tom was part of a team ministry. Faith was often reinvigorated when people became parents, and it was then that Lisbeth began taking Miranda to cheder at a congregation not too far from their home, a pattern that might have ended with Lisbeth's death, so shattered was he, but for the kindness of a student who shared a flat in a neighbouring house, who fetched Miranda—religiously, you could say—every Saturday morning, until they upped sticks for Thornford Regis. Tom felt blessed that Lisbeth's sister slipped with ease into Lisbeth's guiding role, taking Miranda to Exeter to the monthly family services at the synagogue and having them to Friday Shabbat dinners. But he and Miranda had been in Thornford barely four months when Julia ended her marriage to the village doctor and moved to Exeter, another in a string of losses in Miranda's young life.

These thoughts swam in and out of Tom's mind as he made his way towards the High Street, tucking his scarf tighter around his throat. Echoing was a remnant of his conversation with Miranda in the car.

"Daddy," she had said, "didn't Mrs. Ingley's husband die because he had . . . something . . . a sort of . . . ?"

"Yes, Parkinson's." He supplied the name of the debilitating disease, startled by the thought and its possible implication. "Yes, he did."

Or so Judith said.

Why, he worried, as he turned off the High Street, through Broadgate, and began crossing the broad expanse of Cathedral Green, had Judith been researching mercy killing? General information? News items? Surely not a blog. "Why I appeared at your Burns Supper, I can't tell you," she had told him the day before in the churchyard. Could she possibly be in flight from Stafford, the subject of a police investigation into her own husband's death? Yet she had also indicated she had purposely planned to intrude upon the ceremonial dinner.

He glanced up unseeingly at the sculpted screen of the cathedral's west front and considered, Was that a feint? Or—and the thought sent a frisson of alarm down his spine—had someone taken Will's life in the twisted notion that it was in Will's best interest? *Judith? Is it possible?* She trained as a nurse. She could administer medicines—or poisons, as the case might be. She could calculate dosages. Yet it was she, in the reception room that night, who had voiced a concern about Will's appearance. If she had malicious intent, why would she show her hand? And had she not only just arrived at the hotel? She would have had neither time nor chance to tamper with Will's food. Unless she had arrived rather earlier and been loitering in the hotel longer than she claimed when Tom discovered her gazing at the portrait of Josiah Stanhope in the reception room. But why? She knew nothing of Will to wish to kill him—with mercy or without. If she had any animus—and she did—it was towards the Stanhopes, to whom Will was aligned only by marriage.

And, of course, why would she be looking up mercy killing on a computer *after* the fact?

It was all too loopy. He had set his mind to a few hours of pleasure, with his daughter, away from the confines of the winter village, and damned if he was going to ruin it with further rumination.

He had reached Briggs-Ellery, the Christian bookshop, set into a pair of timbre-frame, gabled houses of fifteenth-century origin, steps away from the Close. As he glanced unseeingly at his reflection in the window glass, another unpleasant thought intruded: Madrun was alone with Judith in the vicarage and forever inquisitive, of course. Might she ask some needlessly provocative question of Judith? He focused on the books in the window display. He was letting his imagination run away with him. Judith was a woman in her late sixties, little threat to anyone, at least physically. Suddenly he felt unaccountably anxious. He fumbled in his jacket pocket for his mobile, but before he could ring the vicarage, he heard someone speak his name. He turned to see a young man and woman, arms interlinked, smiling shyly at him, while his mind fumbled for name, date, and place.

"I thought you'd be on your honeymoon," he remarked in as much cheer as relief that his memory hadn't put him to embarrassment. They were Todd and Gemma, the very pair he had married the week earlier at St. Paul's.

"So did we," Gemma replied, absently sending a hand across the bulging front of her coat.

"Of course! The snow."

"If the reception hadn't carried on so, we might have got to Exeter—"

"If your dad—" Todd remonstrated.

"Never mind about that."

"What a great shame," Tom interjected, hoping to quench the rising bickering. "Barbados was your destination, yes?"

"We're still going, Vicar," Gemma said smiling, "only it's all been pushed up a week. The tour company was very accommodating. So we're having our night at the Royal Cumberland"—she gestured to the hotel across the narrow lane from the bookshop—"and flying out of Exeter airport tomorrow noontime."

"Lovely."

"We were about to nip into Drake's for a coffee. Would you care to join us? I don't think we thanked you properly for everything you did for us."

"All part of the service," Tom responded lightly, groping for a suitable excuse, but failing to find one as he himself was headed to the very place. Purchasing ten copies of *The Marriage Book,* handouts for his marriage preparation course, from Briggs-Ellery, would take all of five minutes, and refusing their invitation seemed churlish. Gemma and Todd seemed like they were practising the niceties of wedded coupledom. "I'd be happy to. Go on ahead, and I'll join you shortly." He gestured to the shop. "I have something I must get here first."

"We'll order. What would you like?"

"That's very kind. A dark-roast coffee and, oh, something thoroughly bad for me. You choose."

As it happened, fetching the books consumed a little more time than estimated. Six copies were on the shelf, on the first floor, up a set of rickety steps, but Mr. Ellery, the proprietor, was certain more were in storage. While he waited, Tom set Tamara's shoes on the floor and glanced through *The Marriage Book.* Turning the pages in the section on the restoration of intimacy in marriage, his eyes fell on a snippet of text that gave him pause: *Very often people are waiting for justice to be done before they forgive.* Oh, further unwanted rumination! His mind flew to the Kaifs, each of whom seemed to be imprisoned in that worst sin of marriage, unforgiveness. Was Will's quietus the "justice," however perverted, one or the other of the couple sought to restore a loving relationship? If so, it wasn't working, and rightly so.

Still, Tom mused, shivering a little as the question formulated in his head and Mr. Ellery returned with the extra copies, what were the limits to marital love and protectiveness?

Moments later he was inside the warmth of the Drake, grateful for its atmosphere redolent of castor sugar, cinnamon, vanilla, and chocolate, plunging him into a torrent of childhood memories of visits to his Grannie Ex's cottage in Sevenoaks where his grandmother was always, it seemed, up to her elbows in flour. There, at one of the tables near the window, were Gemma and Todd, talking with a young woman, seated at the next table, with a music case propped on a chair beside her like a misshapen lover.

"Oh, hello. Do you all know each other?" Tom asked, recognizing Tamara Prowse as the lone figure and wondering why she wasn't bustling about serving.

"Tamara was—what?—three years behind me at school, I think." Gemma motioned him to an empty seat before which sat a steaming mug of coffee and a plate with two Chudleigh buns, strawberry jam, and clotted cream. "I remembered Tamara because she was brilliant as . . . who were you again?"

"Olivia Twist."

"Of course. In *Olivia Twist,* the musical. You were only fourteen." Gemma sipped her coffee daintily.

"Your father asked me to bring you these." Tom handed Tamara the carrier bag with the shoes. Tamara peeked in, frowned, then rolled her eyes.

"Dad's forgotten I'm coming home for the weekend."

"Of course! Your aunt told me that. That's why you have that with you." Tom nodded towards the case.

"Well, partly . . . " Guilt flashed in her eyes.

"Are you busking, then?"

She nodded. "I managed to get a pitch here on the Close when I moved here in September. Didn't you once busk, Mr. Christmas? Aunt Madrun told me you did."

"You were a busker?" Gemma seemed to regard Tom for the first time as if he were something akin to a normal human being.

"Magic, not music." Tom sat, set his bag of books on the floor and lifted the mug of coffee, savouring the aroma. "I busked through England and parts of Europe for a time when I was around Tamara's age, between terms and the like. Sleight of hand, card magic, a bit of mentalism. I had a little fold-up table." He grinned. "Great fun."

"Ooo, gives me shivers thinking about singing—or doing anything!—in front of a bunch of strange folk in the middle of the street. My stomach was in knots just saying my wedding vows, and I knew most in the church, didn't I?" Gemma smiled at her husband and reached for his meaty hand with her pink pointy fingers.

"You did well." Tom tore a piece off one of the buns and slathered it with clotted cream.

"Don't tell Dad I'm busking, Mr. Christmas. Please. He thinks I'm working here at the Drake." Tamara pulled her mobile from a pocket and frowned at it. "He doesn't know, and he'll have a fit if he does. He'll think someone's going to rob me . . . or worse. And please don't tell my aunt. You know what she's like."

She glanced up from her mobile and caught Tom's eye. Her mouth widened to a generous grin. He could see why she might have gained a prime busking location in the city, jumping some regulatory queue or other. Tamara had thick honey-coloured hair pushed up into a glorious Medusa swirl framing the broad, pale expanse of her forehead. Her jawline was delicate, but determined; her green eyes warm, radiating a kind of nervy intelligence. Really, he thought, she was remarkably beautiful, yet seemed somehow unaware of her effect (Todd stole shy glances at her), which only added to her charm.

"Your secret is safe with me," Tom replied.

"It helps pay for the extras, and I love playing, but . . . "

"It's not music you're studying, is it?"

"They closed the music department some years ago. I'm studying conservation biology."

"A practical course is much more sensible," nurse Gemma piped up, offering the wisdom of her advanced years.

But Tamara had returned her attention to her mobile.

"Still nothing?" Gemma enquired.

Tamara shook her head. "Adam," she explained to Tom. "He's supposed to be coming to drive me to Thornford. I thought he'd be here by now." Her thumbs danced over the mobile's tiny keyboard. "There. I hope he hasn't switched his off." She looked pensive a moment. "Poor Adam."

"I'm sure he has a lot on his mind." Tom glanced through the Drake's window towards the cathedral, veiled in a thin mist.

"My boyfriend's father died last weekend," Tamara explained to the newlyweds. She dropped her mobile next to her empty mug.

"How awful!" Gemma gushed, then frowned. "He can't have been very old."

"Not very," Tamara replied. "That's what makes it even more sad." She looked over at Tom as if seeking permission to elaborate. "It seems someone may have poisoned him."

Gemma gasped. "I read that in the paper! Do they know who yet?"

"I'm afraid it's all very much a mystery," Tom answered for Tamara, hoping to stem further speculation.

Birdsong suddenly punctuated the Drake's ambient clatter of clinking china, silverware, and low conversation, stopping only when Tamara snatched up her mobile.

"Here he is," she said brightly, her eyes darting over the message on her screen. Her face fell. "Oh, he hasn't left Noze yet!" She looked at her watch.

"Then why not come back with us," Tom offered. "Miranda's at synagogue with Julia Hennis. I'm fetching them in about twenty minutes or so. You could come with us to lunch at Julia's. She'd be delighted to see you. And we wouldn't be long. We'd have plenty of time to get back to Thornford in time for the Wassail."

"Well . . . it's very kind of you, Mr. Christmas. I would like to get home sooner than later. I haven't seen my bandmates since before . . . it must have been early December for a concert at Ashburton. We need to go over a few numbers."

"That's right. You were scheduled to perform at the Civic Hall at Totnes last Saturday?"

"The show did go on, but much reduced in performers and audience, I think—mostly to those who could walk to the hall. But Adam and I were trapped here in Exeter, what with the snow and all. We couldn't get out." Tamara's thumbs flew again over her mobile. "Hard to believe the difference a week can make."

"Isn't that true!" Gemma murmured silkily, glancing at her new husband.

"You were to join Adam's mother . . . ," Tom began.

"They're readjusting the gun pegs at Noze," Tamara interrupted as birdsong alerted her to her screen. "Some American shooting syndicate is coming on Monday. Those poor pheasants," she muttered. "So wasteful."

"But—" Todd shifted in his seat as if roused to counterargument.

"Adam says he won't be able to leave for half an hour." She looked towards Tom. "Yes, Mrs. Moir was to join us. I don't know how she made out. By the time we knew we wouldn't be able to leave Exeter, the mobile service stopped working. Anyway, Mr. Christmas, I'd be very grateful for the ride. I'll text Adam and tell him I'm coming with you."

As Tamara concentrated on her task, Tom puzzled over her words. Adam said he had brought his mother to Thornford from Noze on Sunday morning, but clearly that couldn't be true. Trapped in Exeter on Saturday, but able to navigate the roads Sunday? Unlikely. How, then, had Caroline returned to the village that morning? If she had reached Totnes and attended the concert alone, how had she managed to travel to Noze? And did she have keys to her son's quarters on the shooting estate? Much as he loved his mothers, Tom wouldn't have given a key to Dosh or Kate when he moved to London. What young man wants to live independently knowing his mother might barge in on him unexpectedly? Where *had* Caroline spent last Saturday night?

"There!" Tamara said with satisfaction. "I'll just nip into the loo first." The birdsong sounded yet again. "That was fast." Standing, she adjusted the screen away from the window light. Tom noted her eyebrows climb.

"He has another idea?"

Tamara appeared discomfited. "I don't know if I should say this. It's very strange."

"What is it?" Gemma asked.

The pink of embarrassment touched Tamara's cheeks. "He says I'm not to talk to you."

"To me?" Gemma frowned. "He doesn't know me from—"

"Adam?" Her husband laughed.

"No," Tamara replied, her expression grave. "You, Mr. Christmas. Adam doesn't want me talking to you."

CHAPTER TWENTY-FIVE

*T*om followed Miranda through the vicarage gate onto Poynton Shute and around to the entrance to the Old Orchard, two and a half acres of glebe land sloping gently down to the millpond, which had been ceded to the parish decades earlier. The last rays of the weak winter sun silvered the gnarled branches of the apple trees either side of the beaten, muddy path and cast pale grey shadows over the grass wet with a welter of dead leaves and mashed husks of decomposed apples. Tom inhaled the fermented air and shivered in the damp as they took the fork in the path that dipped under a bower of dark trees and squeezed through a crude opening in the boundary hedgerow to the adjacent property where the Scout Hut blazed like a cottage on a lonely moor. Ahead of them, other villagers trailing the same path blended into the jostling revellers. Some joined the queue at a tented food stall to one side of the hut offering barbecued fare and plastic cups of hard cider. Others gathered under a tented stall opposite the hut where various baked goods were on offer, which is where Tom glimpsed Madrun and Judith as he reached for Miranda's lantern, raising it high so it wouldn't be crushed as they threaded past a merry chorus singing,

> *Here we come a-wassailing*
> *Among the leaves so green,*
> *Here we come a-wand'ring*
> *So fair to be seen*

and made their way into the shelter of the hut, a drafty single-storey stone building whose damp was barely vanquished by single-bar heaters high on the walls and the body heat of a hundred parents and children.

"Old Twelfth Night, Father," a voice muttered in his ear as Miranda settled happily onto a chair before the musicians arranged at one end of the room under a swag banner trimmed with fabric apples.

"So it is," Tom responded agreeably over the hubbub of music and chatter, turning to find Old Bob hovering by his side. "The end of the twelve days of Christmas, in the old calendar."

"First for you and your daughter?"

"Yes. Not something we had in Bristol."

"I had a talk with Judith Ingley 'bout—"

"Yes, I know."

"Told you, did she?"

Tom nodded.

"Tha's all right then." Bob nodded.

"Bob, good on you for doing that." He happened to glance at Tamara, guitar in hand, who smiled at him as he caught her eye, then noted Adam, seated in the front row with his sister, turn and regard him warily. "Miranda, do you want to sit with Ariel?" He leaned down and pulled up one of the earflaps of her wool hat.

She twisted her head up to him, blinking. "No," she said abruptly, pulling off her hat.

"Are you off?" Tom turned back to Bob. "I wanted to talk to you about something."

"Thought I'd watch morris dancers outside."

"Are they on?"

"Aye. In a bit."

"Oh, well, them I've seen before."

"Not this lot. They black their faces."

"This isn't Eric Swan's group?"

"No, this lot's out of Bovey Tracey. But, Father, if you—"

"I'll come and see you tomorrow or Monday, if that suits."

Blackface, Tom thought, watching Old Bob leave. *That should put someone's PC knickers in a twist.*

"Do you want to eat something? Hot dog?" He bent once again to Miranda, but she shook her head, seemingly concentrated on the music.

"I'm full from Aunt Julia's," she replied as Tom placed the lantern in her hand and considered whether to treat himself to some hard cider, just a little; he didn't want to mount the pulpit with a throbbing head as he had the Sunday before. He noted the Kaifs—Victor, Molly, and Becca—easing their way down the crowded entrance corridor into the hut's main room, Victor with Becca's lantern in hand, Molly struggling to balance a pair of what looked like hatboxes. Tom followed Becca with his eyes as she shot to the empty seat next to Ariel, then noted Miranda's head turn sharply in their direction, then back to the musicians again with equal force. He sensed sides taken in the rift between his daughter and Ariel Moir.

"Make yourself useful, Vic, for God's sake." Molly's sharp tone pierced the bright clatter.

"I have Becca's lantern, Molly. I don't have three hands."

"Here," Tom offered, moving towards them. "I'll take the boxes."

Molly thrust them at him, then swept her hair back with a the-atrical gesture. "I have to find the king and queen. Where *are* the king and queen?"

"The king's over there, Molly, if you simply look." Victor ges-tured towards a lad posing for his sniggering mates in a purple man-tle trimmed with silver.

"Then where's the queen? I must have the queen!"

"If I know Emily Swan, she'll be late," Tom remarked, casting a worried glance past the top of the boxes at Victor, who was regard-ing his wife with barely controlled fury.

"She can't be late!"

"Molly, when we passed the toilets, the door to the ladies' opened and I saw Belinda Swan inside," Victor said with barely concealed exasperation. "Emily's probably in there with her mother, getting into her . . . whatever!—coronation robes."

"Perv, looking in the ladies' loo." His wife cast him a baleful glance as she shouldered back through the crowd.

"Oh, for Christ's—" Victor's cheeks flushed. "Take the bloody crowns with you, Molly!" he shouted after her. "Oh, never mind! Sorry, Tom. I'm . . . I'm getting to the end of my tether."

"Molly seems a bit . . . intense this evening."

"She's decided to go off the medication she was prescribed and which was doing her some good."

"Homeopathic?"

"Even I admit homeopathy doesn't cure everything. No, a doctor in town prescribed them. Here, give me those boxes." Victor set Becca's lantern at his feet, took the boxes, and put them between two jam jars alit with candles on the shelf that ran along three of the hall's walls. "Celia Parry was doing Molly some good, too, I think, but then she and Colm flew off to Barbados—"

"But only for a week."

"Molly feels . . . abandoned nonetheless."

"You haven't abandoned her, Vic."

"No, but . . ." Victor flashed him a guilty look. "On top of it all, I had the police around today." He lowered his voice. "Have they talked to you about last Saturday?"

Tom nodded.

"They've taken my computer and my printer—or, I should say, computer*s* and printer*s*, from the clinic in town and from home. They had a warrant. They wouldn't say why, despite my protests, but Molly says your housekeeper had a letter asking her to make some of her yew tartlets for the Burns Supper."

"Yes, she did."

"But why would they *think*—" Victor's voice rose sharply, then he caught himself. "Why would they think," he began again, his voice reduced to a murmur, "that I would write such a thing?"

"They didn't say?"

"No. Have they taken anyone else's computer? Nick's? John's? *Yours?*"

Tom shook his head. "Not mine at any rate." He paused. "Victor, I think their interest likely stems from the colour of the paper used for Madrun's note. It was that lavender shade—or violet, some version of purple—the same shade as the paper and cards in your case, when I bumped into you on Tuesday."

"It's madness!" Victor exploded through clenched teeth. "If I were to hatch some plot that involved your housekeeper's baking, I would never use my own computer or my own printer . . . or my own paper, come to that. How stupid do they think I am? And how do they know what colour the clinic's stationery is? Don't tell me *you* shopped me to the police?"

"I must admit I was surprised when your case flew open and scattered it about. But no, I said nothing to the police. I thought it was a coincidence, then I started to see that colour of paper everywhere—it's on the crowns Molly made, for instance." Tom gestured to the nearby boxes. "And the girls were using it to decorate the lanterns they were making at school. Mrs. Lennox says it's the colour fad of the season."

Victor gestured impatiently. "I gave a box of the paper to Becca, yes, but if paper that colour is so bloody widely disseminated, that doesn't explain why those detectives would single *me* out. It was horribly embarrassing having my computer carted away like that—as if I . . ." His eyes roved the room wildly. " . . . looked at kiddie porn or something equally appalling."

Tom took a cleansing breath. "I'm not sure it was only you they were singling out."

"What do you mean?"

"There are two adults in your household, aren't there?"

"Yes . . . ?"

"Well, you more than I know how Molly has suffered since . . . Harry's death. She hasn't been quite herself, has she." He watched a shadow pass over Victor's face. "I went to your cottage yesterday afternoon to return Becca's torch. She left it at ours last weekend. Those two detectives, Bliss and Blessing, were coming from your cottage . . ." He paused, noting Victor's eyebrows knit with perplexity. "Molly didn't tell you they had visited? She didn't say that she had—"

"No."

"Oh." Tom's heart sank. "Victor, please be mindful of Molly's state of mind when I tell you this: She confessed to the detectives—and she told me—that she had poisoned Will."

"*What!*"

A few heads had snapped in their direction. Tom gave them reassuring smiles, then said to Victor, whose face was shot through with anxiety and anger, "Victor, it's a measure of their disbelief that they didn't fetch her in for further questioning. They're not complete monsters. They do know what your family has endured and Molly's state of mind."

"Then why have they removed *my* things?"

"Eliminating all possibilities, I'm certain," Tom replied, though he wasn't at all certain. Bliss and Blessing may have had a change of heart.

Or of mind.

A large white plastic cup filled with a cloudy brown liquid passed under his eyes.

"You look like you could use a wee drink," said a lilting voice in his ear.

"I wouldn't describe this as 'wee,'" Tom responded as he took the cup from Màiri. He sipped the local scrumpy. It tasted both earthy and vinegary. "But thank you. I was considering going out to fetch one myself."

"Was that Victor Kaif looking furious as a box of badgers?"

"He's had rather a bad day, I gather, and I think I've made it worse." He explained. "But perhaps you know more than I?"

"Not really. I'm merely the village bobby."

"You *do* know something."

"All I hear is that the DI Bliss is not a happy bunny. He and Blessing have few leads and I'll wager someone is breathing down their necks. Is that Tamara Prowse on guitar? She's very good, isn't she?"

Not immune to deliberate subject-changing, Tom asked, "What brings you to this event on a dreary winter's eve?" Over her shoulders, Màiri wore a thick woolen ruana of a deep royal blue that accentuated the bright blue of her eyes. Nice. Her dark hair, released from its workday braid, fell naturally in deep long waves over her shoulders. Nice, too. He noted leather boots, as well, not the wellies everyone else was shod with. Smart.

"I could say my car brought me—and it was no easy task finding parking, I'll tell you—but I came for the great pleasure of this ancient ceremony. Thornford's Wassail is known the length and breadth of these blessed isles, from Land's End to John O'Groats."

"It is not."

Màiri laughed. "I came because I was at a loose end. A girl likes to get out on a Saturday night from time to time."

Tom glanced at his watch. "It's all of five fifteen. The Wassail'll be finished by seven."

"The night will still be young, then, will it not?"

"Well—"

"Och, Tom Christmas, for a man with a Cambridge education, you're thick as two short planks. We'll go have a proper drink after, and not at the Church House, aye? I know an excellent pub down Yealm Road, away from prying eyes, and don't worry, I'll have you home in good time. I know Sunday's your big day."

His under-rehearsed sermon tripped through his mind, as did finding some excuse to Miranda and Madrun for an unscheduled break in his—albeit dull—Saturday routine. He felt a tickle in the pit of his stomach, a surge farther south, and his nose seemed to discover some subtle scent from Màiri that vanquished all the prosaic damp smells in the hut. He smiled at her. He knew the pub she meant. The deanery met there once, in the autumn, for its monthly whinge. It was more country inn than mere pub.

"I expect I could be persuaded," he responded with a feint at nonchalance, moving his left hand reflexively to the clerical collar peeking from his open jacket, nearly spilling his scrumpy with the other.

"I've noted you still wear your wedding ring." Her eyes followed his hand.

"Difficult to remove," he said, aware that ambiguity freighted the words.

"The collar comes off, though."

"Yes, it slips off."

"I'd hate to think you were sewn into it. Does it ever choke you?"

"Only sometimes."

Slightly unnerved by his little spurt of lust, by the possibilities of the evening ahead (*it's just a drink!*), and by the challenge temptation presented (*is it just a drink?*), Tom laughed nervously. But Màiri's attention had been drawn to the middle distance, where two figures were cutting a swath through the swarm of parents and children in good measure because each had a shotgun cocked in the crook of his—and her—elbow. One of them was Penella Neels, a resident of the farm at Thorn Barton who had been an adult confirmand in Tom's confirmation class in the spring. She smiled broadly and greeted him with a silly finger wave. He couldn't hear her giggle above the general hubbub, but he could interpret the gesture and the blush that rose to her pretty cheeks.

"She fancies you," Màiri remarked over the rim of her plastic cup.

"Oh, quite unlikely."

"They're not all disinclined to men at Thorn Barton, you know."

"I know." Thorn Barton, the former manor farm, was owned collectively by eight women dedicated to organic produce and humanely raised dairy cows. "Besides, it appears she might be with Nick."

"Lucky old her," Màiri murmured dryly. "I'm not happy their bringing shotguns in here with all these kids running about. I've a mind to go speak to them."

"I'd be surprised if they weren't fetching Adam. I'm told he's one of the Guns."

"Nick was last year, too. Will was the third, of course. The Moirs contribute generously to this event. I wonder who recruited Penella?"

"I would have thought weaponry would have violated the spirit of Thorn Barton somehow." As Nick leaned to tap Adam on the shoulder, Tom noted the weapon in his hand gleam with a menacing beauty in the hut's flickering light.

Màiri hooted. "Fat lot you know about country ways, Tom.

There's vermin galore on a farm, and they're not likely to hang about on the off chance some man will happen along."

"I expect not," he replied, chastened, suddenly aware of a shift in the atmosphere. Tamara and Shanks Pony continued their plucking and piping and strumming, but attention to them was waning as people shifted towards the Scout Hut door. "I think the lantern procession is to start soon. Miranda," he called, "sweetheart, are you ready?

"Are you joining us?" he asked Màiri.

"I wonder who's minding Ariel, if Adam is going to be off firing his shotgun. There, the idiot's gone and left her alone. What is he thinking? Is Caroline here? Of course she isn't." Màiri answered her own question. "She's just lost her husband. Tom, Ariel knows me from my . . . interlude with her uncle. Shall I suggest she come with us?"

Tom lowered his voice as Miranda pushed out of her plastic seat. "Perhaps not. Miranda and Ariel are having a sort of . . . tiff."

"I won't ask why. Never mind, I'll take Ariel on my own."

"Well, there's Becca's father." Tom gestured towards Victor, who was shouldering against the tide to fetch his daughter. "He might take Ariel with them. Bugger, I've nearly stepped on Becca's lantern."

Gingerly, he took a step back, nearly colliding with Molly, who had bustled up behind him, shouting, "The crowns, the crowns! I need the crowns!"

"Don't worry, Molly, they're right there." Tom gestured to the shelf. "Here, let me get them."

"Never mind!" Molly surged past him and snatched the bottom box by the string.

"Careful!" Tom shouted, but it was too late. Molly swept several of the jam-jar candles off the shelf, sending them cascading to the floor like falling stars. One shattered noisily into a dozen fragments, which skittered across the concrete, the snuffed candle rolling to the wall, while another hit the dowelling edge of the lantern, which seemed for a split second to act as cushion, but didn't. The jar tumbled to the hard surface and split with an ugly crack, releasing the candle's living flame, which leapt greedily at the flimsy paper, in an instant transforming the lantern into a blazing, crackling orange ball of fire. Molly released an agonised shriek that arrested all movement in the room for the second. In the collective gasp that followed, Tom sensed a surge of panic, a spark to a stampede that would crush into the confining corridor. He gave Màiri the quickest of glances and together, as if they were toasting the New Year, they raised their cups in unison. Cider had more alcohol than beer, but much less than the brandy that flamed many a Christmas pudding. Onto the tiny pyre, they dashed the liquid—no loss, scrumpy did taste a bit nasty—dousing the flames and sending a plume of odiferous black smoke curling to the ceiling. They stared silently at the sooty puddle for the moment it took to detect a child's wrenching sob above the renewed hubbub. It was Becca.

"Mind you don't set yourself on fire, Vicar," an older man with long sideburns quipped, handing Tom a sturdy stick on top of which was nailed a flaming tin can to make a crude cresset.

"It wasn't my daddy's fault." Miranda glared up at the man, but he had passed on down the motley parade of villagers queued outside to make their way into the orchard, handing the cressets intermittently to whomever seemed to catch his eye.

"Thank you, darling."

Indeed, it wasn't Tom's fault that Becca's lantern had been reduced to wet ash, but he felt an accessory to a crime nonetheless. A sobbing child rends the heart, and when that distraught child is accompanied by a hysterical mother, then it seems there isn't anything one won't do to put the world right, even if there was nothing one could do. Miranda, who had joined the circle of woe, had looked doubtfully at her own lovely bell-shaped lantern, and then, in a gesture that clutched at Tom's heart, held it out to Becca in offering. Becca, surprised into ending her tears, reached to take it until Victor gently pushed his daughter's arms down, thanked Miranda, and led Becca and his wife away, taking the boxes of crowns with him. Màiri smiled at Tom and as she passed to fetch Ariel whispered in his ear, "You've a treasure there."

Yes, he did.

"And thank you for being so thoughtful to Becca," he added to Miranda, consoling himself that nothing worse could possibly happen at this quaint village gathering. He glanced over at the food tent. Madrun, dressed in a weathered brown corduroy coat, her head wrapped in a scarf like the Queen's, appeared to be remonstrating with Judith Ingley, who was adjusting paper trays of baked goods covered in cling film. No tainted tartlets to spoil this evening, he thought, though he couldn't help noting that rather fewer of Madrun's offerings had been sold than those of the other ladies of the village.

"Daddy . . . " Miranda's tone was cautious.

"Mmm."

"Do you like Màiri White?"

Bugger, but that tripped him up. His daughter was telepathic: He was only about to let his mind settle on the very subject. "Yes, she seems quite nice." He bent to murmur this banality into her ear, conscious of the growing crush of people around them. He was sure the woman in front of him, quite short, her head stuffed into burgundy wool, her back unrecognizable, had begun to subtly tilt in his direction. "Don't you think she's nice?"

Miranda shrugged, didn't say anything. He knew if he ever entered into a new relationship what—or, rather, who—his biggest hurdle would be.

"Goodness! Your lantern still isn't lit!" Tom looked up and down the ragged line, seeing glimpses through the deep shadows of villagers he knew who might smoke, then glanced at the blazing cresset he was holding. Catching a light off that would certainly set off another debacle. "Someone must have matches."

"I wish I could help you, Vicar." The figure in front of them turned. It was Violet Tucker.

"Hello," Tom said. "Mark not with you?"

"I left him at home with Ruby. He's working on—" She lowered her voice and rolled her eyes. "—you know."

"We had a good talk after the PCC meeting Tuesday."

"So Mark said, and thank you. At least he's gone off that daft Harvey Porter, Pigblisters notion, but I don't know." She sighed heavily. "I really don't know what to make of it all."

"Best to let people try and fail." Tom offered the encomium, eager not to take up pastoral work on the hoof, as it were, not at this minute. "And you never know, he might have a wonderful success. Anyway, I understand congratulations are in order!"

Violet's eyes narrowed into a glare.

"Did you win something?" Miranda piped up. She bobbed her lantern impatiently on its pole.

"I . . . " Violet appeared at a loss for explanation.

"Mrs. Tucker won a year's supply of loo paper in a magazine contest," Tom improvised.

Violet's eyes widened, then she fumed, "Mark shouldn't have said anything. It's bad luck to tell anyone in the first trimester!"

"He was that chuffed, Violet. He couldn't help himself. Anyway, I won't say a word, and neither will Miranda. Will you, darling?"

Miranda turned away from Violet and rewarded him an expression of consummate boredom and impatience. She jiggled her lantern again. "Daddy! The others are all lit."

It was true. Up and down the line, peeking from behind knees and coats, he could see wondrous fat shapes—fish and birds and spaceships and flowers, glowing red and blue and green and yellow—along with more conventional glass lanterns, shop-purchased, held by older children and adults.

"You might need these." Judith Ingley joined them, proffering a box of matches. "Madrun said you might forget, so she brought these with her. Hello," she added, introducing herself to Violet. "Madrun suggested I join you. I thought sales might be better served if I stayed at the stall and she joined you instead." Judith caught his eye as he bent to light the tea lights nestled inside Miranda's lantern. "But she insisted."

Tom opened his mouth to respond, but the tenor of the crowd changed at that moment, alert to an assertive voice rising above the jabbering voices and reedy accordion near the front of the line.

"The sleep of winter lies over the land," the voice declared in a the-atrical cadence, as the music stopped and a hush settled. *"We must wake the orchard to new life!"*

A throaty cheer went up and excitement, like an electrical cur-rent, shot down the line, racing up Tom's spine. Miranda squealed. As if by common consent, everyone at once took first steps down the path, wellies slapping and slurping in the ooze, chitchat rekindling then swiftly shifting to verse as a chorus of the Wassailing Song drifted into the dark thatch of tree branches above their heads and grew louder. Tom received the cresset back from Violet and added his own poor, sad, unmusical baritone to the massed voices, feeling a tickle of joy as he took Miranda's hand and shuffled along with her and Judith down the slope, through the crumbling gate, and up the slope into the Old Orchard, pitch-black now, the twisted outlines of the trees faintly—very faintly—limned by a crescent moon cold and silver as ice. The children's lanterns, swaying and bobbing, marked the passage through the darkness, while flames from the blazing cressets flickered over the faces of the revelers.

A halt was soon called by the assertive voice, the owner of which, in light afforded by four newly lit torches set in the ground at the cardinal points of the chosen tree, was revealed as a short, plump man in eighteenth-century costume, a blue velvet frock coat, and a matching tricorn hat. The villagers encircled the tree, its branches so gnarled and moss-covered that it blazed in the darkness like a burning bush. Tom watched the top of a ladder fall against its trunk, then the king, wearing the golden crown Molly had finished the day before, scramble into the branches followed at a more regal pace by Emily Swan, imperiously tossing back her encumbering cape a time or two before turning and settling herself on her woody throne, draping the green velvet fabric around her white frock fetchingly, and adjusting her crown just so.

"That child has airs," Judith murmured, though Tom thought the spectacle of the two children in the tree, crowns gleaming, costumes glowing jewel-like, young faces shining, held an atavistic charm. He could sense Miranda was captured by the scene, too. Her lantern drooped; she stood attentively still.

"Changing your mind about royal service?" Tom asked his daughter, reaching to restore her lantern. In the spring, at the May Fayre, Emily's older sister, Lucy, had been queen of the May, a role Miranda had dismissed as feudal.

"No," Miranda replied in a sharpish tone that was an echo of Lisbeth caught in a contradiction.

Tom experienced the dawn of understanding, and smiled. "Who's the king, I wonder? Is he in Year Four, too?"

"He's in Year Five."

Ah, an older man, Tom thought. "Does he have a name?"

"Garner."

"Tait? Must be the postman's son," he remarked, adding teasingly, *"est-il agréable?"*

"Daddy!"

Tom caught Judith's eye.

"I do know a little French, Vicar," she murmured.

"Sweetheart, why don't you push in a bit, so you can see better," he murmured into Miranda's ear.

But the costumed man, master of ceremonies, seemed to forestall further movement, barking out the running order of the rite, as though none of the villagers, lo these many years, had the faintest familiarity with it.

"I'm going to dip this bread," he shouted, holding up what looked like a grilled piece of Mother's Pride in a plastic bag, "into the cider and give it to the king and queen, who are not to eat it, but put it in the branches of the tree!"

"Curious," Tom muttered, watching the emcee reverently remove the slice from the bag, dip it in a bowl offered by an assistant, and hand it to Emily, who received the dripping thing with an unqueenly moue of distaste and slid it onto a branch.

"It's for the robins," Judith explained, "who sing the apple trees back to life."

"Of course." *Silly me.*

"And now"—the emcee lifted a ceramic jug for all to see—"I'm going to pour cider around the base of the tree and we'll sing the Wassailing Song. You should all join in, loudly. *Loudly!*"

"Oh, good, you've both got programmes." Tom shifted his cresset to illuminate the sheet of paper Judith held between them while Miranda opened hers.

"Old apple tree we wassail thee," voices began tentatively.

"Louder!"

"Here's hoping thou wilt bear." Voices grew more confident.

> *For the Lord doth know where we shall be*
> *When comes another year*
> *For to bloom well and bear well*
> *So happy let us be*
> *Let every man take off his cap*
> *And shout to the old apple tree.*

I should have worn a cap, Tom thought, noting that no one, man or woman, removed his or hers.

"Now shout!"

"Old apple tree, we wassail thee!" everyone shouted, breath streaming into the chilly air.

> *Here's hoping thou wilt bear*
> *Hats full*
> *Caps full*
> *Three-bushel bags full*
> *And little heaps under the stair!*
> *Hip-hip-hooray!*

"Well, that was inter—" Tom began as the third hip-hip-hooray was overtaken by a staccato of explosions ripping through the darkness of the orchard, the force of which seemed to shake the air and certainly made him jump. "Oh, my God, what was that?" slipped from his mouth before he realised it was, of course, the dramatic finale—the Guns firing off rounds to chase away the evil spirits and wake the trees from their winter slumber. He realised, too, in that second, he had crushed Miranda to him. She was now wriggling free. "Sorry, darling. Daddy isn't completely attuned to country life."

As the quartet of cressets around the apple tree was extinguished, a new set flared into life around another tree farther down the orchard's slope towards the millpond.

"Do we do this more than once?" Tom watched the throng drift through the darkness towards the new light while a squeezebox somewhere played impish melodies. Through the flickers of flame, he could make out Màiri's uncovered head bent, to Ariel no doubt, the Kaifs in some uneasy truce as they shepherded Becca forward, and the red tip of Old Bob's bobble hat bouncing along like a little jelly.

"Three times, if I remember," Judith replied, slipping from the partial shadow of light cast by Tom's cresset.

"I'm going to get closer!" Miranda darted away.

"We'll be right here at the back," Tom called after her. "I've got this . . . torch thing," he added, glancing at Judith's pink jacket. "You can't miss us."

"You've been blessed with a fine daughter," Judith remarked as Tom caught up to her and they trailed after the villagers over the spongy grass.

"You're the second person to say that to me tonight."

Old Bob caught his attention again. Remarkably for a man his age, and condition, he was helping one of the lads set the ladder against the tree. Tom had a question for Judith about Bob, though the middle of the Wassail probably wasn't the best time to voice it. Nevertheless: "May I ask, did Bob talk of anything else with you yesterday?"

Judith stopped with him at the edge of the crowd, and fell again within the penumbra of light from his cresset. "Well," she said, lifting the hood of her jacket over her head, "he told me of his prognosis, of course. Didn't we talk about this yesterday in the churchyard?" She gave him a swift elliptical glance. "I think that's what spurred him in part to tell me the details of my father's death, which had been weighing on his conscience all these years. But you know how ill Bob is, despite appearances, Tom. Other than his doctor, I think you're the only person he's told."

"You say, 'in part.'" Tom glanced over to the radiant apple tree, into which the king and queen were climbing. "Was he seeking something else from you? You are a nurse."

She was tying the strings below her hood, but she turned her head again. This time her eyes in the flicking flame were gimlet-thin. She said evenly: "You're fishing for something, Vicar."

But the crowd began again the Wassail chant, sparing Tom for the moment. He was uncomfortably aware that Judith might very well think his enquiry intrusive and unwelcome, but he felt morally bound to offer his dissent and caution her. As he absently recited the Wassail verse for the second time, he formulated in his mind what he would say, but when the final cheers were followed by another shattering volley of shotgun fire, he flinched again. The words flew from his mind.

"You are a townie, aren't you?" Judith observed as she led the way down the grass towards a third tree, again lit against the obtruding darkness. Stopping, she hunched her shoulders and moved her arms protectively across her chest, as if drawing in against the cold.

"That looks more like a mulberry," she remarked as the ladder was raised into the branches.

She wasn't alone. Tom could hear similar mutterings around him until finally one voice—sharp, female, and recognisable—rose above the chorus: "You ridiculous man! That's *not* an apple tree!"

"Florence?" Tom scanned the backs of heads and profiles visible in the tenebrous light. He and Judith were standing on a gentle rise in the orchard's uneven terrain, which climbed behind them to the vicarage wall. "How did she manage to hobble down Thorn Hill?"

"She probably made poor Venice carry her."

But Judith's remark was lost amid the titters and Florence's triumphant declaration: "That's a *mulberry!*"

"The Wassail," the emcee interrupted, then raised his voice as the crowd hummed like disturbed bees, "the *Wassail* is not just about apples—"

"Nonsense!"

"—it's also about pears and other fruits. It wasn't just about getting cider, it was about a good summer full of fruits." His voice gained in confidence. "This is probably not an apple tree, but it is, however, a berry tree."

"You don't wassail a mulberry tree! You might just as well wassail a yew tree and you wouldn't want to give a leg up to those poisonous beggars, ha!"

The buzz became a collective gasp.

"Florence! Really!" Venice's voice broke through but then subsided into a jag of coughing.

"Yewberries are *not* poisonous, and you know it, Florence Daintrey!" a new voice snapped. Madrun's. From his vantage point, Tom could discern his housekeeper's face dancing in flame on the other side of the tree and the thunder in her expression. "Only the *seeds* are poisonous."

"Oh, dear," Judith murmured.

Emollient words formed on Tom's lips and he was about to step forward when the emcee, by now choleric—the uncooked dough of his face had grown blotchy with patches of red and white—began to shriek in a way unbecoming a gentleman.

"Ladies, it doesn't matter! It doesn't *bloody* matter! We're wassailing *this* bloody tree and I don't care if it bears *coconuts*! *Poisonous* coconuts! Now *shut up*!"

Everyone was stunned into silence, as if their normally proper schoolmaster had been revealed a champion swearer.

"Well, get on with it then!" Florence snapped, her voice slightly subdued.

"Thank you, madam!" He jammed his hat forward on his head.

This time Emily Swan scrambled up the tree (whatever its genus) after the king with something less than regality and the whole rite began a new cycle, with the emcee, his hand shaking in the aftermath of rage, pulling a new slice of bread from a bag and dipping into a proffered bowl of cider. But the atmosphere had soured. Tom sensed an eagerness to get it over with and get back to the warmth of the Scout Hut and the promise of more food and drink.

"After all these years," Judith remarked, "how could they not know which trees in this orchard are apple and which are not? Anyway," she continued, regarding Tom speculatively. "You were on a fishing expedition about Bob Cogger."

"Please don't take this amiss, but earlier today my daughter happened to mention—quite innocently—that you had been . . . researching something, well, disturbing on my computer—"

"Yes, I know what you mean. I'm sorry, I'd had a call on my mobile and forgot to sign out. You've been so kind to let me use it. I realised my mistake about an hour later, but it was too late. I didn't think it would be Miranda who would come upon it."

"She had questions in the car this morning. Mercy killing, assisted death—they're novel concepts to her."

"And I apologise for putting you in an awkward position."

"That's all right. I don't mind talking with Miranda about such things. It was simply . . . " He couldn't find the words.

Judith lifted the programme. The others had begun to recite the Wassail verses again, albeit in a somewhat desultory fashion. She opened her mouth to join in, then dropped her hand and turned back to Tom.

"I think I understand." She held up a gloved finger. "Because I'm a nurse and because Bob is old, diabetic, and suffering from chronic renal failure—and because of what I was looking at on the Internet— you thought I might be helping him to end his life."

"Well . . . "

"I wouldn't really need to look on the Internet specifically for that, Tom. I do know how. When Trevor was moving into stage three of Parkinson's and unable to walk or stand, we talked about it, looked into it." She raised the programme again. " 'Old apple tree,' " she began reciting with the others, then glanced up at him, "Shall we continue . . . ?"

"But you didn't—with your husband, I mean."

"No. We couldn't. I couldn't. I'm a Christian woman, Tom, despite spotty church attendance. I believe in the sanctity of life."

"Then why . . . ," Tom began, his voice lost in the final eruption of hip-hip-hooray. "Oof," he grunted, flinching as one gun went off again, blasting into the night sky, one shot following sickeningly— though less rhythmically than before—on another.

But his mind was arrested by a curious anomaly in the third—and frighteningly close—volley, what to his townie ears sounded like a slightly different resonance. And in that second, before he could even think to grasp his meaning, he heard another sound, a hideous groan, and felt Judith's body slam against his own, crumple and pitch forward onto the grass, an ooze of pink on the outer edge of an inconstant ring of firelight.

CHAPTER TWENTY-SIX

The tea was hot and sweet, much hotter than his tongue should accept, much sweeter than he would normally take, but Tom sipped at it greedily, hungry for its restorative powers, welcoming the glorious warmth radiating from his solar plexus outwards up through his chest and along his arms. Brooking no argument, Madrun had settled a blanket around his shoulders, though warmth enough seeped from the kitchen's Aga and the vicarage's central heating. Thus cosseted, he could feel himself begin to sink into a kind of torpor of relief, as if he were a child back in Gravesend settled by Dosh or Kate back into sleep with hot chocolate and Jaffa cakes after waking from a particularly savage nightmare. He fought to keep his eyelids from descending, but they did, and when they did cascading images of the last hour jolted him awake with new horror.

In his first heartbeat, he had thought Judith had fallen into a faint, shocked by the proximity of the third shotgun blast, but at the second beat, as a spray of hot liquid touched his throat and hands, he understood this was nothing so quaint, though his brain refused at first to make sense of what was passing before his eyes in the flickering light of the cresset—the spreading stains along the yoke of her jacket like dark wine newly spilled, the pink fabric split and shredded, its downy filling burst and spilling. And when, by the third beat, all the disparate details coalesced into a vision of horror sprawled at his feet, he was seized by a shock so sweeping in its intensity, he felt his knees buckling. Some good part of that, he understood now, as he gulped the sweet tea, was the hideous echo of his own wife's death, flickering images like an old silent movie of a woman's body, Lisbeth's, fallen in a wash of blood, images that still haunted his dreams and intruded into his waking thoughts. On the fourth beat, barely conscious of the nasty damp penetrating to the skin of his knees, he was crouched over Judith, dipping the flickering light of the torch close in desperate search for some vestige of life.

There was none.

And then tumult. Like a rogue wave, alarm coursed through the revelers. The varied pitch of the explosion, perhaps, the varied direction of the shot, some incongruity below the radar of consciousness, sent those on the periphery of the crowd, those nearest Tom, twisting their necks in puzzled enquiry, a few eyes coming to rest on the ground, now a bier for Judith's body.

"Someone's been shot!" a voice bawled. A hush of disbelief contained the orchard for a second, and then a thrum, like the susurration of disturbed bees, swept through the crowd, but unlike bees agitated in their hive, none swarmed in a single direction. Though barely conscious of anything behind the light encircling him, Tom could sense a pandemonium of movement, hear the tramping boots and the brush of fabric, glimpse the frail light of lanterns fading towards the Scout property or towards the gate to Poynton Shute and the village centre. But others raced towards him, drawn by the spectacle of the fallen body and the crouched figure.

"Oh, my Lord!" one woman shrieked. Tom looked up to see her spread her hands over her face, then looked at the other downturned faces, each one wearing some expression of horror and disbelief, some glancing quickly away, others staring hard into the darkness as if in search of the source of this outrage.

"Is she—?" said one.

"I'm afraid so," Tom managed to croak, rising unsteadily, lurching to his feet still grasping the cresset. He noted faces before him flinch.

"Vicar, you've blood all over you."

Tom swiped at the wetness along his neck above his collar, then stared at his glistening fingers, smeared and viscous. Without thought, he rubbed them down his trousers, over and over in hard, repulsed motions until he felt his skin chafe.

"Has someone a mobile?" He surveyed the stricken faces in the flickering light.

"I've called emergency, Tom." Màiri's calming voice broke through. "Perhaps we should all give the vicar a little room," she added, slipping through a breach in the phalanx of villagers.

Tom watched her eyes travel to the lifeless body at his feet, watched her flinch, watched her eyes return to his, full of disquiet. But all she said was, "Madrun has taken Miranda away."

He nodded, grateful, but suddenly sick at the notion that this frightening episode had erased from his mind for even a moment the most precious thing in his life. As his eyes, unbidden, returned to the corpse, two new figures shouldered into the circle of light.

"Oh, my God, what's happened?" Penella's voice was strangled with disbelief. One arm went to her middle, as if she were trying to keep herself from crumpling. But in the crook of her other arm, almost obscenely casual, rested a shotgun.

"What's happened," a voice barked from the crowd that recoiled from the sight of the weapon, "is that you've killed this woman."

"I don't even know who she is!" Penella stared goggle-eyed at the body. "I didn't . . . " She gestured helplessly to the male figure beside her, similarly gripping a shotgun. "It's impossible. I was—"

"We were over there." Adam Moir motioned down the orchard, in the direction of the entrance gate to Poynton Shute. He gaped at the ground, his face blanched, a sheen of sweat breaking over his skin. "Over there." His hand trembled. "And—"

"And we shot in the air! We shot in the *air!*" Penella's face crumpled in tears.

"They're blanks," Adam insisted, his voice cracking. "We shot blanks."

"That weren't no blank used, lad." The belligerent voice intruded again, rich with country authority. "That weren't shot, neither. Look at her! T'were a slug in one of yours and—"

"There wasn't!" Adam began to rally.

"All right!" Màiri broke in. "There's no point in arguing this now. We need to clear the orchard. Any of you who think you saw something or heard something that might be useful, go and wait at the Scout Hut or give me your names now. You lot"—she turned to a few of the younger men—"pull up those torches and bring them here. The rest of you go to your homes . . . or back to the Scout Hut, if anyone has the heart to keep this poor sad Wassail going."

Folk glanced at each other with distress and hopeless resignation.

"We were all turned the wrong way," said the woman who had kept her hands over her face through most of the exchange. "And it's too dark to see anything."

"But it did sound more like it came from over this part," said another.

"There!" Adam said. "I told you."

His antagonist gave him a sour glare, then everyone began to shuffle off, gathering up other folk who'd lingered, curious on the periphery, their voices fading into the darkness.

"You two will need to stay." Màiri addressed Adam and Penella, glancing at their shotguns. Penella nodded, crying fat sobs, leaking mascara down her cheeks. Adam offered no succour; he glanced at Màiri, then stared sullenly at the body.

"I don't expect we'll be having that drink," Màiri murmured as the young men returned with the cressets and planted them in the grass around Judith's fallen body, as if preparing the ground for some primitive midnight ritual.

Tom glanced at Màiri, grateful for the bonhomie. "No, I expect not." He sensed his smile wobbling.

"You've had a wee shock, Tom. Why don't you go back to the vicarage? They can find you there when they need you."

"Best I stay, I think. I'll be fine, really. I feel I should keep a vigil of sorts." *Because I didn't with Will.*

Màiri raised a doubting eyebrow, though she said, "Of course. I understand."

Now, in the kitchen, Tom took another gulp of tea and considered what he was going to say to the detectives when they arrived. In the orchard, by a body uncomforted by anything but the dross of leaves and putrefying fruit, unmarked by anything but crude tin-can torches, unwitnessed by anyone but himself, he had begun a simple prayer for Judith Ingley, asking the Lord to receive her soul, have mercy on her, pardon all her sins and shelter her soul in the shadow of His wings. The invocation, murmured into the still air, was almost reflexive in its choice of the words, burnished as they were by vigils at other deathbeds. And it was just as well the words slipped without difficulty from his tongue, for his mind, fuelled by a spasm of pure anger, had flown to un-Christian thoughts of hate and reprisal: The outrage of shooting into a crowd where children—*his child!*—were present. The outrage of a public execution, for this was no accident. And then came the terrifying thought—he couldn't block it; it rose on beating black wings—that *he* may have been the target. Had he and Judith shifted stance as the trigger was pulled? He was certain they hadn't, and he felt a moment's guilty relief that he had been spared, but the thought of Miranda rendered fatherless as well as motherless left him nauseous, suddenly gasping for air, and it took an effort of prayer to steel himself and allow a regular measure of cold night air to cleanse his lungs, clear his brain, and restore him to the shattered world. Peering into the shadows, he spotted the silhouettes of Penella and Adam waiting, as they all were, for the klaxon of the first emergency vehicles to sound down the Pennycross Road. They were in muttered argument when he approached.

" . . . you were, too!" he heard Penella say.

"I just went for a pee, that's all!"

"Adam wasn't with me when we did the last round." Penella addressed Tom with a look of frightened fury on her face.

"Shut up, Penella. I went for a pee, Mr. Christmas, that's all. They were arguing about what sort of tree they were wassailing so I went over to the wall in the dark and, you know . . . Then they started again and I only had time to zip up so I fired from a different . . . "

"Where's your uncle?" Tom snapped at Adam, cutting him off. "I thought he was one of the Guns."

It was Penella who replied. Wiping her puffy eyes, she croaked, "Nick had an emergency and had to leave. A call came through on his mobile."

"What kind of emergency?"

Penella flicked a glance at Adam, who remained mute. "I don't know. He didn't say."

"And when was this?"

"Half an hour ago?"

"Be more precise—there were three shots after each tree was wassailed. Did he—"

"The call came a little before we fired the rounds for the second tree—that's right, isn't it, Adam? He left as soon as we'd finished."

"And you have no idea where he's gone?"

"No."

"Were you expecting him back, Penella?"

Penella frowned, as if confused. Then understanding dawned in her wet eyes. "Well, no. I mean . . . we're only . . . friends. But, you can't think that Nick would—"

"He was smiling." Adam found his voice. "When he picked up the call he was smiling—grinning. I could see his face in the light from the screen on his mobile."

"And what," Tom asked with asperity, "is that supposed to mean?"

"He was happy, like. He wouldn't . . . " Adam's voice trailed off.

Disgusted, Tom had walked off, into the dark. The first of two cars, blue lights flashing, arrived outside the gate of the Old Orchard. With Màiri, he had greeted the officers and relayed a gloss of the events. At her insistence, he returned to the vicarage, feeling, as he glimpsed the cosy golden lozenges of light that were the windows of his home, like a weary traveller returned after years abroad. His heart gladdened as he passed through the unoiled gate and walked the stone path to his well-lit door. But his hand stopped at the door handle. Suddenly he was conscious that once inside the vicarage and bathed in its homely light, his appearance would telegraph to his daughter and his housekeeper his frightful proximity to the evening's tragic event. He fumbled at his neck and stripped off his clerical collar. He stared for a second at the violations to its pristine surface, then stuffed it in the pocket of his splattered jacket, which he could only hope to bury in the back of the vestibule closet. But what of his skin? His hair? He glanced towards the Church House Inn and gave a passing thought to washing in its men's loo, but it was too late. Bumble, attuned to the creaking of the gate and the idiosyncrasies of his footfall, was in a lather of barking, dashing to snuffle around his feet as Madrun flung open the door. He could see the strain behind her glasses give way to relief.

"Where's Miranda?"

"In the kitchen. I've given her some rice pudding." Madrun moved to shut the connecting door to the hall. "We had something to eat outside the Scout Hut, but I thought it best we not tarry. People were talking."

"Does she know?"

"Only that someone's been hurt."

"Do you know?"

"Yes. Mr. Christmas, you don't look at all well. Someone told me you were standing very near Judith."

"Very." Tom stepped into the vestibule and struggled out of his jacket as Madrun switched on the light. When he turned, Madrun was rubbing her fingers along the fabric of one of its arms. She peered at some residue on the skin of her thumb, frowned, then shot him a horrified glance.

"Mrs. Prowse," he said, "Miranda mustn't know—about me being . . . nearby."

"But—"

"Daddy?" came a muffled, faintly querulous voice in the direction of the kitchen.

"But Mr. Christmas, you've got blood—"

"Daddy's got a bit chilled, darling." Tom opened the door and called down the hall in what he hoped was his best cheery voice. "I'm going up for a nice hot shower and then I'll be right down."

But the shower, though cleansing, had been insufficient restorative. Afterwards, after he had changed into fresh clothes, after he had joined Miranda in the kitchen and answered her blunt questions as best he could, after he had hugged her tightly and she had gone to her bedroom, Powell and Gloria trailing after her, after he had brooded with deep unease and not a little astonishment that his daughter took this cursed event so in her stride, he began to shiver like a juddering kettle with no cutout switch. Only the cocooning blanket and the hot, sweet tea began his restoration and the onset of new thoughts:

Surely police enquiry would move quickly to the absent Gun. Who else in the orchard, besides Adam and Penella, was in possession of a shotgun? But was Nick Stanhope so arrogant, so impulsive that he thought he could pull off this outrageous act and somehow escape scrutiny? A simple forensic examination would quickly determine that the slug, if slug it was, came from his shotgun, would it not? Unless he had tucked away a second shotgun somewhere in the orchard, accessible at an opportune moment, then quickly abandoned—that, at least, would indicate some forethought.

But surely motive would elude investigators. Why would Nick seek to execute a woman he barely knew?

Tom had a notion why, but if it were true it gave him no satisfaction. He would have no qualm passing along to the police what Judith had told him: that Nick had threatened her, yesterday, outside the Church House Inn. This he could do with a clear conscience. He had no reason to believe she was dissembling; her telling him was a bare fact and a starting point for an investigation. What he could not—and would not—do was speculate in front of the police about the nature of that threat. In truth, he had no details about the content; Judith had provided him none. But he could guess. As he nursed his tea and waited for the vicarage door chimes to herald Bliss and Blessing's arrival, he reflected on the fine line he felt obliged to tread.

The Vicarage

Thornford Regis TC9 6QX

Dearest Mum,

The most awful thing has befallen us! Much worse than ruined Yorkshires or perhaps even wandering yew seeds. And I've hardly slept a wink! Yesterday at the Wassail our houseguest was shot. You recall how shotguns are fired into the air after each tree is wassailed. Well, this time someone didn't shoot into the air. ~~They He They~~ Someone shot into a human being—Judith Ingley, as I said, and upsetting as it is to sit here and type on this piece of paper, she was killed. Instantly, which is a blessing, I suppose, though at the time most thought there'd been an accident of sorts. I hadn't even intended to join the wassailing last evening, but I'm glad I did now. I stayed behind to mind the cake stall, but as sales weren't brisk, I went into the orchard as the third tree was being wassailed in time to hear Florence Daintrey ~~impung inpune~~ criticise my baking in front of everyone—I gave as good as I got, I must say—but minutes later, after the guns

*went off, someone shouted that someone had been shot, which set
everyone into a bit of panic, it being so dark and all and of
course you wonder these days with all sorts about if some de-
praved soul hadn't happened upon the orchard with evil intent.
Anyway, I could see Miranda near the tree and thought it best to
get her away, back to the Scout Hut at least, as I couldn't see
where her father was, but I had barely enough time to buy her a
hot dog (awful things!) before someone whispered to me that it
was the* VICAR *who had been shot. Well, I was very nearly reel-
ing, horrified for Miranda, and knew I had to get her home before some addle-brain blurted it out in front of her. I have to say
I was almost quite relieved when Rab Sorley, who does the
MC'ing each Wassail, announced in the carrying voice of his
that a visitor to the village had been shot—accidentally, he
said—but then, Mum, I had a worrying thought who it might
be, and Bob Cogger confirmed it when we were turning into
Poynton Shute. He was* VERY *upset, poor man! Mum, I was so
glad when Mr. Christmas arrived at the door, but oh he looked
shattered. He cleaned up before talking to Miranda—there were
telltale spots of blood on him, awful!—but I'm not really sure if
she understood what happened, as some of their conversation was
in French, ~~as usual~~. I'm not sure I understand what's happened
either. Mr. C told Miranda that nobody knows yet if it was an
accident or not, which I expect is true, but he told me after Miranda had gone up to her room that the shotgun contained a slug
rather than shot. Mr. C didn't say, but of course that means
someone deliberately had it in mind to take Judith's life, which is
the most appalling thing! Or perhaps someone else's life, which is
even worse, though Mr. C seemed certain the intended victim
was poor Judith. Why and who would do this, I asked, but I've
told you before how ~~circomspec cercum~~ he'll go all quiet about
what he's thinking sometimes. Anyway those two CID, Bliss and
Blessing, arrived before long and Mr. C had a longish chat with*

them in his study. I took them tea ~~and listened at the door~~
thought I might glean something but no chance. I phoned Karla
to tell her the incredible news as she thinks the Wassail is un-
Christian and so never goes and isn't at all happy that the vicar
put in an appearance and said if he was going to attend such
nonsense then he should be prepared to suffer the consequences,
which I thought was rather harsh, but then she was a bit short
over the phone as I had caught her in the middle of watching
coverage of the select committee proceeding on the Parliament
channel, which is one of her favourite programmes. She said she
thought something was askew as she had only finished closing the
shop when someone raced past the door, then not much later, all
kinds seemed to be moving through the village, on their way
home and such, and she thought the Wassail went on past 7 and
here it was barely 6. Anyway, she thought what with Will
Moir's poisoning only a week ago, Thornford was going to get a
reputation, and it occurred to me maybe if we did that would
put a stop to Thorn Court being turned into housing, as no one
would want to move here, but then I thought I was being very
uncharitable to think that way. I wondered to Karla if we really
ought to go to Tenerife Tuesday, given what's happened—I hate
to think of Miranda coming home from school and no one here
with some gunman loose about the village—but Karla's deter-
mined the only thing keeping us away from a sunny beach would
be another snowstorm or some volcano erupting in Iceland and
making a mess of everything. Cross fingers then they find the
gunman in time, Mum. Anyway, after the two CID left, Mr.
Christmas remained a long time in his study—revising his ser-
mon, he said—then went up for an early night, though I could
hear him talking to Miranda when I went up to my bed. I usu-
ally sleep like a stone, but I've had the worst sleep since that time
last June when there were those doings in the churchyard, if you
remember, when Sybella Parry died. I woke up about three and

couldn't get back to sleep, so I listened to the World Service for a bit, then I drifted off, but I woke up again before five, and thought maybe some warm milk might do the trick, but then I realised my Teasmade would go off in an hour, so I thought I might as well give up trying to sleep. So I had a nice cup of tea, after which I had the brilliant notion of going down and making a start sorting and packing Judith's things and putting the guest bedroom to right, being that the rest of Sunday is so busy as I'm trying to prepare enough ready meals for Mr. C and Miranda while I'm away. So I did, though it did feel odd and sad and so very final and even a little eerie—almost as if Judith's ghost were there when I took her things from the wardrobe and folded them into her suitcase. She did like bright solid colours, I must say. A change from the drab things she had to wear when she was a nurse, she told me. Anyway, I ~~was going through~~ happened to open her purse to put back some pills she'd left out on the bureau (for blood pressure, I think) when a wallet tumbled out that had a number of papers, driver's licence and so forth, in it which scattered onto the rug. One was quite an old piece of folded paper with a slight tear that I thought I might have caused, but when I unfolded it, I realised it was one of those heavy linen-backed birth certificates with the handwriting they used to give out. Do you remember? (I've got mine tucked away in a box in my bedroom.) I assumed it was Judith's. I wasn't sure precisely how old she was, so I glanced at it just to see, and wasn't I surprised, Mum, to see that the certificate wasn't hers, but her son's! I suppose some mothers keep their children's birth certificates or only give them to their children when they need them, like getting a first passport or the like. Anyway, it had the Registration District—Leeds—and her son's full Christian names, William Anthony Sean. But what was odd was that the father's name had been left blank and Judith had only recorded her maiden name. Then I looked at the date of birth and thought, AHA! *So her son living in China isn't her husband's natural child at all, which made me think Judith must have been pregnant when she left Thornford all those years ago. Mum, do you remember any of this? Of course, I couldn't help wondering who Tony Ingley's father might be and then it sort of crept up on me as I sat down on Judith's bed and had a think that it might have been that tearaway Clive Stanhope. After all they were the same age, and Judith lived at Thorn Court then. What do you think? Anyway, all in the past I thought and was about to return the certificate to her purse with her mobile and other things, but then I began to think that if Tony Ingley was Clive Stanhope's child, then he's a half brother to both Caroline Moir and Nick Stanhope and might this mean something? Could it be that Tony Ingley could make some sort of claim on his natural father's estate, even five years after Clive's death? I'm no solicitor, so I haven't a clue, but I began to wonder if it all linked in some way to Will Moir's death (and Judith's, perhaps), but I couldn't at all see how. Anyway, I have the certificate with me right beside the typewriter, and I'll show it to Mr. Christmas later this morning. Perhaps he will be able to make sense of it. I must tell you before I sign off that I had a nice chat with Tamara before all the terribleness happened. Mr. C drove her in from Exeter as he happened to be there with his daughter visiting poor Julia Hennis, though I gather Adam was to fetch her, but didn't or couldn't or wouldn't or something, which she seemed to find very vexing. Young people! Anyway, her studies are going well, Miranda was very complimentary about her and Shanks Pony, which I didn't get a chance to hear, minding the cake stall as I was. Jago might have shown up to hear his daughter, but then he probably had his head stuck in a motor, as usual. I hope Tamara is writing to you regularly. And Kerra, too. Anyway, must go. I think poor Mr.*

Christmas has a hard day ahead, so I must be sure he is fortified. The menagerie is well, though Bumble is a trial sometimes. Love to Aunt Gwen.

Much love,
Madrun

P.S. I spotted Màiri White at the Wassail looking very glammed up for a little village ~~affair~~ event! You have to watch these women like a hawk. At least with Mr. James-Douglas I never had to worry about that sort of thing! Also, Penella Neels, who was hovering around Mr. C last year at her confirmation classes, seems to have taken up with Nick Stanhope, which certainly tells me what poor judgement she has!

word, Father?"

Tom turned from the small mirror over the vestry table where he had been examining the dark circles under his eyes, the effect of a night of fitful sleep. Colm Parry, St. Nicholas's choir director and organist, was leaning around the door, his caramel, glazed skin such a visible rebuke to Tom's cheerless winter pallor Tom couldn't help remark on it.

"Not a cloud in the sky in Barbados, I have to tell you." Colm stepped into the cramped vestry, its chill barely vanquished by a wall-mounted electric fire. His hand grazed his spiky gelled hair, as if checking it was still there. (Whether Colm's hair was his own remained a village controversy.)

"And I thought we weren't seeing you this Sunday."

"Otis has come down with something, a cold, flu. I could barely understand him. Didn't he phone you?"

"He might have." Tom had stayed in bed later than he ought and

Madrun had trailed after him through the vicarage, plying him with toast, coffee, messages, instructions, queries—none of which he had been able to properly ingest before racing off in his car through the mizzly rain to Pennycross St. Paul. Returning to Thornford from Pennycross, the engine light on his car had flashed on. Worried, he had dropped the car with Jago at Thorn Cross Garage and ran most of the way through the village to St. Nicholas's. Tom felt extremely fizzy and tired, rather as if he had stepped off a plane himself after a very long flight. "Good thing you were available."

"Well, Otis would have struggled in, if he had to, so he must be *quite* under the weather."

Tom caught Colm's meaning. Otis Croucher, St. Nicholas's new assistant choir director and organist, was a reedy young man from Totnes with a certificate from the Royal College of Organists, no less, but with a whiff of troubled psyche, which seemed to grow more apparent with each quarterly meeting to select hymns and anthems. Finding musicians for small parishes was no easy task, but Otis seemed increasingly wont to go off into little tantrums that evinced a narrow view of music and a generous view of his own importance. That Colm had had a bubble of pop-star fame in the eighties and was loved for it by the villagers buttered no parsnips for Otis Croucher.

"Otis didn't struggle in last Sunday, either," Tom told Colm. "The weather, you know. The choir was somewhat diminished, too, but we carried on. Very Dunkirk of us. Anyway, I thought you—"

"We got to Exeter airport late last evening," Colm interrupted. "And we were going to stay overnight at the Cumberland but I thought I'd really rather sleep in my own bed." He shrugged. "Which, in the end, didn't happen."

Tom stepped towards the vestry's inner corner where his cassock was hanging and shot Colm a puzzled frown. "Why not?" seemed to be the requisite question.

"Oona was in it."

"Is this where I do one of those double takes they do in films?" Tom asked wearily. He really wasn't feeling too clever.

"Yes."

"All right, here goes: Your ex-wife was in your bed!"

Colm had the grace to look discomfited. "She wasn't supposed to be. There are a number of other bedrooms at Thornridge. I told her to use the Yellow Bedroom, but of course she doesn't take direction very well. Never did. It's a wonder her modelling career lasted as long as it did. Anyway, I'll be facing a decorator's bill before too long."

Tom's eyebrows went up a notch as he buttoned his cassock.

"Celia," Colm responded. "Seeing Oona in our bed rather set her teeth on edge. To say the least."

" 'Seeing'?"

Colm nodded grimly. "That and more."

"I thought you and Oona weren't on awfully good terms."

"There's been some . . . thaw—since Sybella's death, you understand."

Tom did. Colm and Oona's nineteen-year-old daughter had been found murdered in the spring, a tragedy that horrified the village.

"It was Celia's doing," Colm continued. "You know, she trained as a psychologist. She thought it would be therapeutic for Oona and me to try and patch things up, and so we have—at least given it a go. We talk on the phone once in a while. At any rate, Oona'd been given the push by someone, that fellow—you might recall. Oona brought him to the funeral. I wasn't happy about it at the time. He was barely older than Sybella."

"Edoardo Lanzoni."

"Very good."

"I credit my housekeeper. She read out an item from one of the papers about their falling-out at breakfast some weeks ago. Underpants model or the like."

"That's right. Not a bad bloke, as it turns out. Thought he might stay the course, but no such luck. Oona's a handful at the best of times. Still, breaking up at Christmas . . ." Colm's mouth twisted. "Oona was miserable, so I suggested last-minute that as Celia, Declan, and I would be away on a mini break that she get out of London, come down to Devon, stay at the house, and have a good licking of her wounds here."

"That seems kind," Tom demurred, reaching for his surplice. "My sense is that it wasn't wise, however."

"Oona has only a passing relationship with housekeeping, for one thing. Celia had cancelled Joyce Pike's cleaning services for the week we were away, so the place was an absolute bloody tip when we walked through the door. Oona couldn't manage to load a dishwasher when we were married, and still can't."

"If she was having parties or the like, I'm sure we would have heard about it in the village. I don't think anyone even knew Oona was in the vicinity." Tom pulled the surplice over this head. "Besides, she would have been snowed in for the first few days. We all were. You were lucky to get out of the country."

"We were one of the last flights out of Exeter airport." Colm's horsy teeth blazed in his bronzed face. "Lucky us." Then his expression grew grave. "But here's why I wanted a word, Tom. When we found Oona in our bedroom—or, rather, when Celia found her, as she went upstairs first, and started in to shrieking—Oona wasn't alone."

"Ah."

"I really do think that new bed linen would suffice, but Celia is set on a new suite, fresh paint, new carpeting—the lot."

"Is it important who Oona was with? You needn't tell me."

"It was . . ." Colm leaned back to look round the door into the sanctuary. The murmuring and cheery hellos of the early arrivers—the bellringers, choir members, sidesmen—echoed along the stone walls. "It was Nick Stanhope."

His embroidered green stole slipped from Tom's hands. "Nick? I wouldn't have thought he and Oona travelled in anything like the same circles."

"They don't. I hired Nick's firm to do some upgrades to our security system, thinking he might best do it while we were off in Barbados. But when we got back last night, half the doors were unlocked, the house unalarmed. Apparently, he was distracted by Oona."

"Was that his excuse?"

"Essentially. Anytime Oona wanted him—and she didn't want him for his way around a fuse box—she'd set off the alarm. Of course, I was furious. It's like going off and leaving two teenagers to mind your house. I've got hundreds of thousands of pounds' worth of recording equipment, and there's the art, and Celia's jewellery. Oona's past reforming, but I was set to give Nick a bollocking for his irresponsibility." He drew a breath. "However—"

"I'm presuming you didn't invite Nick and Oona to stay the night," Tom interjected. "In another bedroom, of course."

"Too right I didn't."

"You wouldn't have asked where they were going, would you?"

"I was past caring. Doesn't Nick have a flat in Torquay? Why?"

Tom reflected on his brief interview with Bliss and Blessing in his study last evening. If they were to act on what he had told them—that Judith told him that Nick had threatened her—then had they pulled Nick in for questioning?

"I should tell you what's befallen Caroline," Tom began, avoiding a direct response to Colm's questions. "Since you'll note her absence in the choir this morning."

"But I do know. That's why I'm hesitant to make trouble for Nick. I hired him as a favour to Caroline, but now that she's suffered this terrible tragedy, I don't want to add to her troubles. But it's not simply that, Tom. It's—"

"But how could you know? Surely the *South Devon Herald* isn't delivered in Barbados."

"I finally gave in and let Declan have an iPhone for Christmas. He spent the whole holiday texting his mates back here. He's the one who learned of it, so I went to the hotel's computer. The paper's online and had a piece about the inquest. It was shocking. *Poisoned?* I take it the police haven't gotten far with their enquiries."

"No, I'm afraid they haven't."

"And then this morning—" The church bells began to ring their changes. Colm frowned. "I should get to the choir vestry and into my kit. I'll be quick: This morning, after Otis called me, I switched on the radio while I was getting some breakfast and heard this appalling story about some woman being shot at the Wassail. Were you there?"

Tom nodded.

"Grim?"

"You might imagine."

Colm appraised Tom's expression, then gave a grunt of understanding. "Before Otis phoned, I did a little tour of the house to see in the daylight what other mess Oona might have made. I went into the gun room—"

Something in Tom's face made him stop. He continued, "You didn't know I had a gun room, did you?"

"Not until I happened across a back issue of *Country Life* at Caroline's earlier in the week—the one featuring you and Thornridge House."

"Celia's idea. I didn't want the intrusion, but she'd had the whole house done up and pouted for days until I gave in. Anyway, the gun room and its contents were entailed with the house when we bought it. Shooting is one aspect of country living in which I haven't the remotest interest, but my financial advisor said the guns—they're all Purdeys and Churchills—are a good investment, and of course Celia finds them . . . decorative. Shall we . . . ?"

Colm indicated the chancel.

"I was in the gun room," he continued, lowering his voice, as they exited the vestry, "and noticed that one of the shotguns seemed to be missing."

Tom halted them at the rood screen. "Are you sure?" he whispered, glancing through the carved oak into the nave to see the sidesmen, John Copeland and Russ Oxley, stuffing copies of the order of service into hymn books. Fred Pike moved towards the choir vestry for his cassock.

"I admit I hardly pay attention to the bloody things, but one of the cabinets looked to have a shotgun missing. I could be mistaken, of course, and there is an inventory list—somewhere—that I could check against. I wasn't overworried about it until I heard the story of the shooting on the radio and thought—can this be a coincidence? According to the story, the police aren't ruling out homicide. If you're going to shoot someone, it occurred to me, best to do it with someone else's gun, am I right, Tom?"

"Yes," Tom allowed, "that does make some sense."

"Of course, all kinds of people have shotguns in the country so I suppose all kinds of people could have done this terrible thing."

"Who knows you own shotguns?"

"Readers of *Country Life*? I don't know—all sorts. Friends who come to stay. Relatives. Some from the village—Joyce Pike twice a week. Molly Kaif's been coming quite regularly for therapy from Celia, which I probably shouldn't say, but I know you'll keep it to yourself."

"Doesn't matter, Molly's told me anyway. But who has access to your gun room?"

"Half the county has had access to my *house*, what with my security system disabled best part of the week."

"Do you keep the gun room locked?"

"No, but the gun cabinets are. Not," he added ruefully, "that the keys are difficult to find."

"And the cabinet wasn't broken into?"

"No."

"Well, there's nothing to do, Colm, but report the missing shotgun to the authorities. You have a firearms certificate for it, yes? Then if they find it, they can examine it and at least eliminate it as the possible weapon."

Colm worried his fingernail. "Which brings me back to Caroline. It's not only Nick who's been hanging about my house. Anyway, I'm not awfully concerned about his fate at the moment. It's Adam."

"Adam?"

"He comes over regularly to service the guns, keep them in good nick and so forth, so they don't lose their value. If I report the loss—particularly while they're investigating this woman's death—then the police are naturally going to turn their attention to Adam. I understand they have a job to do, but I also know from my own experience when Sybella died how . . . intrusive they can be. I'm sure Adam and Caroline—and Ariel—are already suffering terribly. I don't want to burden them with more. The shotgun's only a *thing*. Perhaps I have misplaced it. Besides, if this woman's death is no accident, what motive could Adam possibly have in shooting her? Or Nick, for that matter?"

Tom bit his lip rather than reply. Indeed, he had thought of little else during his fitful sleep. Of course, Nick, of the three in possession of a shotgun at the Wassail, had the best opportunity to shoot Judith. The call on his mobile that had taken him away from the orchard: a setup of some nature? Adam had reported Nick's "smile" at the time of the call. Was Nick smiling in anticipation of a rendezvous with Oona? Or because some plan of his was about to commence? And what motive? Colm asked. Tom could only assume Judith posed some threat to Nick, though she had dismissed his threat to her. And now means. What shotgun had Nick been using? He assumed, as Nick had been a Gun at the Wassail before, that he possessed his own firearm. But only an impulsive fool would use his own traceable weapon. Nick was impulsive, but not a fool. Perhaps there was method in his leaving Thornridge House unlocked and unalarmed. If the weapon used to shoot Judith Ingley were ever found, if it wasn't weighted and thrown into the millpond, and it turned out to be one from Thornridge House's gun room collection, Nick could claim someone, anyone, could have come and helped himself—or herself—to it.

And then, a coincidence. Thinking about it later, Tom preferred the word *coincidence*. In this instance, he didn't wish to use the godly word *providence*. Colm was about to part company for the choir vestry, but the sound of the stout south porch door creaking open on its hinge (most arrived for church through the north porch) caught their attention. And then, before they could carry on to their next tasks, a new and horrifying sight: Miranda stepping up St. Nicholas's crooked aisle in her green wellies and her crimson jacket. On her hands was a pair of remarkably bright yellow gloves reaching well up into her coat sleeves. And in her outstretched arms, carried like a lamb to sacrifice, was a shotgun.

CHAPTER TWENTY-EIGHT

The couch was soft and fat and a few inches too short to accommodate Tom's height—six feet, one inch—or length, when he was supine (or very nearly), as he was now. The choice had been: elevate the feet (over the armrest) or the head (against the other armrest). Even to lie down any which way for a moment was to invite the sleep that his body craved, but the sight of the couch, a marshmallowy confection of blue-and-white-striped chintz, was as tempting as the bed of Delilah and so he was settling upon its gentle surface for a minute—*for just a minute!*—taking care to elevate his head (not his feet) so that he wouldn't sink under the waters of Lethe. Madrun had laid a fire in the grate. It crackled slowly, sending a golden glow over the carpet. Outside, the rain continued in its mizzly fashion, pit-pit-pitting against the panes of the French windows that on warm days opened his office to the vicarage garden. On an ordinary Sunday afternoon, he might have repaired to the sitting room couch or to his bedroom, flopped down, unfolded *The Observer*, cast his eyes over its columns with great intention, and then slipped, without guilt, through postprandial torpor into sleep·full-stop. But this troubled Sunday afternoon, his racing mind countermanded his weary body and *The Observer* fell to the floor. Out in the garden, his garden, amid the shrubs and the very last of the snow, scene-of-crime officers were mucking about looking for some shred of evidence of a killer's presence. They had been concentrated on the Old Orchard in the early morning. It was Miranda's discovery that refocused their attention.

The mental picture of his child bearing a firearm jolted him anew, but at the time, as she moved through the transept, Tom felt constrained to hide his horror and revulsion behind a mask of delight for her initiative. Bumble, scrabbling through the remnant of a snowbank, dissolving in the rain, against the boundary wall between the vicarage garden and the Old Orchard, had laid bare the trace of a curious object, sending Miranda, discerning reader of Alice Roy novels, racing to the kitchen for a pair of rubber washing-up gloves.

"Regarde ce que Bumble a trouvé, Papa, she beamed, straining to raise the instrument, heavy in her child's hands. *"Mais ne le touche pas! Il pourrait y avoir . . .* fingerprints!"

The French word eluded her, which was just as well. Tom had instinctively moved to grab it, desperate to remove the dangerous thing from his daughter's grip. Mercifully, the choir members were at the back of the church in the choir vestry robing themselves; the bellringers were one floor above, busy shadows behind leaded glass. Besides Colm, only Fred, John, Russ, and—inconveniently— churchwarden Karla Skynner bore startled witness to this spectacle, the last entering from the north porch as Miranda entered from the south and casting Tom a glare so censorious he rushed to usher Miranda to the vestry.

"Do you think Mrs. Ingley was killed with this?"

Her bluntness shook him. His heart, already racing at the proximity to this instrument of death, an obscenity in the house of God, gave an uncomfortable thud, and the worry pierced his mind that Miranda was becoming tempered to violent death.

"Darling," he began gently, pulling her to him, "we won't know until the police look at it." He glanced at Colm, who was leaning over the table examining the shotgun. "But I'm sure they'll think you're brilliant."

Colm had phoned the police on his mobile. "I can only presume it's mine," he said to Tom, "and I very much wish it weren't."

While the congregation was singing "O Worship the Lord in the Beauty of Holiness," Tom noted Detective Sergeant Blessing step into the church and take a pew near the back, next to Tilly Springett, who shot him a glance of startled recognition. The sergeant sang heartily—Tom could hear his bass-baritone rumble below the reedy voices of his flock—ending the Epiphany hymn with a full-blooded chord that set a few heads turning. The sergeant appeared to listen, too, with rapt attention to Tom's sermon, or at least he affected the ability to look attentive, which was more than some did, such as Adella Sainton-Clark, who spent his sermons filling in the sudoku challenge cut from *The Sunday Times* as if she didn't think he could see what she was doing. Attendance had been heartening, however; in part—he theorised—a fallout from last Sunday's storm-stayed multitude; in part, too, a visceral response to the sensation and menace of the last week, though he would have preferred villagers drawn simply by the Christian message.

The text for this second Sunday of Epiphany was John 2:1–11, the marriage at Cana, wherein water became wine, the first of Jesus's recorded miracles, the inauguration of His ministry, an opportunity to reflect on the power of Jesus to change things that are ordinary and commonplace into things that are rich and inspired. But as the week unfolded, and as Tom reflected on the dilemmas and tensions of the Kaif and the Moir marriages, he found his mind wandering more and more literally to the institution itself. Were there limits, he wondered, to those declarations at the marriage service to love, comfort, honour, and protect? There was, he thought, to the last.

Later, after the Dismissal, great was the lingering of parishioners in the frosty air outside the north porch remarking on the service (ostensibly), but in reality (Tom noted the furtive glances and rubbernecking aimed past the door) more interested in the dark-suited figure who remained inside, known to a few of them—then, within whispered moments, all of them—as a police detective. "He's come to see a dog about a man," Tom joked to deflect their curiosity, breaking away at last, and stepping back into the empty nave.

"And where's Inspector Bliss this morning?" he asked, leading DS Blessing towards the vestry.

"In the pub." Catching Tom's frown, he added, "He's a martyr to his bowels, as you know, sir, and just between us, of course."

"Of course," Tom murmured, leading the sergeant past Colm, who had been defending the door against a vexed Karla Skynner who was insisting on knowing why a little girl had brought a shotgun into the church.

Blessing flashed his warrant card, informed her he was present on police business, and told her, couched in a kind of officialese, to get on her bike. Inside the vestry, where more than two was a crowd, Blessing scowled at the shotgun glistening coolly in the light from the single lancet window, pitched his eyebrow up a notch at Colm, who reiterated his possible ownership, and said, "Someone from the team will bag it and tag it, and we'll have it tested, of course."

"I can't say I'm anxious to have it back," Colm said after he had explained the security system cock-ups at Thornridge House. "But the paperwork's at home, Sergeant, if you need it. I think everything's Bristol fashion."

"And the last person—or most likely the second-last person—to fire this shotgun, would be you, Mr. Parry?"

"Never fired one in my life, Sergeant. The last person who—" Colm stopped and flicked a dismayed glance at Tom. "My collection is serviced by Adam Moir, so—"

"Who was one of the Guns at last night's Wassail, yes?"

"Yes," Tom replied, "but—"

"But?" Blessing echoed.

Tom had shrugged at that moment. He wanted to say that Adam participating in a violent act seemed unlikely, but he remembered Penella and Adam having words about Adam wandering off for an alleged pee before the fatal shot. Colm had taken his leave, to remove his robes in the choir vestry, and Tom had been left alone with Blessing, who favoured him with a discerning glance.

"Fine sermon, Vicar."

"Just following the lectionary, Sergeant."

"Of course, the lectionary."

"Churchgoer?" Tom removed his stole.

"My work often makes that impossible, as you can see. Mrs. Blessing attends with some regularity, however. St. Mary's, Totnes."

"Then there is a Mrs. Blessing."

"Is there some reason why there wouldn't be?" The sergeant shot him a challenging frown. "Anyway, I thought your aside that the resolution in the wedding vows to protect might bump up against the law interesting. I wondered if you had anyone in mind?"

"I may have."

"I see."

"Has your interest something to do with the recent deaths in the village?"

"You'll learn soon enough, I expect," Blessing grunted. "The inspector and I will be paying another visit on the Kaifs."

"Are you . . . visiting them with a warrant in hand for one or the other?"

"At the moment, Vicar, we're merely pursuing our enquiries. No warrant. Not yet, at any rate."

"Could you get a warrant? Would a magistrate issue one? I can't see that you have much evidence against Molly. Or Victor, for that matter. But, of course"—Tom struggled out of his surplice—"you likely know much more than I do."

Blessing lifted a hymn book with a torn spine from a pile on a chair. "Finding someone with a persuasive motive to poison Will Moir is a bit of a trick," he said, absently turning the pages.

"So your intent is to bother the Kaifs without good reason?"

"Look, Vicar." Blessing snapped the book shut. "The coroner's report says Will Moir was poisoned. There's little evidence it was an accident, so we're obliged to follow whatever leads there are, thin as they are, wherever they are."

"I can understand your frustration, Sergeant, but surely these two deaths—Will's and Judith Ingley's—are connected somehow. I can't see how that connection would turn through Molly or Victor Kaif. I can't imagine either of those two very familiar with a firearm, for instance."

Blessing tried pressing the hymn book's torn spine into place, to no avail. "The only connection is that Mrs. Ingley happened upon the Burns Supper, which Mr. Moir also attended."

"And at which Mr. Moir died, if you recall. As I told you last night, Judith came to Thornford, to the Burns Supper, for a specific reason."

"Which she wouldn't tell you."

"That's true, but her past has a tragic link to the Stanhopes."

"Yes, so you said, but that link is with Clive Stanhope, who has been dead for five years. Even if he did murder Mrs. Ingley's father, there's nothing that can be done about it now—it took place half a century ago and all the principals have dropped off their perches. And if she were bent on some sort of—I'm not sure what, revenge?—after all these years, then it's difficult to understand how

Will Moir comes into the picture. Will *married* a Stanhope, but he *isn't* a Stanhope."

"Don't forget that Nick threatened Judith."

"So she told you."

"Are you suggesting Judith fabricated it?"

Blessing shrugged. "She's not here to be questioned, is she? I suppose making vague threats falls within Nick Stanhope's MO, as I've come to understand it. He was discharged from the army for threatening to shoot an officer, wasn't he? Hotheaded lad."

"Hotheaded enough to shoot someone, perhaps."

"But is he stupid? Shooting someone with your own shotgun would be stupid. Forensics will tell the tale. Miss Neels told us last night that Nick was shooting with his own twelve-bore, one of his dad's. That he left the Wassail at the time he did—some few minutes before Mrs. Ingley's death—may simply be poor timing. And don't forget Adam Moir wandered away, too, at a significant moment. We've taken his shotgun away for examination, and Miss Neels's, as a precaution. Now we have to find Nick and get his. Don't know where the bugger is, though. He's not at his flat, we haven't located his vehicle, and he's not answering his mobile. *That* seems suspicious."

"You might try the hotels." Tom told the sergeant about Oona Blanc.

"Lucky sod." Blessing whistled.

Tom gestured to the shotgun on the table. "Then this is likely a fourth gun."

"It would appear so, unless it's been in your garden all week covered with snow. Wet won't be good for it. Beautiful, isn't it? Look at the scroll engraving and the grain in the walnut. Must be worth a few bob."

"It's more of a terrifying beauty, Sergeant." Tom looked sideways at the thing that may have ended a life, and might nearly have ended his.

"I will grant you, Vicar, that if this does prove to be part of Mr. Parry's collection and prove to be the murder weapon, then those with recent access to Thornridge House will be under greater scrutiny, and that includes your Nick Stanhope, who was also at the Burns Supper."

"He's not my Nick Stanhope, Sergeant."

"But he's *your* prime suspect, isn't he?" Blessing flicked Tom a sly glance. "For me, a man who poisons someone isn't the sort who next goes out and shoots someone else. Two different homicides, two different perpetrators, if you ask me. One planned, the other rash."

"But surely, Sergeant, if this Purdey proves to be the murder weapon, that suggests some planning. If it were Nick, then he would have had to have placed the shotgun earlier in the orchard, or in my garden, which would be easy enough to do in the Stygian darkness of this village, and then fetch it at the opportune moment."

Blessing shrugged. "Possibly. But can you imagine Nick Stanhope slipping taxine into a haggis or a curry or a—"

"Perhaps we underestimate Nick Stanhope, Sergeant."

"Then Nick Stanhope is our man, by your calculation."

Shifting his bulk on the couch, glancing over at his cluttered desk and the tasks that demanded his attention, notably finishing compiling parish statistics long overdue, Tom thought back to his reply to the sergeant: "I can't really think who else."

He had taken a deep breath then and he took one now, though this breath was induced more by self-doubt. Was he shopping Nick to the authorities simply because—he couldn't run from it—he disliked the man? The ground had been laid when he heard that Nick had been partnered briefly with Màiri White, then cultivated at the Burns Supper where Nick proved himself an utter bore by mocking the twinning of his surname and vocation, an opening gambit so unoriginal and unclever that it almost always lowered anyone in Tom's estimation. His dislike had flourished as he bore witness to Nick's boorish behaviour at the dinner, his callousness to his sister, his flirtation with property developers, rumours of gambling and debt—it went on.

Still, he felt a little like David consigning Uriah to the front of battle where odds were good he'd get the chop and leave to mourn his widow, Bathsheba, a *woman very beautiful to look upon,* if he remembered the Scripture correctly. Not that Nick was anything like Uriah, an honourable chap unlucky to have a wife King David fancied rotten. And not that Màiri gave the slightest indication she'd like to resume her relationship with Nick. Màiri was, however, beautiful to look upon.

He sighed again, and thought of the evening past, as it might have been, if the Wassail had been its traditional harmless diversion, if he and Màiri had slipped away to the pub down Yealm Road—just a man in a clerical collar and a very fetching woman who wasn't his wife. People might assume they were meeting on church business, mightn't they? On a Saturday night? Not bloody likely. Perhaps they would assume she was his wife, after all. Why wouldn't they? He wouldn't be the only priest with a wife—what, fifteen?—years his junior. Look at Hugh Beeson. His second wife was well younger than he, the dog!

Or he might simply have removed his collar, ripped it from his shirt, and, possessed by volcanic passions like the hero of a clerical bodice-ripper (if such literature existed), cast it into the tempest raging over the moors, watching it disappear, tumbling and turning, disappearing behind a tor. Màiri had said she'd have him home in good time (as God somehow forgot about His priests when proclaiming Sunday as a day of rest). Oh, no, she wouldn't! He'd have her knickers off quicker than David had Bathsheba's after Uriah's body was DHL'd home on his shield. Oh, yes, he would!

Tom lifted his lids and blinked rapidly. A tendril of some dream vanished. What had he been brooding on?

Moors, bodices, knickers, and collars.

Knickers and collars?

He remembered.

He ran his finger between his Adam's apple and his dog collar, the sign of his consecration, the symbol of his being yoked with Christ, the outward reminder to all he encountered that God was present and that he, Tom Christmas, was His representative. He only removed it for sleep, for showers, occasionally for some grubby task—for honest, practical reasons, not dishonest ones. The collar repelled some people, but it attracted more, opening doors and possibilities for connection, and he was humbled to wear it. Yet there were moments when the collar did feel a little like a tourniquet: He was a floating head, divested from the rest of his body, and set apart from the rest of humanity. If he were single, unencumbered, and employed, say, as one of the workers tearing up Thorn Court's carpeting, then he might explore all sorts of interesting possibilities with Ms. White. But he was not. A man needs a maid, but a priest needs a wife.

He raised his left hand and studied it a moment. He took his right thumb and pushed it along the smooth surface of his wedding ring, twisting it around and around. It was a simple band, purchased from a jeweller on Green Street, a short walk from his rooms in Westcott House, Cambridge. He remembered the afternoon, a Friday near the end of Easter term, the weather sublime, the light dancing along the cobbled lane as he waited for Lisbeth—he was ridiculously early—to join him for their rendezvous. But intoxicated by joy and impatient to get on, he had passed into the shop on his own, where the owly proprietor cheerfully laid out almost his entire selection on a length of black velvet along the glass counter. He remembered dismissing the very ring he was now twisting around his finger. Made of white gold, it had a middle band of pink, a colour that prompted a visceral masculine dismissal. But it's *rose* gold, the jeweller smiled, and Tom was enchanted. Rose gold for Lisbeth Rose.

Who existed only in memory.

Someone—who? he searched his mind unfruitfully—had suggested to him that this day, this minute, would surely come.

It had.

He took a breath to steel himself, gripped the ring between thumb and forefinger, and executed a sharp, swift jerk. The pain was instant, a cutting at the base of his knuckle. He took another breath and tugged again, more cautiously this time, but without result. And then—*bugger it!*—again. He splayed his hands like two starfish and stared at them with dismay. Had time so swelled the joints? When Lisbeth placed the ring on his finger at the registry office in Shire Hall eleven years ago, it had seemed to melt its way down his flesh like butter onto hot toast. He tried to banish the memory of that happy morning, the hasty, giggly, I-can't-believe-we're-doing-this civil ceremony, Richard, a fellow ordinand, his supporter, dropping the ring, Fiona, Lisbeth's maid of honour, just off an all-night call shift at Addenbrooke's Hospital, helplessly yawning, all of them staggering off to The Granta for a quick wedding breakfast, then— weirdly—back to studies and, like a couple of celibates, back to their own rooms in college for a few weeks before they could arrange married accommodation. He couldn't bear to dwell on the first hours of their marriage, not now, not this minute—and this time with ferocity born of determination frustrated, pulled and tugged, squeezed and pinched until his damned resistant knuckle succumbed to the greater damned resistance of the metal band and the thing flew past his fingernail.

It was done.

The ring was off.

Now, through eyes misting with grief and pain, he gazed at his naked fingers, his bachelor hands, as they once were and were again, and at the ring, a circlet of reflected fire, that once proclaimed he belonged to someone else. He drew the band closer, tilting it to catch the light from the flames. Yes, there it was, carved on the inside, only a little worn, a lovers' knot with their initials entwined: TLC & LLR.

Tom Livingstone Christmas and Lisbeth Lillian Rose.

He felt his throat constrict, then a cry, so low it was almost a growl, broke through. He'd said *good-bye my love* to her once, at her funeral. Now, he was saying it again, and for good.

CHAPTER TWENTY-NINE

rs. Prowse, thank you," Tom muttered thickly, rubbing crusted tears from his eyes as he took the proffered cup of tea. "I must have nodded off."

"The rural dean phoned. I took the call in the kitchen."

Tom glanced at the instrument of torture on his desk. "I didn't hear it ring."

"I think you more than nodded off, Mr. Christmas."

Tom struggled to his feet while balancing the cup and shuffled towards his desk, nearly tripping over Powell—or, possibly, Gloria—who had slunk into the room through the open door.

"He did seem anxious to speak to you," Madrun added in a re-minding voice. "May I take this?" She lifted the newspaper from the carpet.

"Yes, go ahead. I'm done with it."

"I do hope they don't spoil the roses."

Tom followed her eyes through the French doors to the garden, where shadows stirred in the greying afternoon light. "Are they still here?" He placed his teacup on a mound of books on his desk and looked at his watch, jolted to register that he had slept more than an hour. He rubbed along his neck, where a crick knotted the tendons.

"I can't imagine what they might find." Madrun turned to the door.

"Have they come for Mrs. Ingley's things?"

"Not yet."

"Then I'll get onto that task."

"Don't forget the rural dean. I believe word has reached him."

"Ah." He shared a meaningful look with his housekeeper. He appreciated Charles's concern, but he feared he would have to wait for a response. "That task" had priority.

Before settling into the office chair, he reached into his trouser pocket and pulled out the folded document Madrun had handed him that morning. He'd barely glanced at it then; now he unfolded it. He sat down, switched on the anglepoise lamp, pushed aside some of the desktop clutter, and smoothed the creases, tufted with age, flat against the oak surface. He should have handed it to DS Blessing that morning at St. Nicholas's, he supposed, but Miranda and the shotgun had driven such tasks from his mind. It was only a yellowed birth certificate anyway, and its content tangential at best to Judith's homicide investigation. Madrun had been terribly excited by her find. She had speculated rather doggedly that Clive Stanhope had to be the father of Judith's child, until finally Tom gave in and admitted it was so, sternly extracting a promise from her *not* to let this juicy tidbit stray from the vicarage for the time being, as news of a new twig on the family tree via the village rumour mill might further distress Caroline Moir.

The certificate usefully contained Judith's son's full Christian names, however, an aid to his task of informing him that his mother had died, which Tom had told the detectives he would undertake, thinking it kinder that the information come from someone who had acted host to her for a week. But it was a cheerless duty, compounded by the violent manner of Judith's death. As he reached for the mobile that Madrun had found among Judith's things, his mind slipped unbidden to the grim phone calls he'd had to make in the hours after Lisbeth's death. How would Anthony Ingley react to this very unexpected call?

He set aside the mobile and reached instead to remove the teacup from its precarious perch on the book pile. He took a sip, and spent a procrastinating moment over the Certified Copy of an Entry of Birth, as it proclaimed itself. Yes, the date of birth told the tale—about seven months after Judith left Thornford for good. Place of birth was registered as Furness House Nursing Home, Leeds, perhaps somewhere near the hospital where she took her training. Name and Surname of Father: blank. Name and Maiden Surname of Mother: Judith Mina Frost. (Certainly not "Judith Stanhope" formerly Frost.) The date of registration was a fortnight after the birth.

Copy though the certificate was, it seemed odd, Tom thought, that Anthony didn't keep it among his own things, though perhaps it was in safer keeping in England, with his mother. Of course, once you've proved your *bona fides* with your birth certificate for your first driver's licence or first passport, of what use was it? He wondered if Anthony had ever been curious about his natural father? Perhaps not. Perhaps Judith had never told him the man's name.

Enough dithering, Tom admonished himself, reaching again for Judith's mobile. He looked at his watch. He had to get on with this. It must be somewhere close to midnight in Shanghai, he realised. More than relaying tragic news, he might be waking a man to it.

Judith's mobile was a slightly vintage model, a flip variety, but in a pink plastic that matched her jacket. He opened the cover to reveal the tiny screen, pressed the CONTACTS button, and scrolled through the names, of which there were many, almost all of them—as was the convention—first names only. The directory was alphabetical, of course, but between *Alice* and *Arthur* there was no *Anthony,* and between *Terry* and *Vera* no *Tony.* A nickname? He scrolled up and down again. Nothing suggested itself.

Odd, he thought. But perhaps Judith only spoke to her son using a landline. That would make sense, as mobile rates to China were probably atrocious.

Still, it put a spanner in the works. He scrolled through the names again. One of these people, surely, would know of Anthony's whereabouts, perhaps have a contact number for him, but who? Of the few entries with last names logged, none were Frosts—Judith's family was thin on the ground—but neither were there any Ingleys. Of course, relatives, even ones by marriage, didn't likely need their surnames recorded.

He was about to phone one at random when the CALL HISTORY button caught his eye. Perhaps Anthony had called her, even briefly, leaving a record of the number. The usual inventory of Christian names greeted his eyes, matching ones recorded in her directory, but most of the newest entries in the log were purely numerical, indicating she had been talking with people who were not among her regular correspondents. Tom recognised the dialing code for his own part of Devon—one number he thought might be the Daintreys'; another looked like the one for Leitchfield Turner estate agents, which always had posters in a display case next to the post office. He recognised the London dialing code. A third code he failed to recognise; he reckoned it might be Staffordshire's, where Judith had lived. But the most recent incoming calls—four of them, from the same number—had a curious succession of numerals, and more of them. The two numerals at the start were clearly country code, not UK dialing code. But what country? Many on the Continent began with thirty-something. France was thirty-three, but this one was unfamiliar. It had to be China.

He looked again at his watch. He could switch on his computer and Google the code to make sure, but he felt impatient to complete this unhappy task. He took a breath, highlighted the number, and pressed TALK. The ringtone had a different sequence from the UK's; four of them passed, and then something happened that, stupidly, he wasn't prepared for. The call went to message. Well, why wouldn't it? It was very late in Shanghai. Worse, the voice speaking the generic, uninformative message—genuine, though; English; not mechanical—was female. Somehow he had expected a male voice, Anthony's. He knew Anthony was married. Judith had said so, but for safety reasons, male voices usually predominated on answerphones. He hastily pressed the button to end the call, then immediately felt stupid, oddly cowardly. He redialed. This time when the outgoing message came on, he asked the recipient to please call him as soon as possible on a very urgent matter.

Must be Anthony's wife, he decided, snapping the phone shut. He could detect a bit of Yorkshire, but a bit of something else, too, that he couldn't quite nail down. The tone was flinty, efficient—there was something formidable in the workings of that voice's owner. And oddly, the voice sounded older than he expected a woman of what?—her late forties, early fifties?—to be.

Doubt rising, he switched on his computer and soon found Internet pages outlining country codes. Bugger! He hadn't been phoning China, he had been phoning Australia! That accounted for graftings of a nasal twang—she was some English expat, probably, whom he had lumbered unnecessarily with the dreaded phone call in the middle of the night. Wasn't Australia at least a couple of time zones farther east than China? Whoever she was—and she surely had some connection to Judith, so making the phone call was not completely worthless—perhaps she was a heavy sleeper or switched off her phone at night.

Tom jerked in his chair. A cat had alit on his lap, claws like needles piercing through the fabric to the flesh of his thighs. They regarded each other with mutual indifference, then Powell—or, possibly, Gloria (as they were both pitch-black with dark gold eyes, the

only detectable difference was buried beneath their backsides)—
contracted into a furry, resonant hummock, irresistibly strokable—
which Tom did, absently running one hand over the warm velvet
curve, as he considered whether to simply phone one of Judith's contacts at random.

He did. He phoned *Alice*, as the list had her name first, using the
vicarage landline; Judith's mobile looked to be on its last bar. She
answered on the second ring, the tone of her voice shifting from
disinterest to curiosity to disbelief to horror in short order as Tom
laid out the events of the last twenty-four hours.

"I can't take it in." Alice's voice came as a gasp. "It's too shocking.
Are they . . . have they found . . . ?"

"It's under police investigation."

"Oh . . . and she just lost Trevor in the autumn. It's too unfair."
Tom could hear her ragged breath. "I'm sorry, did you say you were
in . . . Thornford Regis? I'm not sure I know where that is."

"In Devon."

"Oh, yes, of course. I have a notion that's where Judith was from
originally."

"You didn't know she was coming here?"

"No, no idea. I feel dreadful. I've been meaning to phone all
week. I try to keep in touch, particularly since Trevor passed away,
but this has been such an odd week, the snow and all . . . How can I
help? What can I do?"

"Well, I'm trying to get in touch with Judith's family—"

"I'm a cousin, sort of. Trevor and my husband are cousins, so I
think of Judith as a relative. George will be shocked—that's my husband. He's out walking the dog. We live at Long Compton, a few
miles out of Stafford, and often got together—although that was
more difficult when Trevor became unwell. Anyway, I'm sorry, I
rambling on here. Vicar, I'd be more than happy—well, *happy*'s
hardly the word—to phone relatives and such. Trevor has a sister in
Scotland, for instance."

"That—"

"Oh!" she interjected. "This hasn't been on the news?"

"I'm not sure, but I shouldn't be surprised if there wasn't something before very long."

"So awful to hear it over the television. I must get on it! Thank you—"

"Alice. Mrs.—?"

"It's Ingley, actually. George and Trevor had the same paternal grandfather."

"Mrs. Ingley, there is a way you can help. I would like very much to get in touch with Judith's son. I understand he lives in China, in Shanghai, but I can't find a number for him on Judith's mobile, and wondered if you might possibly have it."

There was a silence, then, "I'm sorry . . . ?"

"Her son? Judith's son, Anthony?"

"But . . ." A kind of embarrassed laughter came over the wire. "Judith doesn't have a son."

"I'm sorry?"

"Judith doesn't have a son," Alice repeated. "She and Trevor were childless."

"No son?"

"No. I'm quite certain. I've known Judith and Trevor for . . . well, nearly fifty years. Goodness, I was at their wedding! Did she *say* she had a son?"

"I must have heard her incorrectly," Tom croaked. "I'm very sorry. I didn't mean to embarrass you."

"That's all right." A certain coolness entered her tone. "I really must get on to phoning round. Thank you for letting me know, Vicar. If there's more we can do . . ."

"You have my number."

"Yes, it's here on the call display." She rang off.

Tom dropped the receiver in its cradle, his tired brain spinning. *But she* does *have a son! It's right here on this document!* He lifted the paper from his desktop, disturbing the cat, who lifted its head and growled. He thought back to earlier conversations with Judith. She had talked very little about her son—though perhaps she had to Mrs. Prowse. What *did* he know? He had assumed since his conversation with Judith in the churchyard Friday that Trevor Ingley had raised Clive Stanhope's child as his own, and that that child had had some suitable education and eventually moved to China for his work. He had, if he thought about it, sensed an estrangement. She was not voluble about her son, the way most mothers are. There was no mention of his accomplishments or his foibles or mention, say, of grandchildren, which might have come along by now. Little wonder: Judith and Trevor Ingley had lived all their lives as a childless couple.

His mind turned to his first encounter with Judith at Thorn Court. He had asked conversationally if she had any children. Why didn't she simply say no? Perhaps he had caught her off guard, obliging her to continue with the fabrication.

And yet Judith Frost *had* given birth to a child nearly fifty years ago in Leeds. The boy had to have been adopted, of course, and was still walking the earth somewhere, if there hadn't been an early, and tragic, death in the meantime. Surely, all her life, she must have wondered what became of this child. Was she now, soon to retire, with husband deceased, plucking an old strand in life's skein? He looked again at the birth certificate, at its details: date of birth, place of birth. Judith had come to Thornford deliberately, specifically, to trespass upon the Burns Supper, and she had done so carrying with her this document. He stared at its yellowed surface and thought back to the churchyard, to Judith's interest in his own adoption, and to her musings on the influences on a child's character, reduced to the shorthand of nature versus nurture. She had seemed, too, somehow resigned to some inevitability, to some sort of loss. Her parents, her husband, he had thought at the time, triggered by the sight of the Frost grave marker. But now, as he pressed his hand along the cat's back, feeling its knobby spine along his palms, he felt the stir-rings of a new and terrible possibility.

And then, at the moment the cat, vexed at being petted with such ferocity, leapt from his lap, Judith's mobile sang a song of six-pence.

lurch, a skipped beat. That was all his heart suffered. She was not dead, thank God, though her posture, prone, was an alarming simulacrum of Will's eight days before. Glimpsing her as he rounded the top of the stairs through the filigree wrought-iron balustrade—a fine architectural detail neither hand nor eye had registered in last Saturday's tumult—Tom had been struck by dread. He'd raced the last steps, almost losing his footing along the twist of carpet. He was behaving irrationally, of course; Caroline's delicate features, even in the dwindling light, bloomed with life; her chest, like a gentle bellows, rose and fell, stirring almost imperceptibly under the cream-coloured throw blanket covering her. He studied her face for a moment, loath to disturb her, feeling faintly like a voyeur when her eyes snapped open. She regarded him, hardly surprised; by the sharpness of her focus, he could see that she had not woken from a slumber.

"I'm sorry if I've disturbed you," he began.

"I heard you come up. I was resting my eyes."

"You knew it was me?"

"I knew it would be someone."

Tom lent a half-cryptic remark a half-rendered smile. "You've been reading," he said, noting a book that slipped from her hand as she pushed off the throw and sat up. He noted, too, the black high-collared shirt she was wearing and the slim black trousers. *"Ariel."* He voiced the title on the dustcover.

"It most likely landed up here before I was born. Some guest left it behind, I expect. I can't imagine any member of my family reading poetry." Caroline took the slim volume in her hand. "I thought if I ever had a daughter I would call her Ariel. I fell in love with the name. It's printed so boldly on the spine. See? It seemed to leap out at me from the bookcase when I was a girl and stole time up here." She handed the volume to Tom and rose. "I doubt I read the poems then. Glanced at them, perhaps. I would have been too young to understand them, in any case."

"And now?" Tom opened the book at random. "Sylvia Plath lived in Devon, for a time, didn't she?"

"Apparently."

"And very depressed, I believe."

"One gets that sense from her poetry. Yes, I can understand them now. Some of them." She glanced at Tom, then moved past him towards the window that looked south over the village to the soft hills. "I'm not depressed, if that's what you're thinking. I know Sylvia Plath is a patron saint of unhappy women, but she was living in a country foreign to her. I'm not. And I loved my husband. There was no disaffection, no estrangement—"

"There was for a period, Caroline."

"Yes, but we chose not to hold the past against each other. Being able to forgive made our marriage stronger in the end. Remember we talked about this in your marriage preparation course? I'm not sure I ever learned if you had a . . . an episode in your marriage."

"We all have episodes."

"You're not going to spill, are you?"

"Not today, sorry."

Caroline smiled wanly. "Never mind. Come and see how beautiful Thornford is in this light."

Tom joined her at the window, still holding the book. He had
once, in a despairing moment, stood on the top of St. Nicholas's bell
tower and surveyed the village in its spring raiment, a thatch-and-cob
jewel set in a sea of luminescent green, but Thorn Court's belvedere
tower commanded the high view, and that view late on a winter afternoon, as the earth turned its farthest from the sun, was of beauty
stripped bare, stark and vulnerable. Dying rays rimmed the horizon
with a soft golden light, flaming the feathery maze of naked trees
tracing the folds of the distant hills and blazing the low, thin clouds
double bright. Above this amber middle band, the ice-blue sky
darkened to indigo; below, the village slipped into bronzing, blackening shadows, a little world folded into a bowl.

"You missed this all the years you were gone." Tom regarded her
in profile.

"Terribly." Caroline folded the blanket around her.

"I had a phone call a little earlier this afternoon."

"Yes?"

"From Australia."

"Not from my mother, I trust."

"No."

"Good, she's supposed to be on a plane out of Sydney in a few
hours." Caroline flicked a glance at him. "It's the middle of the night
in Australia. It must have been an important call."

"It was . . . well, it was important to someone."

Caroline let a heartbeat pass. "And I have a feeling it has something to do with me."

"The call was from a woman named Phyllis Lambert who lives
in Melbourne, but she's English-born. Fifty years ago she was in

nursing school at Leeds. She emigrated not long after graduation. It seems she was a very good friend of Judith Ingley's, and they stayed in touch over the years."

"I'm sorry about Mrs. Ingley," Caroline said, then added when Tom failed to respond: "No, truly. She was a meddlesome woman, and very much had the wrong end of the stick about . . . well, I think you may well know now, don't you. But I wouldn't have wished her dead—not that way." She twisted her head to study his face. "You must believe me."

Tom saw the supplicating shine in her eyes. Sorrowfully, he said, "I'm sorry, Caroline, I'm not certain that I do."

Her expression turned bleak. "Tell me what this woman— Phyllis—said." She spoke without expression.

Tom thought back to the call, announced on Judith's mobile by a few bars of "Sing a Song of Sixpence." He recognised the number; it was the one he had phoned—twice—in Australia. The voice, too, was recognizable. It was the same as the outgoing message, only trembling in anxiety, and it didn't wait for Tom to proffer the usual greeting.

"Judith, are you okay? I was woken by the priest you're staying with. He thinks you're my mother, which is so odd, I thought I'd call you first to see if he's unhinged. Actually, I tried a couple of times yesterday to get hold of you. I found the information you wanted! Judith?"

It had been no easier relating the circumstances of Judith's death to Phyllis Lambert, as she was named, than it had been to Alice Ingley. Indeed, the bonds of affection between the two women ran deeply, as Tom learned in a call so lengthy he thought the phone's battery would die and cut them off before she was finished. They had written faithfully for years; then, when long-distance rates no longer crushed the pocketbook, they phoned with regularity, later adding a little email, though neither cared for its impersonality. She had been planning a summer visit to England. She hadn't been back in nearly fifty years. Her husband, dead two years, hated to fly—they'd emigrated to Australia by boat—and now that Judith had buried her poor husband, so sick, you know, with Parkinson's, well . . .

She burst into sobs. "In fact," she sputtered through tears, "that was our last conversation."

"What was?" Tom had asked, bewildered.

"About Parkinson's and such illnesses, the strain they can put on a marriage. Any road," she'd continued, when she'd recovered her voice, "she asked me to look into something for her, as I nursed for many years all over the country. Ken—that's my husband—was often transferred with the bank he worked for. She wanted to know if I could take a peek into something in the medical records here that pertained to someone living in your village. She was a bit mysterious about it, actually, and I was reluctant, as it meant me violating confidentiality, but Judith seemed to think it was to some good purpose, so . . . " He could hear her blowing her nose. "I'll tell you, Vicar," she added adenoidally, "I'm sure I can trust in your discretion and perhaps it will do some good after all."

Tom's thoughts returned to the present, prompted by Caroline's reiterating the question, "What did Phyllis Lambert tell you?"

He tapped the book of poems absently against his chest. "You never knew your mother-in-law, did you?" he asked instead.

"No. As I think I said on a previous occasion, I met and married Will in Melbourne some time after she died, and soon after we were here in England."

"What did Will say his mother had died of? He must have mentioned it."

"Of course." Caroline tightened the blanket around her. "He said she had died of an embolism, a sudden, horrible, freakish twist of fate."

"Which you never questioned."

"I had no reason to. We were young, in love, soon to return to

England, looking to the future. Who would I have asked anyway? His father he never knew. He had done a runner years earlier. Will had almost no other family—and I'm sure you understand why, now. We wed in front of a JP. My mother and a girl I went to school with stood up for me. Will brought a couple of mates from his old college team. I doubt they knew. Well, I know they didn't, because years later I asked Will if they did. He had gone to some pains to keep his secret from me."

"May I ask when Will's birthday is?"

"He would turn forty-nine October twenty-seven, if . . . " Caroline's brow knitted. "Why?"

"I just wanted to assure myself of something. It's not important." He paused, then asked, "When did you learn that Will wasn't an adopted child, as he claimed to be?"

"Can't you guess?" Caroline shivered, despite her warm wrap. "At your marriage preparation class, we did mention a brief period of separation, about ten years ago, remember? We weren't forthcoming about the reason—we could *never* be forthcoming about the reason—but the point was we overcame it.

"You see, we had had Adam early in our marriage, but I wanted another child. I simply assumed we would have one, as there were no complications conceiving the first one. But years went by and nothing happened and I began to worry something was wrong. I suggested we be tested, then urged, then insisted. I became rather obsessed about it, I'm afraid. Hell to live with, though I didn't much care at the time." She flicked Tom a glance. "Finally, I had made an appointment for us at a private fertility clinic in Harley Street, and had Will believe we were meeting for a late lunch in Portland Place—he was at Sport England then. But as soon as he read the brass plate on the clinic door, he bolted. We sat on a bench in Regent's Park and he told me he had been . . . snipped years earlier, after Adam was born—and he told me why. He told me the woman he claimed was his adoptive mother was, in truth, his birth mother.

I don't know why I never twigged. I've seen a picture of her. The resemblance is quite marked."

She paused. "I presume Mrs. Lambert told you Will's mother died from nothing so out of the blue as an embolism?"

Tom nodded grimly.

"As you might imagine, my world was turned upside down. You know, don't you, that anyone with a parent with Huntington's disease has a fifty–fifty chance of having it himself? That there's no cure? I didn't know at that moment in Regent's Park, but Will told me."

"Suddenly," she continued bleakly, "I was faced with the prospect that not only might my husband be struck down by this cruel disease in the prime of his life, but my son might one day, too. I think I lost my mind for a time. Will told me this a few days before I was to attend a hospitality conference in Torquay. I went early, fled really, and stayed a week after the conference was over, taking long country walks, making a nostalgic visit here, trying to decide what to do. I had a ten-year-old boy at home in Toot Hinton, whom I loved, and despite the deceit and the awful shock, a husband that I still loved. There was nothing to do but carry on."

"Stiff upper and so forth."

"In effect." Caroline smiled weakly.

"There are tests that determine—"

"Will refused to be tested. Ignorance allowed for hope, he said. Even inventing his own adoption was a way of distancing himself. He didn't want to know, didn't want the idea of a death foretold to colour his life. But it did, in its way. Thinking that his life might be shorter than most is why he lived so intensely. Why he worked so hard on building up this hotel, and threw himself into sport, into the cricket he loved so, and running, and being in the amateur dramatic society, and in the Thistle But Mostly Rose, and on the parish council. It's what made him so . . . " Her voice broke. "So . . . "

"Wonderful?" Tom supplied. Caroline nodded mutely, her face crumpled with restrained tears. Tom let his eyes drift to a rook ascending, a black thing losing itself in the darkening sky. He could think of instances in the recent past when Will had shown himself less than wonderful.

"We carried on," Caroline continued, wiping at her eyes. "You do, don't you? Look at you. You've carried on in the wake of your wife's death. Life seems a meaningless succession of days and nights as you crawl your way out of something you didn't think you could bear, doesn't it? And then the pain lessens. Will accepted my pregnancy by another man. I think he was not unhappy that I had somehow evened the score—somehow matched his great hurt to me. He knew that this child would escape the disease's shadow. The years went by—Ariel's ten now—and after a time it doesn't seem possible that anything could seriously alter your happy life. HD symptoms usually begin to show in your late thirties or early forties. Will was in his late forties. We thought we had been spared. And then, one day, suddenly, everything changes."

"Suddenly?"

"Yes, although your mind refuses to believe it when it happens—at least mine did. One day more than a year ago Will cut himself shaving—"

"A common enough occurrence."

"It was more than a nick, though. And he told me it was the way his hand trembled holding the razor that caused it. He had come back from the bathroom, ashen. When I questioned him, he replied, 'It's beginning.' He looked . . . I can't quite describe it—haunted, I suppose, stunned, frightened. I dismissed it, of course, as you do. Laughed it off. As you say, a man cutting himself shaving is a common enough occurrence. But then other signs started to appear—a tic in the eyelids, a hand tremor, episodes of clumsiness, and he was not a clumsy man. More frightening were the changes in mood. Will could be forceful, he could get angry—don't we all at times?—but his was a clean anger, a squall that would pass swiftly. But now he would brood.

"Then there were these sort of mood lurches, a new irritability, and then came one or two episodes of rage, which he seemed helpless to control, and which afterwards filled him with such remorse. It was like he was watching himself undergo transformation, and so quickly. His mother's decline had been swift.

"Of course, the worst of these was the incident with Victor and Molly's boy. Will had lit into Adam over something at one point, but Adam is a man. But Harry's death, and the thought that his outburst might have precipitated it, shook Will to the roots of his soul. Well, you know all this, of course. You gave him good counsel."

"Caroline, if Victor and Molly had known that Will's outbursts were involuntary, they might not have blamed him so—"

"I know, I do know that," she interrupted him softly. "But Will didn't want to be excused. He wanted to believe he was in control of himself. But more, he didn't want to be pitied. He didn't want anyone to *know*, as I said. And there were . . . there were practical considerations. We have yet—*I* have yet—to tell Adam that he may have . . . distorted genes. We maintained the fiction that Will was adopted. It's what we had told him when he was a child. We—Will and I—decided to wait until he matured before telling him. Will's mother told *him* when he was fourteen. It was too soon, he said, a terrible shock, much too much a burden for a teenager to bear. He would reproach his mother for giving birth to him at all, then watch over her like a hawk for signs. We both wanted Adam to grow up without those sort of worries."

"But he's grown now, Caroline."

A shadow crossed her face. "While Will was healthy, there never seemed a good reason to tell Adam. There was always the fifty percent chance that Will *didn't* have Huntington's, and if he didn't have it, he wasn't a carrier, and the chain would be broken. We let ourselves live in a bubble."

"But Will, you say, has been exhibiting signs for what—?"

"More than a year."

"Adam's in a relationship with a young woman, Caroline. They could have—"

"I do know that, Tom. I do worry about it, very much. It's just that . . . " Her eyes wandered the room, now almost engulfed in shadow. "It's that there have been other complications."

"It's money, isn't it." It wasn't a question.

Caroline's eyes found his. "Isn't it always? Isn't it most often money worries that tear away at a marriage?" She looked away. "You know we're in a spot over money. When Daddy died, he left just enough for a down payment on this property. We borrowed from the bank, and Nick lent us part of his share of Daddy's money. He was in the army then, and didn't seem awfully concerned about how he would invest his inheritance. Perhaps we took advantage of him, I don't know. But now he has his own business ambitions, of course, and he owes money to some dubious characters because I'm afraid he's found Torquay's gambling culture more alluring than is good for him—or good for anyone trying to launch a new home security firm. He's been adamant that we accept an offer from Moorgate Properties to invest in the hotel."

"Invest? I thought—"

"That's the rub, Tom. Moorgate offers loans at decent rates, they affect to be helping you out, caring about local business and so forth. There's proper contracts, it's all very aboveboard, but then there's the fine print. If you don't meet certain conditions, pay back the loan in a timely fashion, they give you the chop and you're forced to sell up. And you end up selling to them or one of their subsidiaries. Will saw enough of it when he sat on the parish council to know what their scheme is, and in this instance, their scheme is to tear down this wonderful building, *my home*, plough under the beautiful gardens, and turn it all into squalid little cottages. I'd rather *give* Thorn Court to the village for a park than see it end this way."

Caroline shivered.

"But the web is more tangled," she continued. "And now that you know about Will's condition, you can probably guess. In our arrangements with financial institutions, banks, insurers, we gambled—foolishly, it turns out—by not disclosing the . . . genetic time bomb in Will's family medical history. I'm as much to blame for this. I didn't insist on telling the truth. The savings in our premiums, for instance, was much too tempting."

"Will purchased additional life insurance recently, I understand."

"How did you know?"

"I'm afraid someone let it slip."

"I think I can imagine who."

"Mark meant no malice, Caroline. And it would have gone no farther, except for the extraordinary events in the village this week. I can only ask whether you knew Will had done this."

She gave him a flinching smile. "We've each bought additional insurance. It's a normal business practice when you're renovating and increasing the value of your business property. Nothing to really raise a red flag here, Tom."

"I see." Tom bit his lip. "But, of course, it's not unknown for the death of one spouse to financially benefit the other."

"A truism that hasn't completely eluded those two detectives. Though I understand they've concentrated their attention on Molly. I suppose they think I lacked the opportunity, even if I had a motive."

Tom opened his mouth to respond, but Caroline turned to him with shadowed, exhausted eyes. "Do you think I poisoned my husband?"

Startled at her bluntness, the very question an echo of his own thoughts, he struggled for an even tone: "Caroline, very frankly, from what I know now—or what I think I know—I simply don't know what to think."

Caroline remained silent a moment, then said, "That day, ten, eleven years ago, in Regent's Park, when Will confessed his secret, he told me he would never, ever endure the suffering that his mother endured."

" '*Would* never'?"

" 'Would,' not 'could.' He said he wouldn't let himself become so enfeebled, slip into dementia. He . . . would never put his family through the suffering he endured while his mother suffered."

"But, Caroline, isn't it the sort of thing people say when they're young and healthy and witness the debilitating death of a loved one? In the end, most people, however profoundly they are disabled, vote for, yearn for, life. Life holds all sorts of possibilities, including a cure. Surely, Will was very much one of those people. "

Caroline turned her face towards the window. Tom followed her gaze. Colour no longer stained the horizon. With the sun dropped behind the folds of the hills, the sky had turned leaden, the few thin clouds sombre smudges, while below, in the vale of the village, the contours of tree, wall, and cottage blurred to black, pricked here and there by small, bright squares of curtained window. Towards the eastern extremity of their view, their eyes were drawn by a cascade of light flaring St. Nicholas's square tower and spilling over to the crown of the ancient churchyard yew visible above the dark cluster of cottage roofs along Poacher's Passage. The waxing crescent of the moon, pale in the vanquishing floodlight, seemed to brush the crenellations of the tower as it made its slow passage higher into the night sky.

"It doesn't really have a Gothic shape." Caroline broke the silence.

"What doesn't?"

"The yew tree—or at least our yew tree. In one of her Ariel poems, Sylvia Plath describes a yew as having 'a Gothic shape.' "

"You didn't answer my question."

"We need some light. There are candle lanterns." She looked to a pair on a nearby shelf amid the books. "They lend a lovely atmosphere. We would come up here, sometimes, Will and I, if we had a moment—which wasn't often—and have only that for illumination. Have you a match? I didn't think so. There are some in a drawer somewhere." She moved away.

"Caroline . . ."

"Tom." Her voice floated to him out of the shadows. "Will did vote for life while he could live it to the full, but he would not vote for life as a state of being barely above a breathing, demented vegetable."

"You talked about the advance of the disease, yes? You talked over what you might do . . . ?"

"We discussed everything, Tom. Of course, we did."

Homely sounds followed in rapid succession, the soft scrape of an opening drawer, a rustle through papers, the scrape of glass against metal, the rasp of a match.

"Caroline," Tom said, watching the match head flare, colouring for a moment the pale contours of her cheeks. "Forgive me if this is abrupt, but you didn't pass last Saturday night in town, did you?"

"Damn!"

The flame vanished. The acrid smoke curled into his nostrils.

"I dropped the match."

"There are halogen lights. We used them—"

"No, I don't want that. Candlelight is more . . . soothing."

The rasp of a match sounded and again brought a flush of warmth to Caroline's face. This time, she held the match and pushed it into the neck of the lamp. The wick flickered then flamed, casting dancing shadows around the tower room.

"No, to answer your question." She regarded him doubtfully. "I wasn't in Totnes at all. How did you know? Did someone tell you?" she added with a touch of bitterness.

"No, not as such. I was getting petrol at Jago's Thursday, and he said your car had been towed in from the lane leading to Upper Coombe Farm, which seemed to contradict what others were saying. And yesterday, when I was in Exeter, I met Tamara. She told me the snow stopped her *and* Adam from making their way out of the city. I thought the snow had only trapped Tamara. So you were with neither your son nor his girlfriend that night. I suppose you might have made your way into town somehow—got a ride from someone in a more snow-worthy vehicle on the A435—but where would you have spent the night?"

Caroline placed the lamp on one of the corner tables and moved to light a second one. "I thought when I heard your footsteps on the stairs it might be one of those two detectives—Bliss or Blessing—having given up on poor, befuddled Molly Kaif, newly armed with fresh speculation about me. I have one of the oldest motives in the world to have away with my husband, don't I?—but what I seem to lack was opportunity. I said I was with my son. He said he was with me. The police are concentrated on those who were here at Thorn Court for the Burns Supper, not those who weren't. But if they had taken the trouble to check Adam's story, they would have learned what you learned, that Adam was in Exeter with Tamara, not in Totnes or Noze with me. I thought Tamara might have spoken with them."

"She has no reason to. I said nothing to her that would make her speculate about your whereabouts that evening."

Caroline scratched the match and lit the lantern. "Adam told her I booked a room at the Seven Stars. Of course, if need arises, that can be easily checked, can't it?"

She blew out the match and flicked him a glance that seemed to question what he intended to do with the gleanings of this conversation. He didn't know himself. He felt in an invidious position, his mind deeply resistant to the notion that Caroline Moir, sweet soprano of his choir, angelic in her robes, was drawn to this deceit. But he had to face its implications.

"Then," he asked, "would I be correct in presuming you spent Saturday night here, at Thorn Court?"

"Where else?" Caroline placed the lantern on the table. "I had few options. My car slid through the stop where Bursdon Road meets the A435. I almost hit a lorry, then hit a bank of snow by the lane into Dave Shapley's farm. The man in the lorry very kindly stopped and we tried for a time to shift the car, but the tyres only dug deeper into the snow. Finally, he offered me a lift into town, but I decided to come back to Thornford—walk back, as it happens, through the snow."

"And no one saw you?"

"No one was out driving on Bursdon Road. It was pitch-black and the snow kept falling. I had my torch, but it was a struggle to walk without slipping or falling."

"And you reached the Annex and went to bed."

Caroline hesitated. "Shall we sit down? Why don't you remove your coat?"

He could sense her searching his face as he pulled off his jacket.

"If only there had never been this freakish snowstorm, Tom. Everything would be so very, very different."

"What do you mean?" He sat down at the other end of the banquette and looked at her face in the flickering light.

"I was exhausted and freezing by the time I descended into the village. I came down Thorn Hill, which led me by the back of Thorn Court. Rather than trudge all the way around the little memorial garden and up the drive to the Annex, I went into the hotel through the back delivery door to get warm. I have keys."

"But that leads into the kitchen, doesn't it?" Tom frowned. "No one saw you?"

"It must have been after the haggis was piped in but before you had the curry. I passed the chicken jalfrezi simmering on the cooker. All of you were in the private dining room, including Molly—I presume. Kerra might have been in the serving pantry. I slipped quickly through the kitchen, into the lobby—through the other door, the one nearest the east reception room, not the one that leads to the dining rooms," she explained, "then outside to the forecourt, and along to the Annex. I was glad I didn't see anyone. I didn't wish to be seen."

"Why not? I mean to say, Caroline, you wouldn't have been unwelcome. Why would you be chary of being seen?"

"But, Tom, I *was* seen. Though I didn't know it until later. When I stepped out of the front door into the light from the entrance lamps, someone coming from the garage area took note of me. I didn't hear anything. The snow was so muffling. And I saw nothing. It was pitch-black all around and I'd aimed my torch towards the Annex, and so—"

"It was Judith Ingley."

Caroline nodded.

"And yet she said nothing of seeing anyone that night. How peculiar. She might have guessed it might be you. When we were frantic to find Will—when he didn't come back to table after pudding—and after we found him, here, in this tower room, and couldn't reach you by phone—she never volunteered that you might—*might!*—be fifty yards away."

"I think she quite quickly got it into her head that she had stumbled onto something . . . significant. It wasn't, of course. A conjunction of events she thought meaningful was, in fact, meaning*less.*"

"I'm not sure I understand."

"Mrs. Ingley called on me Thursday evening to offer her condolences—at least that was the pretext. I didn't know the woman, so her visit seemed a bit odd. Nonetheless, I invited her in. She told me her family had worked for mine in the past, and once she told me her maiden name—Frost—I recalled the name being mentioned, though there were no Frosts here when I was a child. Judith had left Thornford before I was born. Her father had died before that . . .

"The true purpose of her call, however, began to reveal itself. After some harmless reminiscences, she told me an outrageous story about my father deliberately contriving her father's death—somehow pushing him off a ladder that was leaning against this very tower." She gestured towards the smaller, east window. "No one had ever breathed a word of such an incident to me before. I could hardly believe it. Did she tell you this?"

"Caroline, I'm sorry, you know I feel duty-bound to keep my conversations with others private."

"She *did* tell you." Her eyes hardened. "I know my father had a certain ruthless streak when it came to business, but this is really too much.

" 'Then why wasn't he charged and tried?' I asked her. Deference was still very much alive in those days, she said. A quiet word with the local constabulary, a bit of money thrown the way of this or that person. I don't believe it. I don't believe my grandfather would behave so . . . so sordidly any more than I believe my father would!"

"People sometimes go to extreme measures to protect those they love," Tom interposed gently.

"Are you suggesting my father committed this crime after all?"

"I don't know, Caroline. How could I? The information was given to me secondhand." He hesitated over the next question, for the answer to it would open a road of enquiry he dreaded. "Did Judith say what she thought your father's motive would have been?"

Caroline shifted on the banquette. "No. Which made the entire interview even more outrageous. Do you know she insinuated that such conduct was part of my family's nature, that there was an inborn Stanhope taint. 'Taint'—her expression, a quaint way of saying members of my family can't help ourselves behaving atrociously because of some genetic legacy, as if human behaviour were like Huntington's—you have a fifty percent chance of behaving like a madman, if you inherit a particular gene from one of your parents." She took a sharp breath. "It's utter insanity."

"I presume she didn't visit simply to rake over old coals."

"No. Her concerns were very much wedded to the present. She

was quite candid. It seems she had spent a good part of the week gathering intelligence about Will and me in some fashion or another. She certainly had a good idea of our finances, gleaned in part from the Leitchfield Turner estate agent who was trying to sell her the Tidy Dolly—if, in fact, that's why she was in Thornford at all in the first place. And of course the village knows our business, doesn't it? But, more sinister, Tom, she seemed to know about Will's . . . health." She looked at him and lifted an eyebrow. "You're not surprised."

"Well, of course, she trained as a nurse and managed a sunset home. Her own husband died of—"

"Tom, I know all that. She told me that's how she was able to make such a quick assessment. She couldn't have been more than an hour in Will's presence. I was stunned, of course. No one knew of Will's prognosis but me. But I couldn't say anything. I couldn't confirm it. I just told her she was being absurd. Before I told her to get out of my sight, she accused me of poisoning my husband to put him out of the . . . out of the misery that would shortly be his life."

"And did you?" Tom realised too late he had given voice to his darkest thought.

"Tom! Why would you ask that?"

"I'm sorry, Caroline, I must tell you I came here fearing the worst. That phone call from Judith's friend in Australia was deeply unsettling. Since I arrived here this afternoon, you've admitted you weren't in town last Saturday night. You were here at Thorn Court. Which you've gone to some lengths to keep a secret, including having Adam lie. I can't imagine what he thinks you're doing," Tom added, watching her mouth open to reply. He held up a cautioning hand. "You've told me before about your financial distress. Now I know about Will's condition, which is truly heartbreaking. All these things Judith knew or suspected. As much as I deplore her coming here and intimidating you with her knowledge, her conjecture isn't unreasonable, is it?"

She regarded him stonily.

"Anyone with this knowledge," he continued, hating what he was saying, "might conclude that you somehow contrived Will's death. With his consent. Or not. I don't know. In either case, Caroline, it's a crime, and though I'm not confounded about what action I need take, I *feel* confounded. I've come to know you well enough these months I've lived in Thornford. You sing in St. Nicholas's choir, our daughters are friends, you and Will have dined with us at the vicarage, people in the village think of you as a sort of golden couple—nothing about you suggests a woman who would . . ." He couldn't say the word *murder*. "And I'm disinclined to Judith's notion that folk are fated to certain behaviours by accident of birth. But I can't look into men's—or women's—souls, however much I may try. I don't know what desperation may drive them."

"Are you intending to go to the police?"

"How can I not? Not unless you can assure me that you had no hand in Will's death?"

She bit her lip. "There's still formal confession in the Church, isn't there? I don't mean the confession we make at the service Sundays. I mean—"

"Yes, I know what you mean—formal confession under the seal of the confessional. Caroline, to receive absolution, you would have to acknowledge your culpability, which would mean going to the police yourself, first."

"I see. Well, as it happens, there's no need for me to make that acknowledgement. I swear to you that I had no hand in Will's death—none. I won't say we didn't discuss the idea of assisted suicide. We did once—it was a horrible and frightening discussion. Will broached it. There had been something in the papers about a couple going to Switzerland, to one of those clinics that help people with terminal illnesses commit suicide. But I couldn't do it. I couldn't see how I could bear to witness Will take his life. There, or here, or anywhere. You see, I hadn't the courage."

Tom studied her eyes, which remained trained beseechingly on him, compelling him to believe her. "Then Will's death remains a mystery."

"Oh, Tom." Caroline's expression softened. "It's no mystery. It's no mystery at all. Don't you see? No one took Will's life."

"But—"

"Will took his own life, Tom. He took the poison himself. He knew I couldn't help him, knew I couldn't be a party to an assisted suicide without endangering myself, without consequences to our children, to our home, everything we'd built together. So he . . . arranged his own death. Do you see now?"

"Took his own life? How can you be sure?"

"It's the only explanation. Once we'd had the assisted-suicide discussion, he must have brooded on . . . taking his own life himself."

"And you had no inkling? People sometimes leave clues to their thinking, their intentions . . ."

"Other than that he was unusually loving and attentive the week before the Burns Supper?" Her eyes glistened a deeper blue. "Perhaps that should have alerted me. But I welcomed any lifting of the depression that seemed to come with the onset of the disease. I only realised what he might be planning last Saturday, when I dropped Ariel off at yours, and you said something about you, as their chaplain, being a restraining presence."

"Yes, I remember the look on your face—wary, a bit frightened."

"It suddenly occurred to me that everything was just so, everything was fallen into place . . ."

"Fallen into place to what end?"

"To disguise his intent. The hotel would be empty of guests because we were closed for renovation. It would be empty of workers because it was the weekend. Ariel would be with you at the vicarage, Adam would be in town, with me. And yet there would be a few people about, a circle of friends and acquaintances, coming and going. There would be plenty of food and drink—too much drink, of course, with memories blurred." She shivered. "I remember thinking if you were a restraining presence, Tom, then perhaps . . . "

"Perhaps Will would change his mind? Caroline, if you thought, at that moment, that you could change the course of these awful events, why didn't you?"

A shadow crossed her face. "Is a simple, straightforward answer possible? I don't know, Tom. An unwillingness to believe it could possibly be true? I think that lay at the root of it, at least in part. You do, in a way, go into . . . well, I suppose Celia Parry would call it 'denial.' That's the fashionable word, isn't it? I thought how ridiculous I would be interrupting your supper and embarrassing Will, and all for nothing. And perhaps at a deeper level, I thought that if he were set on doing this thing, if he had made his plans, then I had to honour them."

"Caroline—!"

"No, Tom. I had to. We agonised about the disease, Will and I. I knew what the future held. So did he, and he was determined not to live his mother's life. I had to steel myself to the belief that what he might do was for the best, for him, for all of us." She stared hollow-eyed into the dark centre of the tower, then put her face in her hands and moaned. "Oh, God, I don't know if I believe that! We would have managed . . . somehow. Or maybe Will would have just found another opportunity. I don't know. I simply don't know!

"Tom, when my car got stuck in the snow and the man in the lorry offered me a lift to town, I nearly accepted, but I changed my mind, thinking I must go back and make sure my fears were baseless. Adam wouldn't miss me. I presumed he and Tamara were probably stuck somewhere themselves anyway. I couldn't get a signal on my mobile to find out. So—"

"But when you got back—"

"Tom, it all seemed so normal, so ordinary. I crossed the kitchen and I could hear laughter coming from the dining room—like any day in the hotel. Or perhaps I was willing myself to believe nothing was out of the ordinary. I don't know. I can hardly account for my actions. I just remember passing quickly through the lobby, out the door, and to the Annex, where I gulped down a glass of wine with some cheese and biscuits and went to bed." She flicked him a guilty glance. "I also took a sleeping pill and was oblivious to the world for the next twelve hours."

"Do you normally take something to help you sleep?"

"Horlicks, occasionally, but rarely a pill. Will had some. He didn't always sleep well. I wanted to shut out the world."

Tom looked away, out the window. From his seat, he could see that the moon's journey had taken it well above St. Nicholas's tower; now the crescent was suspended in the black sky, God's fingernail. A week ago, when he and Roger had walked through the snow to Thorn Court, that moon had been invisible. His mind returned to that evening, to the flow of food and drink, to the sequence of courses, to the comings and goings of the guests. Which of all those moments was the fatal one? Which forkful of haggis or curry contained the poison? Will was the only one to eat from the ceremonial haggis. Had he somehow doctored it earlier, out of view? Or that glass of whisky Will dropped? He had reached for a fresh glass from the sideboard, pouring himself a drink from a new bottle. Was that the moment? Was the taxine stirred into the whisky? Or into the cranachan. Could it be? Or the yewberry tartlets after all. He had had two; Nick had given him his. *"Are there nuts in these?"* Will had murmured. But how could Will have possibly tampered with those?

He returned his attention to Caroline. "Then it was Will who asked Mrs. Prowse to provide some of her yewberry tartlets for the meal."

She nodded. "I think his plan began that moment a fortnight ago when we all rushed into your kitchen to see if your housekeeper had been hurt when she cried out. The berries were on the table.

Her pastries are famous in the village, and though no one has ever doubted her vigilance, the possibility, thin as it is, remained that a damaging seed or two might miss inspection."

Tom took a breath to temper his rising indignation. "Mrs. Prowse has been shattered by this, Caroline. Some people in the village think she either set out to poison your husband or was shockingly negligent."

"I know, Tom, but can't you see how desperate Will was? Everything he did, he did to obscure the fact that he was taking his own life, to divert attention from himself, but not direct it so pointedly on another that he or she would be damaged. I believe he thought of that. Madrun had no animus against Will—everyone knows that—and she was nowhere near here that evening. She was at the vicarage, with the girls, so how could she really be involved?"

"Then what about the Kaifs? The note Will sent to Mrs. Prowse was on the same sort of violet-coloured paper that Victor's clinic now uses for its stationery. It's very unfair to draw them into this. They've suffered a terrible loss of their own."

She laughed mirthlessly. "Tom, Will is colour-blind, remember? Years ago he caught a cricket ball in the back of the head where the . . . I think it's called the occipital lobe rests. The effect is, his colour sense was completely wonky. I don't think he thought for a moment that the paper had anything to do with the Kaifs. Really, I don't. He probably thought it was ordinary blue writing paper. I haven't seen this note, but Ariel brought some violet-coloured paper home the other week."

"She brought it from the Kaifs'."

"But I've also been looking at that colour for our own new hotel stationery. It seems to be the fashion. It was Farbarton's, the stationer in Totnes, who directed me to it. Will wrote his last instructions on paper that colour, remember? He likely pulled it from Farbarton's samples down in the office, thinking it was a standard business blue, but"—she cocked her head in thought—"he most likely used a printer at Totnes Library or somewhere other than here to print the note to Madrun."

"If you were going to send someone an anonymous note, you wouldn't use distinctive paper—a paper that could be traced to someone."

"But it wouldn't be distinctive to Will. He probably chose it thinking it might be linked to many people and therefore sow more confusion. Will wouldn't have set out to hurt Victor or Molly. He was too aware of their suffering. Victor had reconciled with Will—"

"Molly hadn't—not really. And unlike Mrs. Prowse, she was present at the Burns Supper."

Caroline frowned. "I can only guess that Will thought no opportunity could attach to her. And how could it? I know how food is plated and served at banquets, which the Burns Supper was. It's almost impossible to direct a particular plate to a particular person in food service of that nature. And Kerra was serving, not Molly. Molly would have left trays of plated food, about four or six per tray, in the service pantry, which Kerra would pick up and take into the dining room, but it would be impossible to say with any assurance which guest would get which plate. If Molly herself had carried a single plate of food and put it in front of Will, then I suppose suspicion would fall on her. But she didn't, did she? You were there."

"No, Molly was only seen when the haggis was piped in. But don't you see that a cloud hangs over everyone who was there? Your brother, for instance, left the dining room to use the loo, but exited through the serving pantry. Perhaps he tampered with the food. He and your husband were not getting along at the supper."

"But, again, Tom, how would that plate arrive in front of my husband?"

"Victor, John, Mark, too—at different times each left the private dining room on some task or errand."

"But people do move about at banquets, don't they? And that's why Will decided the Burns Supper was the best chance to meet his end, an event so public that a private act would be lost in the confusion. I asked Nick to take me through the sequence of events. I think Will took a sufficient quantity of taxine during your break after the supper and before the toasts began, and came up here, knowing that by the time you found him he would be . . . gone."

"He looked unwell earlier. Judith remarked on it. Thought it was his heart."

"I can't begin to imagine the stress he would have been under that evening. Surely that affected his appearance. Or perhaps he took some earlier—to test its effect? Perhaps he was acting. You didn't see his performance in *Abigail's Party*. He was very good. He played Laurence, who suffers a heart attack.

"I regret all this deeply," she continued. "I think Will was single-mindedly concentrated on what he thought best for me and our children. That any cloud hanging over others in the village was nothing compared with the cross we would bear, the suffering we would endure—the loss of our home, watching him grow slowly mad. I can only presume he thought any inquest would eventually bring in a verdict of accident or misadventure at best, or an open verdict at worst, but that no one in Thornford would suffer unduly, and that Ariel and I could go on living here with some financial security."

"And then came Judith Ingley."

"The snow and Mrs. Ingley, yes."

"Did she threaten you?"

"She preferred to tantalise, I think. She said she would go the police, if and when it suited her. I have no idea what those circumstances might be."

"I'm puzzled. She didn't want anything from you?"

"I think she saw herself as some sort of avenging angel. Tom, I don't think my motive, or combination of motives, to murder my husband mattered to her in the slightest. She said she was only interested in ensuring no Stanhope got away again with murder—the Stanhope being me, in this instance. And of course I couldn't tell her I was certain Will had commited suicide." Caroline turned to him. "What will you do?"

"With what I've learned this afternoon?" Tom pinched the bridge of his nose so hard it began to hurt, a pain preferable to what he had to say. "I don't know how I can do any other than report Phyllis Lambert's phone call to the police. It's information that sheds light on Judith's death, at the very least. I don't know what to say about this conversation with you. I was shocked at the inquest to learn Will's death was neither accident nor premature death. Now I'm deeply grieved to learn that he took his own life. I understand his reasons, I do, Caroline, but it's not the way. You must know that as a Christian yourself. I urge you to go to the police and make a full statement."

"I can't do it. It will ruin us. It will make a mockery of Will's sacrifice."

"But I have to think about the needs of others in the village. Mrs. Prowse is not out of the woods. Bliss and Blessing are focusing on the Kaifs. If you say nothing, and the inquest arrives at an open verdict, then they—and the others at the supper—will always have a cloud of suspicion over them. It simply isn't fair or right."

"Tom, you're the only person in England other than me who knows about Will's HD—or the only living person. Can't you—"

"But once the police find Nick, it will all start to unravel anyway."

"I don't understand? Why should it?"

"Nick shot Judith to protect you, surely."

"Protect *me*? That's absurd. Nick has little thought but for himself. Why would he shoot Judith?"

"But surely you told him that Judith menaced you."

"I've seen little of Nick since Thursday morning, the day of the inquest. I can't imagine how he would know of my conversation with Judith Ingley."

"Then how—"

"It wasn't me, Mum."

The new voice brought involuntary gasps from both of them. Tom's head jerked towards the shadows at the top of the stairs. Peering through the darkness he could barely discern the contours of a figure in a bulky jacket, and then he saw candlelight glint along the barrel of a shotgun and he leapt unthinkingly to his feet.

"Adam, darling," Caroline said, rising at the same moment, "why do you have that out of the cabinet?"

"I heard voices. I thought—"

"It's the vicar," Caroline continued soothingly, moving towards her son. "We're just having a little chat."

"No, you're not. You're talking about Dad and Nick."

"What have you heard?"

"That something will unravel when the police find Nick. Mr. Christmas said it."

"And that's all?"

"Yes," he replied with a hint of petulance, stepping into the pool of light afforded by the lamps. Tom glanced at the shotgun, its muzzle pointed to the ceiling, and at the heavy scowl that creased Adam's face. He'd had his fill of firearms and couldn't quell the shiver that ran up his spine.

"Are you sure?" Caroline pressed.

"Yes, Mother." The scowl deepened.

Caroline flicked Tom a glance of relief, adding to her son, "I wish you'd put that down."

"I asked Tamara not to talk to him." Adam jerked his head towards Tom, dropping the shotgun so it rested in both hands.

"Adam, I know your mother wasn't in town last Saturday, and, no, Tamara did not tell me—at least directly."

444 · C. C. BENISON

"Tom deduced it, darling. I do wish you'd put that thing away. I've told him that Mrs. Ingley knew I was here at home the night your father died and that she had been rather obnoxious about it."

"Mum!"

"Adam's aware of your meeting with Mrs. Ingley?" Tom turned to Caroline in consternation.

"Well, yes. Adam spent Thursday here. He wasn't party to my conversation with the woman, but he saw her come and go. He could see I was troubled. I couldn't *not* tell him." Tom could see a horror dawn in Caroline's eyes as she turned back to her son. "John knows I was here last Saturday," she murmured, as if in a trance, "but he doesn't know—"

"*John* knows?"

"He saw me slipping out the front door from the lobby," she replied absently. "He was coming out of the men's."

"What! He knew Adam didn't fetch you back? Did you ask John to say nothing?"

"Yes," Caroline replied impatiently, her attention riveted on her son. "But John doesn't know that Judith Ingley also saw me. I haven't spoken with John since Tuesday. Only Adam knows Mrs. Ingley met me Thursday. Oh, Adam, please tell me you haven't done anything foolish." She reached for her son, but he drew back, alarm flashing in his eyes.

"Mother, what are you saying . . . ?"

"You told someone? Please tell me you told no one else. Nick? Was it Nick you told?"

"No, *no*. I wouldn't tell Nick. We don't talk about that sort of stuff."

"Then you told no one?"

Adam's lips formed a thin tight slit. He had told someone.

CHAPTER THIRTY-ONE

Some small animal, its pin-bright eyes briefly exalted in the beam of the headlamps, pulled Tom from his black thoughts. His eyes refocused on the rampart of hedgerows, strobing pale gold as the car hurtled down the narrow lane. A road sign leapt from the darkness then vanished, a cottage wall blazed briefly only to be extinguished. Now well past the village confines, Adam had set his Rover into high gear, but no youthful bravado could account for this reckless acceleration. Helplessly Tom's foot pressed against an imaginary brake.

"Killing us both will solve nothing," he gasped as lights from an approaching vehicle reared up and Adam jerked the steering wheel, slamming them into a bend in the hedgerow. Branches thrashed against the passenger windows. As they lurched forward, Tom glimpsed in the interior glow of the other car a silvered face like a furious moon pressed to the glass.

"I don't know why you think John would shoot that meddling

old cow," Adam snarled as he plunged the car back into the endless tunnel.

It was a variant on the very question he had asked in Thorn Court's tower not many minutes earlier, only the tone then had been wondering, unbelieving, without belligerence. Caroline had turned her face from her son at that moment, but Tom, who caught her gaze, witnessed a daze of emotions navigate her features—relief, then disbelief, shock, then horror. It had been his task to address Adam and reply with an equanimity that couldn't be further removed from the tumult of his own emotions.

"I don't. We don't." He had stumbled over the words. "How could John? The weapon's been found, it seems, and it appears to be one of Colm Parry's. Did you not know?"

Adam had blanched. Caroline whipped her head around. "Adam?" she said querulously.

"Mum, I haven't been to Thornridge since before Christmas!"

A new relief seemed to soften Caroline's features at that moment. Tom knew what was passing though her mind: If the murder weapon had come from a place as inaccessible as Thornridge House, out in the country, locked and alarmed, then what opportunity would anyone in her circle have to acquire one.

"You didn't tell me the shotgun came from Colm's." She frowned at Tom. "Surely that absolves—"

"Caroline, your brother has been working much of the week on a security upgrade at Thornridge while Colm and Celia have been away."

Her frown deepened. "I didn't know that. Did you know that, Adam?"

The young man shook his head impatiently. "Ariel's calling for you. That's why I came over from the Annex. I have to get back to Noze. We have an American syndicate arriving in the morning and I need to—"

"I'll come with you," Tom interrupted. He felt a terrible urgency.

"But it's impossible," Caroline murmured to Tom, her eyes flashing a warning. "The shotgun comes from Thornridge."

"I have other things to talk about with John," Tom replied in a low voice. "Adam?"

"How will you get back?"

"I'll get a ride."

"You've Evensong in little over an hour." Caroline extended her wrist towards the lamp and frowned over her watch.

"I won't be long. I'll ask John to drive me back. He sometimes comes to Evensong."

"Not this time," Adam protested. "We've got things to do."

"Nonetheless. If you don't mind. My car's at Jago's being serviced."

Ungraciously, Adam permitted him passage in his Land Rover, one of the estate's older models. Now Tom was confronted anew with the freighted question.

"I don't think John shot Mrs. Ingley," Tom replied, though he recognised the bluff in his voice. In truth, he prayed fervently that John had done nothing so foolish, so criminal. And yet he couldn't keep from his mind the ambiguity wrought by an inquest's open verdict around the death of Regina Copeland, John's wife, who flung herself off St. Hilda's tower at Noze Lydiard Castle. Or was pushed. Was John—taciturn, sensible John Copeland—capable of cold-blooded murder? Gamekeepers were familiar with the death and disposal of the unwelcome, shooting foxes, rabbits, and other vermin with a kind of impunity that Tom, who had never held a shotgun, found repellent.

"I'm seeing John on an entirely private matter." Tom's feet once again pressed an invisible brake as the car accelerated dangerously between the hedgerows. "Would you bloody slow down!"

The car slowed, but only a little.

Tom glanced at the young man's profile in the dash lights and noted the grim set to his mouth. "I'm sorry, Adam. I've made you angry. That's not my intent. I know this is probably the worst week of your life."

Adam's response was to grip the wheel more tightly. The car careened around a twist in the lane, its headlamps briefly blazing through a gap in the hedge black winter fields.

"You're going to grass me up to the police, aren't you," he responded in a sullen tone after a minute.

"No, why would I do that?"

"Because you know my mum wasn't with me last Saturday. Tamara told you."

"Tamara said you were with her in Exeter. What she knows of your mother's whereabouts is what you told her—that your mother stayed over in town at the Seven Stars. Besides, your mother and I have discussed this."

"But what if the police ask you?"

"About your mother's . . . movements that evening? They won't ask me, Adam, because they wouldn't imagine I had firsthand knowledge of such a thing. What I do know, really, is hearsay."

"But they're not thick. They know you're friends with my mother. You're her priest. She talks to you. She doesn't talk to me."

"Your mother has much to deal with," Tom responded, then realised too late how anodyne the observation was.

"And I don't?" Adam snapped. He banged the steering wheel with his fist while a wounded-animal sound, heart-wrenching to hear, seemed to come from the centre of his gut. They were stopped now at the junction with the A435, where Caroline had ploughed into a snowbank the week before. Light from the streetlamp turned Adam's face a sickly green. "My father is *dead*!"

"Adam, I'm so sorry—"

"Poisoned, *murdered*! And my mother may have—!"

"Adam!" Tom cut him off. "It's not true. It's simply not true. Your mother is not responsible for your father's death."

"Then why does she want me to lie for her?" Adam turned to

face him. In the confines of the cab, Tom could smell the other man's hot meaty breath. *"Why?"*

Tom recoiled instinctively from the eruption of fury, struck by his incapacity to offer balm to Adam's confusion and grief. The cruel truth of Will's broken health and plotted death, not his—*never* his—to disclose, would allay the confusion, but only send the dead man's son into a maelstrom of grief, worse than any ripping his insides now.

"I think you'll have to trust that your mother has your best interests at heart," he replied, unhappily aware that this unique circumstance squeezed from him again the most threadbare of utterances.

"What about *my* interests?" The question came as a shout. "If I say my mother was with me last Saturday, that makes Tamara a liar. If I say I was with Tamara, what will happen to my mum?"

The shattering blast of a car horn made them both jump. Adam scowled, wiped the sleeve of his jacket across his eyes, and executed a sharp left onto the A435, tyres protesting. After a few feet he turned sharply across the highway onto a new country lane, narrowly avoiding an oncoming car.

"Stop the car."

"What?" Adam seemed blind to the danger of his driving.

"I said stop the car. I can walk to Noze from here with less chance of dying along the way."

Adam said nothing, but he slowed the car to a speed respectable for a night-shrouded country lane. "You haven't even got a torch," he muttered after a moment, and a moment later: "I'm sorry."

They travelled in silence through the hedgerows, Tom acutely aware he hadn't responded to the younger man's agonising conundrum. What would happen if Adam were scrupulous with the truth about his whereabouts that fateful Saturday? *A righteous man hateth lying,* wrote the author of Proverbs. Yes, he should do, if he were on a quest for righteousness—and he was, really—but Tom felt himself edging towards the slope of moral relativism. Might truth unraveled bring about a greater suffering? Caroline had lost her husband, and now she would lose her home. Adam had lost his father, and now he would learn of his cruel genetic legacy in the most abrupt way. Ariel had lost the man she called Father; now the fact of her paternity would be brought dangerously near to revelation. It was this that Tom, more even than Caroline, wanted desperately to keep vaulted now that he was certain of Judith's true mission in Thornford. Was all this worth more than some miasma of suspicion that might trail after those present at the Burns Supper, more than the loss of money to some faceless insurance company?

"I take it you've talked with John about your whereabouts last Saturday." Tom broke the silence as they turned off the lane.

"When we're checking the rearing sheds or cutting rides through brambles or the like, we talk a bit. He's a good bloke. Easier to talk to than my dad of late." A wide gate discreetly marked with the coat-of-arms of the earl of Duffield loomed before the headlamps. Adam braked the car. "I shouldn't say that about my dad, sorry. John thinks I should say my mum was with me, if I'm asked."

"Does he now."

"What do you think I should do?"

Tom took a deep breath. "I think you need to make up your own mind."

"That's no answer."

"Adam, you become a wiser person when you wrestle with your own conscience and come to decisions rather than go through life following other people's advice."

Adam grunted and stepped from the car. Tom watched him move into the light from the headlamps, unlatch the gate, and push it open. He returned to the car, drove it forward past the gate, then got out and closed it behind.

"I have a question for you." Off to the right, past Adam's head, Tom could glimpse in floodlight the ruins of Noze Lydiard Castle on its outcrop overlooking the valley. "Mrs. Ingley indicated to me that your uncle had, in some way, threatened or intimated her—"

"Now you think Nick shot her."

"I'm thinking no such thing." Not now. "But you were with your uncle last night. Presumably you talked—"

"But we didn't talk about some old lady."

"What about Thursday? At the inquest?"

Adam shrugged. "Maybe it has to do with the Tidy Dolly. He said he was thinking about buying it. I heard she was, too."

"A tearoom? Your uncle?"

"He has a notion of turning it into holiday flats. He's full of schemes, Uncle Nick."

Adam slowed the car and turned into a large farmyard, the twin lights sweeping past motley forms and shadows of country-use vehicles—a quad bike, a small tractor, game carts, a couple of trucks—past a few old stone buildings—barns, store sheds, perhaps—and others clearly intended for human occupation, notably a rambling, thatch-roofed structure that was surely John's. Adam parked next to John's Rover and cut the engine. The yard plunged into darkness, barely broken by a single security light over the barn—which clicked off as quickly as it had clicked on—barely bested by an inch of brightness peeping through the cottage's drawn curtains.

Tom stepped from the car to the furious welcome of dogs—penned, he presumed, as none came dashing along his legs—and caught in the faint breeze a pungent whiff of animal life, of the dogs, and of game birds collected somewhere off in the darkness in sheds or pens. Out of the cocoon of the car interior, the darkness of the yard seemed very nearly impermeable and he felt as if a heavy mantle had descended upon his shoulders impossible to shake off. In Gravesend, in Cambridge, in London, in Bristol—in all the places he had claimed home—he never experienced night the way he did in the deep Devon countryside. In Thornford, caught after sunset well away from the vicarage without his torch, he occasionally experienced a ludicrous moment of panic if no friendly lighted window came into view as he groped his way down into the village, his brushing hands grateful for the Braille of the stone walls lining the lanes. Now with the moon's crescent vanished behind gathering clouds, the wind rising in short gusts, he felt prickling along his skin an almost atavistic fear of the dark. No wonder that apparitions of wronged women and phantom presences so easily attached themselves to the ruined castle nearby. What he had not detected in the blend of night noises, the crunch of their shoes on gravel, the snap of Adam opening and closing the boot of his car, the now half-hearted barking of the dogs—and what he had not been prepared to hear when the noise stopped—was an unearthly wail, distant yet strident, like that of some creature, a ghost perhaps, suffering fearsome mental torment. His hackles rose in an instant, then subsided as he realised what he was hearing.

"John likes to practise his pipes before supper." Adam's voice came through the dark, followed by a scrape and the dull thud of a heavy object dragged along the cobbles. Torchlight broke the darkness suddenly and Tom could see in backshadow what looked like a bag of animal feed slung over Adam's shoulder.

"John's is over there." Adam waved the torch. "Take this, if you like," he added, proffering the torch to Tom. "I know my way around."

"Thanks," Tom said, taking it. "Where do you live?"

"That way." Adam gestured into the darkness. Tom directed the torch, which limned a small cob dwelling. "I can drive you back, if you like," he added contritely. "That's if John can't. He's likely meeting the shoot captain later this evening."

"That's very kind, thank you." Tom turned and waved the light beam over the cobbles, conscious that Adam was staring after his retreating figure. As he approached the cottage, the skirl of the strange, mad thing amplified, the sound uncannily thrilling, setting the hair to bristling on the back of his neck. "Flowers of the Forest"—he recognised with a start the plangent air, a funeral choice usually. He reached the door, a windowless wooden affair surrounded by a wreath of untrimmed ivy, inky spikes in the blackness, and hesitated.

"Lord," he murmured under the drone of the pipes, bowing his head, "make me an instrument of Thy will." He let another moment pass to quell the thrumming along his veins, then knocked. He waited for the wail to cease, then rapped his knuckles more firmly against the door when it didn't. The force of his hand nudged the door open an inch; it wasn't locked, little surprise in the country. He stepped onto the limestone flags of an entrance hall, his torch picking out waxed jackets hanging from pegs, boots and shoes tidily arrayed below a wooden bench, a closet, a metal gun locker, and a glass cabinet filled with colourful rows of shotgun cartridges that looked antique even to Tom's untrained eye. He moved towards a thread of yellow light spilling across the flags from a door slightly ajar and poked his head through into a large lime-washed parlour, a log-burning hearth with a fire-blacked surround at the farther end. He had half expected the room to express a bachelor austerity, but John was widower, not bachelor. A quick scan suggested furnishings with an origin in a grander house—heavy mahogany chairs, shelves, a desk—and décor guided by a discriminating feminine hand—rose curtains, lamp shades, and pillows, slate-blue sofa and chair covers, united by a faded Axminster carpet. Regina Copeland's legacy and little changed in ten years, though an absence of china ornaments and silver frames and the presence of a motley assortment of stuffed wildlife, including a stoat and a sparrow hawk, suggested a more recent victory for masculine taste.

John's broad back was to him, his legs spread wide in a footballer's stance, the tenor drone of his pipes pressed almost to his bull neck. In the low-ceilinged room, the primitive sound seemed to fill every corner; it crept like a tick under Tom's skin and burrowed into his nerves, magnifying a new-minted unease. John seemed lost in concentration. Uninvited, loath to interrupt, Tom could only abide in the shadow of the door well and consider how the next minutes would unfold. The thought came to him unbidden that if John turned, the composition of his face, the subtle shift of tiny muscles around the eyes, would tell him all he needed to know, and he shrank from the possibility.

But it did not come to pass that way. As John came to the final notes of the dirge, a door on the left opened and a lean woman of middle years with fox-red hair stepped through wiping her hands on a tea towel. John turned his head to her, but her eyes took in Tom's presence in that instant, and she flinched, dropping the towel. The reed fell from John's mouth and he twisted around to take in Tom's presence. His face was unreadable.

"Please forgive me," Tom said as the bagpipe released an unlovely squeal. "I didn't mean to startle."

"Tom . . . ," John began, then looked to the woman, who moved swiftly to his side. "This is Tom Christmas, the vicar at St. Nicholas's . . ."

"Oh," she murmured, her eyes suspicious.

" . . . and this is Helen Lander." John finished the introductions without elaboration as he bent to snatch the towel off the floor.

"You're likely starting a meal," Tom continued, advancing into the room.

"Not . . . for a bit." John looked to Helen for confirmation as he handed her the towel, then with furrowed brow at Tom. "I . . . Is there? . . . Did we arrange—?"

"No, you've not forgotten anything. I came because I . . . wanted a word." Feeling constrained by Helen's presence, he affected a light tone, though his heart beat a hard tattoo.

"Jago wasted no time on your car."

"Adam drove me. I was speaking with Caroline earlier this afternoon at Thorn Court." He sensed rather than saw Helen stiffen.

"Perhaps I should leave the two of you," she interjected.

"I'm sorry, I didn't think you might have company," Tom began as she flicked John a coded glance and slipped back through the connecting door.

"Helen organises the shooting lunches." John stepped over to the door, pushed it shut, and twisted the knob. "At the lodge. It's . . . Never mind, you wouldn't be able to see it from the road even in daylight," he added, relieving himself of his pipes, the bag protesting with a feeble wheeze. He placed them on top of a case at the corner of the sofa, and with strong, even strokes straightened the sleeves of his loden pullover. His eyes returned to Tom's with a brief, assessing squint, then resumed their characteristic imperturbability. "You were speaking with Caroline," he echoed. "About . . . ?"

"The events of the last week. May I take off my jacket?" The room seemed to Tom unnaturally warm, though the fire was burning low. He suddenly thought he might be coming down with a cold.

"As you like," John responded, moving to a drinks table under a painting of a hunting scene. "Whisky? I was about to have one."

"I'll join you then." Dutch courage, he thought, not really fancying a drink. He dropped his jacket over the top of a wingback chair.

"Water? I'll have to get some from the kitchen."

"Neat is fine."

John handed him a crystal tumbler with an inch of amber liquid at the bottom. "Caroline?" he prompted.

The smell of the whisky met Tom's nose and repulsed him a little. He *must* be coming down with something. He took a polite sip, which seemed to burn along his tongue, and began.

"I know, for instance, that Caroline did not spend last Saturday night snowbound here at Noze, as she claimed, or in town. She was in Thornford, at home, though she was out in the storm briefly. You know it, too. In fact, you knew Saturday at the Burns Supper she was at Thorn Court, and I think I know when you realised. You went out for some antacid tablets before the curry course and came back with a strange expression on your face, as if you'd seen an apparition. I recall it clearly. But you didn't say anything then . . . "

John sipped his whisky and shrugged.

" . . . and you didn't say anything the next morning. In church, you didn't *say* you had fetched Caroline at Noze, but you left me with the impression you had. Only when I mentioned the absence of tyre tracks did you say that Adam had fetched her back, and, of course, that wasn't true, either." Tom ran his finger around his collar. "Why," he asked, though he felt certain he knew the answer, "did you not mention you'd seen Caroline? You must have witnessed her crossing the lobby."

"What if I tell you I don't know."

"I would have trouble believing you."

"But it's true. There was something about the way . . . I'm not good at this."

"At what?"

"With words. Describing things."

Tom frowned. "About the way Caroline—what? Looked? Seemed?"

John nodded. "I could see her as I opened the door of the men's—her having come through from the kitchen. She couldn't see me. She stopped for a second. She looked . . . like a doe who'd heard a branch snap in the woods."

"Frightened?"

"Maybe. Alert, more. I thought perhaps she'd planned some sort of surprise for the supper, and I didn't want to spoil it, so I didn't say anything."

"But after, John, when we'd found Will . . . ?"

"Seemed odd to say I'd seen her hours ago, for one thing." He shrugged again. "And I thought there being no surprise at the supper after all, what Caroline had wanted was not to be seen in the hotel, so I thought, she must have her reasons . . . "

"And then the next morning," Tom prompted, taking another sip of whisky.

"The next morning . . . well, I didn't need my car, did I? I went to the Annex. I told her . . . well, after I told her about Will, I said I'd seen her the night before in the hotel—"

"Her response to that?"

"Hard to say. She was already shaken by Will's death. She asked me if I wouldn't say anything."

"And you complied."

"If it helped her. It seemed harmless. I didn't ask why. We didn't know then there was anything unusual about Will's death."

"But after the inquest, we did. You must have wondered why she sought your collusion."

John's mouth formed a thin line. He set his glass on the mantel and lifted a poker from a rack by the fireplace. "I'm not certain what you're getting at, Tom," he said, stirring the logs so they tumbled and flared.

"John, you recall our conversation in the vestry Thursday. Ariel's well-being was very much on your mind, and why? At the time, your concern seemed to me outlandish and misplaced. But then I began to see why you—you, the most phlegmatic of men—would rise to such passion. Will, it turns out, had ingested poison last Saturday. At the time, Caroline had been in the hotel, not here at Noze, not in town. At the inquest, I'm sure, it struck you that Caroline may have had a hand in her husband's—"

"I never—"

"And that's why she sought your cooperation. She knew you had a . . ." Tom groped for understatement. " . . . soft spot for her."

"I never thought Caroline was responsible."

"Wives kill husbands. Husbands kill wives."

John's face flushed. "What are you on about?"

"John, I'm not referring to your late wife, to Regina. I'm merely saying that spousal homicide is not uncommon."

"Caroline wouldn't have poisoned Will."

"Are you quite certain?"

John looked away. "She's not the sort," he said thickly, adding in a defensive tone, "Why? Do you think she did?"

"What I think won't matter. What others think will. Once police learn Caroline was at Thorn Court, once they learn she asked people to keep this a secret, she'll be their prime suspect. Caroline stands to benefit financially from her husband's death, and it seems half the village knows Thorn Court is in financial peril."

He watched John continue to poke at the fire, which now sparked and blazed.

"John, I went through the hell of a police investigation myself when my wife was killed. So, you told me, did you. I know the police must do what's asked of them, but I wouldn't wish the experience on anyone who is innocent." Tom paused. "I think anyone who loved, or was in love with, Caroline wouldn't wish it on her, either."

John looked up from the fire, his eyes steady but now watchful.

"Caroline is an attractive woman, is she not? And she seems in her way to get what she wants from men. Will left a good job in London to come down here and run a hotel with her. I'm sure it was she who persuaded Nick to lend them part of his inheritance to finance Thorn Court. It can't have been Will. There seemed little love lost between the two. Adam, too, is prepared to lie about his mother's whereabouts, even though he is deeply troubled as to why. His mother won't tell him. But I'm sure he fears he'll lose her, too. That she'll be arrested, tried, jailed. And what will become of Ariel?—your concern to me in our Thursday conversation. But it's not simply your natural daughter's fate that worries you, it's Caroline's, too, isn't it? You are, after all, in love with her."

"What of it?" John glanced towards the connecting door. "I didn't poison Will, if that's what you're on about."

"No," Tom murmured, "that's not what brings me here."

"Then what does?"

"John, you weren't the only person to see Caroline at Thorn Court last Saturday."

"I don't know what you mean."

"I think you do. Judith Ingley saw Caroline come out of the

hotel entrance moments after you saw her cross the lobby. Later, Judith made sure that Caroline knew what she saw—"

"Blackmail."

"In effect. Then you do know what I mean."

"Yes, all right," John groused, slipping the poker back into the rack and retrieving his whisky. "Adam did say something about it. I'd forgotten."

"Something?"

"We were out wrapping some sack around one of the barbed-wire fences Friday and he happened to mention it. The lad was a bit upset, needed someone to talk to, I suppose."

"And did you tell him that you, too, had seen Caroline at the hotel?"

"No."

"John, there are only two people who knew about Caroline's disturbing conversation with Mrs. Ingley. One was Adam. I expect Caroline felt she needed to tell her family at least part of what Judith had to say, since they would be the ones to suffer if anything happened to her."

"And Nick."

"Caroline says not. She had almost no communication with her brother since the morning of the inquest. It wasn't until Thursday evening that Judith arrived at Thorn Court. John, the second person is you, of course. Adam shared his worry with you. He couldn't very well with Tamara, since he's trying to protect his mother, and he couldn't with Nick, who is hardly a steady, sympathetic character, and his sister is a child—so he told you."

"Well, what if he did."

"Last night, as you know, Judith Ingley was shot dead by someone who knew his way around a shotgun."

John frowned. "Folk at church this morning were speculating about Nick Stanhope."

"Anyone carrying a shotgun at the Old Orchard last night is being investigated. But the direction of the shot, the type of ammunition, and the discovery of a shotgun in the vicarage garden suggest the involvement of another party. It might be Nick. A phone call apparently prompted him to leave the Wassail a little before Judith was shot, so he may have had the opportunity, but . . . "

John glanced again towards the communicating door, as if someone on the other side might be listening. "Is this why you've come?" He dropped his voice, shifting his eyes, now steely, to Tom. "Are you suggesting that I shot Judith Ingley?"

"I pray that you didn't, John."

"The gun was Colm's, not mine. I don't own a Purdey."

"How do you know the gun was Colm's?"

"It's certain, isn't it? I saw the look on Colm's face when your daughter brought it in, then you and he closeted yourselves in the vestry with that detective. If it wasn't Colm's, why would he be bothered? And how would I have got hold of one of Colm's, in any case?"

"Thornridge's security system has been inoperative much of the week. Nick was supposed to have been doing an upgrade. Access wouldn't have been difficult."

"I only ever see Nick Stanhope at band practice. I know little about his work or his whereabouts."

Tom ran his finger absently over the rim of his glass. "Was Helen with you last night?"

John reddened. "I'm not sure that's any of your business."

"I agree it isn't," Tom responded evenly. "But her presence here would establish an alibi for you."

"I don't bloody need an alibi."

Tom stepped towards his jacket, turned it to its tartan lining, and slipped his free hand into an inside pocket. "John, my purpose in venturing out on a winter's eve isn't to spread accusation—"

"Don't you have an evening service?"

Tom glanced at a clock on the mantel. It was almost six; Evensong was in half an hour. "They'll manage if I'm delayed." He pulled a piece of folded paper from the pocket. "I came for another reason, although . . . "

"Although . . . ?"

Tom hesitated. "Perhaps we should sit."

Regarding him with new unease, John settled onto the sofa. Tom sat opposite, in the wing chair.

"You recall previous mentions we've made about our parentage," Tom began. "We're both adopted. We've each wondered from time to time who our natural parents were, particularly when we were teenagers, but neither of us has pursued it as an adult. When my wife and I were planning a child, we thought of exploring my parentage, for the usual reasons, genetic legacy and so on, but somehow it fell to the wayside. Life crowds in in other ways."

"Yes." John frowned at him over the rim of his glass.

Tom placed his tumbler on a table beside the chair and ran his thumb unthinkingly along the paper's folds. "Mrs. Prowse found an old document among Mrs. Ingley's belongings earlier today. It's something that should properly be placed with the police, but . . . "

"What is it?"

Tom studied John's watchful, weathered face a minute, dreading what the next few minutes would bring. "I want very much for this document to be utterly irrelevant, but I believe very much that it isn't. Actually, I thought about simply destroying this, but I have my reasons—good reasons, I think—for showing it to you." He straightened the paper along his lap and read from it. "Were you born April second, by chance?"

"Yes." John's brow furrowed. "I'll be forty-nine this spring."

Tom glanced at the stated year of birth in the second column, and made a swift calculation. "Your mother—your adoptive mother—never said where you were born, did she?"

"Near Leeds. Or in Leeds."

"At Furness House Nursing Home?"

"That I wouldn't know. Or remember. I know it was a private adoption." He shrugged. "It's been many years since I've had this sort of conversation with my mother."

"Your parents—your adoptive parents—had you christened John?"

"Yes. What are you on about, Tom?"

"And they chose John? Adoptive parents often change the name of the child."

"My parents apparently liked the names my birth mother gave me. Most of them, at any rate—the traditional ones, William and Anthony. But they didn't care for Sean, which was the third one. I think they thought it too trendy . . . or too Irish, so they changed it to John, and I suppose I was always called John because it was the name they more or less chose. Why?"

Tom stared silently at the aging document with its entries in tidy cursive handwriting, now faded. He considered for the second time that day tossing it into the fire—the flames were so near—but desperation to protect the welfare of two people stayed his hand. Silently, with foreboding, he passed the certificate to John and watched as the man's eyes below their heavy brows scanned the information.

"Are you suggesting . . . ? Frost?" John glanced up from the paper, his features creased with perplexity. "Should the name be familiar? I don't understand?"

"Frost is Judith Ingley's maiden name. She said so at the Burns Supper."

John frowned again at the document then lifted his eyes once more, only this time they were narrow slits of contempt. "But this can't be. It's a . . . coincidence. There must have been another baby born that day who was named . . . " His heavy face, turned the colour of ashes, suddenly pricked with red. "Did she tell you this? That I was her . . . "

"No, she—"

"There you go then."

"John, listen to me." Tom leaned forwards. "Judith said she came to Thornford with a notion of buying a business and moving back. That might be true, but I think in the end it would have depended on another factor. You see, she told me that she had travelled to the village last Saturday very purposefully to arrive at Thorn Court in time for the Burns Supper. She wouldn't tell me why, but we had a provocative conversation about adoption and children and in what combination they are products of their parents' nurturing or their own inborn natures. This afternoon I made an attempt to get in touch with Judith's son to alert him to his mother's death. You may recall her saying she had a son working in Shanghai."

John gave him a quick assenting nod.

"She doesn't have a son working in Shanghai. I talked to a woman related to her by marriage, who's known her well for almost half a century, who told me Judith had no son. None. And yet"— Tom gestured towards the certificate—"she did have a son, born almost forty-nine years ago, with the same three Christian names you have."

"That doesn't—"

"I'm certain she came to the Burns Supper to see the man who was her son, to see what life had made of him, and what he'd made of his life."

"They're not to make direct contact like that! They're supposed to—"

"I know. Make contact through some intermediary agency. And maybe Judith would have in time, but . . ." He didn't voice the obvious. "At first, this afternoon, I thought that Will might be the child. He"—Tom chose the next word carefully—"said . . . he was adopted. He's your age, but the dates and places don't match. Yours do."

As he spoke, Tom observed a succession of emotions struggle for supremacy on John's normally stolid visage: incredulity, shock, fear, cunning, and, finally, horror. He stared at Tom, his mouth wrenched open, seized in a rictus of disbelief.

"It can't be." His eyes had a feverish shine. "It's impossible." But as the seconds passed, the full implication seemed to seep into his expression. "Why?" his voice rasped as he lurched from his seat. The certificate fluttered to the floor. "Why are you saying this? She's dead! You didn't need to tell me this. I didn't need to know."

"John, there's something more," Tom began, his heart sick, watching the man stagger past him and dart his eyes around the room as if in search of something, an exit, a drink, a weapon. Tom jerked forward in his chair in readiness as John stumbled along the carpet, crashing into the drinks table, steadying himself by grasping the edge of the mantel with one hand. With the other he clutched his stomach and bent towards the fire as if he were about to be ill.

"Jesus Christ," he groaned. "What have I done?"

A muted keening, more terrible somehow coming from a man, seemed to inhabit the room in that moment. An echo of the bagpipe's chill lament, it pierced Tom's eardrums and travelled his spine. Helpless, horrified, he watched John struggle to stop. The connecting door flew open and Helen burst into the room like an avenging virago. She stared at John speechlessly, then turned to Tom.

"What's he done?"

Her phrasing, her knowing tone, nonplussed him. He looked to John, who raised his head.

"Get out." He had recovered his voice. *"Get out!"*

She didn't blanch. She stayed her ground. "You did it, didn't you?" Her voice was cold. "You shot that woman."

"Helen, shut up!"

"He was gone for about an hour last night." Helen turned to Tom, her eyes blazing. "And in my car! And when he got back, he was—"

"Shut up, I said!"

"John Copeland, what have you done?" Her jaw thrust forward, her teeth bared. "All because of that bloody woman—that bloody Caroline." She spat out the name. "I'm calling the police."

"No!" John howled, lunging towards her.

Tom was on his feet in an instant. Helen struggled towards the door, her hand straining for the knob, John tearing at her shoulder. Tom wedged his body between them, seeking purchase on John's arm to pry them apart, but John was powerfully built and it took all Tom's mettle to separate him from the woman. In doing so, he slammed John face-forward against the wall, knocking a picture off its nail, sending it cascading to the floor with the resounding shriek of fragmenting glass.

"Helen," Tom gasped, winded, his heart crashing against his chest as he squeezed John's wrists in a lock with both his hands, "please, leave us for a few moments. Do nothing, not yet. Please, I beg you."

She regarded them as if they had both lost their minds. "I'm leaving! I'm getting out of here!" She darted towards the door to the hall. The decisive slam of the outside door failed to move John, who slumped against the wall, the fight gone out of him. Tom let go of John's wrists, and caught his breath. Outside, a car could be heard roaring to life, then receding over the cobbles. He waited, anger contending with pity for this foolish, troubled man.

"You knew Colm's was wide open."

John regarded him hollow-eyed. "Yes, Nick happened to say at the inquest the alarms were off at Thornridge House when I asked him what he was doing with himself. I knew from Adam about Colm's collection. It was nothing to walk into Thornridge last evening unseen."

"There was someone staying there."

"A few lights were on. I saw no one. The key was in a drawer. Perhaps if the access hadn't been so easy . . ." He trailed off. "I thought no one would ever think I had . . ."

"But why, John? Were you so in love with Caroline? It's a perverse love that leads a man to do the terrible, terrible thing that you've done."

"I couldn't protect Regina from her demons, you see. I thought I could protect Caroline, then maybe one day . . . "

"John, you have to give yourself up to the police."

"Do I?"

"Of course. Have you lost your mind? Do you think you can get away with this?"

Beads of sweat glistened along John's hairline. "But no one knows but you."

"I can't treat this as private confession. If you don't give yourself up willingly, then I must. John, you've trespassed against God's law, and man's. A woman has died. You shot into a crowd of people, with children, *my* child—and your child, didn't you know? Didn't you think Ariel would be among them . . . ?"

" . . . and shot the woman who gave birth to me."

"You shot and killed another human being."

"But the world will know if I confess."

"The world will know if you *don't*. There can be no bargaining here. Helen has guessed. Before long Tamara Prowse will question Caroline's alibi. If there's a police investigation, don't you see that everything will unravel? Your kinship to Judith Ingley will be un-earthed and exposed. And, John, there's something more, and this is why you must be quick and make a clean breast of it."

And now came the moment he dreaded most. He picked up the certificate from the carpet where it had fallen from John's hands. "Caroline must never know about the woman . . . and the man who gave you life."

"Man?" John spoke listlessly. "But . . . that column was empty, wasn't it?"

"Judith didn't wish to record the name on the certificate, but of course she knows who the father of her child was—your father, your natural father."

"Who was my father, then?"

Tom took a deep breath. "Clive Stanhope."

"Clive Stanhope? You mean . . . Caroline's father . . . and Nick's?"

"Yes, John, and yours, too. Do you see why Caroline must never know, why there must be no protracted police investigation, why this must be kept from the world?"

John stared at him, his full unblinking gaze, his blood-drained face, horrible to behold, yet Tom could not look away.

"Do you see?" he intoned with greater urgency.

"Merciful God," John's voice fell to a low groan. "Ariel. Caroline's daughter, my daughter . . . A child of . . ." He brought the back of his hand to his mouth, as if he could stifle the truth by stifling its utterance.

A silence enveloped the room broken only by the intermittent snap of the burning wood in the fireplace. A dog's bark intruded, but heralded no trespasser; no chorus arose in the wake. John dropped his arm after a minute, the set of his mouth revealed as a grim line. Straightening his spine, as if gathering resolve, he said to Tom, "I must have some air. I need to think."

He gave Tom no opportunity for rebuttal. He stepped towards the door to the hall. He did not stagger.

Tom sank back into the wing chair, labouring to calm his roiling mind, bend it away from the harrowing events of the last few minutes, the last few hours, the last few days, towards prayer and contemplation—and to a decision. He had no fear John would take flight. Following the usual hall sounds of gathered jacket and hurried exit, no noise announced retreat from the estate—no car door slammed, no ignition turned over, no gravel crunched along the drive. Only the dogs set to an excited yowl, but soon they abandoned their quest for attention, leaving Tom to the crackle of the fire and the thrum of his own blood. Even if John did try to vanish, tramping through the dark to some road, to some village or town, eventually to some great conurbation, he would be found in time. Britain was a moated nation and the drawbridges were well manned.

His hand still clutched John's certificate of entry of birth and he turned his attention to it, smoothing it on his lap along its resistant folds. Somewhere in some file in some office in England, presumably, a similar certificate existed for him that declared his natural parentage. An odd thought struck him: Might Dosh have a copy that she had kept from him all these years? His had been a private adoption, too; perhaps the paperwork had travelled to places it normally wouldn't, or shouldn't. Had he ever asked if she had such a document? He couldn't remember. And then a brooding thought: Might there be some telling detail about his natural mother or father that Dosh was keeping concealed? She was always the more watchful of his two adoptive mothers, as if she were bracing herself for that certain trait bred in the bone to come out in the flesh.

He was being fanciful.

At last, he rose from the chair and bent to the fireplace. He smoothed the certificate once again and placed it on one of the dying embers. The paper glowed, flared yellow-red, then burst into full flame. Seconds later, it was a wisp of grey and black, but marked by ghost text that still declared its content. Tom took the poker from the nearby rack and stirred and stirred the remains of the certificate into the anonymity of the wood ash. Satisfied that nothing remained, he lifted himself off his haunches and reached into his pocket for his mobile to make the unavoidable call. As he switched it on, he heard several sounds in near quick succession: cars—more than one—beating along the cobbles then halting, doors opening, and the voices of men. John's expected guest, the shoot captain? And colleagues? Barely a moment had passed when he heard, muffled but still detectable, farther off at some distance, a sound he hoped not to hear again soon—a shotgun blast.

He raced for the door.

Hotel Playa de los Doce Días

Tenerife

21 JANUARY

Dear Mum,

Here we are in Tenerife. I can hardly believe we managed it
after the events of the last ten days. I felt quite horrid leaving
Mr. Christmas and Miranda yesterday, even though I'd filled the
fridge with ready meals and made sure everything was washed
and ironed. Mr. C has ~~contacted~~ contracted a wretched cold, so I
can't imagine the state of his speaking voice at yesterday's funeral
for Will Moir. Like a death bell, Karla said. I should very much
like to have gone to the funeral but Karla had us to the airport
hours in advance of the flight as usual, as the airline says you're
to do. I always think it unnecessary, but Karla is a stickler for
the rules. Jago, however, was VERY put out and was quite short
with Karla in the car. He had said he would drive us to Exeter
airport as he always does, but he hadn't counted on there being a
funeral and the Thistle But Mostly Rose part of it. Since there
was no time to arrange other transportation, he was a bit stuck,

though as I say I think there was likely time enough. It wouldn't have mattered if Jago had driven us wearing his kilt, knobby knees showing and all! Anyway, what's done is done. I expect we'll be finding another way to get to the airport next year! And I'm not sure who will be fetching us when we fly back next week. Oh well, worse things happen at Seaford, as Dad sometimes used to say, though had he ever been to Seaford? Before you were married perhaps? In the car going up, we couldn't help talking about the last few days. Jago said John always seemed like such a regular fellow and couldn't believe he had shot himself over some woman. SOME WOMAN *was how your son put it, Mum. I said to him, didn't you know John had a soft spot for Caroline? No, he said. It came as a complete surprise. I thought him (and his kind—men!) very thick, and said so, which only made him shirtier. But I have to say, Mum, I've thought to myself that John Copeland's doing what he did—poisoning Will Moir, shooting Judith Ingley, and then taking his own life—*seemed very over the top too odd *quite extraordinary. Still waters run deep was my* hipothes *view. Or volcano—John was a volcano of passion set to explode! I think I said to you in my last letter, or maybe it was Monday's, that I thought there had to be more to it, especially as Mr. C was* VERY *offhand when I broached the subject. As I wrote earlier, I was so very relieved that my lovely tartlets were innocent (what a shame I tossed all the berries I had put down last autumn!) but I couldn't help wondering how John managed to get whatever that poison's called into Will's food. Well, Mum, imagine my surprise when I learned the truth! I was packing for the trip after breakfast and getting Miranda off to school yesterday morning when Mr. Christmas came up to my rooms and asked if he might have a word before I leave. I told you there was more than what met the eye, and there was! But it's terribly sad. Will Moir took the poison himself. He had the early signs of Huntington's* Korea cor chor *disease and didn't*

*want to suffer or make his family suffer. Do you remember
Moira Docherty who was the landlady at the Roundhead in
Hamlyn Ferrers? Isn't that what she had? I remember folk said
she had completely lost her mind at the end. So cruel! Anyway,
Will planned his death for the Burns Supper so that it would
look like an accident or at least anything but suicide so that Caroline could collect the insurance money and not have to sell the
hotel and give up the family home. The plan might have worked,
Mum, but for the unwanted snow and an unexpected guest
which threw a ~~Spaniard~~ spanner in the works. (More on that in
tomorrow's letter!) I don't know what will happen to Caroline
and the hotel now, as Mr. C says she has told the police everything and given them a private letter that Will wrote to her and
had left in his safe box at Barclays and I do feel sorry for her, despite what Will put me through the last week, but the only thing
I could think of was your granddaughter. What if Tamara mar-
ries that Adam Moir and has a baby? I remember from Mrs.
Docherty's instance, how Huntington's ~~Kor~~ disease runs in families and how chances are 50/50 of ~~catching~~ getting it. Does
Adam have it? I asked Mr. C. There are tests for it now. But
Mr. C said Adam and Ariel know nothing. Caroline has yet to
tell them, or at least Adam since Ariel is so young and perhaps
can't take it in, but will have to tell them very soon, as it will all
come out when the inquest into Will's death resumes later this
week. What a trial that will be for Caroline! Anyway, I didn't
say anything in the car to Jago, as I thought he might go off, and
anyway Mr. C asked me to keep it to myself as he didn't want
Adam hearing it from anyone's lips but his mother's, which is
quite correct of course. I haven't even told this to Karla, but I
thought by the time this letter gets to you, the inquest will be
over and it will be in the papers. You mustn't worry, Mum. Tamara is too young to settle down and even if she should settle
down with Adam, which she won't of course as she is a smart girl*

and will have a brilliant career, then you can be sure she will be completely sensible. Judith Ingley's parents are buried in St. Nicholas's churchyard, but of course she is to be buried at Stafford next to her husband. Mr. C said he thought he might attend, if the funeral is held after I return to England, though I suppose if it isn't Miranda could stay for one night with the Swans while he is away. I feel very sorry for Judith's son who has lost both his parents in less than 6 months and has to come again all the way from Shanghighai for another funeral. Of course, as I mentioned, Anthony Ingley has a natural father and I told you who I thought it might be! Yesterday, when Mr. Christmas was with me in my rooms, I asked him, was Clive Stanhope Anthony Ingley's natural father? Well, I could see I had quite shocked him. I don't think I've seen such a peculiar look on his face before. After a minute, he said no, it wasn't. He had had a long conversation with Judith one afternoon and they talked about their lives. Judith happened to say to him that Anthony was not her husband's natural son. She had brought him into her marriage. Mr. C said Judith had mentioned the lad's name who was the natural father, but it wasn't any of the old Thornford names and he couldn't remember now. What a shame Judith never wrote it on the birth registry! Any guesses, Mum? I would have been too young to pay attention to what a couple of teenagers were up to. Someone likely at least Judith's age now—late 60s—or maybe in his 70s or I suppose 80s. I just had the most peculiar thought! Could it be Old Bob? They had been seen having a long talk in the pub and he was VERY distraught when she died. But he would have been old enough to be her father! Is it possible? I've always had a feeling Bob had once set his cap at someone in the village and was disappointed. Funny he never married. Well, I best end this letter. I can hear Karla roaming about and we'll be going down to breakfast soon. We haven't stayed in this hotel before. It's new and looks quite nice, though this is the third room we've been in since we arrived yesterday. Karla didn't think the other two were at all what was pictured in the brochure and of course made a point of saying so. I had a bit of trial finding stationaery, too. I suppose folk send messages on their phones now, but I can't say I've ever wanted a mobile. Anyway, I'll send you a postcard of the hotel with our room—our NEW room—marked with an X. We have an ocean view now, as promised. The weather is wonderful. So sunny. I shall be brown as a berry when I get back to dear old Thornford R. All is well here. Love to Aunt Gwen. Glorious day!

> Much love,
> Madrun

P.S. I was thinking on the trip here that I'd be happy to help pay for a mobility scooter for you. I hate to think what the NHS has on offer. You and Aunt Gwen could get one each and be sort of a dynamic duo about town. What do you think?

P.P.S. I forgot to tell you I made Yorkshire pudding Monday. I'm not sure Mr. C was happy to be having roast beef again so soon, and on a Monday of all days, but I simply couldn't leave unless I was sure I hadn't lost my touch. And I hadn't. Such a relief. I thought if it came out flat again, then I'd have to stay put in Thornford, as something awful would be sure to happen. Anyway, Mr. C and Miranda have lots of cold roast beef for sandwiches.

P.P.P.S. VERY interesting this, Mum: I happened to look at Mr. C's hand yesterday morning as he fetched my big case to Jago's car. He's moved his wedding ring to his RIGHT hand! I think you know what that means!

P.P.P.P.S. In the first post yesterday, I had a letter from Ellen Maddick. Do you remember her? We went to Leiths School together, but then she went back to Shropshire and we only stayed in touch through Christmas cards for a time. Anyway, it turns out she has a new position as cook-housekeeper for the earl of Fairhaven who owns Eggescombe Hall, which isn't far, at the edge of south Dartmoor. She says Lord and Lady Fairhaven spend a fortnight at Eggescombe every August and that I must pay a visit, which I may do. I'm sure Mr. C said the earl of Fairhaven was one of the Leaping Lords and had volunteered Eggescombe for the summer parachuting fund-raiser. Great fun, I expect. As long as Mr. Christmas doesn't expect ME to step out of a flying airplane!

Acknowledgments

I'm a member of a band of sorts, though it doesn't play the pipes, and there are more than eleven of us. But you need a band to write and publish a novel and I'm very fortunate to be joined with people who play in perfect harmony. (If anyone's off pitch at times, it's muggins here.)

I am particularly grateful to my redoubtable editor at Random House, Kate Miciak, whose enthusiasm for Tom Christmas and his world keeps my mind buzzing and my backside planted where it needs to be—in front of my computer. I am grateful, too, to her colleagues Randall Klein and copy editor Laura Jorstad for the expertise they bring to turning manuscript into finished book, to designer Marietta Anastassatos and illustrator Ben Perini for the truly delightful cover, and to Kristin Cochrane of Doubleday Canada for her championship in the true north proud and free—which also happens to be the home of my agent, Dean Cooke, to whom I am also most grateful.

Thank you, too, to Sharon Klein and Leah Johanson, of Random House, for zeal in the name of publicity, and to those who aided and abetted, among them Rory Bruce, Gil Doll, Cathy Tippett, John Toews, Jack and Wendy Bumsted, and Michael and Susan Hare.

I am also grateful to those who read and criticized portions of the early drafts of the manuscript of this book—Rosie Chard, Sandra Vincent, Frances-Mary Brown, Perry Holmes, and Spencer Holmes—and to those who have lent their help in various ways—Michael Phillips, Clark Saunders, Barbara Huck, Peter St. John, Bill Blaikie, Carl Antymniuk, Pierre Bédard, Bradley Curran, Neire Mercer, Sara Raymond, Gerry Convery, Jill Treby, Barbara Robson, June Milloy, Faye Sierhuis, and John ("Pigblisters") Whiteway. Lastly but not leastly, thanks to The Queen's Own Cameron Highlanders of Winnipeg for an excellent—and really most scrumptious—Burns Supper.

I remain most grateful to the Reverend David Treby, vicar of St. Mary and St. Gabriel's Church in Stoke Gabriel, Devon, England, for his readiness to answer all my questions about the finer points of the Church of England. All inaccuracies and curious interpretations in that quarter are entirely mine.

Finally, I am very grateful to the good people of Stoke Gabriel whose splendid village set in Devon's soft hills provides me with much inspiration.

About the Author

C. C. BENISON has worked as a writer and editor for newspapers and magazines, as a book editor, and as a contributor to nonfiction books. A graduate of the University of Manitoba and Carleton University, he is the author of five previous novels, including *Twelve Drummers Drumming* and *Death at Buckingham Palace*. He lives in Winnipeg, where he is at work on the next Father Christmas mystery, *Ten Lords A-Leaping*.

www.ccbenison.com

About the Type

This book was set in Caslon, a typeface first designed in 1722 by William Caslon. Its widespread use by most English printers in the early eighteenth century soon supplanted the Dutch typefaces that had formerly prevailed. The roman is considered a "workhorse" typeface due to its pleasant, open appearance, while the italic is exceedingly decorative.

FIC
BENISON

Benison, C. C.

Eleven pipers
piping.

DATE			